SHALLOW ENDS

SHALLOW ENDS

a novel

DAVID JAMES KEATON

Podium

Some parts of this novel were previously published in substantially different form in the following publications:
"Queen Excluder" in Gamut, Issue Six, Spring, 2017.
"The Smile Police" in *Mystery Tribune*, Issue No. 2, Summer, 2017.
"One Caprice at a Time" appeared as "One Piece at a Time" in *Just to Watch Them Die: Crime Fiction Inspired by the Songs of Johnny Cash* (Gutter Books), Fall, 2017.
"Spin the Throttle" in *Tales from a Talking Board* (Word Horde), Fall, 2017.
"A Prayer for the Surfer Boys" in *Dead Bait 4* (Severed Press), Winter, 2017.
"Wreckless Eyeballing" in *It's a Weird Winter Wonderland*
(Coffin Hop Press), Winter, 2017.
"Dolla Dolla Bill Wall" in *Tough*, Winter, 2020.

Cover design by Amanda Shaffer

ISBN: 978-1-0394-6747-7

Published in 2024 by Podium Publishing
www.podiumaudio.com

Podium

To Veronica, who says it all with one word.

SHALLOW ENDS

If the bee disappeared from the surface of the Earth,
man would have no more than three years to live.
—Larry Irwin Einstein

Nobody's getting off.
—Ric Ocasek, "Jimmy Jimmy"

CHAPTER 1

THREE PUMPERS

That's it?"

The monstrous vehicle was rumbling around the corner, huge wheels lunging with every pothole, and it thundered toward her like a drunken parade, the teeth of its grill gleaming, red-white-and-blue beacons blazing, and the waves of music from the speakers were throbbing deep in her chest like palpitations as it continued to lurch and lumber to the curb, a tattered and limp American flag waving feebly from the railing. Heads turned, confused by the contradiction, the promise of rescue and disruption. Noxious exhaust and alcohol fumes preceded the beast, and, as she stood in its unyielding headlights, the grotesque patriotism and boozy promise of such a spectacle somehow simultaneously terrified her while also inducing a queasy excitement to get this crazy show on the road as soon as possible.

"Where's the fire!" someone laughed, running up from behind the truck.

"Where's the party!" came the response over her shoulder.

This is the worst idea I've ever had, she thought. *But the night's still young.*

And so were they.

Eight hours earlier, when the dying honeybee fell from the ceiling, Angie's last class of the semester still had a half hour to go, but she knew she'd lost them for good.

Her students howled as the dazed intruder dropped and began drunkenly rebounding off their desk legs like a buzzing bumper car, and she ran to open the nearest window to hopefully steer it outside. The fresh gust of post-thunderstorm breeze should have calmed everyone down a bit, but they'd already been wound up so tight watching a countdown-to-summer on the wall all day (almost as closely as she had). Even before their surprise guest turned her classroom into a free-for-all, tensions were high with her students locked in a fierce debate regarding *Lord of the Flies* and how *they'd* never succumb to such savagery. They'd almost come to blows at one point, without any sense of irony, which meant that the honeybee currently spiraling down into the center of their circle like a helicopering maple pod was goosing an already unstable argument straight over the cliff of rational discourse. Some students laughed and dove for cover, some dug through backpacks for overpriced EpiPens, and the rest pressed in closer. Angie's best students tried to shield the bee from the boots of their bullies, always intent on hastening the demise of anything vulnerable.

"I'm *Lord of the Beeeeees!*" Jack shouted, the first to try to stomp it into oblivion. But before his heel came down, Angie was standing over him with two fists full of his soda-stained soccer jersey.

"Do *not* do that," she said with a calm authority that shocked both of them, and only half the class dared to laugh.

"Lemme go," Jack said, his grin morphing into a grimace. Though they were both technically adults, Angie knew manhandling a student would likely lead to a sit-down with her department chair, or at least the loss of her hard-earned chili pepper on Ratemyprofessor.com. But today was the last day of class. A good day not to care about such things.

The day before Spring Break is supposed to be fun, goddammit, she thought, staring down the kid in her clutches. And it had been fun, for a while, anyway. That morning, she'd let the students indulge in YouTube clips of fictional classrooms in films, springboarding from their previous activity of analyzing their room as a "text." *Dangerous Minds*, *Good Will Hunting*, and *Dead Poets Society* seemed to be favorites, the last two especially. Just the sight of Robin Williams's benevolent goblin face got the kids very excitable, even if he wasn't particularly funny in those movies. But they did understand that this was a man who seemed scientifically engineered for humor, leaving mugging gaps in his delivery where they could react, that universally recognized pause indicating that anything resembling a joke may have occurred, and they always filled that space eagerly. And the honeybee seemed to represent one of those conspicuous pauses, the disruption of a routine. And, as the filmgoing world had been trained to do, they filled any vacuum with aimless, youthful energy.

Miraculously, Angie had time to consider all this as she *yoinked!* Jack up by the sticky handle of his jersey, mildly surprised by both her strength and his lack of density. When it came to fulfilling Angie's assignments of looking for visual arguments in the film clips without getting stuck on the plots, Jack was the worst, and she'd gotten more tired of him as the semester wore on. It was just another reminder that, though college freshmen were already drinking, driving, and presumably fucking with some dexterity, they were still kids where it counted, with attention spans as fleeting as a mayfly. Or a poisoned honeybee.

Even before today, she'd felt her control slipping, and she understood the bee, as much as the book, were excuses for them to riot. She chided herself for not realizing any kid named "Jack" would push every bad-faith argument to absolve the evil deeds of his fictional counterpart. And just like there was apparently no visual representation of a realistic classroom in the history of cinema, there were thousands of bad "Jacks" in postmodernist literature, as well as the back rows of schoolhouses.

But grabbing a kid was crossing the line. She'd honestly wanted to make the most of her last day with them, and if pressed, would have admitted to being relieved by an interruption. She loosened her grip on Jack's jersey, noting with pride that his sneakers were lowering from his tiptoes back down to his heels. She could smell the onions from the Togo's roast beef sub he always brought with him to class, despite the note on her syllabus saying: *No food unless you bring enough for everyone!* He'd laughed and asked her if she *really* wanted a room filled with twenty-five reeking sandwiches ("Because I'll go get them right now," he'd threatened).

Not that they couldn't all use a little more rare meat to make them grow. "The students get smaller every year!" she told anyone who listened (or anyone who called *her* short), never admitting it was likely the ever-tightening squint of her glare that was shaving the inches off these kids. Or possibly it was the increasing amount of time she spent lecturing rather than questioning, pontificating rather than actually talking, never with any eye contact, directing it all at an invisible cloud of collected sighs floating just above their heads, rather than row after row of gape-mouthed faces that this dead air had leaked from.

It didn't help that, deep down inside, she knew she was no different. They were her. She was them. And they were all just getting worse.

Finally free from her grasp, Jack backed up fast enough to stumble, as he waved other students to back up, too. Angie strode through the gap like the Red Sea and cupped her hands around the writhing bee. It rolled into her palm, lurching and sputtering like a tiny backfiring jalopy, and she held it at arm's length as she walked back to the crisp, breezy suction of the open window. She knew this effort was futile, not just because the creature's sluggishness betrayed the effects of the pesticides coating their quadrangle (now, *that* was a space the students liked to read as a "text," as flower-blinged as a Rose Parade float as the administration suckered the yearly deluge of awe-struck parents), but simply because the bee had stung her during her attempted rescue. Effectively gutting itself as the black stinger, still trailing its stomach and bluish-green blood, pulsed furiously to pump what little venom it could muster into Angie as it slowly lost all remaining muscle control. She felt almost nothing. She would have normally flinched at the sting, but instead she happily took this transient pain with a smile, feeling the opposite of animosity toward the insect's gory parting shot at the world, or maybe, just not wanting to give any little bastard the satisfaction.

"I can't teach anymore," Angie said into the phone balanced on her shoulder as she walked to the bus stop.

"Why not?" Jill asked on the other end, though she'd heard all the reasons before.

"First off, they're too young. And I swear they're getting younger by the minute. I'm pretty sure they're shrinking, too," Angie said, as if it just occurred to her.

"Oh no, not the shrinking thing again," Jill said, laughing. "You probably shouldn't feed them any more sugar, though."

"Wait, what?" she said at first, thinking of the bee. Then, "Hey, that was your idea! 'You catch more kids with honey than vinegar,' remember? Or whatever the hell you said."

Angie originally endorsed Jill's initial recommendation to pass around peppermint candies to reactivate the class after their usual noon slump, but now she wondered if this hadn't contributed to the mutiny.

Sugar infusions and the specter of stings had to be a volatile cocktail for any red-blooded kid's pulse rate.

"Always write off the last day," Jill said. "They're not going to give you anything while watching a clock."

Angie thought about that clock again. During the workweek, her thoughts were never far from it, either. At the beginning of today's class, she'd reintroduced the lesson where they were tasked to come to a consensus regarding what sort of "argument" their classroom made, and the students got stuck on a couple key details: the hole in the clockface that they were convinced housed a camera; the dangling microphone hanging from the ceiling tiles, which they were *definitely* convinced recorded their conversations; and, of course, a surprise moment when the video projectors had filled all four walls with the naked emotion of Angie's unprepared expression a split second before she projected the film clips of fictional classrooms. But that inert, glassy-eyed clock with the mystery hole was the worst, and she couldn't help glancing at it, either. Since she was a kid, she'd always been convinced a stopped clock foreshadowed death.

"We're being watched!" her students had declared, and she believed them. The bee and the clock, and even the phone call, had conjured up an unexpected hat trick of memories from her childhood, but a quick bite of her own tongue pushed these thoughts away before they could coagulate into anything tangible.

For now.

"I just need to find myself another line of work," she told Jill. "Maybe a career involving actual adults? Or grad students! Yeah, anything with my peers would be fine."

"Yikes," Jill said. "Be careful what you wish for, sister."

"Hey, wait a minute, *you're* the one who should be making wishes today."

"Ding ding ding! You are correct!" Jill said. "So are you on your way?"

"Give me about fifteen minutes," Angie said, hanging up, the back of her phone smearing the stinger barb and deflated venom sac across the lifeline of her palm. Any lingering pain was gone. And work was finished, at least for now. She had just one more phone call to make.

For tonight's surprise.

* * *

It was Jill's crazy leap-year birthday, and to start things off, everyone was meeting at Papalino's, her favorite pizza joint in Kentucky. Towering and surly, Papalino and his three shiftless but omnipresent sons (brothers? cousins?) would all be gone in a year, soon to be replaced by a nutty artisan Popsicle "restaurant." But for now, Papalino's was the last-remaining New York–style pizza place on Baxter Avenue, jam-packed every night due to its flat, floppy slices, as well as its proximity to the popular Bardstown Road strip and its tireless nightlife.

Angie knew it was going to be an odd mix tonight, more friends of friends than usual, so she wasn't shocked when she walked in and nobody was talking. Three tables had been pulled together, and most of the revelers were already seated and tucked in tight, but everyone (except a grinning Jill) was as stone-faced as Easter Island statues.

No, maybe more like Stonehenge, Angie thought. Easter Island faces always looked oddly content to her. In fact, when it was revealed in the news that those heads had always been connected to massive bodies nested cozily beneath them, she thought this made perfect sense.

"I thought this was a birthday, not a funeral!" Angie clapped her hands and headed for the lone empty chair someone had awkwardly positioned between Amy and Jill. Angie's long-suffering "best friend" and sometimes doppelgänger, Amy, was likely the culprit. Once, Angie had tried to explain to her that she didn't believe in best friends, that she was actually suspicious of any grown-up still insecure enough to label them, and this, of course, ensured Amy would declare them best friends for life or longer.

"I think you overestimate us," Beth said from across the table, lips pursed tight as usual. Angie sometimes joked she'd be a great ventriloquist act without the dummy.

"Well, thank Christ she does," Jill said. "Our poor Angie, always shooting for a cozy *My Dinner with Andre* situation when she sets up these things. Intense, revealing conversations? She'll have ten of those by lunch. Big, life-changing topics to ponder? Get ready . . ."

"My dinner with who?" Amy frowned.

"The dude from *The Princess Bride!*" Jill said.

"Duh, that's *My Dinner with Andre . . .* the Giant," Amy said. A Wallace Shawn fan she was not.

"Actually, I prefer more of a *My Dinner with San Andreas* situation," the new kid, Lund, muttered from his corner seat. He was a chubby, gamer-hunched recent hire who worked feverishly in the University of Louisville writing center to help athletes squeak by in their classes (so they could continue squeaking their shoes on the courts), and Angie couldn't remember if she invited him or not. They were all crammed together, but with the shoulders and faces of the other guests angled away from him, Lund still appeared to be seated alone.

"Nope, I don't get it," Beth said to Lund while looking at Angie.

"You know, like an earthquake waiting to happen?" Lund shrugged, laughing nervously.

"Still don't get it."

"Well, it's not your *fault*," Lund said, so proud of his punch lines that everyone refused to acknowledge them just on principle. "Get it? *Fault?*"

"Check, please!" Beth snorted with a brutal dismissal.

"Can I see your invitation?" Dan asked him, leaning in from Lund's left with one of those a-little-too-hard shoulder slaps, then standing up abruptly to cut off his stuttered response.

"So who invited this guy?" Amy asked Angie.

"Dan or Lund?" Angie whispered back.

"Either."

"Who knows."

"Can people invite themselves?"

"Maybe," Angie said, then added, "I think it's like the opposite of tickling."

"I can totally tickle myself," Amy said, sheepish.

"Time to get this road on the show!" Dan shouted, jumping up, and one of his lackeys, Jeff "Janky" Janks, got up to follow him to the restroom. Angie guessed drugs were involved.

"Don't spoil the surprise, jerk," Angie practically hissed as they walked past.

Jill, playing along, stuck her fingers in her ears, singing, "La la la la la not listening . . ."

"You know, I'm starting to think the bee today was on purpose," she said to Jill, plucking her friend's fingers free.

"What? That scene in your classroom? Are you nuts?"

"What bee?" Sherry asked from the far end of the table, somehow sounding simultaneously bored and insistent.

"A hornet dive-bombed her class today," Jill said.

"It was a honeybee," Angie corrected her.

"There was a hornet in your classroom on the last day?" Gaddy asked, elbow-to-elbow with Sherry and sounding a little too incredulous. "Wow, that does sound premeditated."

"Maybe," Angie shrugged, and Jill leaned over to Angie and isolated their conversation.

"Seriously, how would those little brats know anything about your past? Or your brother, for that matter?"

"They are a 'hive mind,'" Angie said, laughing.

"What about her brother?" Gaddy asked, eyebrow up like she almost gave a shit. But it was way too early in the night to start talking about all that stuff, and Angie was always leery when her name change came up, so she changed the subject instead, which was always easier.

"So . . . have you guys looked yourselves up on *Rate My Professor* yet? Kids know everything these days. It's too freaky. I think I'm going to quit."

"Oh yeah," Holly said, draped over Sherry's shoulder. "It's all out there now; *Rape Your Professor*, *Draw Your Professor*, *Dissect Your Teacher*, *Teacher Eviscerator* . . ."

"*Teacher* Evaluator," Lund announced, getting his usual groans.

Back from the restroom with hooded eyes, Dan and Janky sat down for about thirty seconds, then pushed their chairs away from the table and headed straight back to the restroom again. Ruck, another flunky even lower on the food chain, followed them this time, and Angie sighed.

"Someone tell them not to get fucked up yet. We got a long way to go, and all night to get there."

"I'll do it," Holly said, slapping her thighs and standing up to march after them.

"Oh my God," Beth said, pointing toward a patron bursting out of the men's room seconds later, fumbling with his braided belt.

"Hey, this shitter ain't gender fluid!" the man yelled in the general direction of the register, and one of the Papalinos ran into the restroom with a cook trailing him for backup. The partygoers arched their ears at the ruckus in the stalls, then Dan crashed back out and ran to hide behind Lund's chair.

"Gender *fluids*, ewww," he said.

The collective eyeroll from the table was practically audible, but it didn't slow him down.

"Hey, what are you doing . . ." Lund protested as Dan reached down the back of his shirt and past the waist of his acid-washed jeans to give his Fruit of the Looms a brutal wedgie. "Come on!" he squealed, falling backward to escape the indignity as he furiously tried to feed the lolling 50-inch elastic waistband back into his pants like a magician's never-ending string of soiled handkerchiefs.

"Knock it off!" Jill yelled at them as more of the staff, presumably related, approached their tables. "Let's get some grub going."

"Any more trouble over here, and I'm calling the cops," the oldest son (but more of a mid-tier Papalino) told them over a wrinkly finger wag, and everyone glumly rejoined the table. Dan waved down a server for some beers and one of their infamous pizzas with its delicious lake of grease, and he led the group in scarfing it down, every so often sharing a glance with Holly or a "bro squeeze" of Lund's shoulder, which seemed to be the most heartfelt apology his species was capable of.

"Yeah, hurry up and eat," Angie said, tapping her wrist where a watch would have been. "There won't be food where we're going, guys!"

"And we won't need any roads!" Lund said, laughing as he misquoted another movie.

"Oh no," someone said, and everybody concentrated on fueling up.

To escape the latest awkward silence, Beth stepped outside for a cigarette, and Angie watched Holly whisper something to Sherry, who then whispered something to Gaddy. The "triplets," as Angie sometimes called them, weren't afflicted by the "best friend" syndrome that plagued Angie, but that's only because there were three of them, so their triangle was practically a family, as impenetrable as the Papalinos. Rumors abounded they were addicts, though no one had ever actually witnessed them in the act of shooting up. But Angie occasionally found herself scanning their arms for track marks, or the rubber-band remnants of a bicep choke-hold, any evidence at all of those secret golden pumps of a shared hypodermic needle. And tonight, not just because of everyone's sneaky trips to the restroom, Angie was looking extra close at the roadmap of veins on their long limbs, thoughtfully rubbing the red stigmata and dull memory of the sting to her own palm. To numb the pain, she'd creased it twice with a thumbnail, just as her brother had taught her when they were kids. She always suspected this alleviated nothing and only distracted from the venom by slicing it with a deeper injury. But it usually worked well enough. For some reason, however, this sting was harder to dismiss.

Ten minutes later, after tableside conversation was finally picking up, someone reported a paper-towel dispenser with a fist-sized hole through its plastic face, and the youngest Papalino (but somehow the largest) called the cops. And even with the red and blue lights suddenly filling the windows, Gaddy, Holly, and Sherry were ducking back into the restroom again, with Dan dragging Lund by the collar in right after them.

"What is going on in there?!" the brawny Papalino shouted, banging on the door.

I'll tell you what's going on in there, Angie thought. *Either talking smack or doing smack.*

Then Beth came back in from her smoke break and waved for Angie's attention, silently mouthing the signal:

It's here.

Apparently, those red and blue flashers outside weren't the fuzz after all.

"Let's go," Angie said, a little bummed that Jill's birthday dinner was starting in such disarray, but satisfied a few of them had put something in their stomachs before the drinking got going for real. She stood up to wave the remainder of their party—some who were arriving fashionably late and were now doubly confused—right back out the door they'd come through.

"Everyone, out! Out out out!" Angie said. "No, Jill, you wait here a second, spin around, cover your eyes . . ."

Jill turned to face a corner as ordered, stomping a foot as if she was being disciplined, but also doing a happy little golf clap in anticipation. The advancing lightshow was blinding now, staining the restaurant with dazzling color, and even the Papalinos were shielding their heavy brows. The windows rattled in their frames. Customers steadied their wine glasses.

Something big was coming.

"What do you mean, 'That's it?' What in the world were you expecting?"

"I don't know. Something else?"

Angie had no good answer to Amy's reasonable question as the seizure-inducing flashers and the pulsing music painted their teeth alternately red, white, then blue, while triggering the car alarms around them.

They called it a "party bus," but it was just as much a real bus as the garish Popsicle stand in Papalino's near future would be considered a real restaurant. But the second life of things was sometimes the most interesting, Angie decided, briefly remembering her childhood again, and despite her trepidations, she was eager to climb on board.

It was one of those old-time, decommissioned fire engines, but jazzed up with strips of neon, a new coat of candy-apple gloss, knotted strings of Christmas bulbs, and a row of ragged, diesel-stained American flags dangling over the wheel wells and fenders. A gold plaque nailed to the driver's door labeled it a 1955 AMERICAN LAFRANCE SERIES 700 pumper, one of those ancient fire trucks with a pug nose for a cab and more than a passing resemblance to the hippy buses popularized in the psychedelic '60s. Angie did a lap around the vehicle, and despite the haphazard Dr. Moreau attempt to stitch the old beast into a garish, rolling celebration, she was still not sure why they called it a "party bus" on the website instead of flaunting the more unique history of the truck. The "party" aspect was fairly accurate, though, as she caught a glimpse of the huge, churning hot tub nested in the back, sunk down where a thick coil of fire hose would normally be piled high, surrounded on all four corners by the flashes of the brain-numbing beacons and the thumping, madly celebratory beat.

Angie signaled Beth in the growing mob to send her back into Papalino's and grab Jill for the big reveal. Beth, a part-time librarian and part-time pain in the ass, who'd just started working with Angie at U of L, was a brown-eyed, girl-next-door type, also known as *Jill's* type (Jill being a black-haired, broad-shouldered, striking former rugby champ), and Angie was kinda playing matchmaker by bringing her along. Beth hadn't had a lot of time to talk to Jill over dinner because of the restroom nonsense, and she could be uncomfortably shy with strangers, but Angie hoped she'd been so inert this evening because she was taking the potential hookup very seriously. Angie figured she and Jill would have plenty of time to bond once they splashed around town in the fire truck's hot tub and did a lot more drinking. Angie figured Beth had to loosen up a bit and lower the muscular tension twitching perceptibly along her jawline before she cracked a tooth.

Would a smile kill her? Angie thought.

Amy stomped up behind Angie, thumping her back with her shoulder. She was always underfoot at any given moment, small arms crossed tight, signaling she was feeling left out again. She was also becoming more skeptical by the second as she looked over the vehicle.

"No, seriously, that is it, right?" Amy said, throwing Angie's own question back at her.

"Yep!" replied Angie, now happily resigned to their fate, if only to annoy Amy. "Could be fun! Or at least funny."

"I guess I thought it would be bigger?" Amy said, deciding to make the best of it, too.

"It'll be good for us all to cram in the back." Angie shrugged. "Like one of those corporate retreats. This is our bonding weekend!"

"This better not last the weekend," Amy said, laugh slipping. Angie always seemed concerned with welding disparate groups of friends into some sort of cohesive whole, and without turning toward her, she gave Amy a half-hug of reassurance in light of all the forced camaraderie. Though both young women looked remarkably similar from a distance (dirty-blonde hair, shorter than average height), their laughs were so distinct that, ironically, it made them even harder to tell apart, meaning Amy laughed way too big and full for someone their size, while Angie opened her mouth wide but silent when she thought something was funny, seemingly content to let Amy do that emotional labor for both of them. This was a role Angie was always happy to surrender: designated laugher, designated driver, you name it. Sometimes letting Amy play the best-friend card had its advantages.

"Sooo how did you hear about this rolling monstrosity again?" Amy asked her.

"I caught wind of it creeping around town during Derby season last year. It did a drive-by past Cherokee Road when we were down there doing trivia, and people on board were friggin' screaming. But I don't think I've ever really looked at it up close . . ."

They both turned toward the sound of the driver's door swinging open with a rusty creak, and a large, round-faced man hopped down to the street to greet them, the acrid odor of gasoline rippling from his body to reach them first. He sized up Angie and Amy simultaneously, one eye squinting shut as he chewed the corner of his lip, the other eye circling them like a cockroach trapped under a shot glass.

"Is he at least what you expected?" Amy whispered.

"Yeah, no, he's exactly what I thought he'd be," Angie snickered, chewing a thumb.

"Hello, ladies," the driver said, giving no indication he heard their exchange, but almost kicking Angie with a work boot as he brought a toe up to scratch his leg. He handed her a business card, then used a greasy thumb to clear the opposite nostril of mucus and gesticulate impatiently to the gathering crowd.

"Over here! Hurry up!" Then, to the two of them, "So is this your charter? M'name's Winston, but you can call me whatever."

Angie turned the card over in her hand. On the front, it read:

Mr. Winston Payne: Raconteur. Available for Party Buses, Party Boats, Party Planning, Promenades, "Paybacks," and Landscaping.

"Why is 'Paybacks' in scare quotes?"

"Uh, why is 'Paybacks' on there at all?"

On the back, underneath a sweat-soaked, folded-up dollar bill with a tiny hole through it where they'd once been pinned together, the card read simply, *Turn over.*

Angie and Amy shared an amused glance, and the driver moved away from them to count heads as more people came up the street and streamed out of the restaurant toward the truck.

"What's a 'Rocketeer'?" Amy asked, stifling another laugh.

"Did he just give me a dollar?" Angie giggled.

"Hey, at least it doesn't say 'turn over' on both sides," Amy said, and Angie elbowed her to keep her cool. She shook the dollar bill open, and the odor of stale cigarettes and skunked beer wafted from its folds.

"Maybe it's the first dollar he ever made," Angie said.

"Or his last," Amy said, and Holly swooped in, always interested in other people's conversations.

"The driver gave you a buck?"

"No, his business card. I don't think he knew there was a damp dollar stuck to it."

"I had a quarter stuck to my ass once," Holly said wistfully, then moved on as Amy shook her head.

"You ladies have a question?" Winston Payne barked from behind them, and Amy jumped.

"So how much do we owe you, Mr. Payne?" Angie asked him.

"How many y'all . . . uh . . . baker's dozen? Let's call it three hundred even," he said flatly, eyes still sizing up the group as they all milled around and stood on toes to get a better look at the enticing party pool just over the rails of the truck.

"Hey! Everybody!" Angie shouted at the gang. "Cash! Now!"

Holly shoved her way up between Angie and the driver before anyone could ante up, almost knocking Amy off-balance. Angie spit out a mouthful of Holly's huge yellow mane, peering through, then parting her thick tresses with an exaggerated motion like she was opening a robe.

"Don't worry, Angie, we got it," Holly said, untangling Angie from her cascading hair with a practiced shake of the head. Gaddy and Sherry, her partners in crime, moved in to keep blocking out Angie and Amy, smiling as they took turns skinning a huge wad of green dollar bills thick as a burrito.

"You gals strippers?" Winston asked them without much interest.

"Yeah," Holly said, with a snort. "We'll strip whatever you want. Wallpaper, siding, inhibitions, sunburn, you name it."

"Whassat?" Winston scratched a leathery ear.

"Sir, can you please play the CD I brought?" Angie stepped back in front of Holly, Sherry, and Gaddy, desperate to get the party rolling. Jill was a big Prince fan, and Angie had burned thirty-five of his biggest hits for the occasion, one song for every year Jill was alive, each adding a layer of biographical significance. The mix began with "Raspberry Beret," a song Jill had recently become convinced was an ode to circumcision, and ended with the bizarre dolphins-squeaking guitars of "Animal Kingdom." Angie didn't delude herself into thinking everyone was going to appreciate her mix, but she didn't care. It wasn't their birthday.

"'Fraid not," Winston said, turning away from Angie and the CD in her hand. "Friar Tuck will be supplying the music." He pointed over her head.

Angie frowned, looking back at the red flashers and strobes on the truck's trailer until she finally got the joke.

Friar Tuck . . . the fire truck? Woof.

She couldn't imagine anyone defining the tuneless thudding she felt in her chest as "music," but she decided to give it a chance. She clapped her hands to keep things moving, and the driver, too, her cue to start hollering again.

"If yer going, let's go! Let's get got!"

Angie held up a finger to ask one final question about the length of the trip, but the energy was ramping up and everyone was shoving past her to climb aboard. She was pleased to see Beth leading Jill by the hand, up between the headlights to lean triumphant against the gape-toothed mouth of the shimmering chrome grill. Then she saw Winston give their group a final disapproving assessment, and watched Beth do a double take when he strode slowly through the high beams, frozen as if she was trying to place the man in her memory. In the moment, Angie forgot to ask her about this, and she would kick herself for it later, but Beth had one of those perpetual sour and frazzled expressions, the kind of person who she suspected might struggle to recognize her own face in a rearview mirror.

Lucky for her, this fire truck doesn't have any, Angie thought nervously, noting the painted-over holes near the driver's side window as it slammed. Everybody was yelling now, pushing Jill to the front of the mob so she could get on first. As the cheers grew, the party grew less coherent and they struggled to figure out how to climb aboard.

"Oh my God! Party Bus! Whoo-hoo! Last one in is a rotten eggplant!"

"Party booooooooooosss! Whoop! Whoop!"

"Party berz in tha herz!"

"Ermergerdpurtyburssssssssss!"

Leading the frenzy to mount the truck was Dan Villareal, and unfashionably late Reeves . . . something or other? Angie could never remember if "Reeves" was his first or last name and never cared enough to solve the mystery. Most people considered him Dan's trusty shadow, or maybe it was the other way around. Dan Villareal, on the other hand, was very distinctive, that strong, silent, sportsman with a helmet of majestic hair like Clint Eastwood in 1971's *Dirty Harry*, and the kind of kid that beet-faced asshole coaches liked to claim was a "born leader." He always seemed a little lost without a beach around, hard to come by in the middle of Kentucky. Angie had fallen for his confident, sunburned-and-barefoot shtick, too, until she met more West Coast goofballs at U of L just like him and stopped being impressed by the facade. Still, Angie and Dan dated for three months, with him crashing at her apartment weekly but never quite moving in. Then one day he was rude about something insignificant (so insignificant she retained only the residual memory of irritation), and the next day she stopped caring about their relationship entirely. Even if Angie didn't remember the reason for the breakup, she did remember their last conversation, when she came home early and caught him in her apartment alone, and at first she thought he'd been crying. Then he gave her a hug, and she realized he was soggy due to sweat, not tears, due to the exertion of packing up all his shit as fast as possible. She wasn't sure why they'd remained friends after that, but somehow they had.

Reeves Something or Other was a smidge shorter than Dan, but way more muscular, and, as far as anybody knew, sported a similarly hazy, surf-and-sun-addled origin story. But he also had one of those mean little ferret faces, angular and suspicious, and he was generally disliked, though no one could ever pin down any instance of him actually *doing* anything wrong. Angie had considered trying to solve that mystery, back before her booty calls with Dan, but all she could figure out was that Reeves simply had a face that was tough to trust. Once Amy described his face as having "the kind of mouth that would keep smiling after it was smacked," and Angie never shook the image.

Ruck ran up between Dan and Reeves, trying to get them both in a headlock, which they slipped easily. Angie had almost forgotten he was there, this prissy, annoying kid who walked on the tips of his toes and was also in the sad position of shadowing Reeves, who was already batting cleanup for Dan. Tellingly, if "Ruck" was a bastardization of any normal name, Angie was pretty sure no one had ever bothered to ask what it was.

After they dumped Ruck to the pavement, he picked himself up and sat on the fender of the fire truck, shaking something suspicious out of his shoe and looking around anxiously as he wondered what to do with it. Winston rolled down his driver's-side window and leaned out to smack the top of the cab with a huge, calloused catcher's mitt of a hand.

"You!" he said, pointing at Ruck, who was straddling the wheel and still looking at his shoe. Winston put two thick, oily fingers into his mouth and whistled hard, an alarming, almost mechanical blast of noise, like he'd whistled so much it was both second nature and a violation of the natural order.

"Hey, boy!" he said. "You take off your clothes when you're on board and not before! And if anybody leaves any shoes on the sidewalk, that ain't my problem! We will *not* be coming back."

"We won't, huh?" Gaddy laughed. "Spoooooky."

Away from the restaurant table, Angie got her first good look at Gaddy, noting that she was almost two-thirds legs, a tall, blonde wisp of a WASP who moved much faster than Angie thought possible. Angie watched as she stole Jill's hand away from Beth and dragged Jill around into the glow of the red lights at the ass-end of the truck. As Gaddy soaked in all the excitement with the air of someone who needed to claim it, she waved Angie over to lock fingers and put an arm around her waist, too.

"Was this your idea, Angie? Oh my God, you are so hilarious."

"It was everybody's idea, I guess," Angie lied, not sure what was so hilarious, exactly. Her hectic semester wrap-up dominating her days, tonight's plan had been put together so fast she barely remembered making the phone calls.

"Yeah, I've heard about these dumb things and always wanted to rent one," Beth said, sheepish. "I've just never had enough friends to make it worthwhile."

Still don't, Angie didn't say.

Jill put her other arm around Beth so that they all were in a huddle. Everyone wanted to be Jill's friend, for obvious reasons. She always had a surplus of goodwill to go around. This made the awkward combo of revelers easier to stomach, though Angie still worried about how half-ass she'd organized this thing, especially her slapdash manner of telling people to "go ahead and bring a friend or whatever!" which clearly resulted in a confusing telephone game of invites and now some borderline strangers soon to be crammed into a hot tub together.

Telephone game . . . she thought, biting her tongue to bury another unwanted memory.

"Well, kids," Jill said to them all, but mostly to Beth, "I don't know about having enough friends, either, but we definitely got a crowd here tonight! And these nuts are keen on somethin'."

"We sure are," Holly said, all wound up and practically hopping up and down in the gutter. Angie saw Holly's size 10s stamping toward a fluttering bit of insect life riding the breeze near a candy wrapper, and, panicking as she suddenly remembered the dying honeybee from her classroom, unhooked herself from Gaddy's grip to head her off.

"Whoa, careful there, killer," Holly said, holding out an arm and almost tripping her as they collided.

"Careful yourself," Angie said, low and much more serious than she intended.

"Excuse me?"

"Sorry, it's just that we're lucky the bees bounced back this year. Let's not tempt fate any more than we already have, okay?"

"Oooookay," Holly said, sarcastically, prodding the Bit-O-Honey wrapper with her toe instead of the insect, which appeared to be a maimed dragonfly after all. "Bitch thinks I'm in her class," Holly said to Jill while keeping eye contact with Angie, but Angie decided to let it go. Jill gave her a grateful smile and started clapping again to keep the energy high, as Angie watched the dragonfly's crumpled body glide into the stream of garbage and ride through the bars of a sewer grate. She followed the line of water back to the idling fire truck and only then remembered the promise of the pool.

"Line up! Let's go! Let's go!" Angie said in her best Winston impression, and the rest of them mostly did as they were told, ignoring the driver's instructions as they unzipped their jeans and stripped off their shirts right there at the curb, revealing young, wiry bodies, bikinis, swim trunks, or skivvies previously concealed underneath. Angie imagined them as superhero sidekicks getting ready for the undercard skirmishes, and some passersby whooped at the surprising display of skimpy swim-wear, undergarments, or roadside skin. Angie tried to corral everyone away from traffic and was getting close to forfeiting her assumed leader-ship position. She steered bodies and mentally checked off names, and had another reminder that even though she'd dug deep into her address book for just half of the dozen people needed to book the bus, about a third of the friends of friends tagging along Angie didn't know very well at all.

Fuck it, how bad could it be? she thought, slapping Jill's high-toned ass as she slinked by. *As long as they're all friends of Jill's, or friends of friends of Jill, they gotta be friends of . . . somebody.*

As far as the rest of the main-event partiers queuing up, extra tips on some remaining love triangles (*quadrangles?*), there was Jill's old rugby nemesis Sherry, another Cali transplant, as well as the snarky new adjunct in the Communications Department who moonlighted at nearby Elizabethtown Community College, appropriately branded "Gaddy." And, of course, her wicked Siamese twin, Holly, who seemed to hate Angie (and possibly everyone), for reasons undetermined.

She suddenly locked eyes with Beth, whose confidence must have peaked early, as Angie noticed she was either scared or shiver-ing. Beth's swimsuit definitely had the accent on "suit," being almost indistinguishable from her work clothes, a little like one of those sleeved, striped getups you'd expect to see in a Roaring Twenties beach scene, or maybe prison. This more formal/institutionalized look was offset, however, by three white flowers pinned behind her ear, a detail that Sherry, Holly, and Gaddy were already focused on and occasionally trying to flick loose when she wasn't looking.

The triplets are going to be a problem, Angie was now realizing. But sometimes a "problem child" or two made for a memorable birthday? Apparently, all three of these beaming bullies had gone to undergrad together back in California, transferring to the University of Louisville halfway through the semester for undisclosed reasons, and remained glued together at the hip, or at least the phone, because of the lingering hint of a scandal. But today, Angie hoped there might be a slim chance to actually get to know them, due to the unusually close quarters of such a wacky party. The scuttlebutt around school was that Holly had gotten thrown out of Santa Carla University for plagiarism. Or maybe that was Sherry. Actually, come to think of it, Angie remembered Reeves swearing to Amy that he'd heard from Ruck that Gaddy had somehow been "arrested" for copying something? Which didn't make any sense at all.

Can someone really be arrested for that? She wondered, eventually relegating such hearsay to her pay-no-mind list, at least until one of them pissed her off again. Which would no doubt be tonight.

The driver's-side window squeaked again, and Angie watched Winston crane his head out to glare at the crowd rubbernecking and bottlenecking and just generally pissing away his night for as long as he could stand. Finally, he sighed and jumped back out of the truck to pull open a side gate and reveal a set of glistening steel steps, polished as mirrors.

"Thought you kids were educated!" he spat, then shambled back toward the cab, dropping a ring of keys onto the street in the process. Angie kept watching him, fascinated, as Winston refused to pick them back up, instead just kicking the keys ahead of him until he was around the passenger's side of the cab and out of sight. She looked around to see if anyone else saw this display. But instead, she heard the unmistakable sound of multiple throat clearings, threats, and the usual masculine puffery, as most every male in their mismatched crew roughhoused with each other in a desperate attempt to get noticed (an inevitable result of spontaneous shirtlessness). Angie sized up the boys, remembering a riddle Jill asked her once: "Is it grosser to watch some dude position himself to see or be seen?" Angie had answered "Seen," and Jill had explained the actual answer to this, as well as all riddles, was, "The doctor was a woman."

"Calm down, losers!" Jill shouted into the cloud of testosterone. "It's my goddamn birthday."

But people were so electrified, they were prolonging everything, that giddy euphoria of expectation and mass "edging" before an unknown activity inevitably turned to shit. Angie saw the guys flinch at her voice, and she was glad this was Jill's party, as Jill would be a valuable asset for keeping the boys under control. Especially their "classless" clown, ol' Janky Jeff. Her earlier classroom fiasco back on her brain, Angie clocked Lund to see if he'd bailed after his tormenting in the restaurant, but she saw him at the back of the bunch.

Always at the back of a bunch, this kid, she noticed. And someone who was clearly very nervous about taking off his shirt, let alone his pants. Angie had only met Lund once or twice on campus, and his skittish lack of eye contact was infectious enough to keep him at a social distance whenever their paths crossed. Angie wasn't sure if the name "Lund" was short for anything, and, as always, it was tough to care about young men of a certain age. To be honest, even if friends had called friends had called friends, Angie wasn't sure how he could have possibly ended up at this party. But the triplets had already paid for him, along with everyone else, so it was too late now.

Even farther back, beyond the hinterlands Lund was using for cover, there were some hushed tones as the crowd parted, and Carlos emerged, sort of the group's caboose tonight, someone sturdy who always laid low even though he didn't have to, and, in fact, hadn't even sat at their table in Papalino's earlier, choosing to chat up the kitchen staff instead. He was the most intimidating dude on campus, a Mexican power lifter with a flattop from the sports-medicine program, who was bigger than any two of them combined, even bigger than the driver, which made sense because rumor had it that Carlos used to drive a bus, too. Angie heard he'd arrived earlier than anyone, chugging his patented three (!) overflowing glasses of milk with his own personal all-meat pizza. "For protein," he'd say, arm like a moat around the pie, until there was nothing left within those greasy castle walls except a smoking crater and some crust rubble. The guys called him "Godzooky," and he worked weekends with Ruck on the campus maintenance crew for some extra cash. Angie assumed Ruck had invited him, and honestly thought Carlos was a little scary, but she would never admit this out loud because of the racial implication. Fascinated, she watched him slide through the rabble, eying the swirling red lights on the back of the fire truck like he might devour them next.

"This is gonna be so fun," Jill said, ascending the squat silver ladder onto the back stairs to the pool deck beyond, peeling down to her sports bra and undies as she went. "Except I didn't bring a swimsuit, ya jerks!"

"Don't worry about it," Angie said.

". . . because Beth didn't, either!" Amy added.

"You guys are nasty."

Carlos circled the throng one more time, not ready to climb up just yet, and several of them watched his thick hand stroking the lines of the fire truck like it was alive.

"I think he's going to fuck this truck," Dan snickered.

"Goddamn it, we are on a schedule!" Winston squawked from behind his wheel, patience gone, and everybody finally hustled up the ladder into the crisp, open air of the back trailer to start dipping toes into the water.

"Don't leave any y'all's phones on the sidewalk!" the driver yelled before he rolled up his tinted window for good. Angie hoped this was the last she'd hear from him.

She'd later regret that wish.

"Yeah, don't leave any phones!" Amy said to Angie with an elbow.

"And don't prank-call anybody, either!" Dan said to Angie with another elbow, and Angie frowned, thrown a little by this particular joke, secretly loaded as it was.

"I don't get it," Angie lied. But she got it, all right. She was sorry she'd told Dan anything about her childhood when they were together, but especially the stuff about her strange relationship with telephones.

"No, seriously," Reeves added, wanting to join in, but nudging Amy instead. "Never prank-call this chick's parents' house after midnight. They'll literally rip your head off."

"Literally, huh?" Angie said.

"Yes, literally!" Ruck said, jumping in front of her face, and Angie held a hand out to block him from getting on the truck.

"You called my house and literally got your head ripped off, huh? Prove it," Angie said.

"Okay, watch . . ." Ruck said, making a move like he was going to remove his own head, and for a second it seemed like he might. There were even some gasps when some of the more inebriated locals bumbled around the corner, which quickly turned to groans of disappointment when Ruck's cranium didn't go flying down the street after all.

"And don't leave any shoes!" came the penultimate muffled order from the cab.

"Yeah, don't leave any shoes!" Amy said, laughing.

"And don't leave any heads!" Angie added.

"We will not be coming back!" was the final announcement.

"Jesus Christ," Angie muttered, stepping up the ladder. "We get it."

"Did you hear that, guys?" Dan said, ducking in front of Angie and shouldering her painfully in the breast. "We won't be coming back."

"*You* won't be coming back," Angie snapped. "If we're lucky."

Up top, shaded from the fire truck's flashers, the shimmer of the street lights reflecting on the pool danced in their eyes, and the monotonous beat grew deafening to drown out their banter completely, vibrating loose the beads of nervous sweat from shivering backs as the pulse of the speakers synchronized their heartbeats.

Tonight, they all felt a little lucky. But that wouldn't last.

CHAPTER 11

SOUP-CAN TELEPHONES

Nahla's Story

We were sitting down to dinner when the phone rang, and my father sucked in a sigh, his throat swelling like a lizard. He didn't breathe until he allowed the receiver to ever so slowly touch his ear, then he held his blink just a little too long and hung the phone back on the wall. He never flinched from the calls like he used to, or even from the frequent bee stings (two reactions that used to be synonymous). We noticed he seemed less rattled by everything these days, maybe because he was surrounded exclusively by all of us females, but we were surprised to find ourselves missing the peripheral bluster that used to come with a brother-and-father dynamic in the house.

Our mother was passing around the honey-glazed carrots when the phone rang again, and my dad marched over and picked up and slammed down the receiver in one quick motion (but still not as hard or fast as he once did), never bothering to pull the spoon from his mouth. Our mother gently asked the table whose turn it was to change the number this week, and my dad sighed again, muttering through a mouthful that we might have to change it *twice* a week now.

"We all have to do our part if we want to keep it in the house," he said.

My little sister crossed her arms, demanding to know why we needed a phone at all, and she received a mystery kick under the table in return. I couldn't remember my last important phone call, but our mother once said a house without a phone was like a house without windows, which sounded worse than the alternative we were living with now.

"We're the last family in a thirty-mile radius who gets dinner interrupted every five seconds," my little sister hissed as she stabbed an unruly carrot, rolling and mashing it flat under her fork. I kicked her under the table again, harder than I meant to, and my sister spit out a stem in disgust. Our house was a lot tougher on carrots this year. The new honey our mother had used to flavor them (the cheap industrial version that most families had been reduced to) wasn't helping to ease the always tense dinner-table experience.

"Mom, Nahla's wearing her boots inside!"

"That's not true," our mother reassured everyone, ignoring my boots, just as we all ignored her eyepatch, which covered the hole of an eye she'd lost for reasons unknown. I couldn't remember her ever having two eyes, actually, but neither she nor my father would discuss it. In-house rumors included "errant bee sting" and "toothpick incident," though he insisted it was absolutely *not* due to an accident, as if that would ease our minds.

"There are people besides us who still keep phones around, just in case," our mother reminded us. "We just have to stay ahead of it, that's all. I'll change the number tomorrow. Everyone remember to write the new one on your hands!"

My dad sighed again, corralling his food into sectors like a jailhouse lunch tray, then sighed twice more before taking a bite. We once calculated he had exactly nine distinct sighs. And this particular high, sputtering example, Sigh Number Five, we'd baptized "Balloon Knot Slipping from Fingers."

Just when our forks were clicking and picking up speed, the phone rang again. This time, I made my move before my father, pushing out from the table and cutting the corner easy with the extra traction that adorned my feet for just such a chance. But my dad was always ready. Being closer to the wall, he slid my brother's empty chair into my path, bringing me crashing into the stove with a solid hip-check. My elbow clipped the wall mount on my way to the floor, and the phone followed me down, a lonely screw rattling on the linoleum next to my nose as my dad breathed his shuddering Sigh Number Three, or "Final Thumbnail Release Before Tire Properly Pressurized." He held out his thickly calloused hand to help me up.

"Nahla didn't hit her head again, did she?" our mother asked without looking.

Directly between my father and myself, the receiver twisted angrily on the floor, the hateful force of the voice coming from the phone keeping it squirming and whirling like a sadistic game of Spin the Bottle that had no real interest in playing Cupid and was instead just shooting random arrows for the hell of it, wanting more than anything to hurt anyone who remained to be tormented in such a circle.

But the spinning phone receiver would never stop, so the game could never start, or end.

The voice, however, was very clear.

"Can you hear me? I'm gonna kill every goddamn one of you . . ."

My brother, Greg Junior, had worked at the prison because it really was sort of exciting to have one so close by, even if most of the locals would never admit this. My father also did not agree.

"Wow, what a great idea," he sneered. "A huge, glass-and-steel highrise with a beautiful, riverfront view." He would insist that their town could have easily rented out high-end apartments on the same spot, opened some shops, brought some money back into their local economy. But we all knew he was mostly upset about his son betraying the family business.

We would park our bikes by the river, the closest we were allowed to get to the prison (making it our all-time favorite spot), and we'd try to glimpse any shadows behind one of a thousand heavy-duty, riot-glass windows. We couldn't know if it was an inmate or guard moving around in there, but we crossed our fingers that it was prisoners, hopefully continuing to do things they weren't supposed to, even while incarcerated.

"If they had built apartments on that property, maybe your brother could have been happy as a security guard," my dad said the last time our family was all together at the dinner table, his most loaded taunt since he challenged Greg to tear the phone book advertising supplement in half when he was nine years old, not even bothering to offer the phone book itself. My brother was convinced our father had turned on him simply because his new job required he showered before work instead of after work, the latter being a ritual he swore was the best indication of a man's worth, which made more sense than anything either of them did.

"A guard," he'd snort. "That's worse than a cop. Is my son really dead set on deserting our family legacy just to pretend a flashlight is a gun?" he would ask anyone who listened. But my brother wasn't the only family member in town to suddenly go AWOL on family traditions or societal norms after the prison showed up.

"You know what, Smalls?" my dad said to him, having recently regressed to a nickname he'd abandoned when chubby little Greg Junior first cried in recognition of the insult (or finally saw the movie it came from). "You don't realize what you've signed up for. A prison guard? Come on. That's like the pro golfer of law enforcement."

"Like the what?"

"Golfers aren't no goddamn athletes!" he railed. "Or baseball players, for that matter. Out of shape, haphazard grooming, too much jewelry . . ."

"That's firefighters, Pop."

". . . shit, I saw a pitcher at least ninety pounds overweight on a Wheaties box once. Two hundred fifty pounds counting the gold chain. Almost as ridiculous as football. In fact, the only thing that could make baseball watchable would be lighting home plate on fire, maybe throw in a shark or two. Use a hornet's nest for a ball . . ."

I remembered smiling at my father's last suggestion, though I knew he'd never abuse a valuable pollenating insect like that. I tuned out the rest of his rant, instead studying the two men in our family in what would turn out to be their final side-by-side snapshot. My brother really was just a smaller version of my dad, and "Smalls" suited him even better than the "Junior." Weirdly enough, our mother was a smaller version of my little sister, too.

But me? I forget about me sometimes. We were all small, but I didn't really look like anybody else, the reward for being a middle child and, as a result, the odd number out, a girl who looked like other girls, mercifully free from expectations and most people's memories.

Balancing on my kickstand and pedaling backward along the Alleghany River, I kept a lookout for cars. Even ten miles away from the prison, cops regularly cruised by, hanging out their window with their weary "move on, move on, *you*, yeah you, move on . . ." After the initial curiosity, some adults wanted the kids to avert their eyes from the horizon completely. But for anyone around my age, or maturity ("Elementary or below," my junior high teachers would sadly inform our parents), it was as if someone had placed a giant ant farm on top of a television set during the dullest Saturday morning cartoons, then insisted I never glance up.

But fascination was inevitable. The prison peering at us through the fog was all us kids could think about.

There was the initial outcry of potential dangers, of course, as well as the grumblings like my father's regarding the prime real estate wasted and the new sewage and oil slicks visible along the river's edge. But newspaper editorials assured everyone that private prisons were really just the next logical step in US incarceration, and that they would bring jobs and money to our town. And with the loss of most families' huge honey revenue, the townspeople truly wanted to be believers.

Before it got bad, there was even a time when only excitement was buzzing through the phone lines, when prison trivia filled dinner-table conversations without any sense of dread at all. My brother, Greg Junior, was one of the first guards hired the day they opened the doors (then closed and locked them just as quickly, of course), and he could always be counted on to bring home stories from that mysterious giant ant farm looming in the distance. One of the first nights, Greg Junior informed our wide-eyed mother there was the exact same number of prisoners as townspeople, and ol' Greg Senior scoffed at that notion.

"Impossible."

"No, it's true," my brother swore. "But they're keeping it secret. Freaks people out."

Our mother told the neighbor this gossip, and then that neighbor told *her* neighbor, and with only our matching populations in common, there was this sudden, strange compassion growing in naïve townsfolk such as myself for these mysterious, unseen inmates in our midst, as well as in the mist. So we started mapping the prison bus routes. And most of us kids could have told you who was coming in and going out and how close those statistics might also match the number of births and deaths at the local hospital. My little sister even reported that her classroom had started a project where they were writing letters to the inmates, as if these criminals were enlisted men at war overseas and not serving eight to ten for bashing a drug dealer's head in with a toilet lid ("Probably," my dad said). But instead of cutting off this line of communication, or firing the teacher responsible, the town debated how most of the incarcerated were likely the victims of unfortunate circumstances. And these weren't dewy-eyed California locals. This was goddamn Pittsburgh, the rustiest buckle of the Rust Belt.

But this prison was somehow romancing us all.

"Toilet lids are very hard," our mother shrugged, her one eye still smiling from the extra paycheck and the subsequent cost-of-living decrease. It was a small but significant cash influx that could easily be recognized at our dinner table, where all four food groups were finally represented again.

"Yeah, people don't kill people, toilet lids do," my dad sneered. He sneered almost as much as he sighed some days.

Later on, when blame was flying around and looking for somewhere to land, many people thought that it was this teacher who encouraged such an irresponsible correspondence that had started all our troubles. But she'd had little effect on our lives, if you don't count subconsciously inspiring my own dead-end career in academia as a fruitless "fuck you" to the educators who underestimated me. My brother, however, was the only one who really knew what it was like *inside* the prison, and it was his observations that always haunted me.

One night, long after the calls started, when everyone else was sleeping and our cordless phone was tucked in my pillowcase like an ornery bird (leaving it off the hook was somehow inconceivable), my brother crept into our room to explain to me that the town was being harassed over dinner every night with these calls because of him and him alone. Because, he explained, in a moment of weakness, he had loaned his cellular phone to one lonely prisoner.

"He wanted to call his girlfriend," my brother whispered. "It seemed important, Nahla, and he swore he'd give it back before they left the cafeteria. I guess someone killed him for it."

My heart fluttered, the importance of the phone in my pillow suddenly magnified by a thousand. I was relieved my little sister was sound asleep and heard none of this. She would have been worse at keeping the secret than I had been, and I was terrible at it.

"I didn't tell anyone," he said. "I was thinking I'd lie and just say I'd lost it. Hell, I figured the battery would be dead by morning. But snagging my phone got all those prisoners thinking, and they started passing it around before I could cancel the service. And when the bill showed up in our mailbox, it was showing numbers for half the houses in town.

Maybe they smuggled in a new battery? Renewed my minutes? I really don't know how it happened so fast. Maybe phones can multiply, from snacking on earwax all their lives. Maybe it's just inevitable. But hey, on the upside, at least it distracted them from their other horrible hobbies."

"What horrible hobbies?" I asked, spellbound.

"Ever heard of 'chemical warfare,'" Greg Junior asked, eyes practically pinwheeling in excitement. He loved grossing us out almost as much as we loved him doing it. "Or 'gassing,' as they usually call it."

"What's gassing?" I asked, my hands squeezing the ends of my pillowcase like handlebars.

"Gassing is what they call it when an inmate flings fermented piss, blood, and shit in your face when you walk by. So sure, there's probably a phone for every prisoner by now, but we were, like, 'Come on, there's worse things they could be doing, like gassing . . .'"

"Nasty!" I whispered, eyes dilating along with his.

One phone for every prisoner, I thought. *And one prisoner for every one of us.*

"That's nothing, though," he went on. "One dude with hepatitis Z, who we'll call 'Encephalitis Steve,' well, he likes to crush up light bulbs to stir in with his drool-and-fecal stew so you cut yourself and get infected when you try to wipe that shit off. 'Getting stung,' is what they named that one. Or as I like to call it, 'The Worst Fuckin' Day of Your Life!' Blood and piss concoctions are actually a little more rare, though. But, Nahla, you can't flinch for any of it. Not unless you want it to keep happening. You just cannot flinch."

"Flinch and you're dead?"

"Flinch and you're weak! And maybe that leads to dead. Or worse."

He seemed to really notice me for the first time that night, peeling me off from the collective "we" of our family, my identity taking shape right there in the echo of his sordid prison tales.

This change also caused him to suddenly reconsider the stories he'd told me.

"I shouldn't be telling you this stuff. Okay, listen, Nahla, don't tell anyone about any of this. Swear?"

I crossed my heart, lied about hoping to die, all that nonsense. Then the phone was screaming again, and Greg Junior reached behind my back and gripped its neck through the pillowcase, picking it up, thumbing it off, and flinging it back down like it was never there, a smooth self-defense move our family knew well, but one I was doing less and less lately.

But fast as my brother was, like the nasty little invincible genies they were, some of the threats always escaped the bonds of their tiny speakers and slipped into the rooms with us:

"Kill fuckin' kill, you fuckin' cock fuckin' motherfucker, I'll fuckin' kill you and you and you and you and you . . ."

I kept my brother's secrets as long as I could. But I almost squealed that weekend, when the most skittish families in the neighborhood started throwing phones out their windows. In desperation, some people even decided to try those ridiculous soup-can telephones. Then someone's son, the newest and therefore the most beautiful kid in our town (up to that point), got together with some other sixth graders and, inspired by their parents, tethered a private primitive phone line through the trees between their houses. Unfortunately, this beautiful new kid made the mistake of using a soup can that still had a little soup in it, congealed around the rusty edges, and a week later, the raging infection cost him 90 percent of his hearing in one ear. When he finally came back to school, none of us thought of him as the Beautiful New Kid anymore. Still, he tried to convince everyone that his father was the only one in town who'd stopped getting terrifying phone calls from the prison because of their "very special number," some nonsense about a combination of digits that made their house the most statistically unlikely to be dialed. It was a good idea in theory, but none of us believed him, and, like the little monsters we were, we pretended we couldn't hear him by cupping our hands over our own perfect ears when he was talking.

But soon after his disenchanted return to school, I decided I needed to whisper my brother's big secret into his ear. And in the one class we shared, while we were all watching a black-and-white movie on color-blindness of all things, I was careful to target the side of his head with the hair still cut high from a recent surgery, knowing that this way my confession wouldn't count as a betrayal to our family, even if he *was* awake during that movie, which was impossible. He heard nothing, and I felt so good afterward that I wished I could have kept using that dead ear as a repository for my deepest, darkest, most confidential disclosures. But the new kid and his father finally moved away for good a week later, the kid taking his dead ear with him, which was fine, because I really didn't have much else to confess. I'd later understand that secrets needed a circle of friends, and connections withheld from the most interested parties, facilitated by cupped hands over receivers, up and down the two-way street of that electronic umbilical. But at that point in my life, my street was a cul-de-sac, with voices coming in and not out.

Okay, that's maybe a bit too ambitious to consider myself a dead end at that age, but I was certainly on a road to nowhere. But maybe I did have one secret:

For me, the terrible ring of our telephone was welcome, and my eager tongue, which hovered over all the tiny plastic holes of those receivers, was always ready to roll out its red carpet.

CHAPTER III

A WATERPROOF WATCH

Once they had a chance to let everything (and everybody) literally sink in, the back of the fire truck turned out to be a bit of a disappointment. The bubbles around the border of the hot tub were crowned by oil-slick rainbows and a toxic yellow tint, and, upon closer inspection, the AstroTurf outlining the edges of the deck had visible black mold along the seams. And when everybody first eased their bodies into the churning pool, they discovered the depth of the water to be oddly inconsistent, sometimes coming up to the waist or neck of most of them, then seeming to be practically knee-level on Dan and Reeves, as if the pool contained its own tidal system, but its orbit was spinning wildly out of control. But when Angie saw the water fill Ruck's mouth as he splashed about, briefly choking off another rambling story about Lord knows what, she stopped worrying about water levels, for now, anyway.

Jill yelled, "Come on!" and guilted the last few stragglers (mostly the girls) into tossing their shoes and clothes into a pile on the plastic grass near the bottom of the silver steps; then the rest of them bounded into the pool like a string of ducklings chasing their mom's tail feathers. Most of them started out sitting down so their bodies could acclimate to the water temperature. Like the rest of the world adjusting to a rash of impossible-to-predict climates, the night was unusually warm, even for the Blue Grass State. But the seasons still changed in Kentucky just like anywhere else, so once the truck started moving forward, and the night wind started whisking the water off their backs, it became clear that it was going to get chilly if they stuck to half measures. Most forced themselves to at least dip down to shoulder-level to adapt, but the shivering was bringing them together, at least physically. According to the website, the "Party Bus" rolled year-round, rain or shine, touting its heated pool as "a slippery blanket to share with a dozen of your closest friends!" but Angie was starting to suspect this was overselling the fire truck's capacity for comfort. However, Angie figured someone like Jill, with a birthday that only came around every four years, was going to be happy tonight no matter how chilly things got. And they'd only be riding around for what? An hour?

Generic dance music pumped hard from speakers bolted to the top of the cab, rattling the truck's metal shell along with their brains, and Angie lamented her immaculate Prince party mix once again. The engine sputtered and revved up to gain speed on a hill near an overpass, and Janky held up his arm and tapped a huge Invicta wristwatch to note the time, mostly just an excuse to show off the unsightly puke green-and-chrome timepiece with a face almost as wide and shiny as his own. Every one of Janky's big-ass watches was more hideous than the last, but this one was something special, sporting a dial made from recycled Mountain Dew cans. Somehow, Janky thought being a "Bartle Skeet" junky also made him environmentally conscious.

"Okay, we're leaving late, people," Janky yelled. "It's quarter after nine! Make sure we get the full hour we paid for, baby!"

No one acknowledged his *Dirty Dancing* quote, and Reeves threw a lifeguard cross-chest rescue move around Janky's thin torso, slapping him onto his back. The *crack!* of the water sounded like it hurt, but both of them laughed when Janky thrust his dumb watch up high and triumphant.

"Waterproof to fifty meters, bitches!"

It was always a challenge for Reeves, or anyone, to successfully bully Janky, though the claim to fame that usually immunized him from ridicule was almost a decade old by now. He'd become sort of famous, one of those newspaper "miracle babies," though at the time he was a teenager who'd survived a bad landing when a passenger plane's landing gear failed to deploy. The story was, he had just upgraded his seat to First Class right before takeoff, and this seat change is what saved his life, making his close call the perfect fable to accidentally illustrate how important a privileged position was in life. It *did* stop people from calling him "Jinx," however, a nickname he'd hated all his life, even if "Janky" wasn't much of an improvement. Still, within a year, everyone but himself was sick of hearing about how he'd "cheated death."

Janky also had a congenital hand defect, and the huge wristwatches were an obvious overcompensation, but he gesticulated so often and so quickly when he told that story that the anomaly was usually invisible anyway.

The fire truck lurched forward under them as it found a higher gear, dumping most of the party onto their knees and elbows, then the ride smoothed out as it cruised down Bardstown Road past the busiest bars. Dan dragged his camouflage backpack to the middle of the pool, where it bobbed between his knees, and with some deft flicks of his wrists, started tossing cans of Natty Ice to the group like he was dealing cards. Some tiny hotel bottles of Jack Daniels and Jim Beam floated out of his bag, too, clinking against the sides of the pool and, like feeder fish, tapping everyone on the shoulder for attention. Some of the bottles twirled in lazy circles between them all, and Ruck started smacking at them like mosquitoes, finally snatching up two mini-bottles to crack open the tops.

"Jack and Jim . . . climbed out on a limb . . . to get a drink of water . . ." Ruck sang between sips, a can of beer in one fist and the snouts of two minis peeking out from between his other knuckles.

"You know what they say about mixing drinks," Amy warned him.

"That's not what that means," Ruck said, tossing a baby Jack Daniels at her belly button. "They mean don't mix them *up*."

"Are you really that dumb, dude?" Angie asked him.

"No, seriously, they just mean don't confuse one for the other! It's less of a warning than a reminder, kids!"

"Clearly, you are confused, yes." Angie twisted off a top and winced after a swig.

"Fuck off," Ruck said, spitting some beer her way, and some of the group blinked in surprise at the sudden venom. But, as usual, Ruck was grinning so wide, they couldn't tell if he was joking or not. He seemed to be trying to usurp Janky's role tonight as the tiresome "wild card," and nobody needed two.

This could be a problem, Angie thought. *Assholes are hard enough to tell apart* before *people get naked.*

Equally frustrated with Ruck's attempts to hog the spotlight, but much less likely to suffer fools, Jill grabbed one of his ankles and pulled him under the water again. Just to remind him whose party it was. He came up sputtering and coughing, maybe ready to swing at her, but Jill just stared him down. She had about ten pounds of muscle on him, but, more importantly, a confidence few ever challenged. Ruck blinked with the music for a moment, then just slinked back into the crowd to pass out more bottles.

"Thanks, birthday bee-otch," Angie said, and then she and Amy shouted together, "Happy birthday, Jill!" and the pool party cheered as everyone slapped the waves, suds bubbling over onto the fake grass and splashing over the rails.

"Yeah, happy birthday, queen!" Sherry said, as Holly and Gaddy joined her in the center of the pool. The three of them stood up tall, tanned skin gleaming in the streetlights as they clanked their cheap beers together. There was some howling from people on a nearby curb, and the partiers realized their fire truck was cruising in front of Shenanigans, one of the unruliest bars on the strip with a permanent health inspector's grade of C proudly displayed in its window. Angie squinted and saw that someone had taken the time to draw a plus sign on the glass next to that score, then a smiley face, and finally a *Good Enough!* above it all, and she secretly wished her grade-grubbing students would be satisfied with that grade.

The guys in the pool stood up to flex and answer the drunken call to arms, waving their beers and bottles at the street, whooping and whoo-hooing as the mammoth red engine picked up speed toward the next intersection. Angie thought they were going a little fast for Bardstown Road, but maybe the driver was just trying to catch all the green lights. As she peeped over the side and saw fewer taillights ahead, she thought Bardstown didn't seem as crazy as it usually did on a Saturday night, but there was time for that.

"Sorry we didn't bake you a cake," Gaddy said to Jill.

"No, that's fine," she said, laughing. "Like our mamas always said, you get cramps if you don't wait an hour before swimming!"

"Well, I get cramps when I combine pizza and beer. Or maybe that was pizza and milk," Amy said, looking around for Godzooky, their power-lifting poster boy for Muscle Milk and weird weekend dairy consumption. Then Ruck was there again, slowly rising up from the water in the center of their circle, goonish grin still intact, like a coven had conjured him up by mistake. He shouted over the music.

"Hello, ladies! So I was thinking . . ."

"You are truly terrifying, dude," Amy said.

"Yeah, what's gotten into you, Ruck?"

He just kept smiling at Angie as he nursed a mini-bottle of Jack like a pacifier. After a couple awkward seconds, he cleared his throat and turned back to Jill.

"Anyway, like I was saying, I think you may have a point."

"And what point is that?" Jill asked, cracking her knuckles, ready to dunk him again. Besides her ten pounds, she also had a good eight inches on him, and this was all in the arms, where most men didn't realize eight inches was the most useful.

"What Angie said! About getting confused! About combining too many things!"

The music dropped out for a second as the sound system crackled from some shortwave feedback, and things were oddly quiet as they rumbled to a stop at a red light. More of the group tuned in to the conversation at the center of the pool, and even a soggy Lund came up from his corner, his yellowing, half-soaked OUTPOST 31 T-shirt dangling and his acid-washed jeans hanging off him like a loaded diaper. A pink-and-yellow trail stained the seams of his back pockets and leaked into the water's surface behind him, and Angie looked around to see if anyone else noticed this stain. He was the only one of them still fully dressed, and she really didn't want to shame him into stripping down. Instead, Angie just watched him struggle with the decision of whether to scratch his head or cross his arms, then attempt both like he was trying it out for the first time in his life. She pretended to stretch to turn away from Lund, spotting Godzooky leaning on the rail, seemingly uninterested in pools or parties.

Everyone pressed in again when the music kicked back on.

"Think about how unusual all of this is!" Ruck shouted. "We are combining drugs, pizza, alcohol, animosity . . . and an old-timey fire engine. Madness! And you know what today is, right?"

"Hold on, what drugs?" Gaddy said, eyes moving left and right like a cat clock.

"Joking about the drugs! Calm down. I'll ask you again, what is today?!"

Of course they knew what today was, but they waited for him to say it anyway.

"It's Leap Day!"

"What can you do?" Jill shrugged, smiling. Growing up, Jill always hated being born on Leap Day because her parents used her unusual birthday as an excuse to get her a present every four years. But worse than that, it gave her a feeling of limbo, like she wasn't really maturing as fast as her peers. This was one reason she hit the gym early, when back home in South Carolina, most of her friends, girls *and* boys, were only interested in hitting the beach.

"I'm just saying that combining all these factors is unprecedented and could potentially be dangerous enough to influence temporal perception." He pretended to adjust a pair of invisible glasses.

"Riiiiiight."

Ruck kept beaming, but something in his eyes betrayed the earnestness of this claim.

"So wait, what are you saying?" Lund asked, suddenly interested enough to bumble forward and receive a vicious shove backward in return, a push that seemed to come collectively from the group.

"Watch where you're going, shit bag," Reeves said. "And pull up your pants." Lund said nothing, and Reeves added, grimly serious, eyes a little wider, "And stop looking at me."

Lund sloshed away into the dark. When they first climbed in, Angie had thought the pool seemed too small for everybody, but it seemed to be growing larger with every turn of the truck.

"What did he say?" Dan gargled through a rapid froth of beer around his lips. Being half-submerged was affecting their ability to drink in any reasonable way.

"I think he said, 'Let's get back to the party!'" Reeves squeezed Dan's cheeks to eject the foam, then they both peeled off to go back on the rail and hoot and holler at some high-heeled women on the road teetering dangerously close to their wheels. Reeves took a second from his catcalling to give Angie some side-eye, and Angie remembered how performatively obnoxious he could get, like it was a burden to always be such a prick. But in that moment, she also realized Reeves reminded her a bit of her brother, with an attitude her family had labeled "stagecraft," that fascinating disconnect with the expectations of any current situation, coupled with a self-awareness he never fully utilized.

Or maybe they both just liked to smirk.

Either way, she wasn't quite sure how she felt about these newfound connections between childhood memories and this party, or any link between Reeves and her brother, for that matter, but she decided that, psychologically, this revelation wasn't as terrifying as the day she discovered Dan had reminded her a lot of her *dad*. Shudder. At one point, she chalked up all this to the simple fact that Reeves and Dan were, at one point, the new kids at the University of Louisville, and she had always been into the new kids (except for Lund, of course). She heard these two had even arrived in the same car, with a broken horn no less, leering villains right out of an '80's movie, so Angie could justify being infatuated with them for a minute, along with everyone else, in that *Pretty in Pink*–era James Spader sort of way.

But if someone wanted to get technical, the *newest* New Kids on the Chalk weren't any of the boys. It was actually Holly and Sherry. Or was it Holly and Gaddy? Angie could never remember. And they were tougher to love than anybody. Maybe not as tough as Ruck, though, who was yammering again.

". . . all I'm saying is, if it wasn't February 29, and if this was a normal, modern-day fire truck doing what it was supposed to be doing, we'd have a much better handle tonight on our passage of time."

People were splashing him hard to try and shut him up, but Ruck was really stuck on this.

"Hey, I'm serious!"

"Well, thank Christ for Janky's fifty-pound watches, am I right?" Dan said, looking for Janky's scrawny arm that was always lugging around such a ridiculous anchor.

"Fifty *meters*, bitches!" came a small but excitable voice from the water.

"I have a watch, too," Lund offered.

"Oh yeah? Well, *watch* this!" Dan shouted, and with both hands rammed Lund down onto his ass. Then again. Then again.

"I was just trying to . . . I was . . . trying . . ." he tried to explain, finding himself underwater over and over, sucking and bubbling and struggling to get up.

"What did I tell you about looking at me, punk?" Reeves asked the writhing shape under his knee. Then Jill was running toward them, and Reeves quickly pulled Lund up to his feet, in the process stretching the collar of his T-shirt so far that his slick, bony shoulder popped out of the hole like a pale wing.

"Yeah, *watch* this!" Ruck yelled, shoving Lund again, but nobody was laughing anymore. Sherry got between Ruck and Lund to stop the harassment, then handed Lund a mini-bottle to take his mind off the indignity of it all. Reeves peeled off to do a top-rope wrestling dive from the corner rail, already over it.

"Stay in your lane, *Lord of the Fries*," Dan said to Lund with a final chest bump, knocking him onto his back one last time. The reference made Angie's heart skip a beat as she couldn't help remembering her cursed final class. But one or two warm beers later, everyone was dancing again, and the territory skirmishes seemed mostly forgotten, at least for now.

Except for Angie, who was thinking about what Ruck had said as she continued to drink. She looked around until she caught Beth's eye, who seemed to be the only other person at the party to consider this equation:

Leap Day plus interpersonal conflict plus mind-numbing music plus historically charged object (and maybe some drugs) equals . . . potentially unforgettable, otherworldly celebration?

Then Beth was looking away, and only Angie was considering these disparate elements of a previously undiscovered ritual. But if they really were to summon something in that pool, what would it be? And would they even know when it happened?

Lower Bardstown was the wildest street in Louisville, second only to Lower Baxter. However, Lower Baxter didn't get the army of motorcycles roaring their engines at the Speedway at the corner of Bardstown and Grinstead, drunk from the heavy pours you got at the Back Door.

Approximately fifteen blocks into the party, as the fire truck slipped through the nucleus of midtown revelry, dance skills were starting to be affected by some noticeable shivering.

"I don't think this pool is actually heated," Angie said, hugging herself and vigorously rubbing her upper arms, the universal declaration of "It's kinda fuckin' cold, right?"

Besides some holdouts, the mingling of the cliques had formed a double ring of bodies in the middle, with many of them crouching low or sitting to maintain body heat. They weren't ready to admit just yet that they were having slightly less fun, but they were starting to ask some more questions.

"Hey, can somebody ask homeboy to turn up this piece?"

"The heat or the music, Dan?"

"Your mouth."

"Your mom's mouth."

"Your mom can't come to the phone right now," Dan said to Janky, bobbing his hands like she was in his lap. "If there's a message you want to leave her, let me know."

"Fun fact," Lund said. "On a long enough timeline, two people exchanging 'your mom' jokes will eventually result in the legal adoption of the losing participant."

Everyone considered this a moment.

"You hear that, Janky? You're my son now. How do you want me to make up your bed? I had trains, but I want it to be just right."

"No, you're *my* son now. So I'm going to need you to bring home ten job applications every Friday or you're going to start paying rent."

"I live rent free in your balls," came the response, which was confusing enough to end it for now.

"Well, if we *were* talking about this horrible music, how about we get him to turn it off for good?" Amy proposed.

The volume of the music had increased steadily once they passed the Mid-Town Mall parking lot on another borderline-alarming turn, and Amy wasn't the only one gritting her teeth because of the beats. Angie's head was only a foot from one of the speakers, and she had to make a conscious effort to keep from flinching, but the rest of them had almost grown used to it, close enough to forcefully project their voices at more reasonable volumes.

"No, I meant turn up the heat!" Dan said, laughing. "I've had enough of this rave shit for a lifetime."

"I'll do it," Reeves said, looking for any excuse to spring dolphin-like from the water and show off his abs and the swim trunks clinging tightly to his groin. He stomped and splashed his way out of their circle up to the back of the cab and leaned down to knock on the driver's back window.

"What the hell . . ." Reeves muttered, and the others turned toward Reeves and saw something they hadn't noticed before: The tinted, oval window on the back of the fire truck's cab was covered with iron bars, sparkling fresh welds attaching them to the frame. And the glass behind the bars wasn't just tinted, it was mirrored, reflecting back their confused faces. Reeves rapped on the metal bars until his knuckles hurt, then he tried pounding on the roof instead.

"Yo! Action Jackson! How about you stoke that fire, boy!"

The truck slowed somewhat, and Reeves stood straight and proud, probably expecting applause. But the truck was only making another tight turn onto Eastern Parkway, quickly accelerating back up to speed.

"Do you think he heard me?" Reeves asked the group as he spun around to let his body collapse into their waiting hands for a fairly effective stage dive. They lowered him into the water, laughing, and Angie snorted. It was a move they'd done at her faculty retreat the previous summer, and despite all attempts to resist, she found it impossible to not catch anyone who did that sort of "trust fall," even if it was staff members she despised.

Or maybe it was a "trust jump," she thought.

The worst part was the sweaty retreat coordinator explaining it was "very much like tossing someone a basketball," then proceeding to hurl Nerf basketballs at them. He told them that only two percent of the world's population will allow any ball to hit them in the chest, and that number seemed high to her. But here she was, catching Reeves with the same trust she'd give a greasy foam basketball.

"I don't know," Dan said to Reeves, squatting next to him to spit water up at his chest. "Does it feel any warmer?"

"I'm pretty cold," Beth sighed, perma-frown locked on.

Janky crawled over to Beth to imitate her sour expression, then leaned backward into a kind of *Exorcist* crab walk, his head almost completely inverted, half-submerged and laughing.

"There! Now you're smiling!" he said.

Beth slid away from him, and Lund took this opportunity to move in, shifting his body slightly closer to hers, and Beth moved away from him, too, bumping into Godzooky's formidable frame on her way out of the circles. She leaned her head on his massive bicep, and Angie frowned at this exhibition, knowing that Beth's displays of weakness might turn off Jill, even more than Beth's backslide into gender norms. But Angie saw Jill nearby, oblivious to it all as she checked out Holly's long legs and her dripping ringlets of hair, and Angie figured her attempt to play Cupid tonight with Beth and Jill was already screwed.

"I firmly believe the only thing keeping us alive right now is global warming!" Ruck announced, opening another mini-bottle. Spirits high, he ran forward to pound on the cab like Reeves had done.

"Hey, Argyle! You in there?"

"What the hell is going on with this guy?" Jill mumbled, turning from Holly's legs to finally take stock of their situation. She pushed past Ruck and peered through the bars into the mirror.

"Maybe the driver's wearing headphones?" Lund proposed, protective arms crossed so tight they sank into the damp shirt draped over his soft torso. His acid-washed jeans were now sagging so low, they appeared to be melting into the waves.

"It's like that Prince song . . ." Amy started to say.

Some of them obliged her with a "go ahead and tell us the dumb song" sort of sigh.

"You know. We sang it at our house all the time. Where they go, 'Amy?' 'Yes, Lisa?' 'Is the water warm enough?' 'No, Lisa.' 'Also, the bathtub is clogged.' 'Okay, Lisa.' 'Do you have the Drano?' 'Yes, Lisa.' 'Whose turn is it to clean the tiles?' 'I don't know, Lisa, is it Thursday?' 'Let's both do it, then.' 'Shall we begin . . .'"

Angie and Jill appreciated the joke, and Jill gave Amy a high five. Like many of the post-grad-age students she knew (and presumably some of the others currently hopping around the pool), Jill, Amy, and Angie had been every combination of roommate, tenant, and sofa squatter at some point, but they'd always remained friends.

"I'm talking to you, bro! Can you hear us out here?!" Ruck was punching the roof of the cab. "Fix that jukebox! Shovel that coal! Unclog that drain!"

"Great," Dan said, laughing. "This crazy crackerjack at the wheel is probably drunk, listening to bluegrass murder ballads or some shit. And now he's cleaning his gun."

"I didn't notice an accent when he was yelling at us on the street," Lund offered, sheepish.

"I think you lose your accent when you yell," Ruck said. "That's science."

"I think it's the opposite," Lund said.

"Well, this suicide music is no accident," Reeves said as he double-fisted more liquor.

"What do you mean?" Amy asked.

"I mean, I think he's torturing us."

"Do you think he wants us to jump?" Ruck asked him, and Reeves cracked two more beers and drained them completely before answering.

"I think he wants us to jump."

He spiked one can in the water and crushed a second one in his fist. At least five dented empties were bobbing around him as he reeled his camo backpack up to his body for more alcohol.

"What the hell are you looking at?" Reeves asked Godzooky, who had moved much too close to him for comfort. But Godzooky, as always, seemed like he was looking through the crowd instead. Then Godzooky found Reeves's gaze and held it, and a momentary quiet cut through the incessant beat as the music hiccupped and cycled back to the beginning.

"Who wants to play chicken!" Ruck shouted to break it up.

"Is the water deep enough to play chicken?" Jill asked. "We're not all pocket-sized like you, Ruck."

"Okay, how about Spin the Bottle!" he said, laughing, skipping a tiny whiskey bottle toward her like a pebble on a pond.

"How about we tell some campfire stories instead?" Beth said sarcastically, grabbing Godzooky's telephone-pole of a forearm for stability. "Because I'm freezing, y'all!"

"Try smiling," Dan sniggered. "Maybe that'll warm you up."

"Do not *ever* tell me to smile," Beth said, letting Godzooky go, sloshing toward Dan, hands on her hips like a gunslinger. Her eyes blazed with almost murderous intent, and Angie had to wriggle in to separate them. She put a hand on Beth's shoulder and steered her over to where Jill and Amy were claiming a corner. She had never seen Beth like that before.

This night is getting weirder with every turn, she thought as the fire truck lurched again.

"It doesn't feel like you're shivering," Angie said to Beth. "You feel hot, actually."

"I am shivering so fast it's undetectable to the naked eye," Beth corrected her, and Angie looked Beth over and believed it. There was an energy coming from her body that tonight was even more palpable on their aquatic dance floor. Angie looked around to find Holly, Sherry, and Gaddy watching the two of them very closely. Gaddy was taking turns whispering in each of her friends' ears, earning her "Gadfly" nickname.

Or is that her real name?

Once, when they'd been stuck in a weeklong writing-lab seminar together, but before all the plagiarism accusations, Ruck told Angie that he heard through Amy that the "new girl Holly" had "sticky fingers." And if Angie had wanted to suffer through an actual conversation with Ruck that day, she might have asked him to clarify whether this was a slur against Holly's sexual preferences or an accusation of shoplifting. She hoped to never solve that mystery. To an outsider, the alliances and web of gossip might have been hard to follow, but on the party bus, things were getting simplified, reducible to the precise number of bodies confined on the fire truck; a mostly insignificant number of bickering dude bros, give or take a loner, and exactly two regiments of three women each. Oh, and there was Beth.

"Get naked, you say?!" Ruck hollered at them. "Yes, great idea, girls."

This talk of nudity reminded some of them of their clothing, or maybe just the possibility of being warm again one day soon. And that's when Angie finally noticed it.

"Wait, where is our shit?" she said.

"Huh?" Jill said, turning from picking a sliver of pepperoni out of her teeth in the mirror of the cab's back window to look where Angie was pointing.

The stairway that divided the cab from the trailer—the area where they'd left their stuff—was empty.

"Our shirts, pants, shoes, everything. They're gone."

Everyone else followed Angie's finger. She was right. The mound of clothing that they'd bundled and stacked and pinned down on the metal steps with their shoes was missing. Everyone pushed forward to look for their belongings. Elbows jabbing. Voices rising.

"Did the driver take our stuff?"

"Did that guy seriously steal our shit?"

"Maybe he put them up in front with him? For safekeeping?"

"He fuckin' stole our shit!"

"No way, we would have noticed that."

"Where's the hell's my purse?!"

"Seriously, guys, my Aquaman Converse high-tops were vintage. Irreplaceable."

"He totally stole our shit!"

"Man, I had a harmonica in my jeans."

"A harmonica? Jesus. Thank God he stole your shit!"

"What's wrong with a harmonica?"

"Better question! What good is having Aquaman high-tops if you don't wear them in the water?!"

"No, think about it. If you don't want airport security to search your ass, carry a harmonica. Shows up on the X-ray real good, but they won't risk drawing attention to it because you might take it out and *actually start playing*. They'd rather risk a bomb on the plane. This has worked for me for five years."

"He's right. Harmonicas are the worst."

"Your Aquaman high-tops were knockoffs anyway. Pretty sure they said 'Aqua Dan.'"

"Why the fuck would he take our shoes after reminding us not to leave them behind?"

"He terk our jerbs!" Janky shouted, and most of them laughed to break the tension.

"Maybe they just got dumped off the truck on a turn?"

"We haven't had a hard turn yet."

"Uh, yes, we have. Like, ten of them!"

"Okay, is our hour up? I'm about done with this party bus."

"Yeah, what time is it anyway?"

Several of them looked to Janky, and he thrust up his heavy-watch arm, but he held his breath before he answered, eyes shifting as a passing streetlight illuminated their faces.

"I . . . don't know," he said finally.

"What the hell do you mean 'you don't know'?" Reeves asked, grabbing his wrist to get a look at his Invicta.

"I mean, it's got a lot of dials, man . . ."

"You never set this watch, did you, Janky?"

Reeves and Dan began fighting over Janky's arm, squinting at all the microscopic numbers on the overly complicated watch face, then Dan shook him by the shoulders and pulled the comically huge timepiece up to his ear, dragging Janky's entire body along with it.

"Hey!" he protested.

"Yeah, I don't hear nothin'," Dan said, shaking Janky like a scarecrow. "This thing's broke."

"My watch is working! It's a limited edition! Runs on good vibes!"

"Hold on a second." Reeves sounded concerned. "What time does that bullshit say? That can't be right."

"Waterproof to fifty meters, bitches . . ."

Reeves slapped Ruck hard across the face and was shocked that the strategy worked. He shut up and held his wrist straight under their noses.

"No. Way," Dan said, turning Janky's arm around and showing the watch to the rest of the party.

"'No way' what?"

"No way we've been driving for three goddamn hours."

"Does anybody have a phone?" Dan was asking. "A phone! Who kept their phone?"

"And where would we be hiding our phones, genius?" Amy said, laughing, and Lund absently patted his sagging jeans.

"Your watch is broke as fuck, Janky," Reeves said, patience gone as he struggled to rip it free from his wrist.

"Ow!"

"Or maybe this is just some of that Leap Year sorcery I was talking about," Ruck said from behind them.

"What was that?"

"He's right," Jill nodded. "Whenever it's my birthday, the world remains in limbo until tomorrow. Four years will pass in one night."

"Wait, fer real?" Janky asked her.

"No, not 'fer real,' stupid," Dan said, arm back and considering a slap of his own.

"Holy shit! A four-year party?! What will we drink?"

"Ninety-five proof to fifty meters, bitches!"

"Everybody shut up about the goddamn watch!" Reeves said, snapping the leather wristband free of Janky's arm with one last tug, while Janky went flying.

"Hey, give that back to him," Angie said, not so much worried about the theft as she was about losing control of the party. Godzooky crept in close again to shadow Angie, and she appreciated the backup. Reeves eyed the veins in Godzooky's forearms cautiously, but scoffed to save face. Then he side-armed the ludicrous watch over the railing, and everyone watched it detonate against a stop sign that the fire truck was currently blowing through without slowing.

The music had stopped again as it recycled, the colorful flashers dimming as the glow of civilization faded into the intangible dark beyond their taillights.

"Is this a joke?" Angie asked everyone.

"Cocksucker . . ." Janky sneered at Reeves as he got back up, and he surprised everyone by hauling back and taking an ambitious round-house swing at Reeves's angular, chiseled face. He missed by a mile, however, and Reeves caught him by the back of the neck like a puppy and hauled him backward into the pool, winding up his free hand for a good smash to possibly flatten Janky's princess nose forever. But before he could follow through with the punch, Reeves found his wrist locked tight in Godzooky's throbbing beef-heart of a fist. The music was back, joining a series of potholes that thumped out a drumroll under their feet.

After a tense five seconds of deadlocked stare down, swallowed by the deafening return of the mind-numbing trance beats, Godzooky lowered Reeves's arm, slow enough for him to change his mind about trying another hammer fist, at least for now. Some of the partygoers looked Godzooky over from head to toe for the first time, noting the heavily muscled chest bursting under the construction-orange tank top, and some of them wished this chest had their back, too—or even maybe their pillow—though they had no idea how much strangled snoring that extra meat marbling his pectorals caused its owner every night. Being big always came with a price.

Someone handed Godzooky a congratulatory beer, and he drained it like it was a balloon, and most of the party followed suit. Godzooky was the kind of guy who didn't need to crush the can afterward, though sometimes he did accidentally, like now.

"This is definitely the strangest birthday yet!" Jill shouted, shaking her head, her voice echoing as they cruised under an overpass, throwing them into temporary darkness with just the flashers and strobes on their faces. "Who paid for this bus anyway? Just so I can thank 'em!"

The three coconspirators in the corner laughed and flipped their wet hair around, looking at Jill slyly, and, for once, all three of them were eager to answer a question.

"We did?" Sherry said, tying back a ponytail. "Sort of." More laughter and shady giggles.

"What do you mean, 'sort of'?" Lund wanted to know, surprised by his own indignation. But they'd all chipped in for the rental, and no one would be happy with their hard-earned student-loan money being pocketed.

Sherry pulled a remarkable wad of bills seemingly out of thin air and started fanning them off the stack and into the water like she was rewarding a particularly agile striptease.

"Where the heck did that come from?" Lund was awestruck.

"God *damn*, are you made of money, girl?" Amy asked her, raking her nails gently across Sherry's abs to see if more cash flew out her navel.

"You just have to keep those muscles strong," Sherry said, cryptically.

"Oh no," Ruck said, looking down at her bikini. "Is that where you hid it?"

"Don't worry about it . . ." she started to say, but Ruck was already diving for the dollars and cramming them into the waistband of his swim trunks.

"Whoo-hoo!" he yelled as Holly moved in to grab Sherry by the collarbone, swinging her around to stop the rainmaking with their stash.

"Are you nuts?" she asked Sherry through her teeth.

"Just having some fun, dang," Sherry said, flicking a final dollar across the tip of Holly's nose. Holly's tongue rolled around just under her lips, like she was considering saying more, but thought better of it with everyone looking on.

"So you gals are sorta new here, right?" Angie said, eager for a distraction from the new information she couldn't help but add to her ever-growing equation:

Unresponsive driver plus plummeting temperature plus all our shit stolen equals . . . human trafficking?

"Yeah, you never told us how y'all met," Amy said.

"Hell, yeah, what brings you lanky freaks together?" Janky asked, inciting the rest.

"I would love to hear that!"

"Me too."

"You would."

"Me three."

"Tell us a story, Mommy!"

Gaddy held up a hand, playing coy, and Sherry and Holly shared a look like they were contemplating letting a cat out of the bag. Ruck hopped up and danced around them with their dollar bills bulging in his shorts and filling his cheeks, twirling himself dizzy until he dropped with a plop.

"Spin me a yarn," he bubbled and slurred around his mouthful of slushy money, "Pretend we're sitting around that campfire, warming up them butts."

"Gross," Angie said, trying not to look at him.

"It's actually easier to start a fire than you think," Sherry said, laughing, getting comfortable in the water and motioning for others to gather around. She looked like she really was going to weave them a juicy tale after all.

"We burned down a bar once, didn't we, girls?"

Feeling a real good story threatening like a thundercloud, Janky's feet stopped kicking to the nerve-wracking reverberations of the electronic music and he sat down a little too hard and stayed there. The other partiers joined him. The drunkest of them so far, Ruck struggled hard to listen, however. Hands on his ears, he looked like he was at rapt attention, but he was actually holding his own noggin erect, delirious but also confident his head might come unscrewed and bounce off down the road behind them.

He'd soon learn how accurate this premonition was.

CHAPTER IV

DOLLA DOLLA BILL WALL

Sherry's Holly Story

Okay, ready? So there's this bar back around our old college haunts called The Hut, and the first night I walk in there, I can't believe what I'm seeing. I try to get people to talk about all this money I see pinned to the walls, but everybody acts like they're over it.

"Oh, that money?" Chuck the bartender looks up when I ask the obvious. "That's nothing. Just the first dollar SCU students make at their first job. They come back here to celebrate and pin up a buck."

So yeah, this dive bar with literally *thousands* of one-dollar bills all along its walls and ceiling is within sight of Santa Carla University's campus, and the location is probably one of the reasons patrons would think walls covered in cash is no big deal. I mean, how privileged do the locals have to be to shrug off money that's almost literally growing on trees, right?

"What's with all the little notes stuck on all their dollars?" I ask Chuck.

"Those are their first business cards."

Aha! *That's* how privileged. I try to imagine a world where kids are so spoiled that their first job comes with a business card. With a blue-collar upbringing and years of union strike food filling my lunch box, this all sounds like science fiction to me, and it helps to say "imagine a world" with a deep announcer's voice to not laugh out loud. Which is kind of like the bartender's voice, come to think of it.

Now, Chuck is lingering near me longer than his job requires, so I know I'm looking good and getting ready for hours of free beers. But then I almost blow it with my next question.

"Don't you guys worry about someone stealing them?"

"Who the hell would steal them?" he says, walking away from me, all disgusted, not even taking my drink order, let alone offering me a freebie, which is fine, really, since I never know what I want. But I *do* know that I have all sorts of bad ideas now.

The next morning, I drive up to San Francisco for the long Memorial Day weekend, struggling to avoid the scourge of tollbooths. I originally grew up in Northwest Ohio, where toll roads were a real problem, where spending every weekend feeding dollar after dollar into the greedy mouths of those way stations between Toledo and Chicago (with sometimes less than a mile of highway between stops and starts) was as depressing as feeding them into a stripper's G-string. Both come with exactly the same sad lack of progress.

What I'm saying here is *I* didn't pin my first dollar to any walls because I'd no doubt wasted it at a fucking tollbooth.

So when I get home to San Fran, I tell my dad I've been kicked out of another school for plagiarism. Yep, you heard right. And it seems like he doesn't care as much as he did the last time, but he sure doesn't get the joke when I explain it was my class on postmodernism, of all places, where I got busted , so, actually, plagiarism in *this* instance should have been rewarded.

Let me back up a little further. By that I mean jump ahead . . .

The second night I end up in The Hut is about a month later, and by now I can't take my eyes off all that cabbage growing on those walls. I stare at the money on the ceiling so long that drunks peepin' up my nostrils start feeling a little too intimate, but after 2:00 a.m., I finally get a chance to lie down on the pool table and calculate the money on the ceiling to add to the grand total on the walls, and a little cash register is *ka-chinging!* right along in my brain. Normally, people might do a double take with me stretched out on the table like that, but half the balls are missing, and no one's playing, and I'm so tall, I'm sprawled out with my hands and heels in the pool table's pockets.

So while I'm staring up at this canopy of limp but leafy greens, I'm reminded of my dad's favorite novel, *Black Sunday*, and the part when the Secret Service stops by Tulane stadium for their security check before the President's Super Bowl visit. But security is so used to checking just the doors and locks and windows that no one ever thinks to look up to the sky.

"They *never* looked up," my dad used to remind me, every summer he reread it.

But I'm lying on this filthy pool table for a long-ass time, okay? Picking at one of the deeper cigarette burns in the soft felt as I count every dollar above me, and it's like trying to count the stars, and it gets pretty late, so I know I'm going to be left with what we used to call the "trail mix peanuts," meaning all the desperate, unwanted rejects who are left at the bottom of the bowl when the lights come on. It's *always* the peanuts. It's never just you and a hot Brazil nut, you know? And while I'm working on calculating my grand total, some dudes in bright, shiny shirts (more like *circus* peanuts, which are the worst) start circling the table to hit on me, pretending they want to get in on whatever game I'm playing, and I'm good at letting people run their mouths while I just nod along.

There is one particular honey-glazed cashew eyeing me through the barroom detritus, however; leggy, blonde, sort of an exaggerated *me*. I make a note to find her later when they sweep up the rest of the nuts.

I'm finally able to finish my rough count of the money through all this unwanted attention in just a couple hours. And as I do this, I suddenly realize that counting each dollar is the exact amount of time it would take to pluck one off the wall.

I'm up to $5,000 dollars when I finally get up off the pool table and Holly grabs my face and spins it into a kiss.

The third night, I head to The Hut to meet Holly again. My lips are still chapped from our first smooch and "meet cute," but this time she's all talk, no action. We waste time blathering about how she was a biology major at SCU until she pilfered someone's chemistry project for her final exam. I don't tell her about my own adventures in academic dishonesty, but now that I know she probably *can't* be trusted, I figure it's safe to confess my obsession with the dollar bills on the walls. She's well aware of them, and together we marvel at how no one else seems to think this is odd. We also talk about Santa Carla being like a gingerbread house of cash or something, and how only losers like us think walls made of actual money is something strange enough to draw attention to.

"It's like the 'Emperor Has No Clothes,'" Holly says, trying and failing to blow her thick blonde hair out of her face and off her nose, fighting with it way more than necessary.

"You mean 'The Emperor's New Clothes,'" I say, laughing. "And it's kind of the opposite?"

"Right."

"So what do *you* think about the cheese all over these walls?" I ask some slaphead drunk who's trying to gently elbow between us for attention.

"Welp, I've been coming in here since the '80s," he says. "So that means Chuck must routinely rip these dollars off the walls to make room for more. He must be making bank!"

"So you think yoinking this money would be a victimless crime?" I ask him. "Sorta like a Robin Hood situation?" I shrug, and he shrugs back.

"Sure. And I'm Friar Fuck!" With this, he makes a reach for my ass.

"Yikes," I say, pinching his bottom lip hard with my thumb and forefinger. This particular drunk has been trying to get on our radar for an hour, and he's regretting it fast.

"It's a trick, I say!" the drunk yells, falling backward, one hand down his pants and the other flicking the corner of a dollar bill like he's testing it for weaknesses. Chuck looks up to make sure the drunk knows he's being watched, then shakes his head and swabs a swirl of swill puddling near the resister with his rag.

"What do you mean, exactly?" I ask the guy, and he angles his head in to whisper, his swamp breath making me switch to mouth breathing.

"Them there money walls? It's like a . . . psychological experiment?" he says conspiratorially, and more young men gather round. Not to hear more prattle from this wheezing slapjack, but because Holly and I don't realize our stools are blocking the lane of the Atomic Dunk basketball game. Feeling ornery and enjoying our new roles as obstacles, we both spin our knees toward the drunk, an unmistakable signal to him to "take your time and shoot your shot."

"Okay, okay, okay," he says, excited. "You guys ever see that movie *Witness*? Where that cop is hiding out with the Amish, and he's up there on the roof pounding in big wooden nails with toy wooden hammers and wiping his brow while the comely womenfolk pass around big sweaty lemonades?"

"Probably not." It was on Netflix a couple months ago, actually, but I turned it off right at the beginning when the hero wrecks a birdhouse. I knew I'd just keep thinking about homeless birds for the whole movie.

"Well, back home in Ohio, I saw that movie in the theater when it came out, and afterward I start thinking, 'I wanna help an Amish family build a barn!' So I get a map and it's only a three-hour drive to the Amish stronghold of Shipshantucket or wherever, but it's a total tourist trap, right? And I find exactly one horse and one carriage and that's it. But they pretend they can't see me! Even though I'm yelling out the window plain as day, 'Got a barn?! I'll friggin' build one for ya, chief!' So I eventually settle on eating a tuna sandwich in an 'Amish-owned' diner." He gives us the air quotes. "'Amish-owned' according to the sign, anyway . . ."

"Awesome story, my dude," Holly says, starting to spin her stool back toward me, and he speeds up.

"Wait, wait, so I go in the diner, right? And on the floor is this silver dollar. And I go to grab it, but it's one of those gags where you can't pick it up, right? It's freakin' nailed to the floor! But is that to trick the tourists or the locals? I ask the Plain Jane waitress, who, it should be noted, is wearing a suspiciously colorful hair clip. How's that 'Amish'?! And if they aren't allowed to use nails and hammers and, like, electricity, how are they able to hammer silver dollars into the floor? Or toast my goddamn sandwich? But apparently, besides invisibility, another Amish superpower is refusing to answer questions, and she just gives me my tuna melt without a peep. But before I leave, I ask her one more time, 'Who's that silver dollar really for?' And she sighs and says, 'It was for you.' So sure, maybe I didn't exactly build a barn, but I built a *bridge*. And I passed their test, you know? So now you know what I'm thinking? I'm thinking maybe they do the same thing the kids do here. And that silver dollar in the floor was just the first dollar that joint ever earned."

"Cool story, bro."

"It wasn't bad, actually," Holly admits.

"I'm basically Amish now," he says.

"Well done."

Chuck stifles a laugh from behind the bar, and we spin back toward the basketball hoop, tiny umbrellas falling and our new drinks in hand. We don't even look to see who bought them for us because we're already having fun planning our caper. And over the next hour or so, we talk about how we need at least one more person to pull it off, how Holly would prefer it if we had four, but Honorary Amish Guy is currently our only sad prospect for a third man, and he's still lingering near this basketball game like he wants to feed it dollars off the wall and blow our cover. So I freeze him out until he leaves. But apparently, I've smiled at him one too many times without realizing, and he comes right back, stuck to us like honey. First, he wants to shoot baskets again, but soon enough he's back onto his theory about the money being fake, like it's been pinned there to test our resolve or something. "We're practically next door to Stanford!" he says. "Zimbardo?! The Stanford Prison Experiment? Come on, everything is a test!" Later, he even confides to us that Chuck has secretly raised the temperature in the bar precisely three degrees, and that "someone, I ain't sayin' who, has released exactly three bees in here!"

We look around, but we don't see any bees.

"Did you know that adjusting the temperature or releasing a bee into a closed environment is a classic study?" he asks. "A test of what, I'm not sure. And who knows by whom. But obviously don't sic a bee on anyone you don't trust."

"We appreciate the heads-up, buddy," Holly says.

"That's a waste of three perfectly good bees, dude," I say.

After he's gone, we're feeling nice, and we drag our stools out of everybody's way, then the two of us spend the rest of the night hogging the game and shooting hoops and fantasizing about our big heist. And by the time we're drunk and the basketball game eats our first and final dollar, all the big bad talk turns serious.

We're still looking around for a more suitable final recruit when Holly's ex-girlfriend walks in.

I'm hoping she'll be our third, but not at first, because Steelheart's ridiculous power ballad "I'll Never Let You Go" is hitting just the wrong note when this lanky vixen named Gaddy swings open the door. But once she starts talking and someone puts some boozier Tom Jones on the jukebox, it suddenly feels like this chick will be down for anything.

And this is even *before* she starts telling us—after some extra goading from Holly—about her own adventures in expulsion. So it's fate! And I'm thinking this makes us the ultimate squad. Three genetically perfect women who, in the injustice of the century, have been somehow bounced out of school for "conduct unbecoming a Santa Carla University student."

Then she clarifies; this bitch actually got kicked out of the fucking Secret Service. Not school. Dinner dinner, chicken winner.

Some time passes. The Hut is dead, but we're still shooting down our share of suitors.

"Another day, another dollar, another shitty free drink," Holly jokes.

It's weird, but there's something about women hanging together that makes young men bolder. To them, we're probably indistinguishable on our own, as indistinct as three extras in the background of any film. But together, we're the silent kinda sirens, and it's as if we only exist when they make their approach. But to be fair, we rarely pass the Bechdel Test ourselves. You've heard of that, right? Where a movie must have three women in it, and they have to talk about something other than money?

One more thing. Being "three women" who are seen as one also means we're allowed precisely one character trait each. Even if it's the same one. To make it easier on everyone, I really wish that we were one blonde, one brunette, and one fiery redhead (or some other color not found in nature), but this is California, not *The Witches of Eastwick*, so we're mostly just variations of "blonde," dirty through platinum, although Gaddy's tint technically is a little more "pink lemonade," in emergency room fluorescents, anyway. So it's handy that we at least have increasing levels of height and hue to tell us apart, which means Holly, the Big Hair of our squad, fields most of the propositions from drunken strangers and, therefore, sort of becomes our leader by default.

But besides the odd, awkward come-on from the Honorary Amish, action trickles off to a ghost town in the bar soon after that. Until a graduation party from a neighboring school floods the place around midnight. See, when June hits, because SCU is on quarters instead of semesters, students go home every weekend to hang with friends who've already been on summer break for weeks. This drives SCU kids mental near the end of spring quarter. To be fair, I was never able to get used to this system, either, and not just because of the extra reset button you had to hit after Spring "Whoo-hoo!" Break, when everyone starts post-ing their beach pics and you still have eight excruciating weeks of classes left. Though I'm not sure that not buying a single book didn't help. Was that a triple negative? So tonight we decide Santa Carla University isn't on semesters just because the word *quarter* sounds too much like money. And there's money *everywhere* on this campus, not just on the walls of The Hut.

I step outside to pretend like I'm smoking so I can chew on my finger, and from five blocks away I can see the green glow of campus, the perfect lawns with grass carpets like golf courses, even though the surrounding neighborhoods are on all-year water restriction because of the droughts. The administration knows this is shady, so they water everything in the dead of night. Seriously, I know they do this, I've heard it hissing! And one time, I saw this gnarly palm frond pinwheel down from the sky and *bloop!* plop down right in front of Mission Santa Carla, smack dab in the middle of all that glistening emerald grass, and it finally gave me something interesting to stare at for once . . . until an under-the-table, underpaid Mexican maintenance man in a golf cart zipped over and gathered it up without even stopping. It was like the poor bastard was one of those long-suffering *Flintstones* dinosaurs. Remember when those prehistoric critters would stop trimming hedges with their toothy snouts and shrug at the camera with the hint of an accent, "Hey, it's a living!" Or maybe that was just one of those weird "forgot to study" dreams I had when I lived in the dorm freshmen year.

Anyhow, my point, if you guys are still listening, is this all had something to do with why I stopped trying to do school "the right way."

Because one night, sometime around when that palm frond dropped down in front of me, I knew I would never again hand over any work that was my own.

I'm heading back in when I see the Honorary Amish and Gaddy by the grease trap. She's pulling him in by his limp denim collar, and thank Christ it's not a kiss, but whatever she whispers is scary enough to make him march straight out into the night, eyes blank as a Man-churian Candidate.

"What'd you say to him?" I ask as I hold the door for her.

"I said the worst thing you can say to an Honorary Amish," Gaddy says, cackling.

"And what's that?"

"'One more word and you're shunned.'"

"You went Full Amish on his ass."

"And I'd do it again."

I don't push her for any more info, understanding that whatever we do with these dudes, it's always for us, never for them.

When the graduates get too noisy and even the most inhospitable corners of the bar are jam-packed and crop-dusted with Azzaro Chrome body spray, we escape outside so Gaddy can smoke, or vape, or whatever she's secretly sucking on in her fist. We talk about the lack of security at The Hut and how no one is even checking IDs at the door. Holly says she was eighty-sixed from SCU bars before for underage drinking, but never from The Hut. The odd location has made this bar an anomaly, we decide. When we were still enrolled, the shittier students called this end of town "the dark side" of campus. They were certainly being racist, but it could also be the lack of streetlights. This unfortunate reputation would help us, regardless.

I pick at the dog-eared corners of the flyer on the window, where The Hut's score has been posted by the Santa Carla Health Department. I'm excited to see it matches my grade-point average the quarter I was kicked out the first time, a full letter grade worse than Shenanigans, as if this is possible. Clearly, we're made for each other.

We keep drinking until they close, and at 2:30, we're outside the door again, under the street signs at the corner of Franklin and The Alameda (always that ridiculous West Coast "the" in so many of the street names). Holly jokes that "Alameda Franklin" sounds like Aretha's Spanish cousin as we watch Chuck the bartender cram red and white balloons into the dumpster until it's overflowing. The graduation party on the patio is finally winding down, and we're surprised to learn the place even *has* a patio. But a patio doesn't have walls, so we knew there'd be no dollar bills outside anyway, so who gives a shit.

Chuck struggles to pull the lid down on the dumpster, balloons bulging out three sides, and Holly walks over to pop one with her long-ass pinky nail. *Pop!* Then three more in succession, *pop pop pop.* Chuck keeps flinching even after he knows they're coming.

"You know, there is a way to make all those balloons fit, ya dummy," she says, and he goes back inside, ignoring her. She just drums her razor-sharp nails and keeps on popping, *pop pop pop pop pop . . .*

In so many ways, The Hut is ripe for the picking. Or the popping. *Pop.*

Two dozen pops later, the balloons turn out to be just the siren song we need, because two drunk frat bros think they're fireworks and stumble up to our street corner to sway back and forth, looking us over like we're the proverbial steaming turkey leg on a desert island. I tense my old rugby muscles, getting ready for a scrum when they ask what we're doing, but, as usual, the questions are directed at Holly. The biggest hair.

Holly smiles and pulls one kid close and makes all sorts of promises, glistening lips a half centimeter from his earlobe. They barely hesitate to agree to whatever craziness she's asking of them because she's saying it like it's just "one little favor," and she's actually hot enough to define what constitutes "little" or "big," so they'd have probably done it even if they weren't hammered, which they are. We start walking away while they stick around the bar, working up their nerve to do this deed, and we figure we got a 50/50 chance of them pulling it off.

We're a block away from the bar and trampling through some jade bushes when we hear the glass shatter.

CHAPTER V

SPIN THE THROTTLE

So . . . did you guys rob all the money off the walls or what?"

"Sort of?" Sherry said, looking to her crew for help. But Holly ignored her and Lund's question and took another drink, while Gaddy just danced off in another direction. No one said much for a while, as the music had settled on a slightly more soothing house beat and everybody seemed to have adapted to the cold water in the pool. Sufficiently entertained by the story of the money on the wall, at least for now, most of them seemed to have forgotten about their intentionally inaccessible driver, or the inscrutable Leap Year ritual they might have unwittingly set into motion.

Except maybe for Angie, who was thinking about the "trust jump" exercise.

Or was it a "trust leap" . . .

Beth cleared her throat to snap her out of it.

"Back in undergrad, I would go to these off-campus parties, and this group of friends-of-friends-of-friends lip-synched that same Steelheart song she was talking about. Then they'd sort of crowd-surf the living room and laugh, being all ironic about it. But they did this every weekend, and they all clearly loved the song more than each other."

"Cool story, Beth," Reeves snickered.

"I'd rather hear that song right now," Angie said. "Any song right now, actually."

It was almost quiet, except for the ominously subdued throb of the speakers and the slosh of their bodies.

"You know what you should have cranked on the jukebox while you were robbing that bar?" Godzooky finally said to Holly to break the spell. Nobody had noticed him saddle up to the group. "Johnny Cash."

"Huh?"

"What did he say?"

"I didn't know he could talk," Holly said, backing up against the rail as she gave Godzooky an awkward smile.

"Get it?" Godzooky said. "Johnny *Cash*?"

"Oh, we got it," she lied as Gaddy and Sherry slipped around his thick arms to glide away toward Holly.

Angie stuck around the rail to listen in as Godzooky explained to Beth and Lund that he loved Johnny Cash, as did his whole family. He was the only musician his uncle would listen to who didn't sing in Spanish, though Godzooky always felt the mariachi horns in "Ring of Fire" made this boast a bit of a cheat. And don't get him started on that fucked-up song about the guy who builds a car from the parts of other cars . . .

"You guys are missing the point!" Holly interrupted. "The moral of our story is that men can't drink a beer with their penis, no matter how hard they try."

"What?" Jill asked, doing a classic spit take with her beer.

"Okay, *eventually* that's the moral," Holly said.

"Can we hear the penis part, please?" Lund asked, shifting his feet and hauling up his drooping drawers over and over.

"Nah, maybe later," Holly said as she sidestroked around them.

"Nonsense!" Janky yelled as he pulled down his briefs and slid a mini-bottle under his balls, swinging his hips and the beer to the music.

"Absolutely not," Beth said, giving him a wet punch in the chest in protest.

"Okay, okay, obviously I'm not drunk enough to drink with my penis," he said, pulling his underwear back up. "Not yet, anyway."

Reeves came up behind right then and tried to finish de-pantsing him, and they tumbled into the side of the pool, both fighting for fist-fuls of each other's shorts. Sherry and Gaddy were wrestling around a bit now, too, and the pulsing music seemed louder again. Holly was dancing almost out-of-control, blonde tendrils whiplashing, and her seemingly endless limbs swimming through the air. Angie thought of a giraffe trying to paint a house. Occasionally, a beer can or a mini-bottle would slip from Holly's hand, but one of the guys was always near, scrambling to give it back before its contents got dumped and mixed into the gray cocktail of their roiling hot-tub stew.

"Maybe I could ask a question?" Beth had moved to the murky middle of the aquatic dance floor, waving for attention as if everyone wasn't three feet away. They made room for her and pretended not to listen. Dancing and drinking seemed to have been the unspoken short-term remedy for everyone's strange predicament. The music ramped up even more.

"Hello?" she said. "Hey!" Some finally turned but didn't stop moving.

"We haven't really been on the road for three hours, have we?" Beth yelled over the ruckus, eyes beginning to water. Only Angie seemed to notice her increasing distress.

"No way, it's been a half hour tops!" Angie shouted back. The speakers were a steady hammer on her nerves but she tried to keep a brave face, like everyone else, as if the party was more important than possibly being abducted right out in the open for all to see.

"How long was this tour supposed to be?" Beth asked. "An hour, right?"

"Whoa, a three-hour tour means forever!" Ruck said, laughing a little too hard. "Haven't you ever seen *Gilligan's Island*?"

"Actually, it was canceled after three seasons," Lund said, trying and failing to dance.

"This party will take as long as it takes!" Jill said, oddly defensive.

"Insanity," Beth said, shaking her head, and Jill pulled Angie close.

"Okay, real talk! How long can this thing go before it runs out of gas?" Jill barked in Angie's ear, half-yelling, half-joking, but still making Angie hunch in alarm.

"Probably until dawn?"

"You know what?" Jill said. "That sounds amazing! So let's make the most of it. You, too, Beth. Loosen up. Have some fun. Right. Now. It's my birthday, losers!"

"Yeah, happy birthday!" Angie gave her a hug and waved at everyone to join in, as if they hadn't already done this. Amy dutiful slinked over and hugged Jill's muscular arm.

"Hell yeah, happy birthday, bitch!" Sherry and Holly shouted together, mini-bottles clicking.

"Get it, girl." Gaddy tried to clank a bottle with them and whiffed, but Dan caught her before she fell. She slipped away from him, dancing with her neck craned up at the country-dark sky, presumably tallying up the starlight like dollar signs.

"To another successful journey around the sun!" Lund said to tumbleweed stares, and he lowered his arm.

"Happy birthday, my ass," Reeves sighed, cracking open another beer and staring at the raised welt on his wrist, still branded red with the snake bite burn of Godzooky's grip. Thoughtfully, he tapped the handprint on his skin as if it were another stopped watch.

"More like Happy Forever Day," he shrugged, crushing the can as he drank it, jetting the foam all over his face.

"I wish that, just one time, there was a scene in a monster movie where some huge beast blends in with a parade of crazy balloon floats, so it takes people forever to notice, and they just keep cheering as it cruises on by."

"What made you think of this?" Dan hated Lund as much as anybody else, but this idea intrigued him, and the alcohol was no longer keeping up with their worrying.

"I don't know, but it sounds like us, though, doesn't it? Like if this truck was in the middle of a Macy's Thanksgiving Day parade, with everybody screaming to get off? You'd pay no mind to a line of fire trucks with people freaking out in the back."

"I hope this truck slows down sometime before Thanksgiving," Dan said.

"It'll have to stop at some point. Didn't you hear that throttle grinding on the last turn? There aren't any gears left to strip on this piece of shit."

"That's your brain you're hearing."

"Well, I think they'd still be dancing anyway," Lund said, pointing at the slowly gyrating bodies nearby. Some of them had drunk enough to cross a threshold of not caring about much at all. "Even if the truck never stopped."

"What the hell are you talking about?"

"Next Thanksgiving, look close at those parades. Watch those giant motorized birthday cakes and the backs of those inflatable monsters as they drift on by. Everyone's dancing up there. But they're tired. And they want it to be over."

"You're nuts," Dan said. "We won't be around next Thanksgiving."

"You can say that again," Lund said, leaning against the side of the pool to watch the fracturing party with something like resignation.

"Has anybody looked at their hands?" Janky asked around, but nobody took the bait. Many of them had started forgetting he was there until he spoke, too busy dancing as if their night, and their lives, depended on it.

"Hey now, seriously, check your fingertips for wrinkles. It's better than any dumb wristwatch. Because judging by the level of new tire tread on my thumb, I'd say we've been in this pool for . . . approximately six hours. Maybe more."

If anyone heard his wild estimation, they didn't respond.

"Hey, what was Ruck saying about your job?" Reeves was asking Godzooky instead. Godzooky was one of the few who hadn't danced at all, sticking to the rails and watching them all. They were both leaning back, shoulders touching. Reeves was tall like Godzooky, but not nearly as broad. Godzooky stared straight ahead, listening close, breathing deep, his wide chest inflating like a beefy frog. "Don't you drive a bus just like this?" Reeves wanted to know.

"This isn't a bus," Rucks said from Godzooky's other shoulder. "And I didn't say anything about his job."

"You probably will, though." Reeves reached around Godzooky to give Ruck a slug in the arm, taking the opportunity to get in Godzooky's ear. "So tell us about your bus, bro." Like most guys, the drunker Reeves got, the more mysteries he thought he had to solve, and the worse he got at solving them. He'd get belligerent, asking everybody pointless questions, then ponder the answers all night like the riddle of the Sphinx. But Godzooky wasn't answering right away, just blinking slower and longer than necessary.

"Come on, man. Tell us about your freaky ride."

"There's nothing freaky about my ride," Godzooky said carefully. "It's just a car. Not like it's made out of skulls or anything."

"No one said you had a car made out of skulls, ya fuckin' weirdo," Reeves said. "But your car . . . Okay, yeah, your car, I *have* seen you around town in that thing, parked sideways to get gas? And that is not a car you would normally find in nature, am I right? Is that the freaky car you were talking about, Ruck?"

"No, he drives a bus. Like a bus driver or whatever."

Godzooky cracked his knuckles, and when he spoke again it was slow, deliberate, like he was rehearsing courtroom testimony.

"My car isn't freaky. It's just different. But when it comes to cars, or people, or to be honest, anything in life, really, you can only know what you are dealing with if you take it apart."

"Riiiiiight," Reeves said, laughing and shaking his head. "You been taking people apart again, killer?"

"Have you ever really been hurt?" Godzooky turned to ask him, but the question sounded like it was for everyone. Janky ran with it first.

"I'm glad you asked!" he said. "You know, besides my very famous plane crash, it seems like every injury has involved my hands . . ." Janky offered up a palm. Angie saw that he was right about the water wrinkling it so deeply. Their party had pickled his flesh considerably, and the puckered hand looked almost fake to her, like a toy left out in the rain. And, of course, there was his lack of a thumb.

What has two thumbs and should measure its lifeline? Not this guy! Angie felt bad as soon as she thought it.

". . . and even my childhood injuries that were not exclusively hand-related *definitely* had a hand involved, usually as an accomplice. You just couldn't get hurt without one," Janky went on. "But what about the rest of my body, you may ask . . ."

"Nobody asked!"

"Well, there was that time I scorched the hair off my legs while running through a campfire on a 'Dare' in order to avoid having to choose 'Truth,' or that time I dislocated my jaw when some crazy chick asked me to help stage a fight on a hayride to impress someone's drunken dad."

"That's somebody else's story, dumbfuck!"

"He never had any hair on his legs."

"Were there really that many high school hayrides or that many high school fights?" Janky wondered. "I can't remember. Hmm, okay, what else . . ."

"My turn!" Ruck shouted.

"I'm not done!" Janky said. "There was that time I purposefully cut the hell out of my hand with my thumbnail trying to sabotage a palm reading where she said my lifeline was curiously small—though tonight with all these water wrinkles I should be back up to nine lives . . ."

"I thought he was done talking about his hand."

"Okay, picture this," Janky said. "If someone does chalk outlines of us tomorrow, mine will always be the one missing something. And if we played Hangman? Drawing our bodies like little stick figures? I would win because there will only be four tiny lines at the end of my arm, and everyone else will have five."

"That means you'd lose at Hangman," Dan laughed.

"Losing at Hangman means you won."

"Huh?

"See that?" Reeves said, pointing his thumb and forefinger at Janky like a gun. "This little bitch is living proof why little boys take Hangman so seriously."

"Janky, are you trying to tell us you're missing your thumb on your right hand?" Angie said, splashing some water on her face and rubbing her eyes vigorously. "Because we already know this."

"I don't know, am I?" he said. "I hardly think about my missing thumb. Except for three to three hundred minutes every day. I mean, even though I was technically born this way, I still consider it an injury, not an illness. Hey, speaking of injuries, did I ever tell you about my plane crash . . ."

"Noooooooooo," several of them wailed at once. Only Godzooky seemed disappointed that Janky's seemingly endless list of afflictions was ending, and he mumbled something about his own "roadmap of defects affecting him just as profoundly," which Angie thought made him sound like a car, and was also a hell of a thing to mumble to himself. But Angie only caught the tail end of it, and she watched Godzooky angle himself out of the Janky and Ruck sandwich, then sit down by himself, face to the wall of the pool. Angie thought it was a strange time for the guy who never talked to be having an existential crisis, but then decided his timing was actually perfect.

Lund pointed off into the distance.

"This exact same scene is happening on that drive-in movie screen right now . . ."

"That shit is miles away by now," Dan said.

". . . where one character shows another character an injury, and then that character has to one-up them with crazier injuries of their own . . ."

"Nobody's one-upping anybody," Angie said.

". . . but it's such a tired trope, and nobody would really trade injury stories like that in real life because nobody really wants to see what happens to the human body when . . ."

"Ooooh, speaking of bodies! Feel that groove . . ." Holly said, gesticulating her shoulders toward the speakers as she pretended to recognize the anonymous thumps of the latest tune.

"My turn!" someone shouted, and suddenly everyone was angling for any light and hiking down their swimsuits and shorts, still swinging their hips to the beat, but more eager to reveal any scar, crease, or furrow carved into their bodies by time, unaware that tonight's whirlpool of motion had marinated their skin long enough to truncate every lifeline on their palms into ridged road maps to nowhere, despite these dead ends being the only grooves that mattered.

Maybe a dozen miles later, huddled close in the pool to maintain their body heat, some of them were considering jumping off the back of the fire truck at the next red light, but they hadn't stopped at any intersections for quite a while. The truck wasn't slowing for anything. And although the flashing strobes had tapered off to a dim pulse, the music had climbed back up to dominate their thoughts again, and they could barely hear each other unless they cupped hands around their mouths. Beating on the driver's cab had yielded no results, so they'd resigned most of their efforts to blowing into their hands for warmth and draining as much alcohol as they could from the remaining bottles and cans. At this point, everyone was convinced they'd been trapped on the truck for half a day, but many of them were too incapacitated to accurately gauge time, as well as their predicament. The music, as well as the darkness, certainly wasn't helping them to calibrate any temporal position. So most of them continued to party as if it was the end of the world.

However, behind some of those cupped hands, plans of escape were beginning to take shape.

A sudden light source loomed in the distance, and they splashed over to the railing to get a closer look, ready to try and flag someone down. When they were able to make out the glowing screen of a drive-in theater just visible through the trees, most of them slumped in disappointment.

"I know that movie!" Lund yelled, grabbing nearby shoulders to shake, truly energized for the first time. "It's right in the middle of the film," he said as they all turned away. "Second-act crisis, right where you wonder if they're gonna figure it out!"

"Who cares, dude?" Reeves said finally.

"This is right where the bad guy warns the good guy to 'not attempt to grow a brain.' When I was little, I thought he meant grow one in a jar! Which is scientifically impossible despite cinematic depictions of . . ."

"Somebody shut him up," Reeves warned.

"Look!" Lund pointed, but no one was looking. "See how that actor spit? Ever notice how after a movie punch, the person on the receiving end immediately hocks a wad of blood onto the ground? Why? Are we to assume a fist to the face can give you hemoptysis? Get real!"

"Wanna test that theory?" Reeves asked him, but Jill answered instead.

"Back off, asshole," she said, blinking slow. Reeves hadn't seen her slide up next to him. "It's still my birthday until I say it's not my birthday."

"It'll always be your birthday!" Holly yelled, a concept that sounded much more threatening than Reeves.

"Jill, aren't you getting worried about never getting off this truck?" Reeves asked her.

"Not yet? Maybe? I don't know!" Jill said, shaking it off. "Let's see where this goes!"

Angie and Amy splashed up to flank her and nodded in agreement. Any alignment right now seemed like a good idea, even if Jill's apparent disregard for the revelers' safety seemed to be getting more unhinged.

"We're with her," they said.

"Huh?" Reeves cupped his ears.

"We're with her!" they both yelled, up on their tiptoes to get closer to his level.

"Fucking nuts, every one of you," Reeves muttered, his voice lost in the music.

"I only get to party once every four years!" Jill said, high-fiving a short line of reluctant hands. "Go big or go home, am I right?"

"Go big!" Holly whooped, drunker than most and agreeing wholeheartedly.

Reeves and Ruck shared a glance, then sloshed over to get up in Jill's face.

"Back up a second. What did you mean by that?" Ruck asked.

"What?"

"What did you mean by that?"

"Yeah, what do you mean!" Reeves added, poking her in the shoulder.

"What do you mean 'What did I mean?'" Jill asked, looking at his finger instead of him.

"Is it just me or is she not acting right?" Reeves asked the group, then turned to Jill. "Is all this a big prank?" She snarled and sucked a lip instead of answering. "Seriously, are you punking us, ya daft cunt?"

"What?! Nope, nope, nope," Jill said, stunned. "No way. What are you even saying?"

"Stop this," Angie said, and they did. Beth looked around at everybody, her gaze moving from face to face in the faltering light.

"I don't want to be rude, but . . . who even put this party together? I mean, I know Angie invited me, but, like, why are you here?" She motioned all around her. "And by 'you,' I mean fuckin' *everybody*."

"Angie called them, right?" Jill said, looking to her friend.

"I mean, yeah, I called a couple people."

"Who called you?" Reeves asked Holly.

"Who called you?!" Sherry answered back, defensive, and the rest started talking over each other.

"I don't know, someone called me, and then I called her, and then she called him, and then—"

"Wait!" Amy said. "Back up. Someone called you? 'Someone' who?"

There was silence.

"Raise your hand *right now* if someone here in this pool invited you to this party."

Amy raised her hand to answer her own question, and then Angie did, too. Beth and Jill, and maybe Lund, also began to raise their hands, but then everyone simultaneously thought better of it and dropped their hands back into the water.

"What the fuck is going on here?" someone asked right when the strobes were dimmed again, the music climbing to levels almost too loud to think.

"Hey!" Jill clapped her hands over her head. "For the cheap seats back there! Anybody touches me again and you'll come back with a stump, just like your boy Janks!"

Reeves moved quickly, jamming his finger back into Jill's face, almost but not quite touching her nose. Everyone froze.

"Leave her alone!" Holly said, coming over, the rhythm sloughing off her body as she danced closer.

"Do it," Jill said to Reeves, and he just looked her over.

"Do what?" he asked finally. They were both close enough to hear each other very clearly. "And what are you gonna do if I do it?"

"What are *we* gonna do, you mean," Angie answered from Jill's side as Amy nodded along from the other. Jill took a big step forward.

"Make your move, numbnuts."

"Make your *movie*?" Lund said, laughing, and Dan palmed his face to shove him away.

"Just answer the question. Did you *plan* all this shit?" Reeves's finger was still hovering, but he sounded almost sincere. "Did you tell this guy to drive around for nine fuckin' days?"

"Just do something," Jill said, voice even, and Reeves made a circle with his finger and his thumb to ready a nose flick, but at the last second, he balled up that fist and loaded up a punch instead. But before he could throw it and cross that line with the group, Godzooky slipped a meaty arm around his throat and flipped him hard onto his back, the force of the slam temporarily dividing the waves as easily as he'd divided the crowd on the street earlier.

"Calm down," Godzooky growled, voice box snaked with veins but sounding as calm as Jill. Underwater, Reeves couldn't hear this command, and the bubbles indicated he was going to come back up anything but calm.

"I said, 'calm down!'" Godzooky continued to hold him fast with one hand on Reeves's neck and the other one against his chest. Reeves's mouth pulsed for air just below the surface, and it took a good thirty seconds for anyone to realize the severity of what was happening. Then Dan and Ruck both piled onto Godzooky's back and strained against each heavily muscled arm. But the two of them had been slamming beers and bottles all night, whereas Godzooky had slammed three tall glasses of milk over dinner, so they were fairly ineffective, just climbing Godzooky's torso like kittens.

"Let him *up!*" Angie said, the "up" stressed like it was their safe word, and Godzooky locked eyes with her, considering it. The strobe flash of a sodium-vapor streetlamp surprised their panicky faces as they zoomed under their arch, and Godzooky blinked and reemerged from wherever he'd gone, nostrils still flaring. He straightened up, flinging Dan off one shoulder, then Ruck off the other, then stepped back to let Reeves rejoin the land of the living and breathing.

Coughing and retching, Reeves flopped like a hooked marlin, hacking a lung oyster of mucus at Godzooky's chest as he caught his breath. Furious, he waved away anyone's attempt to help him, then shuffled his way to an empty side of the truck and stared out into the black countryside zooming past, glancing back occasionally, eyes full of retribution. He spit, then spit again, hacking until no more water came out. The group traded glances as the lone streetlight faded, and Angie barely caught sight of Gaddy whispering something into Holly's ear, and then Holly nodding along.

"All that over a car?" Ruck was hitting the side of his head with the heel of his hand to clear his ear.

"Don't talk about my car anymore," Godzooky said to him from the wall, almost pleading. Angie hadn't seen this car of his that everyone was talking about, but she had seen a drawing of it pinned to a refrigerator in the maintenance office. The caricature of Godzooky behind the wheel was recognizable (like the singing demigod from the cartoon *Moana*, but with shorter hair), but the sketch of what was presumably his automobile hadn't made any sense to her. It reminded her of when her grandfather, suffering from dementia, had been asked to draw a clock by his doctors, and how he'd framed the frightening results because it looked like alphabet soup (her grandpa loved alphabet soup).

"A car made out of skulls would be very hard to maintain," Lund said.

"Shut up!" Holly screamed.

"I wanna go home!" Beth cried behind them, fingers in her ears to muffle the music, and the group circled their wagons again in response, not really around Beth, but mostly around a Devil's Cut empty that was bobbing in the water, dead center in the pool. And after their heartbeats and the anonymous music died back down, Jill used the opportunity to spin this bottle once, twice, three times, until it finally slowed to point at her belly, and then everyone started to get the picture.

"Are you thinking what I'm thinking?" Jill asked them, and their eyes were answer enough.

Normally, the problem with spinning a bottle in a swimming pool is it would take too long to stop. But tonight, they had all the time in the world. Angie shoved the bobbing mini-bottles out of her way as she thought about her grandpa's drawing of alphabet soup.

Why not? she thought.

"So are we doing this?" she asked the group, and the strobe lights got brighter again.

"I think everybody's already kissed everybody," Janky said, laughing, then jumped back from where Reeves was bubbling and sliding under the water near his legs. He looked up at them from the center of the circle, his glowering face just visible under the bottle. They pretended not to see him.

"One, that's not true," Angie said. "And two, you'd be the last person to know who kissed everybody or anybody."

"His mom might!" Ruck said.

"Damn bottle will never stop spinning!" Dan complained.

"Fuck it, let's just tell stories, then," Angie said. "Like Sherry did. To pass the time."

"Sherry's fable was ninety-seven percent fabrication," Ruck scoffed.

"A hundred percent 'fab,' you mean," Sherry corrected. "And don't worry, there's more to that one!"

"Great."

Angie looked her over, noticing what they always called her carefully cultivated "Suicide Blonde" style (aka "The Hitchcock" for short), and that she was pretty frazzled. Her head was down, eyes narrowed but shifty, not quite the Kubrick stare, but more like she was speed-reading an invisible newspaper.

"Fuck Hangman. Let's play Truth or Dare," Sherry suggested, and someone clapped the water in agreement.

"Now, that's an idea!" Reeves was back up, rubbing his sore neck, eyes brightening, sputtering water like an outboard motor, then he went under again.

"Don't be so sure," Sherry said. "Most people call Truth or Dare a modern-day lie detector, but you can beat both of them the same way. Ain't that right, Gaddy?"

Gaddy smiled, but said nothing.

"Oh no," Holly laughed, clearly in on the joke. "Watch her butt for bubbles!" she said cryptically, and Gaddy slugged her in the arm.

"What the fuck?" Dan was baffled and angry again, eager to bully someone now that his B-side, Reeves, was staying mostly underwater.

"She's serious!" Gaddy said. "Like, you can totally fool a lie detector if the question is, say, 'Have you been to the moon?' and your answer is, 'Yes!' but then you finish it in your head with 'Moon Township, Pennsylvania.'"

"It's true," Holly agreed.

"*Noon* Township?" Lund asked. He was slurring now, though no one had seen him take a drink.

"Have we started the game, then?" Dan asked.

"I think she already lost," Reeves said from somewhere around his knees, where he was blowing bubbles like a baby.

"You see, the machine, or the group, makes a note of your Truth Profile from innocuous questions like these," Gaddy explained. "So when the lie detector gets to the important stuff, no one can tell the difference. Is he man, machine, or mini-bottle?"

"Riiiiiight," Dan said. "So tell us, Gaddy, have you ever been to Mars?"

"Mars, Pennsylvania, yes," she smiled.

"But you said it out loud."

"Moon, Mars . . . what the hell is going on in Pennsylvania?" Lund whined.

"Okay, ask me anything," Dan said.

"Have you ever been to Uranus?"

"Nope . . . and now I'm thinking, 'because it's ninety-nine percent acid? I mean, ice.'"

The triplets studied his face for an explanation, then threw up their hands, laughing.

"Whoops, there's another loophole to beat the needle," Gaddy said. "Be an idiot!"

"Okay, ask Reeves if he ever dropped acid," Dan said.

"You ever drop acid?"

"Yeah, right here in this toilet, earlier tonight," Reeves said from mostly underwater, and his words came out a bit like a child playing in their milk.

"Can we be serious?" Amy pleaded, then screamed when Reeves breached the surface under her like a shark taking a shot at a sea lion.

"But do you mean drop acid or, like, *drop* acid?" Reeves asked, smiling. "Because I've done that twice in my life. I mean, once, when I went surfing, twice in my life, for the first and last time! Whole goddamn night of firsts . . ."

"If you want to know what we're really swimming in," Dan said, "check ol' Lumpy's shorts."

Lund backpedaled with a protective hand on the ass of his swamped jeans.

"Are people making less sense than usual?" someone asked, but no one wanted to answer.

"I thought you were the surfing king, Reeves, like, all famous on YouTube 'n' shit," Ruck said.

"Not exactly. Maybe more like notorious. You're probably thinking of Dan."

"Yer all the same species," Gaddy snorted.

"Huh?"

"Okay, everybody shut up. It's my turn to tell a goddamn ghost story," Reeves said. "Who's got the flashlight to jam under my chin?"

"If you got a chin, I got Deez Nuts!" Dan said.

"Fuck you, then," Reeves said, disappearing under.

Angie held up a hand and spun the bottle. She spun it hard, more confused than ever, but happy to be making the most of Jill's birthday as long as she could amid the escalating unease of an endless party.

They waited, but her bottle wouldn't stop. They all stared as it spun, not sure if they even wanted it to.

"Who's goin' Ouija boardin'?"

"We's goin' Ouija boardin'!"

"Whoop! Whoop!"

Angie and Amy were rapping their own ICP "Chicken Huntin'" remix to float the idea of a different classic party game, since the spinning bottle had drifted away without showing any signs of slowing down. The speakers and the wind had died down a whit, but people were slumping even more than usual, so Angie figured a new game couldn't hurt.

Or do I mean, 'couldn't help'?

Her friends weren't aware of her unhealthy infatuations, or how, like most reasonably spooky kids, she'd been enamored with spirit boards for a long time. But that was a different life, a different name, back before her mother had to finally give in to buy her an "official" board, back when she had been forced to play her own versions with a variety of other objects, some of them alive. Like the time she gently laid her fingers on the back of a turtle she'd found on the white lines of their street, letting it guide them to the safety of the gutter, all the while thinking: *If the turtle steps on that cigarette, I'll die before I'm twenty. If the turtle steps on that candy wrapper, I'll live forever . . .*

But her favorite incarnation was her earliest, modifying a 1975 Milton Bradley board game called Bermuda Triangle, which had helpfully supplied its own version of a planchette: an inky blue, amoeba-like cloud with a magnet tucked away under the bottom. And when you spun the wrong numbers on the dial (or the right numbers, depending on your recklessness), this ominous dark cloud slid over your tiny, metal-capped boats and plucked them from the game board with invisible fingers, vanishing your fleet from the shipping lanes forever. Very quickly, the spinner was lost, and then the rules, but she was more than happy to resort to a more cooperative form of game play, her shaking fingertips just barely brushing the edges of the thundercloud as it swept the entire game free of ships. Because of this modification, most of her Bermuda Triangle sessions lasted one round, or approximately fifteen minutes, before the storm devoured everyone.

Mercifully faster than their current predicament aboard their leaking lifeboat.

One night, with some help from her brother, she'd created a new kind of board with some magnetic refrigerator letters and a honeybee drunk on pollen as her planchette. The bee spelled out *Blarg*, a perfectly terrifying message from the underworld, and she retired homemade "witchboard" building for a while, distracted by plenty of other childhood projects.

But she still loved messing around with them at parties, and Amy did, too. Partly because Ouija boards didn't pair everyone off, like Spin the Bottle, but mostly because she'd developed a lifelong love for any games that a father would throw into the burn barrel as fast as he would find them, all while shouting, "Sorcery!" convincing anyone who witnessed this that he was trying to summon the spirits himself.

"But how the hell can we play that game back here?" Dan asked her.

"Yeah," Lund agreed, immediately making Dan reconsider.

"I don't know," Sherry said. "Stuck in the back of a seedy, soupy, skeezy, steadily cooling hot tub, whiplashing around on the back roads of the Kentucky countryside? I kinda love it."

"It won't work!" Lund said, pouting. Being the naysayer was a natural defensive mechanism for someone rarely asked to participate.

"Is the hot tub really getting colder?" Beth asked. She seemed to never stop shivering.

"It's all in our heads," Jill answered, and protests were flying. Angie realized that, either deliberately or accidentally, her apparent denial of their predicament was keeping the debate, and maybe their bodies, warmed up.

"Maybe it's just in *your* head."

"Or maybe someone is fucking with us."

"I think the driver is lost."

"This is a big prank. We just have to stick it out."

"No, this is a big party."

"That's right. The party we paid for. Like, maybe the scares are included."

"What part would be the 'Ouija,' though?" Amy asked, bringing it back to the game. "Don't we need the board to play it? Is the game, uh, the *thing* or the board?"

"I think it's the board?" Reeves muttered, half under.

"'The board is the thing . . . to catch the conscience of the king . . .'" Lund said, giggling.

"No," Angie said. "All you need are letters. Or just some way to pick a letter."

"Pick from where?" Amy asked.

"Anywhere."

"So what you're saying is, even if you can play it without the thing, you can't play without the board."

"Planchette!" Angie corrected her. "And yes."

"Sounds like lunch!" Dan said, laughing.

"It's shaped like a heart," Holly offered, smiling.

"Yeah, a heart that gives you splinters," Sherry added.

"We don't need a board!" Angie shouted. "That's what I'm saying."

"The board is the water? But the thing . . ."

"Planchette!" Angie shouted again.

". . . could be a bottle."

"Yes, exactly. It could be a bottle."

Most were still too low in the water to be seen, and Angie felt a grim skepticism surrounding her.

"No, no, this can work," Angie said, a little desperate. "We can just designate one of our bodies 'Yes' and another one of our bodies 'No.' Then we just need the letters . . ."

"I'm so confused."

"No, it's easy, there's, what, nine of us left?" Lund asked.

"What do you mean nine of us left," Dan laughed. "There's all of us left, moron."

"So that's three letters each," Lund plowed on. "Remember how we had to text before smart phones? Same thing! So 'one' is 'A-B-C' . . ."

"'Two' would be 'A-B-C,' bro." Reeves was up and spitting from a wave as the fire truck took another unlit turn. "'One' doesn't have any letters on it. I should know. My phone is old as fuck."

"And four letters were on number 'seven'?"

"Huh?"

"Forget it!" Angie threw up her hands. "We'll just stick with 'Yes' or 'No.'"

"But you can't play Ouija boards without the board," someone bubbled again, possibly submerged, but everyone knew they were going to play it anyway. Spin the Bottle, Truth or Dare, Ouija boards . . . they were going to play all the party games tonight, because every one of them had the same outcome.

Hyperbolic anecdotes masquerading as confessions. Sometimes vice versa.

"All righty! Since we have ten years to burn tonight—Have we done this yet? A toast? I have some toast." Holly was holding up one of the mini-bottles of Jack. "To Jill, and another successful journey around the sun!"

"He already did that," Dan mumbled, wearily angling a thumb toward Lund.

"Well, maybe we're gonna spin around the sun one more time before the night is over!" Holly shrugged, and everybody looked around. She had a point.

"That is some deep shit!" Ruck yelled.

"Yes, we are in some deep shit!" Beth yelled back.

"I can't take much more of this fucking music!" Reeves said, punching the side of the truck hard enough that they felt it reverberate through the water around them. People were used to watching Reeves and Dan for signs of violence, and now that the spinning bottle had returned to stop and point directly at Godzooky, suspense was waking many of them back up. Not so much in anticipation of a fight, but who might tell the next story. But Godzooky surprised everyone by quickly covering the bottle with a massive hand and dunking it back down.

"What happened to all that Ouija board stuff?" he said, the deep bass of his voice activating the rest of them.

"Good question!" Angie said, not hiding her disappointment.

"Naw, naw, your turn to spill it, bud," Reeves said, not looking over and continuing to give the steel wall above the hot tub a series of kidney punches. Ruck moved in to offer an arm like he was considering giving Godzooky a good-natured "Hurtz Donut," but Godzooky flexed as he stood up, and Ruck thought better of it, pulling up short to pretend he was wiping water off his face. The group watched the raised cables of his forearms and neck as Godzooky stretched, but his mouth wasn't as pursed as it usually was. He looked around at them curiously, as if he was really seeing them for the first time, and it seemed like he was actually considering telling the party his story. Everyone held their collective breath, except for the dipshit twins, Janky and Ruck, who were creeping in closer, in case they could pile on or cheap-shot someone if the opportunity arose. Angie was worrying about another brawl brewing as Lund dragged his big Baby Huey of a body almost onto her lap.

"Don't you worry about me," he burbled. "I know I don't look like a fighter—and I'm not—but these are *special* glasses. Springs in the hinges. So if I get hit, they break away from my face, like stripper pants. Live to see another day! I call 'em my Special Spectator Specs. Patent pending."

"Oh my God, who are you? Just shut up, dude," Angie said, adding an elbow.

"Did you see the fight earlier, though?" Lund whispered to her. "There was no blood, Angie. No blood at all. That's how you know we're in a movie. I mean, *not* in a movie."

Angie nodded like she had any idea what he was talking about. If she didn't know better, she would have guessed Lund was as wasted as everyone else. Still, she looked around at the water, squinting at the colors she was seeing. There was no blood in the hot tub, but there was something else swirling around all the empties and the bodies, mixing in with the suds. Mixing in with them. She rubbed her eyes again, indulging in the flash of light from the pressure of her fists. Then it faded to bring her back into the shadowland of the pool.

A rumble strip on the road made her look around, but it was just Godzooky, clearing his throat, getting ready to talk. The rest of them moved in expectantly.

He did tell a story, but the music was deafening, and the fire truck was rattling over miles of tire strips and potholes and roadkill, and no one really heard much of what he was saying. Or maybe they just pretended not to. But if pressed, they would probably admit they had no idea if such a wild story could really happen outside of their heads, let alone whether or not he was telling the truth. But if there was any moral to be learned, it could probably apply to Godzooky's fable, as well as to the apologue they currently shared, and it was this:

If what happened on the road stayed on the road, then this meant them, too.

CHAPTER VI

ONE CAPRICE AT A TIME

Godzooky's Story

A week before I quit my job, I was balancing on the corner of a dance floor at another miserable wedding reception, considering getting drunk for the first time in my life, when the flower girl ran up and swung a glow-in-the-dark sword at my face. "I'm a superhero!" she yelled, and I asked her, "Did you know superhero films are destroying Mexican and American cinema?" Then she pretended to cut off my hands.

That night I learned that the punishment for trying to dash the dreams of children was not knowing how long she expected me to keep acting like I had no hands. Apparently, it was forever, because when I was shuttling the wedding party back to the hotel, the flower girl started screaming from the back of the bus that I should be using my elbows on the steering wheel.

"¡No *puedes conducir si no tienes manos, tonto!*"

As most people already know, I drive an odd-looking vehicle. A home-brew. A "Rat Rod," as the gringo larvae are calling them these days. But I'll come back to that. Most nights I'm just driving a regular ol' bus, and the majority of my week consists of rebounding back and forth from hotels to wedding ceremonies, or worse, to their endless receptions. But that evening, when the last of the stumblebum attendees piled onto my bus after midnight, and I pulled away with both me and my air brakes hissing together, I watched all the half-lidded eyes in my rearview mirror, counting up the forgotten cameras and wallets and cellphones I would be plucking from the cracks of their seats. And that's when I understood that stealing stuff from this job had gotten entirely too easy. I was getting soft, and I knew right then I'd have to look for another line of work. I've had worse jobs, yes, but no job that had ever been so unsatisfying to not rob. All together, I've had fifteen or sixteen occupations in my life.

And I've found a way to steal from every single one of them.

You might not believe it, judging by the car I drive—or the way everybody whispers—but I'm not particularly evil, or even particularly broke. *Quebrado, limpio, sin lana. Roto.*

Okay, at first, maybe I *was* sorta broke, scraping gas money by running what they called an "open drawer" on the register of my first job, a run-down Putt-Putt where I handed out clubs and candy-colored golf balls to entitled suburban Chad wannabes. But it evened out, karmically speaking, as I was also performing a public service by making sure the lil' *pombre hombres* who looked the most desperate around their dates ended up knocking only the blue balls into the holes all night. Tell me that's not a hex.

But later, when I was chewing open the corners of Planters Peanuts bags at my job at the CVS—so I could throw them in the "loss" bin and eat at my leisure—it had started to become a challenge to find something to swipe from *every* low-paying job I held. So when I was way past too old to still be doing stuff like this, I found myself struggling to throw a pillowcase over a small tree to kidnap it from my landscaping job, just to say I did it, I guess. And I realized that somewhere along the way all this stealing had become a ritual.

I think these urges were hereditary. Aren't they always? My father implanted this idea early, I think, with a certain story about his brother stealing a car from the factory where he worked back in Austin, Texas— well, actually stealing a *ton* of cars, or parts of them, anyway, then reassembling a hybrid beast in our garage once his body finally retired him early. Rumor had it that my uncle put together some incredible clusterfuck of an automobile, all cockeyed with the ill-fitting, ever-changing styles of so many models over time, but the truth was he had no idea how many parts a Cadillac needed when he first started this scavenger hunt at age seventeen. And even after fifty years of working in auto factories on both sides of the border, he'd gained no more usable knowledge about car repair or construction, and even less of a command of the English language than his borderline illiterate nephew—that being me. But he *had* accumulated just enough stolen junk to build an incomprehensible pile of nonsense that no one could possibly mistake for a car in their wildest nightmare.

Mi familia tells me I kind of look like my uncle, which isn't much of a compliment. My uncle was a big guy like me, and he wasted a full year of the Hispanic Scholarship Fund, too. And we had both decided to walk around proud with those flattops that were so popular in the '50s among authoritarian white men who scoffed whenever they capped off a Chicano in full cholo uniform. Business casual for the barrio, we called it: white T-shirt, khakis, and a head you could land a helicopter on. This tradition was more due to the shape of our family's skulls than anything else. But my uncle claimed we couldn't be replaced by automation with these haircuts because the robot uprising would telegraph its arrival, with antennas and pointy heads marching over the horizon, not the handsome runways over our family's ears.

So sure, there are some similarities between us, even if his temper was so much worse.

My uncle was smarter than he looked, however, and he got very upset when gringos called him "Frankenstein," but even more upset when they called him "Frankenstein's Monster," which I thought was insane. Didn't he make the monster to look just like him? Meaning, to look just like us? Who's to say the doctor wouldn't look exactly like that monster in the right headlights?

"I'm Frankenstein's Monster's *car*," my uncle would correct them, which makes me the nephew of an automobile? Something like that. Or . . .

"¡Ey, *qué pasa/qué onda, Frankenstein? ¿Puedo usar esos tornillos de tu cuello de manillar?*"

And some evenings, when I'd lie in bed after spending too much time on the road and the wheels of the bus went down and down and down, I would begin to feel the bolts in my neck. This was not a *pesadilla*. I was born to love any dream where I'm walking down an empty street with jumper cables draped over my shoulder, a sizzling car battery slung under my arm like the president's nuclear football, until I awaken from that jumpstart, knowing that I'll now be able to walk the streets forever.

After I ran out of stuff to steal and quit driving buses, my uncle Frank found me a new job in a fertilizer factory. He said it was good money but long hours, and a small enough operation that there was no threat that automation, or less-demanding migrant workers, would replace me any time soon—exactly the kind of job where I could stew and plot and avoid feeling sorry for myself, maybe feel those bolts on my neck again when I dreamed.

Frank ruffled my flattop and said, "Good kid" when I showed him my first paycheck, pinned to a coupon for twenty-five percent off my next box of fertilizer. Now, when I say "fertilizer factory," you might be dreaming of a conveyor belt of butts pooping into boxes nonstop or something. Oh, you're not? My bad. Well, my point is, this was *chemical* fertilizer, not fecal. Just these little toxic yellow pellets. My vacuous, entry-level post was on "The Box Line," where I operated a hot-glue gun and sealed up the boxes once they were brimming with tiny, helpful turds.

I was positioned under a monstrous metal chute where the pellets poured out, and every so often, one unlucky soul would draw the short straw and have to climb a stubby ladder on the side of the chute and shake the grate until the buildup of pellets was busted up and dislodged. I say "unlucky" because even though the grate could be unhooked easily enough, then swung and rattled even easier, the heavy frame turned and tipped in an alarming way. So if you were daydreaming, you could get your hand pinched right off, as clean as a sphincter, which isn't very clean at all. And this is something that must have happened more than once, judging by the two big signs, one in comic sans, with a comic-book dog that warned, WATCH YOUR PAWS, ASSHOLES! and the other one that was sans comic, an all-business military font instead simply stating: **THREE DAYS SINCE OUR LAST ACCIDENT.**

This was not an erasable board.

In other words, the box line was deceptively dangerous work. But old habits died screaming, and pretty soon I was already looking for something to swipe. However, there were only two of us slaving away at any given shift, so I was hard-pressed to come up with anything in that factory worth stealing. At least not yet. It didn't have to be a big heist or anything. In fact, the least tangible thing I'd ever stolen was basically "time," but it was sometimes the most satisfying.

My partner's name on the line was "Joon," like the month but spelled wrong, an odd name for sure, he admitted, and certainly unusual for a boy, but according to him, not nearly as tough to grow up with as you might think. He said the made-up names these days were so goofy that nobody bothered to tease anybody anymore.

"Yeah, but what does it *mean*?"

"It's short for 'Juniper,' the quickest burning wood," he replied in his thin voice, suspicious face like an ostrich. I hoped he wasn't trying to scare me, because it was having the opposite effect. So with a hearty pinch on the back of his neck, I told him he had the perfect voice for the cartoon on the poster, and we would be safe together.

Joon and I were the only ones on the box line, and the only workers in that entire west end of the building, near as I could tell. My uncle said the factory had been much busier when it first fired up, not so many dead zones. On my first day, the oldster who trained me how to run the glue gun claimed that the recent near-extinction of the honeybee was responsible for the downturn and waning factory demand. He said that chemical fertilizers were being linked to the colony collapse and the subsequently under-pollinated and anemic crops. He was sure the demand would rebound soon, once the bees "bounced back," he said, glass eye watering but hopeful. So it was just me and Joon, building boxes at a pace just barely above "inert." But I kept on keeping on, dutifully shooting my goo gun, laying line after line of hot glue on the box flaps like heaping stripes of toothpaste, then sliding the box over to my partner, who would press the flaps together and count to ten to let them set before shoving them down the conveyor belt and through the doggy door out to the waiting truck. As we glued our boxes, we had a lot of downtime to get to know each other—not just during Joon's count to ten, which grew longer and longer each time he did it. Basically, I had Joon's entire life story down after day one.

Whenever I dreamed of factory work—and who didn't?—I always thought it would be a pointless job (check!) that was mind-numbing and tedious (check!) but which would position my body dead center in the bustle of some fascinating and kinetic "The Future of Industry!" Rube Goldberg machinations (nope!). That might seem like a nightmare sentence for most sane people, but this sort of purgatory would give me plenty of time to plan a new scam, and this is where things got rotten in Durango.

The problem was Joon. I'd never be able to figure out what to steal from this space-age poop factory if he couldn't shut the hell up for five seconds. Most gringos loved to hear themselves talk, and this mother-fucker was pure agony.

Did you know Joon owned three cars in his life, but never had an accident? Me either. Did you know that Joon once caught a man in the bushes eating his entire wedding cake? Prove it, right? Did you know that Joon had a collection of shot glasses from every rest stop between Kentucky and South Dakota, every one of them named after a cop that got shot in the line of duty? Well, now you do. Did you know that superhero films were destroying Mexican and American cinema? Did you know that kids sometimes say I look like one? Joon was unconvinced. Did you know Joon was the most unessential human being ever to glue a box shut and count to ten?

His morbid shot glasses came up a lot, but I didn't rib him too hard about them, as I had my own ghoulish collection lining the walls of my garage. But was a collection still a collection if nothing matched? If there was no reason nor rhyme? If it was just a bunch of little something or others that I'd managed to smuggle out the door of every job I'd ever had? Why not? With the uptick on loss-prevention these days, by "door" I mean the back door, of course. First, you threw something in the trash, then later, you rocked up in the dead of night for some dumpster diving. And this is exactly how I got my massive and eclectic music collection out of Media Play, before internal theft put them out of business (Uncle Sam voice: "I'm doing my part!"), or how I got fifty boxes of Godiva chocolate out of Barnes & Noble, actually, my most lucrative covert operation. It did require some extra steps, like a fine-tipped, permanent black pen snatched from the Walgreen's gift counter next door, and just one number altered on each box's expiration date. So after inventory, the manager became my unknowing accomplice, telling me to roll the spoiled candy to the curb. Thanks, boss! I'd kept one box of chocolates to adorn the garage wall (now long expired for real), but I did manage to sell the forty-nine remaining boxes on eBay for fifteen bucks a pop. This was Christmastime, and Godiva (or "Go Deeeva," as the soccer moms called it), was super popular around the holidays. I sampled my own box of candy when the chocolates eventually started turning white, but they gave me diarrhea. But my uncle pounded that shit. Didn't bat an eye.

"¡Estos dulces son buenos! Tiro el resto de las piezas para eliminar el intermediario."

Stealing a box of fertilizer, though? That would be too big to squirrel out with the trash, even if I managed to walk it past the security guards and stuff it through our doggy door. And filling my pockets with pellets for my score wasn't just unambitious and borderline idiotic, it was downright unremarkable, judging by the dusting of yellow lines marking their path like a treasure map through the parking lot. This meant all the men in the factory shook fertilizer out of their collars and pants cuffs every night, like in *Shawshank Redemption*, when Andy moved his wall out into the yard. But why even bother? I never understood it, and I thought I might as well go back to driving buses again if I was going to settle for sad swipes like that.

So I'd have to think bigger. But to do that, I needed to hear myself think. Even working the booth at Putt-Putt during the busiest summers, I would have a good half hour of solitude between customers. And my old landscaping job was perfect for alone time, which was how I had figured out how to forge the purchase order for an upside-down willow tree and plant it next to the shed of a family who was away in Long Beach for the weekend . . . just so I could sneak back, dig it up, throw a hood over its fuzzy head, then plant it next to a neighboring shed so that it would feel like it was mine. To represent the tree on my garage's trophy wall, I settled for a scraggly voodoo doll I made from some branches. I did try to grow a sapling from a cutting to keep on my key chain, but no dice. An upside-down willow was more fickle than the flip of a buttered pancake. Always ending up on the ground, wrong side down.

And back on the box line, Joon never stopped talking. Not even to breathe. I swear, he'd be talking on the intake and on the exhale. I never had a moment to dream, let alone scheme. Joon probably developed this skill to adapt to a lifetime of dull-ass work, but I was cut from different cloth. And I soon realized that Joon felt an urge to fill all this dead air because we were really two men doing a job meant for one. Which meant my uncle had been wrong. A robot with a flattop would be replacing me soon enough.

And Joon would no doubt talk it right into a rusty grave.

Despite all these obstacles, I started plotting. Then after about a week, I figured out how to clog the grate on purpose, to necessitate sending one of us up to shake it loose more often. All I had to do was come in early and splash some milk up there to make the mesh a little tacky (I had plenty to spare). This bought me some time away from him. Then I convinced Joon that I couldn't shake it loose anymore, even when it was my turn in the rotation. You know how in movies, when someone tells an elaborate story to convince someone to do something, and their acting is a little *too* good? Well, I didn't have that problem. And in this instance, my size, square skull, and general aura of untrustworthiness worked in my favor. It got to be our routine, me in the morning clogging up the grate with some of my pellet milkshake, and by midday, Joon up there rattling the cage.

One afternoon, when I was well into a mental diagram of how to fold one of our long boxes into a full-body origami to sneak down the legs and arms of my overalls and out the back door to nail to my garage wall . . . Joon finally pinched off his hand.

He honked like a circus seal, and as I scrambled up the ladder to pull him loose, I would love to tell you that I didn't know what I was going to see up there, and that it was all in slow-motion or an out-of-body experience or whatever, but there was a good thirty seconds of me just staring mesmerized as I watched the chute pitch to the right, then roll to the left, then head straight for poor Joon Bug's skinny neck. Maybe I could have stopped it, but I got distracted by his limp handshake, which was loosening its grip from my hand at the same time as it released itself from Joon's body. I could feel Joon's last heartbeat in that hand, saw the last twitch as it worked to seal the glue on just one more fertilizer box before it lost all contact with command central. But I held it tight, and I couldn't help but imagine how that hand would look on the wall of my garage.

The circus in Joon's throat stopped barking when the grate slammed down again, and Joon's head came off so cleanly that at first I thought there would be no blood at all. Then his neck went off like a fountain of fireworks, and when I kicked the box into position under the chute with a practiced punt, those thirsty yellow pellets soaked up the blood so fast that it was as if there was never any accident at all.

I looked to the sky peeking through the slats of the factory's tin roof and whispered, *"Mi reino por unos cables de arranque . . ."*

I didn't wait to see if anyone accepted my offer.

When the dripping of his lifeblood stopped, I slowly stepped down off the ladder, took my glue gun in my fist, and laid a long, perfect stripe on the flaps of a box. Then I took five steps to the left where Joon used to stand, where the flattop robot would now replace us both, and I did Joon's job of sealing up the box. I even counted to ten, like he always did. Then I counted to twenty. Then I counted to a hundred, because with his head sealed in that box of fertilizer, I had some quiet time to myself. That's when I finally thought of something worth stealing.

Standing there with a freshly fertilized head in my hands, I thought back to when I first turned on Joon. I guess it was when he offered to buy me lunch.

Wednesdays are bad enough, but it was also my first day on the job, and I wasn't hungry because I was used to sleeping until noon for the bus-driving gig. Plus, I always had my trusty thermos of milk, which is really and truly all you need most days. So I was sitting there shaking yellow dust from my hair and trying to lay low, as this was the only time during my workday where it's a room full of people, and I sure don't need any new friends in my life. But Joon makes this big production to walk up and say real loud that he can front me the money for food until we got paid. In that moment, I looked him up and down, at his lemony-powdered beard and his lemony-jaundiced eyes, and then I gazed out at everyone else in their prison-chic jumpsuits, suddenly horrified they thought I was anything like them, or *could* be anything like them. And then that same day—when I was still stewing about this and not watching close—I accidentally pumped some hot glue onto my glove and it started to burn through it and down to my skin, and Joon reached over and yanked it off, smiling like he was the Mexican American superhero I needed but didn't deserve, and I thought, *Al carajo esta mierda.*

So that was probably when I started hating him, but I swear I never wished him dead. There's just something about being stuck together too long at any job, you know? It's an intimacy I just cannot abide.

In spite of everything I'm telling you now, I knew I'd be the number one suspect in his death, so I needed to act fast. This meant some brutal decisions. I imagined that by rotating his body around those dangerous corners at the top of the chute, a few careful tips of the grate could clip the bulk of him into manageable pieces, just as easily as you'd nip the cheese corners to round off your burger. So I did this, and the blood poured down into the boxes crazy fast, but it was nothing I couldn't keep up with it. Even if you make the mistake of bringing me on board, I'll always be a good worker.

I wouldn't call it work ethic, though. Maybe something closer to guilt.

That night, I signed the overtime sheet, and I started sending the smallest parts of him out the back door. Fingers, toes, an ear, all sealed with the pellets doing their job soaking up the excess, and Joon was soon on his way to help some poor farmer's crop grow nice and tall. I envisioned Joon's ghost talking the stalks to death instead of me, or rambling in Kevin Costner's ear until he was convinced to build a hockey rink in his cornfield during an Iowa heat wave and ruin his life in an entirely different way. You ever see that movie? Now, that is some serious white people shit. I remember some kid choking on a hot dog, and a ton of headlights at the end. Roll credits.

Some of Joon went out the back door in those boxes, but the rest of him—the more substantial hunks—still posed a real problem. And insane as it sounds, the closer you got to the parking lot, some real scrutiny became an issue. And there was decent security at this plant for some reason. Later, I heard the rent-a-cops had been contracted by the plant because pharmaceuticals were stored on the other end of our warehouse to help them make rent, and the loss-prevention company's contract built in a couple weeks for them to float. So this meant you couldn't leave for the night with anything more than a reasonable bulge in your pockets, but I knew I could duck out of the factory at least three times that day for "breaks" without arousing suspicion. Why not swipe the drugs, you ask? Instead of swiping pieces of my coworker? Well, drugs would look as stupid on the walls as a dollar bill. And, funny as it sounds, I'm kinda straight-edge when it comes to my body. You don't chug milk for the taste. You do it for the gains.

We were allotted two breaks and one lunch, but it was still early into the second shift. I didn't smoke, but I would have to that day. So I hit the big red STOP LINE button and started at the top. *Go big* and *go home*, I told myself, and I stuffed Joon's head into my jumpsuit, admiring my new beer belly in the reflection of the hopper. On the way out the back, the guard didn't bat an eye.

In my car, I worked Joon out from under my shirt and flung him into my trunk without ever having to pop it open. That was the beauty of '95 Mercury Mystiques and their drop-down back seats: Trunks were just a target to toss all your shit into. After his head was rolling around back there, I found a soggy Salem filter on the ground near my car, and I fired it up with the Mercury's lighter, just in case I had to breathe on anybody on the way back in.

Nobody got close.

On my official lunch break, I took out his hands. Then his arms. I was surprised to find the hands were easier. Hands in your pockets made shapes in your pants that were so recognizable that they were completely ignored, even when there were two too many. This is why everyone spends their time looking for a purple nip slip on Vishnu instead of being freaked out by that whirlwind of limbs. At least I do.

On my final smoke break, I brought out his legs. I'd stuck them down the pants of my jumpsuit, then jogged past the guard like I was having some intestinal distress, which was sorta true at this point. Later I would douse my guilty bowels with a natural remedy, a metric ton of whole milk. Lactose intolerance is a sign of weakness, so I don't tolerate it.

The guards didn't balk at my giant legs and my where's-the-toilet shuffle. They even averted their eyes, not wondering why I wasn't hauling ass to the restroom, instead of hustling out to the parking lot to christen a Little "Deuce" Coupe.

Last up was the torso, his heavy-duty core, the "muddy muddy middle," said *The Piggy in the Puddle*, the part of our body that makes us undeniably human and impossibly messy. It was both the hardest and the easiest. I knew I'd never get it to hang on the wall in my garage— hey, what do you call a guy with no arms and no legs hanging on the wall? Art? June Bug?

Anyhow, for Joon's marbled midsection, I just propped it up on the toilet in the restroom, locked the door on the stall, then crawled on back out. No one used that particular restroom but me and Joon, so I figured I'd bought myself a week before the smell hit the rest of the warehouse. The torso balanced on that seat without any problem, either. Turned out our hefty asses were truly our center of gravity and, therefore, the most important part of our built-in gyroscopes, vestigial tails be damned.

After dumping the biggest chunk of him in the stall, I went back to the box line and hit the big red button one more time. The conveyor resumed, and the dusty pellets came raining back down, and I worked double duty to finish out the day. Turned out, it was easy.

Like I said, this was never a job that needed two people.

I brought all those plump and pink puzzle pieces to my garage, which had previously been my uncle Frank's garage, which was where he was still storing his car. The car that everyone thinks is my car. But I kinda like it when that happens. It's more mine than anybody's now.

I should clarify. By "car," I mean a rolling junkyard masquerading as an automobile, because it resembles nothing else in this world. But that doesn't mean it won't start. You can start any cursed creation on four wheels, as long as you feed it first. A little fuel in the tank. Or a little fool in the trunk. Either way. But while I was gathering up its feast, I was counting all the parts, and my heart skipped when I realized the puzzle was missing a big piece. His foot. I knew I had to go back.

I was a little nervous about revisiting the scene of the crime, but I'd come too far now. And then I realized. Any foot would do. So I slunk back to the warehouse the next morning, at seven sharp, and I punched my ticket. Even had a bit of a fright when I thought I over-heard someone near the bathroom yelling "olfactory" instead of "old factory" because they'd nosed out his nucleus. But I knew that place stank bad enough to disguise Joon's bottom-heavy centerpiece for at least another couple days.

Another day with his torso on the toilet, and me on the box line alone. And when Joon didn't show up, they sent me a twitchy WWII vet to stand in for him, some psycho named "Billy" who thought I was fucking Korean instead of Mexican (Caribbean?), so it only took half the day before I was able to convince him to climb up there and shake out the grate. I did warn him to watch his hands, swearing to him that kick-ing it loose was the only safe way to unclog that filter. And when his foot was crushed and almost but not quite pinched off at the ankle (so close!), then completely removed at the hospital that night, I stopped by to put in a job application at the Emergency Room. Orderly, parking attendant, whatever. "I can start tomorrow, yes, sir, glad to be working with you . . ."

I've worked all sorts of jobs, but the job is never the important thing. Just the collection.

And even if that Second World War veteran flipper is gone by the time I infiltrate my next job, like I said, any foot will do, as long as it's white as a field of daisies in June. Actually, that doesn't matter all that much. America is a melting pot, right? One thing I learned from my uncle is that once you realize you aren't bound by the rules of building the right thing with the right parts, you could dream of building the wrong thing, and do it in half the time.

"Tira el libro de instrucciones y agarra el perro," he would say.

Then maybe, *"Digo, el* día. *"*

If you must know, despite all my hustle on the job, our family legacy as crazy klepto completists finally got the best of me, and I was pulled over in my uncle's "Cadillac" on my way home from my first day in the ER. Busted for stealing medical supplies, they said, if you can believe that. The joke's on them, though, because they didn't even notice my new foot. But the officer knew something was up right away, even without the stethoscope around my neck. It's true that people will overlook extra hands, bolts on your neck, maybe an extra foot or two up your ass, or even a torso strapped to your hood.

But ninety-nine broken taillights will summon the cops from a hundred miles away.

CHAPTER VII

THE NEEDLE

I said, we need to crack a taillight to summon the cops."

"That is not what he said!" Ruck was pointing at Godzooky like he'd cracked the case instead. "And who even invited this guy?"

"Didn't you?" Angie wanted to know.

"No, that is exactly what I said." Godzooky insisted, and everyone in earshot was baffled.

"I have to admit, I didn't catch most of that story about heads and hands and yellow poop pellets, but . . .." Angie was still trying to play it cool, but also actively wondering if there was any coming back from where Baby Godzilla's bloody factory confession regarding *actual murder* had taken them. Luckily, judging by the group's lack of alarm, most of the details had apparently been lost both in transmission and translation.

"Didn't understand a word!" Dan said.

"Hey, we told him to tell a scary story," Janky laughed.

"Did we, though?"

"I think what he was really trying to say was that he stole our shit," Ruck said.

"He terk our jerbs!" Janky couldn't resist.

"Yeah, no, that's not what he said. Was it? Hey man, was that Swahili or what?" Dan asked him.

Godzooky frowned. He'd served up his best bestiary in the King's English, with maybe half a dozen Spanish phrases tops, but he wasn't that surprised how quickly gringos tuned him out at the first rolling *R*. Or maybe, as some sort of unconscious defense mechanism, he'd actually narrated this story in Spanish, with a half dozen English phrases instead? Who could tell?

"Kill one bird with ten stones," as his uncle liked to say. All he knew was that, ever since he started dreaming in Spanish again, he sometimes got his mother and adopted tongues reversed. But his fellow captives should have had no trouble understanding such a universal plan as breaking a taillight to get the attention of the cops, anything to draw attention to their plight. Back when the streets were filled with activity, screaming at pedestrians or cars from their pool prison yielded no results, misinterpreted as trying to get a different sort of attention.

"Do you think a bottle could bust a taillight out, or would it just bust the bottle?" Dan asked, slapping a Natty Light against his palm, liking this plan the more he thought about it.

"Did you catch that part of his story about stealing a dog and jump-starting his head?" Amy mumbled to Angie, still working to translate his story—she was very proud of her Spanish class from two years ago—but Amy shook her off.

"I didn't know you drove a bus," Lund said.

"¡Es un *trabajo!*" Gadzooky laughed, confusing them even more.

"Forget the bus. I got a B+ in Intro to Spanish Literature," Amy said. "And I can't believe everyone isn't more freaked out about what he said about his car."

"Who cares about his car?!" Beth said, slapping the water, and Janky groaned.

"Hey, Beth, do you *ever* smile?" he asked her, bold as hell. He reached for her face, and Beth swatted his hand down with a speed and force that surprised everyone who felt the wake of the blow.

"I told you once already. Do not ask me that question again," Beth said, and Angie and Amy nodded to signal they would reinforce this ultimatum. They were already repulsed by Janky tonight, not just because of his missing thumb, and Jill, half-joking, had confided to Angie earlier that anyone without a thumb would be of little help once they jumped off and had to hitchhike home.

She had a point. Speaking of . . .

"If you were to summarize the point of your story, Carlos, what might you say?" Angie was trying her teacher voice on Godzooky, hoping for better results.

"I guess my point was that I know what things are made of?" he said, after some thought. "Like what this fire truck is made of, and what we're made of . . . and once you know what something is made of, it's nothing to fear. And, yes, that definitely includes all of . . . this."

He pointed so that the "this" indicated Dan and Reeves.

"Okay?" Jill said, still puzzled.

"I'm starting to wonder about something, guys," Ruck said.

"What's that?" Jill asked.

"Maybe we're all here for a reason."

"Huh?" Angie cupped her hand around her ear. The beats were climbing again. Sometimes they didn't notice the music at all, and sometimes it was all they heard. Usually when they tried to hash out their situation. And right now, the vibrations were riding the waves right up their asses again.

"I said, maybe we're all here for a reason!"

"Here in this pool?"

"You mean *here* here, like, alive?"

"Of course you're here for a reason, boys!" Jill said. "My birthday!"

"No, I do mean here on this truck," Ruck went on. "After hearing some of you tell your cursed life stories, I'm starting to think we were brought here to be tested. Or punished."

"Punished by who?"

Don't say it, don't say it . . . Angie thought, but Lund said it.

"I think you mean by 'whom.'"

Otherwise known as Mr. Winston "Don't Call Me Pain" Payne.

"Gonna be punished by *me* in a minute," Dan said on his way to Lund, but Reeves put a hand on his chest to restrain him for now.

"Stop it!" Jill said, looking around the group, which had tightened around this debate. Even Godzooky's eyebrow was up, sending his flattop askew. He'd maintained a poker face while narrating his own wild tale, but now his stoic facade looked ready to crack.

"Maybe he's right," Reeves said. "This might be something like—what's the word?"

"Purgatory," Dan said.

"Yeah, we died from all the urine in this water," Janky said.

"I'm just saying, it might be time for more desperate measures." Reeves pointed off into the dark.

"Dearly beloved . . ." Jill sang, still trying to keep things light.

"We are gathered here today to marinate in our own piss!" Dan added.

"That's not how the song goes, asshole." Jill took a step toward Dan, but then Reeves was up in between them, shaking the water off his back like a dogfish, snorting and reaching for a nearby beer, but settling on trying to get a game of Spin the Bottle going with it instead.

"Who wants to play?" he asked.

"Didn't you hear what we just said?" Amy said, stupefied by their behavior.

"Didn't you hear what *you* just said?" Ruck blew a raspberry at Reeves, amazed by the whiplash of his inebriation.

Godzooky waved it all away and went back to his corner to brood. Amy, Beth, and Angie picked the other corner, watching them all carefully. Sherry, Gaddy, and Holly went up to the rail, bopping as if they were being cheered on by crowds along the streets. Jill surveyed the scene, lost in thought, and the rest were somewhere in the shadows.

But they all knew the party was over.

And for the drunkest boys drifting back toward the rear, like Janky and Ruck, or Dan and Reeves, the red glow of the exhaust was looking a little like exit stage right, and jumping from the back of a speeding fire truck at 60-plus miles per hour onto a bottomless black country road seemed more and more like the reasonable option.

Every time someone spun the bottle, the unseen driver seemed to sense it, and the engine deep in the bowels of their clattering juggernaut would strain as it fought its way back to full throttle. The simmering panic of the group had caused them to circle back around to playing Truth or Dare after all, the absolute nadir of party games. But for whatever reason, whenever it was one of the triplets' turn to ask the titular question, they just ended up trading injury stories all over again, which Angie decided was a game much worse than Truth or Dare, actually. But they were driving through an area approximating civilization again, the regular glow of a gauntlet of sporadic streetlights raising their spirits.

As Holly, Gaddy, and Sherry shared their scars to trump Janky, Angie listened, skeptically, realizing why fairy tales always started with the same word.

"Once, I ruptured a disc in my back from moving boxes of magazines at a bookstore," Holly said. "Ended up having surgery on my spine and spent months of rehab in a pool with weights around my ankles. The retired Olympic dyke in charge of my rehabilitation developed a mad crush on me, and she started piling on the weights, and I started getting worried that she wanted me to stay injured so I'd keep coming back in. I'm not kidding! She totally 'Munchausened' my ass. Is that a thing? 'Munchausen by Pool'? Anyway, who the hell puts weight on your ankles in the deep end? How dangerous is that?"

"Like putting a hot tub on a fire truck?" Janky offered.

Nervous laughter bubbled around them, and Holly went on.

"Now that I think about it, I'm sure she was just focusing all her attention on me because all the other crusty old fossils with their work-related injuries were wandering around like zombies, and any exercises they could handle had to allow a constant eyeline with *The People's Court* playing nonstop above our heads, which was like their gospel hour. The more virile construction workers always acted like astronauts in training, too. And they'd notice me right away and get all real interested why I was there, that 'new sincerity' version of wolf whistling, right? And I'd just change the subject, telling them they should try jogging with my death weights in the pool 'cause 'it's just like running on the moon.' And they'd believe me. Lost three of them in a week." She turned and tried unsuccessfully to point at the small of her back. "See that right there? I still have some scars from surgery where they slipped and—"

"Wait, is that the *moon* moon? Or Moon, Pennsylvania?" Dan asked.

"Shut up."

"Wait, did you say 'scars' or 'stars'?"

"She said stars," Janky said. "But I think she meant her tramp stamp."

"Oh, okay."

Dan gave Janky a short groin punch, then someone tackled someone, who then tackled someone else in return. Gaddy took it as her cue to jump into the fray.

"Once, I knew a bartender who ruptured his urethra trying to piss into a mailbox!" she said. "But the box was too high, so Chuck—that's the bartender's name—he had to straddle it, bending his junk down to, like, *jam* it inside. And I guess he just bent that little junkyard too far! And guess what? Who'da thunk it, but the idea of pissing into a mailbox musta got him a little too excited. And just like Jane Goodall reported after studying men in the wild, it's difficult enough for them to piss without half an erection. Now add a literal red flag to the morning-wood equation? Forget about it. It might be true that you can't tickle yourself, but if you're sitting on a mailbox with your pants down, boys, that little red flag might tickle your balls when you least expect it. And we don't envy you guys that one, no matter what Freud says. By the way, banging wooden mailboxes shaped like animals are best, sure, but they're also a gateway drug. Just ask Chuck. No telling what he'd jam his joint into after that."

"Shit just took a turn," Janky said, mouth slack.

"Ever see those mailboxes shaped like sharks?" Holly asked him. "Where someone thought it was cute if the mailman had to slide his arm into a shark's jaws every morning? Notice they don't last too long. 'Federal offense,' my ass! More like a crime against nature. But you'd know all about that, huh, Sherry?"

"So, are you saying men are out there fucking everyone's mailboxes?"

"Zip it!" Sherry shoved Janky aside, stepping up to accept Gaddy's invisible microphone.

"Okay, I have an idea for a new reality show," she announced. "How about . . . a dozen people in a rolling bathtub . . ."

"And you fill it with beer!" Janky shouted, and got tackled by Dan, hard this time, his head bonking against the fiberglass bottom before he could resurface and try to reclaim the stage by bringing his lack of a thumb into the intermittent incandescent spotlights.

"Some of you may have noticed that I'm missing the thumb on my right hand . . ."

Groans turned to moans.

"We already did this, ya tool!" Jill reminded him.

". . . but this is not a birth defect *nor* an injury, however! This is the result of a spider in my mother's womb." Eyes were rolling real hard now. "Sure, I may look like anyone else, but remember, whenever I'm talking about my thumb, I'm not *really* talking about a thumb. I'm talking about the space where the thumb would be, which is entirely different . . ."

"What's it like being the worst hitcher of all time?" Dan asked him, and Jill gave Angie a knowing "I told you so" look.

"I still love you, freakshow!" Reeves gurgled.

". . . but if it wasn't for that lack of a thumb, no one would know there was anything different about me at all. Besides surviving that plane crash, of course . . ."

"Barf!"

"Cut his mic!"

"Get off the stage!"

". . . there was nothing wrong with me. There was something wrong with *her*. I'm not joking here, people. I was told by a real medical doctor that the reason I'm missing my thumb is because my mother had webs in her womb."

"Webs in her what?" Holly asked, not wanting the answer. "Just stop!"

"That's what I said. And a doctor referring to amniotic band syndrome as 'webs' is exactly the kind of overly simple explanation that can make an impressionable child overanalyze to a very dangerous degree. 'Was there a spider in the womb with me?' I would wonder. 'Did I spin these webs?' 'Is the inside of my mother like those horror movies where the monster's mouth opens up and there's strings of spit dangling down that harden as stiff and sharp as piano wire sealing your mouth so you can't scream?' Totally normal questions! Why is everyone looking at me like that?"

No one was looking at him anymore, except for Lund.

"*Alien* was one of the ten best films of the twentieth century," Lund said sincerely.

"Well, when I was little, I told the other kids that my thumb was removed by scientists to stop me from accidentally crushing things. I told them that after the fiftieth baby bottle exploded in my grip, the government had to take drastic action. I said I could have been the greatest guitarist of all time, or quick-draw artist, masturbator, Major League pitcher, thumb wrestler, tickle monster, you name it! But in reality, the only thing I ever accidentally crushed was a pumpkin I was too lazy to carve and left on the TV. It sat there until Easter. Then the next Easter. And it just kept shrinking, and when I went to chuck it, my thumb punched through the side of the pumpkin with such sickening ease that I almost hurled. Now imagine having a thumb strong enough to do that to *everything*. That's my burden. Okay, it felt really good to get all this off my chest, guys, thanks . . ."

"Tickling is abuse," Beth said, with no hint of irony.

"Speaking of mushy pumpkins, the surgery from my ruptured L5-S1 disc left a spot that feels like it would totally give in if you pushed on it," Holly said, spinning around to try and present her lower back to the group again. "Someone poke me in my pumpkin spot!"

"Ewww . . ." No one took her up on it.

"You know, before the internet, carving pumpkins was so much simpler. Protest signs, too," Dan mused. "They're all too clever now. And it's just an embarrassing competition."

"Like this?" Angie asked him.

"Yep, like this."

"Even though a birth defect is typically thought of as a weakness, or worse, a sickness, the results later in life usually resemble more like a wound, physiologically and psychologically," Janky went on, trying to sound haunted.

"Somebody shut him up before I do it permanently," Dan warned them.

"But there's definitely something comforting to a boy who can turn illness into injury by adding a spider to the recipe. Anyway, I can't prove it, but my brother claims that when I was born, instead of holding me up and spanking me to get me breathing, the doctor screamed because of the amniotic webbing hanging off my fingers. The nurse actually screamed for a fly swatter."

"Enough," Angie said to him evenly, and somehow that worked.

The group drifted away with the tide of another one of the truck's wide turns, and the party was silent for a bit, with only the music rattling their brainpans. Reeves finally stood up, bleary-eyed from the pool, and he clapped his kneecaps like he'd put something off for long enough, and now he was going to work. Then he grabbed Janky's thumbless hand and hauled him over by the rail to turn it over in the moonlight to get a good look. Janky struggled and twisted, feet slipping on the bottom.

"Are you ready to turn that frown upside down and earn your keep, son?" Reeves asked him, getting a better grip on his arm to stop his thrashing.

"Shadow animal king of the world, this guy!" Dan said, slithering next to Reeves and peering over his shoulder. He wasn't sure what Reeves was up to, but he was all in. All of the bottles had been drained, and all of the empties were spinning now, and it looked like the "Truth" part of the game wasn't going to penetrate enough injury stories to help Janky avoid the "Dare" any longer.

"I thought of a real good dare for Thumbelina, here," Reeves said, pulling Janky's head up by the hair. A buzz went through the group at the impending violence, and Holly was clapping giddily. But help was coming for Janky in the shape of the impressive combo of Godzooky and Jill. But they weren't coming fast enough this time. Angie saw the hesitation and sensed the mortal danger of a dare at this moment, and she held up her hand to shout:

"Truth!"

Reeves glared at her a full minute of rhythmic synth bumps, then he let Janky go. Janky shot away like an eel.

"Okay, yeah, truth," Holly said, temporarily impressed with Angie's display of mercy for Janky. "Did you know that one out of every five people has killed someone, whether accidentally or on purpose?" Holly's grin was so big that the ends of it were lost in her hair. "So, with that math in mind, exactly three people here in this pool have killed someone. Or will."

"Don't you mean accidentally on 'porpoise'?!" Ruck said, doing a belly flop.

"This *is* Purgatory," Amy whispered to Beth.

"No, this is Hell," Beth whispered back.

"Nah, the last circle of Hell was ice," Angie said, unhelpfully. "Not piss and Heineken backwash."

"I'll just come out and ask!" Ruck said. "Has anybody here killed anybody?"

There was some more nervous laughter and conspiring in the corners, and even Godzooky shook his head and laughed hearing the question out loud. But if anyone had been sober enough to pay attention, a third of the partiers were conspicuously silent.

No matter how dire their situation could seem, they always rebounded, and even the looming specter of damnation did little to rattle their unshakable faith that no vehicle could drive forever.

* * *

Despite Jill's protests, Angie and Amy decided to try one last time to get the driver's attention, before suspicions of murderers in their midst got too out of hand, and maybe to get "Mr. Winston Payne, Raconteur," to answer their nagging question about why they'd been brought together. They both climbed out of the pool and into the wind and pounded on the roof of the cab together, every so often giving the bars on the back window of the cab a good knee to the teeth for good measure. The truck wasn't impressed with their efforts, and neither was the party.

"You two besties are adorable," Ruck snarked. "You bang exactly the same."

"You wouldn't know," Amy said, still pounding.

Beth plugged her ears from the racket, which had joined the thump, thump, thumping of the music, itself amplified by the canopy of roadside trees they were currently cruising under.

Angie took a break from their hammering to catch her breath.

"So are you, like . . . sisters?" Ruck asked as Angie left his high five hanging.

"Nope," she said flatly, resuming her assault on the fire truck's canopy. She looked over at Amy as she pounded. "But we *have* been known to finish each other's . . ."

". . . sandwiches!" Amy yelled, and there was laughter and more beer cans popping. Angie could have sworn they'd run out of alcohol, either in Dan's backpack or the group's individual stashes. But new beers were appearing like magic. It was almost a relief, however, as she feared sobriety would somehow be worse.

The two of them continued to batter the roof of the cab as hard and as they could, until they were sore and exhausted, teeth chattering from standing high in the wind. They both scurried to the pool to warm back up. Jill stared at them a moment, and then pushed past Angie to give the bars on the cab window one final punt, howling in pain in return. She rubbed her aching foot and scanned the horizon for any signs of headlights. The streetlights had dwindled again, and Angie couldn't remember the last time they'd seen another vehicle on the road. She wondered if they'd soon cross a state line.

"Motherfucker's deaf," Jill slurred, clearly referring to the truck itself.

"Hey, does this ship have a name?" Lund asked them, and Angie's heart soared at the idea they were on a boat. The thought was comforting in its familiarity.

"You know which ships had the best names?" Lund continued. "The *Alien* movies. Every name was doom. It telegraphed their destruction. Like, if you're flying toward the sun, the ship is *Icarus* every time."

"And if you're flying near the toilet, the ship will be called *Skubala!*" Reeves said.

"I don't get it."

"Heathen."

Spirits were up again. Sharing stories about the frailty of their bodies had, for some reason, given them all a second wind. It was almost as if Janky (or more likely the triplets), had done this on purpose, to keep things easy and breezy? Angie didn't understand this investment in the status quo, but with the tension still ebbing and flowing with the turns, and the varying levels of illumination and their oppressive soundtrack, she tried not to make waves.

"Where exactly are we?" Ruck asked the group.

"Whoa!" Beth howled, hanging onto Reeves's arm on a hard turn. For the past several miles, she'd been reacting to every bump like it was turbulence on her first flight.

"Halfway to Elizabethtown, I think!" Dan said, voice echoing around the inside of the aluminum can hanging off his mouth. "Hard to tell, though."

The music was bumping hard again, and escape plans began to fly before they were drowned out again.

"Listen, should we just try to bail out or what?"

"Try to flatten the tires?"

"Yes!"

"Which one?"

"Both!"

"Let's take a vote."

"How about drain the pool?"

"Yes, brain the fool!"

"What?"

"Yes!"

"'Yes' to what?"

"To the vote!"

"Vote on what?"

"I can't hear you!"

"I've got it!" Ruck said, launching himself into the center of the group. He waited a beat for maximum impact. "Let's kill that fucking music."

Everyone cheered. "Fuck yeah!"

"Like, I don't think it's just me when I say the music might be part of the problem," Ruck said. "Not just an annoyance, like the way it goes up and down, hypnotic and abrasive at the same time?"

"I'm with him," Beth said. "Sometimes it's this dull roar, but other times it's a primal electric scream, and it's like I'm always shrinking away from it, only to find myself right in front of another speaker. It's like I'm both bullied and lulled into some sort of aggressive complacency?" Doubt in her voice, she added, "Is that a thing?"

A revelation seemed to settle on their faces, even the most skeptical, furrowed brows. The music had to go. In the moment, it made the most sense. They were sure they could get their minds right without that incessant beat.

And if they had the power to stop the music, maybe they had the power to stop the truck.

Before anyone could hash out a specific plan, Reeves was already on task. Dramatically cracking his knuckles, he turned and savagely head-butted a bolted, ten-inch subwoofer off the side rail and into the road. It exploded behind the truck, and everyone's eyes gleamed at this sudden display of power. They couldn't believe no one had thought to do it sooner.

But as the pieces scattered in the glow of the taillights, the calming effect of lowering the volume was shattered along with it. Perhaps because they found it a little too easy to imagine themselves splashing across that road in the place of the ruined speaker.

"How fast are we going?" Angie asked Amy, who was already onto the next speaker.

"Too fast," she answered. "Help me get the other one . . ."

They all swarmed the next mounted subwoofer, multiple hands fighting to rip it free from its brackets. Most of the party missed the second crash, as they were busy hunting down the remainders of the sound system, their obvious foe.

Lund found a smaller speaker tucked under the stairs where they'd originally piled their now-missing shoes and clothes. Ruck found two more flanking the emergency-strobe siren bar. And in the gap between the trailer and the cab, Janky found a handful of eight-inchers floating in the jumble of hoses and wires.

All in all, they found nine speakers pumping music, and they dug them out like ticks. With the removal of each one, the beats sank down to a more tolerable level, low enough that they all felt uneasy when Reeves sniffed out the final speaker near the bottom of the stairs. He yanked it loose and drop-kicked it into the night, and then there was just the sound of the road, the wind, and the water beneath them.

Facing their dilemma in relative silence combined with the threat of sobriety had definitely made things worse. Before, it had felt like the party was over, and any second the lights would come on over the bar. Now it felt like they were locked in until morning. Or longer.

I guess, thank God for the mystery booze? Angie thought as she watched the shivering and anxiety spread. She found some stray airplane samples of Jack Daniels floating by and passed them around as pacifiers. Some of them, like the triplets (and Reeves, of course), seemed to be under the influence of an even harder substance, but this was no time for a blood test or follow-up intervention.

The truck slowed for a red light, the first one in so long that they almost didn't recognize it. Most of the males hopped up fast to line the rail, asses wiggling like cats as they built up their courage to take the plunge over the side.

But when it should have been slowing down, the truck sped up instead, blowing through the intersection at a ridiculous speed, and the temporary comfort of road signs and streetlights was gone again. The wind cut through their wet skin and gooseflesh, and the group closed ranks, sinking back down into their cold soup of glass, tin, and dwindling heat. As they drove deep into the country, and the moon was lost behind the clouds, the blackness pressed them deeper into the pool. Time passed.

"How warm would it be inside you?" someone whispered into Angie's ear after what seemed like hours. Angie wheeled around, livid. But they were all nearby, and it was too dark to see who'd said it.

To distract herself, she focused on the kitten she'd heard screaming from the alley trash on her way to work that morning. It seemed like something she'd heard years ago. At the time, she thought the animal sounded like a child, which she decided was much worse than a child sounding like an animal. Now, with the anonymous whimpering and giggling in the corners of the pool, she wasn't so sure.

She kicked her legs and rubbed her arms, trying desperately to heat back up. Her motions created a new vortex of bobbing beer cans and bottles, clinking around her like billiard balls, swirling away from her body toward all the glistening, rippled skin as the scheming continued. She thought about Ruck's theory that they were being held captive as punishment for their sins, and she remembered her first time in a similar situation.

It was back in junior high, when Angie knew this girl whose "Hot Dad" ran a hayride around his property every year around Halloween. He would fill a topless trailer with grass and straw, hook it to a tractor, then weave about twenty kids as close to the roadside ditches as he dared, sometimes stopping to hold his flask up to the sky to check how much liquor was left. Between drags, he'd tip the trailer as far as he could into the ditch without flipping, then get mad when the children didn't squeal.

Angie never flinched, let alone squealed, not even when Hot Dad steered them through his gutted beehives and knocked the drawers of dead honeycomb under his wheels. Angie knew the bees were gone by that point, but some of the kids fell for the gag and screamed and swatted at dozens of ghost stings. But even though she never got scared, those rides did teach her something about hay; it hurt. Sitting in hay was like sitting in a pile of half-sharpened pencils, not soft and fluffy as she'd imagined. She'd watch the other girls scratching and shaking the hay loose and wondering how it managed to worm its way down the backs of their blue jeans, and she'd pull her belt tighter. But mostly she'd watch that one particular boy who was new to their school, pretending to look for something she lost in the hay so that he could catch her doing it.

"What are you looking for?" he'd ask. *Sucker.*

"Come on, do I really have to say it?"

But there was never a proverbial needle in the haystack (it just felt like there was), and once the tractor stopped weaving and settled on its long trek around the six-acre property line, most of the kids stopped itching and reflexively formed the impenetrable groups they always had. At that time in her life, Angie considered exclusion the worst form of bullying. Later, she came to appreciate the solitude, but back on the hay ride, she wanted the attention. And she had an idea.

There was another new kid (always another new kid), and oh, how Angie loved her some new kids. At least she used to. Everyone called him "Crazy Miles" even though they were pretty sure he gave himself the nickname after stealing a mile marker off the turnpike. And, despite an unremarkable face, clothes, or build, Angie noticed all the girls couldn't take their eyes off him for more than a few minutes. This was that "new car smell" these new kids always came with, and Angie couldn't help but want to sit next to him. And after one more wobbly lap around the Hot Dad's dried-up bean field, she popped the question.

"Hey, you wanna stage a fight and freak everybody out?"

Angie had never been in a fight with anyone besides her brother, so it felt right. Crazy Miles started tittering and agreed this would be a good way to shake up the trailer (at least two kids were already asleep), and the next time the tractor wheels slotted into the rows tilled into the field and the ride steadied a bit, they both stood up. Angie made sure all eyes were on them, especially snaky girls like the triplets, the ones whose lips were never far from each other's ears, and she gave Crazy Miles a shove in the chest, yelling:

"What did you say?!"

She must have jostled him a little harder than she intended because he lost his balance and started windmilling his arms, looking kinda goofy, and then Crazy Miles totally forgot Angie's master plan and hauled back to punch her in the mouth. He opened his hand at the last second—which was somehow worse—and he mostly caught her in the ear with the blow. But the swat was hard enough to upend her over the side of the trailer and dump her onto the crops like a shovel full of manure. She didn't remember the tractor stopping, or the kids piling onto Crazy Miles, or the righteous ass-kicking he received for hitting a girl, but she did remember being carried in someone's arms, and the swampy alcohol on this person's breath telling her she'd be okay. And she definitely remembered the swollen balloon where her bottom lip used to be, and those invisible pins and needles around her smile when this talking sump pump leaned down to give her a kiss. It was about as wrong as could be, but in that moment, finally free from all the needles and scorn of the other kids, she didn't care.

She ended up with a dislocated jaw and a default friendship with Crazy Miles after all. That is, after she got him back with her own shot to his teeth when he was turned around at his locker (though she didn't open her hand at the last second like he had). After that, he was pretty much her only friend through junior high, even if he turned out to be less interesting than anyone could have guessed, certainly for someone with a name like "Crazy Miles." And after graduation, after he got a job at the new prison like everybody else, Angie sold him her car, a piss-yellow '88 Sunbird, signing the title over to him the day after she made the last payment. And as anyone who has paid off a car can tell you, that was precisely when it started to fall apart. But their friendship had fallen apart first.

The last time she talked to Crazy Miles, he had called to complain about a wheel that flew off when he took a sharp turn, and said something about the gas needle being frozen on a quarter tank forever.

She thought a little about haymakers and told him, "It's your car now. Do I call you and tell you about my car?" and she hung up.

Most of the guys were leaning over the rail, still trying to gauge their chances of a successful leap to freedom, even at full speed, when the leering milk ad whooshed by dangerously close, startling everyone back to indecision. Brilliant with light, the billboard depicted a typically diverse group of partiers chugging heaping mugs of frothy milk on a sun-soaked beach, absolutely the best place for the summer rays to curdle a belly full of dairy into sour cream. Angie saw that some vandals had changed the "Got Milk?" to "Got Milf?" and then painted the grinning teens' milk mustaches black, transforming them into a happy gaggle of little Hitlers, which caused their resident milk connoisseur, Godzooky, to grumble under his own curdling breath, "Show some goddamn respect."

Reeves put a tentative foot on the rail, then Dan did, too. Then Janky. Angie estimated their speed at 70 miles an hour, with no slowdowns in sight. Shit was getting weird fast, and Angie knew it was time. She pulled Jill into a corner and told her about her own plan. The best plan yet. Her memory of the hayride had given her a perfectly terrible idea.

"We should stage a fight."

"Why?"

"I don't know," she admitted, then she snapped her fingers. "To reveal someone as a traitor."

"There's no traitor," Jill said. "Just an army of assholes."

"Exactly, but maybe one of those assholes is laying low . . . or hiding in plain sight." Angie said, tapping her temple, and then she abruptly shoved Jill hard back into the circle, putting the plan into action. Angie caught a glimpse of her smile before her punch and Jill's resulting splashdown, but Jill's game face was on by the time Beth and Amy were helping her up. Angie knew she'd channel her freakish birthday zeal to play the antagonist perfectly. Amy and Angie would have been more evenly matched, but Amy would have never gotten through a fake fight without laughing and giving away the game. Jill was all business when you needed her, even wasted. Especially wasted.

Jill ran back and put Angie in a bear hug, then she threw Angie up onto her shoulders like a WWF titan ready to drop down hard, and though Angie realized she hadn't really fleshed out the plan, it did serve the purpose of stopping the suicidal cannonballs over the rail.

And the party was into it. They forgot their abduction and excitedly watched Jill's savage slam (letting the water cushion the fall), then Jill letting Angie work her arms under her chin and run her back crashing into the hot tub's ladder. Their grappling took them up to the ropes (aka the rail), and it was all total pro-wrestling bullshit, but they were leaning a little far out over the road, and Angie's hands were on her throat, and Jill was giving her a look like, "Okay, maybe it's time to stop?"

And that's when someone showed his ass (for real) and became not just the antagonist they needed, but the one they deserved.

"Do it!" Janky yelled as he pushed his way into the open, accidentally leaving his underwear behind, which had gotten hooked to a screw head on the lip of the tub. He was only aware of his own nakedness when the crowd moved away in revulsion as the wind freeze-dried his testicles to his thighs. He cupped his crotch with his good hand, and Gaddy's eyes practically spiraled in anticipation of the scene getting any wilder.

"Do what, huh, instigator?" Reeves asked him.

"Yeah, what did the Miracle Baby just say?" Dan laughed.

"I don't know, nothing, never mind," Janky said, working to unhook his shredded jockeys with his thumbless hand.

"No, no, just a second," Dan said, finger up. "Did you try to entice her to murder her friend?"

"Huh?"

"He tried to get her to kill her!" Dan said, pointing at Janky.

"You know, yelling 'fire' in a crowded theater isn't as bad as yelling 'do it' in a crowded fire," Ruck said, bafflingly.

"In a crowded fire *truck*, bro?" Dan corrected. "Forget about it."

Reeves moved in, recognizing a new opportunity to usurp Dan's authority, and, for the first time, Angie noticed again how efficiently the two of them continued to swap ranks. It was always when people wanted to hurt each other. She released Jill's throat and let her slowly slide back down off the ladder, then she held up her hands.

"Hold on, hold on," she said. "Jill and I were just screwing around, guys . . ."

"Didn't look like it," Reeves said, one eye shut and the other squinting from the wind.

"Just stop, please."

"Fuck that!" Reeves said, grinning at them all. "Whether or not we're here as punishment for past sins or whatever that crazy shit he was saying, there is clearly something afoot with locked cabins, endless rides, and whatever else is wrong with us." He counted off on his fingers. "Weird drugs and weird drinks and weird music and a weird leap-year birthday and . . ."

"'And,' 'and,' 'and' . . . and what are you even saying?" But Angie didn't really want to know, as it was sounding like Reeves just trying to justify whatever he was going to do.

"Look around," Reeves said, no longer smiling. "If this isn't a cage match, what even is it?"

"No. It's a shark cage full of sharks," Angie said as the truck somehow sped up again.

"You have no idea," Reeves said, his smile back, and he spun on his heels, splashed over to Janky's losing battle with his underpants, and shouldered him hard off his feet.

Janky went up, out of the water, ass over elbows, and seemed to hover there off balance, as his bad hand slipped off the rail, four fingers grasping in vain to stop his tumble.

Then, before anyone could protest, Reeves lunged forward again, shoulder down like a silverback ramming the safety-glass at the zoo, and body-checked Janky right off the back of the fire truck and into the night.

"Oh my God," Jill said, hand over her mouth, and there was a gasp from the crowd.

They all heard the wet *thwack!* of naked skin on pavement, and everyone pushed their way to the back rail. Angie squeezed between a gawking Holly and Gaddy to watch Janky's body bounce high, feet scissoring as if struggling to find a runway for a safe landing, like his ill-fated airplane all those years ago. Then there was a whipcrack as he double-smacked the pavement, hipbone and then head, and now he was breaking, limbs flailing, the blacktop claiming him, modifying his body's perfect symmetry into the hideous, impossible angles of roadkill.

Then he was gone.

A man without a thumb has no business on the road, Angie thought before she could slap herself. Then she did it harder to see if the first slap was real.

Reeves stepped away from the rail and looked around at everyone, as shocked as the group by what he had done. Then he found God-zooky's glare in the back of the crowd and focused on staring him down instead. When that didn't work, he turned to the rest of them, watching as they quietly hunted down some bobbing beer cans to quench their guilt. They cracked them and drank, with nothing but the sounds of the wheels and their gulps. Angie sipped a mini-bottle of Grey Goose as she listened to the deep seams of the highway tap out an SOS no one would answer.

Lund tried to put an arm around Angie's shoulder for comfort, and, still dazed, she almost let him. Instead, she handed him the Goose and slid out from under his soggy T-shirt wing to stand by Jill.

But Holly had gotten to Jill first, eager for that ear. The light from a recent intersection was fading again, and they welcomed the dark. It was easier to pretend nothing too bad had happened.

Before the light went out again, Angie caught sight of Reeves watching Jill and Holly closely, and Angie realized Holly was now on his radar. She was amazed to see Jill clearing a space in the water, pushing away bottles, cans, and bodies for Holly to take center stage, clapping her hands high over her head for attention. There was no time to grieve. It was apparently Holly's turn to tell a story, as if life in the pool could just go on.

Angie scratched lines down the sides of her face with her fingernails to stay focused or maybe just sane, while Reeves belched and wandered off, trudging through the debris, then finally pulling down his shorts to urinate in the corner. Angie wondered how often people had pissed in the water tonight, and now, thankfully, she had something new to worry about. But for a moment, she let herself indulge in the indifference of the deep, dark Kentucky countryside, grateful there weren't any streetlights that would reveal the true noxious hue of their community pool, or the guilt on their faces for how far they'd fallen.

Then she looked back toward the red glow of the taillights and decided that some of them had fallen farther than others.

CHAPTER VIII

HONORARY YOGI

Holly's Gaddy Story

Okay, speaking of peeing in pools, let me tell you my part of our story. Don't worry, it's the best one. It's got full-frontal nudity, real magic, and a man drinking a Long Island Iced Tea with his penis. Oh shit, I buried the lede!

So we go to the bar one final time, a last hoorah before the night we'll be pulling the purloin. I've always loved that word, *purloin*. Sounds delicious. Second maybe to *pilfer*, but way better than *filch*. Gag, am I right?

It's not easy playing leader, so I have my accomplices get on the Atomic Dunk one last time to steady our nerves and our shooting hands before it goes down. We're able to talk about some more of my master plan under the fake electronic crowd noises of the game for quite a while. I don't tell Sherry everything, though, and, as always, the less control Gaddy thinks she has, the better. Oops, did I just say that out loud?!

But it will be an all-night job, this we know. Just the sheer amount of effort spent *depluming* this dive means a real labor-heavy piece of work, and Sherry's obviously into that sort of thing with all her annoying blue-collar fables, or haven't you heard. Vomitus! But, honestly, raking in that money will be more like raking actual leaves than anything. See, in the movies, stolen cash is always bundled into perfect little bricks, and the crooks bring the stacks up to their faces, then run their thumbs along the tight corners like they're shuffling cards. Total bullshit.

"See, when they do that, they're making sure the money isn't marked," is what I explain to my crew.

"Really?" Sherry says, skeptical, but still swishes three rapid-fire shots through the hoop.

"Remember, I used to date a Secret Service agent named Gaddy," I remind her.

"And?" Sherry misses the next shot.

Gaddy half-smiles at any reference to her own scandal, so I know Sherry, silly tramp that she is, will push her to see where this story will go. One thing I learned from (the papers I sold to) my postmodern pop culture class is that modern heist films are expected to have a relationship triangle (just ask Lund!), so the shakier Gaddy seems, the more she resembles the fictional wildcard, and the more excited I get that our job might actually be *real* this time and not just a buncha talk.

And, honestly, this score could finance a big move for all three of us. And we could leave the scandals behind us, maybe try the center of this country for a change.

"Well, technically I dated her while she was still an SS recruit," I say. "And she didn't make it past the probationary period. Did you, Gaddy?"

"Which probationary period?" she laughs, "Theirs or yours?"

"Ugh," Sherry groans as her last ball clangs on the rim, and the game hisses and jeers. She reaches over to give the straw in my drink an unnecessarily adorable suck. "Do tell."

"Okay," Gaddy says, teeth sparkling and cracking her thumbs. "So, first off, did you know that when you join the Secret Service, they give you a lie detector test and ask if there's any time in your life when you've stolen anything, and then keep asking these questions until you cry?"

"Wow. No kidding?" Sherry says.

"Yup! And then when you finally do cry? They go, 'Don't worry, everybody cries.'"

"Fuckin' assholes."

"That is bonkers!"

"Don't worry," Gaddy says. "I got the last laugh. Because what they didn't know was that you can beat the polygraph with Kegels every time."

"Wow."

"This part is true," I nod.

"Weird!" Sherry says. "So, wait, she passed the test, then. Did she ever get to run alongside limos with presidents or whatever? Because that would be insane."

"No, she got bounced out of the Service when she screwed up tagging along on her first stakeout," I say, laughing. "She was new, so they gave her the garbage detail or marking all the bills, one by one. She was supposed to put a little black line in the upper right-hand corner of all the hundreds with a Magic Marker, and they said any mark would do, right? But she had to do this all night with this huge stack of cash. So, like a dummy, she just had to get creative . . ."

"How so?" Sherry asks Gaddy, clearly trying to shut me up and get it from the horse's mouth. Gaddy reluctantly finishes her own story, just as I'd hoped. Good girl. This is why I love her sometimes.

"Ugh! Okay, well, to pass the time, I kinda started doing those flip cartoons instead."

"Where?"

"On the hundreds!"

"A cartoon of what?"

"Three blind mice. Running right up the side of that spooky pyramid."

"Oh my God," Sherry says, covering her snort with her hand. "That is amazing."

"So when the bad guys did that 'movie money move,' you know, running their thumb down the corner of the stacks . . . you know the move, right?"

"Oh, we know the move," I say. Jesus, have we met?

"They got a little surprise. A tiny cartoon where this itty-bitty burglar gets scruffed by the neck like a puppy and tossed into a little cage."

"Daaaaamn. You should have drawn a gallows and a hangman to freak 'em out, though."

"Low-hanging fruit," she says.

"You gotta love her!" I say, and Sherry nods. "Even if she's a pain in the ass."

"But we have to ask ourselves," I go on. "Is this even gonna be worth the effort?" My smile drops a little, but Sherry's nod in agreement speeds right up. Told you she was a good girl. Paradoxically, for a Midwesterner like herself, it's that unusually long heist time that makes the job obviously worth doing. That sort of real *work* work just feels right.

And suddenly she's even got me excited about the job again, because I feel certain that the eight hours it'll take us to pluck those dollars off the walls would be worth precisely that amount of *pluck*. Get it? Like determination? If you have to explain the joke, that means it's a really good one? And that sorta satisfying symmetry does not happen in any other line of work, legitimate or otherwise.

So at some point we scooch our stools away from the basketball game to give other people a shot, so now we're right next to the restrooms. Every inch of The Hut has a toilet smell—the sad, stale air of an old casino—so hanging out around the restrooms is as good as anywhere.

Which makes sense considering their peculiar choice of wallpaper.

Didn't *Mythbusters* prove that seventy-five percent of paper money is speckled with microscopic amounts of piss, blood, sweat, feces, and cocaine? Well, they should have. Maybe scientists just proved that those five things have always secretly powered the world. Money be stinky!

Eventually, we abandon our circle of stools altogether and head toward the bar, which alerts any desperate dudes still paying attention to order us more of those nasty-ass "girly" drinks, stat. We accept them all, smiling, of course. And while we wait, I point out the huge, jagged hole in the mirror behind the shelf of higher-end bottles. The bartender sighs apologetically as he slides me my Smurf-tinged Blue Hawaiian, Sherry's nuclear Fuzzy Navel, and Gaddy's toxic green Mixed Martian Arts. He understands the drill with these losers.

"What happened there, Chuck?" Someone points at the hole in the mirror.

"Two assholes came in here at closing time a couple nights back, screaming about losing their keys," Chuck says as he hands us more drinks. "Then they started brawling with each other, and one of them whipped an ashtray at the other idiot's head. Smashed my goddamn mirror, and that thing costs more than a windshield to get it fixed, so the owner said 'Fuck it, gives the place character.' But it just makes us look ghetto, if you ask me."

"Oh shit," I say, blowing bubbles through my straw, pretending I hadn't sent those morons in to stage that whole scene. "Did you get a description?"

"Description? Yeah, like I said, 'two assholes.' Students, I guess? Dumb faces? But they got bars over those faces now, since I got 'em arrested! Cops and campus security came in, seasoned them with pepper spray, choked 'em out, then dragged 'em off. They'll probably get expelled, for starters."

"I thought it smelled spicier in here," Sherry says, looking a little guilty and trying to steer the subject away from those two marks we potentially flirted into ruin. "A little salt and pepper spray makes everything taste better, right?"

"As long as the snozzberries still taste like snozzberries," I say, laughing, my tongue dangerously close to snarfing the wall. Instead, I run my hand up a trail of dollars like I'm petting a cat the wrong way, then the three of us trade glances as we two-finger-suck our straws and try to look like tiny sexy babies who just learned to drink. I told you this job took a lot of *work*.

After draining three gross Lemon Drops apiece, no one feels guilty anymore, thank God. And when someone tries to slide another Candyland in a fishbowl full of rubber ducks and *Romper Room* bullshit, I have to finally complain to Chuck about his drink selection.

"Why do you even have the toys to put together these goofy friggin' beverages?" I ask him. "And while we're at it, let's talk about your logo. A bronco heel-kicking a martini glass? Hut . . . hut . . . derp! Seriously, so many embarrassingly Junior Cosmopolitan refreshments are offered in here, honey. I thought you were a *dive* bar. Aren't you embarrassed? Show some pride, dude. All you're doing is encouraging fools."

"Who's encouraging who? You guys sure keep drinking them!"

"We're not talking about us right now," Gaddy says. "We're talking about you and this sad sack of a saloon."

"Now, that's where you got it all wrong," Chuck explains. "You wanna talk authentic saloons? That old myth about cowboys just drinking straight whiskey? Lies. Don't believe the hype. Did you know that the most popular drink in the 1800s was a Stone Fence? That's six ounces of whiskey and some apple cider, on the rocks. Maybe real rocks, who can say? But that is some sissy-ass shit if I ever heard it."

"I'm sorry, but that's still a shitload of alcohol," Sherry says.

"Yeah, but still, those cowboys were 'girl drink' drunks!" Chuck says. "So I'm just keeping shit real here. And by 'real,' I mean 'real drunk.' Now, do you want this with or without the edible underwear flowers?"

*   *   *

It's getting late, but we need Chuck a bit more pliable for our plan to go down smoother than his stanky drankies, so Gaddy tries her best to woo him with some key song selections. I already told her that the romantic days of leaning against the jukebox and locking eyes was long gone, but she wanted to try it, probably to keep me from having to mack on Chuck. She doesn't understand that all these "jukeboxes" are just dumb oversized QR codes glued to the wall now, so nobody loiters near them anymore. She put on some Thin Lizzy (don't ask me how or why), but it's so overplayed these days it's invisible to the naked ear anyway. So I finally say "fuck it" and slink around the bar to straight-up nosh Chuck when he's restocking down on his knees and out of sight. It's small, unexpected hiccups like the fact that jukeboxes aren't jukeboxes anymore that suddenly have me worried about our heist, as my lips are trying to get Chuck's dead mouth wet and my canines are tugging on Chuck's weirdly shriveled tongue.

Me going behind the bar without asking (or being asked), is a bold move. It's not *quite* peeking behind the curtain in the Emerald City, but it's close. You're just not supposed to be back there. But it works like gangbusters, and it puts this dutifully robotic bartender into an entirely different state of mind. Suddenly, Chuck's baritone is a whole octave higher, much more susceptible to my flights of fancy than I was to his flights of sugar-coated cocktails. I keep our lips locked tight, and my unruly but secretly obedient hair drapes over most of his peripheral vision, a blinding helmet for my steed. But just to make sure, I crank his head around to face the ragged black hole in the mirror behind the bar.

Totally at my mercy and gazing over my shoulder into nothing, Chuck is none the wiser to the efficient relay line I've organized behind him. I slide a hand down his stomach, unhook the keychain from his belt, and pass it behind my back to Sherry, who passes it to Gaddy, who pretends to head outside for a smoke but instead meets Magic Mike's 24-hour Key Cutters van in the parking lot of the 7-Eleven across the street. Chuck, you just got got.

So while I'm still slobbering on the bartender, Magic Mike grinds a copy right there in the back of his Chevy conversion for a measly three bucks, which suddenly seems like a lot more money tonight, since that will be three more flowers we'll be plucking from the walls while they're still green.

After the kiss, I stay behind the bar to chitchat and help out popping tops for the mooks, just to keep Chuck distracted. And with one or two more well-timed rotations and follow-up kisses for misdirection, and his face buried in my gorgeous wheat field of hair (did I mention how on-point this chick's lettuce was that night?!), and with the two of us haloed by the harsh lighting and shattered void of the smashed mirror over our backs . . . I've got his keys clipped back onto his belt before he closes the bar. None the wiser.

Sure, I basically have to do everything, but I'm used to that.

But now we're ready, and after clocking traffic inside and outside The Hut for a solid week, I decide next Saturday will be perfect for the big finale.

By the way, his keychain was one of those stupid dreamcatchers, which was Chuck's first mistake, really. But not his last. I could have told him those things could never catch shit.

Or us.

The night of the heist, we get there a half hour before closing, and we already know we're in trouble when our trusty bartender Chuck vows he won't be locking up until he's drained a Long Island Iced Tea with his penis.

Until he's what the *what* with his *what*? Lemme rewind.

In retrospect, I should have expected this. Like the teachers always told us in college, there are only three classic tales in literature; man goes on a journey, stranger comes to town, idiots dare each other to drink with their dicks.

The three of us are standing there, trying to decipher what we're seeing, but it's an unnatural scene that takes a solid three minutes for our overworked brains to process:

Chuck squatting on top of the bar, bulging genitals ugly as hairless rats, piling over the lemon spirals on the edge of a frosty mug, his eyes pinched tight while a line of patrons press in around him, whooping and hollering their encouragement. I see the Honorary Amish in the crowd, and he turns toward us when the light from the swinging front door shines a spotlight on the perverse festivities. He gives us a wrinkly wink, and Sherry recoils. I give her shoulders an affectionate squeeze to keep her focused, and then I wink back at him, just to keep Honorary Amish on the hook in case we need him. I pull Sherry and Gaddy back toward the basketball game in the corner, like it's any other night in the bar.

But the way I see it, I expected obstacles, and now *time* has become a new one. The original plan only gave us from close until dawn to do the deed, less than five hours tops. Past that and people would see us through the windows, depluming them dollas and whispering five thousand "She loves me . . . she loves me nots" in each other's ears.

"How long is this clambake gonna go on?" Sherry asks me, and Gaddy bites her lip, worried.

"So who dared Chuck to do that?" Gaddy asks.

"Everybody?" I shrug.

"I think that's just how the locals mark their territory now?" Sherry says.

"Well, to answer your original question, Sherry, hopefully this goes all night." I give her earlobe a pinch, pushing the right buttons as always. Some people think pushing your buttons is a bad thing, but it totally depends on what that button does.

"Why not just swipe one sector of bills at a time and replace it, section by section, over a period of months?" Sherry asks, ready to give up already. I guess I pinched the wrong ear.

"Because I won't give a shit about any of this next week!" I sigh, betraying my impatience. Bad leadership. But when you're on the top, you can't reach every button from where you're standing, you know?

"I feel you, but don't we need Chuck out of here?"

"No, we need Chuck right here."

"I don't get it," Sherry pouts. "We have the key!"

"The key doesn't matter now," I say, shaking my head, always doing everyone's thinking. "Because you obviously missed something . . ."

I cock a finger at the wall behind Sherry, and at first all she sees is the dollars. But Gaddy gets it, and she beckons Sherry closer. Gaddy looks right, then left, then pulls the corner back on one of the bills, and a half dozen dollars peel back with it, taped to a big piece of poster board. Underneath this flap is the keypad to the alarm.

"Oh my God!" Sherry slaps a hand over her own mouth. "When did you find that?"

"I was with him this morning when he opened. One final recon."

"Wait, did you—"

"We don't have the code," I interrupt before she asks about things that don't matter. Any conquest during the job is on a need-to-barf basis.

"So it's off," Sherry says.

"No, what? No way. It is certainly not off," I say, positively frazzled. "That just means we get to go with Plan B!" I cock another thumb at the dick-dipping insanity happening on the bar behind us.

"Okay, what does the morning-after pill have to do with anything?" Sherry asks, and she's only half-joking. Little would surprise her now.

"I think she means Plan 'D,' as in that crazy shit over there," Gaddy laughs, pointing, and we all try not to make eye contact with Chuck's peen. But I see my opening, so I wave at the Honorary Amish again, and Sherry and Gaddy drop in some quarters and grab some basketballs. The balls from the arcade game are dented and slack from overuse, "about as firm as a sixty-year-old testicle," Chuck said once, but he's pushing sixty, judging by his balls, and suddenly the game isn't much fun anymore. But we take 'em for the team, don't we, girls? Still, when it comes to Gaddy? I had no idea! Above and beyond, that one.

Reflexively, the Honorary Amish holds up two crusty hands as if someone would actually pass a ball his way, and I see Gaddy crush her saggy basketball in frustration and brick it off the rim. Honorary Amish is earnestly explaining to a handful of even more perplexed spectators exactly what Chuck needs to do to win this seemingly impossible bar bet. And let me tell you, "mansplaining" ain't got nothing on this inspired speech, This clown was actually "actually-ing" a dong-drinking with his own.

". . . actually, I learned this very same trick in India, back in 1976," Honorary Amish says. "And what Chuck is getting wrong here is you can't just start drinking like that. Not *drinking* drinking, anyway. It takes stamina. It takes training. And I should know—'76 to '77, I'm riding elephants, wearing togas, snorting curry, all that claptrap. Basically, I'm an honorary yogi . . ."

"Drink! Drink! Drink" the crowd is yelling.

"How much is gone?!" Chuck yells, high up on his bar, eyes still closed. The barflies are mystified, but game for anything. Some trad goth loser leans in and takes a quick measurement of the remaining drink-to-rim ratio with his designer cigarette case.

"How much did I drain?!" Chucks wants to know.

"Nothing!" the kid reports.

"Damn it!" Chuck bears down, teeth clenched now.

". . . actually, to successfully accomplish this feat, you have to have non-ejaculatory sex for about a year," the Honorary Yogi goes on, holding our full-court press around the game frozen with one hand. "And that's when you step it up. You practice a disciplined urethra suction, first with water, then with milk, then, sure, maybe a Long Island Iced Tea. But that's final-stage, expert-level shit. Or, as they call it, DEFCON: Wang."

The lushes around us erupt in laughter. Sherry and Gaddy go back to shooting hoops.

"But you gotta understand! Most people believe these muscles can't be controlled. But a yogi like me can submerge his *choda* in a glass of milk and suck it on up. Honest to Vishnu. Ever heard of *bramacharya*? This is a code of honor between yogis, guys; I shouldn't even be telling you this, but . . ."

Even I start to tune him out, and I notice a college kid pinning a crispy new dollar and a thick, off-white business card to the wall, then he clasps his hands and holds them high over his head in triumph. Never mind the jobs, where do they get all the pins? Weirdos.

"Listen to me, please"—oh my God, yes, he's still talking—". . . actually, Dinabandhu Pramanick definitively proved to several onlookers he could completely drain a glass of milk with his urethra, then eject the fluid back out. Most people wrote it off as a stunt, or an overly complicated way to masturbate in public, but the science is very sound . . ."

He locks eyes with me, the only one still listening, and I notice Gaddy has less than no interest in his story, which is just a little too nonchalant. Then I notice her mouthing the words of the Honorary Yogi's script, and I realize that she was the one who actually convinced him to memorize this body slash mind slash penile-alignment horseshit. I know, what a twist, right?! Don't worry, it won't make sense later, either.

". . . you must, in essence, 'breathe' inside your partner during copulation, fully absorbing his or her soul, over and over again. And if you reach the highest levels, one day you could even drink with your finger . . ."

Some distant laughter and demands to "Shhh!" and we look to see Chuck taking a bow up on the bar, zipping his pants, then jumping down to his regular spot at the taps. Sherry stops shooting hoops and strides over with Gaddy in tow, who gives me a wink, and somehow all the basketballs are re-inflated now, hard as rocks. Did you know that thirty percent of us womenfolk can pop a basketball with a thumbnail if it's caught just right? Vitamin B and calcium, baby. Well, what you didn't know is that one percent of us can inflate them back to capacity with just a kiss.

"Anyone want a free Long Island Iced Tea?" Chuck offers. No one takes him up on this.

Now that the three of us are close enough to the actual bar for the insulting girl drinks to start flying again, I announce to any fake ID frosh who's paying attention that, "Yes, I would love a Razzamatazz, thank you!"

"I'll have one, too," Honorary Yogi decides. Chuck frets.

"What's in that?" he asks.

"What kind of bartender are you?" I ask, feigning confusion.

"Yeah!" Gaddy shouts. "I thought you were authentic, barkeep! Start trottin' like them cowboys!"

"Oh, now you're into sugary drank?" he smirks.

"I can't even look at you now." Gaddy laughs at Chuck, staring at his crotch instead.

"Hey, as a woman, I'm well aware of the embarrassing array of ingredients in the candy-colored 'Willy Wonka' libations these frat boys rain down on us," I smile. "But that doesn't mean they aren't delicious."

For the record, in case you ever want to try one, a Razzamatazz is pretty simple, really. Three Olives vodka (but any raspberry-flavored vodka will do), cranberry juice, and club soda on the rocks. That's it. If you add a splash of heavy cream, then you're dealing with a Pink Narcissus, named after the '70's gay softcore porno with the professional belly dancers, so maybe slow your roll on that stuff? Anyway, messing with either one will make your belly ache, so be ready for that, too. But I'm always ready, so I pound mine down before the ice even shrinks. And everybody claps.

Then the Honorary Yogi does something terribly uncouth but totally planned, and the crowd goes wild as he squats, unbuttons his fly, and dunks his repugnant pug-nosed glans into his glass. He begins to hum, and more people swarm his gag than Chuck's. So many, in fact, that they're fighting to get a closer look and almost knock him off his heels. At least until Gaddy "accidentally" tips his Razzamatazz over in the middle of the scrum of bodies and spills his bright crimson cocktail onto the floor.

"Foul!" someone yells. I agree. It would be a foul in any sport, not just Atomic Dunk.

The Honorary Yogi solemnly picks up the empty glass and waves people back over, clutching himself with his other hand.

"It's okay, it's okay. No, don't worry, men," he says. "The deed has been done . . ."

Jaws drop in awe as he proceeds to piss into the glass until it's filled back to the brim with red.

"What kind of place is this?" someone behind me whispers.

"Holy smokes!" I say, genuinely amazed, and now the applause is deafening. Chuck runs around from the safety of his bar to snatch the glass from Yogi's hand and study it, and the crowd draws back in case his loathsome fluid goes flying. Not sure how to investigate the authenticity of this one-upmanship, Chuck just gives it a sniff. His nose wrinkles.

"No way."

"Yes way . . ." is the answer, to even more cheers. ". . . the Yogi Way."

"Fuck it," Chuck shrugs. "Drinks are on the house! As long as pants stay on."

"Meat is not back on the menu, boys!" Gaddy warns everyone.

Then, all eyes on Gaddy, she takes the recycled Razzamatazz from Chuck's hand and brings it up to her lips like she's gonna slam it. Three people gag, I dry-heave, and another guy passes out against the ATM. But instead of downing it, she spikes the glass to the ground, obliterating the evidence.

So, tell me, did you get so caught up in Gaddy's ruse, watching these clowns leaking libations from their schlongs, to forget about our heist? Don't worry, even though it might seem like we did, too, you really gotta give us more credit than that! Come on, now.

Suckers, all y'all. From both ends.

CHAPTER IX

DISPLACEMENT

All the boys were lined up against the rail and hosing off the road with five strong, frothing, yellow streams of urine flickering in the haze of exhaust. Even Godzooky took a spot near the corner of the pool, hips thrust for extra distance, less a sign of solidarity than an understanding that they should keep their prison toilet as pristine as possible from now on.

"Never piss where you drink, or shit where you eat," his uncle Frank would always say. "Unless you're in jail, where you have no choice."

A nervous sixth stream had the expected trouble getting enough velocity to arc up and into the road. Angie watched Lund and the rest of them with interest, thinking about Holly's cock-and-bull story of the Long Island Iced Tea. She had a hard time shaking the centerpiece of her story, even when the boys were finished and sitting back down into the community stew. She checked the water level around her navel, unable to remember how high it had been when they started.

It reminded her of an interesting experiment she read about back in school, where a crow solved the puzzle of how to drink from a skinny glass of water by methodically dropping pebbles into the glass with its beak. She wasn't sure what this had to do with their current predicament, or Holly's repellent story for that matter, but any memory or tall tale continued to be a welcome diversion.

Looking down, she noticed the water was now down to her waist, and she checked the mineral stains on the side of the tub to see if it was really going down, wondering if, eventually, it could all be pissed over the side.

What is the life cycle of a beer in the body these days? Angie wondered. *And is its lifespan much longer than ours?*

But as she cupped a handful of water and saw the foaming beer suds mixed with perfumes and body lotions and hair products, she was even more convinced they were siphoning everything up through their young bodies, sucking away their environment through each orifice, visible or otherwise, only to be expressed over the rail again and again. She resigned herself to this truly endless birthday, when they would all be left standing in the middle of an empty pool after their lives had been literally pissed away.

On a long enough timeline, everything ends up on the side of a road.

With her thumbnail, Angie marked a line into the plastic lining of the pool. Now she'd know exactly how far it was dropping, or filling with beer and urine. But then she realized that, just like the ice cubes that melted in your drink without overflowing, or the skinny glass of water when the crow stopped drinking, the volume of the hot tub would revert, no matter how much of the contents were transformed into alcohol or bodily wastes, and she was never more eager to escape the party than right now.

She stepped out of the pool and put both hands on the rail.

Then a beer can bonked her on the head and, for now, she shook off the impulse to jump.

Blood was swirling.

It was unmistakable. Someone was bleeding, but no one knew who it was. The red whirls dissipated when anyone got too close, and half their bodies were hidden underwater anyway. Angie said they were like the survivors of the *Titanic*, bobbing in the waves while unknown creatures nipped them away to nothing.

"Except instead of everybody huddled on a door, we're all crowded onto a beaded curtain.

"Actually, we're more like survivors of the USS *Indianapolis*," Lund corrected her, and he pointed out the tiny spirals of red were not what they seemed.

"I wish I had my door with me right now," Reeves said. "Coulda saved everybody with that door."

"Fuck are you talking about?"

"See that? That's not the right color for blood," Lund said. "It's like we're in a movie."

Angie pushed him away, craning her neck back to count the trees flying by overhead.

"You know what drives me nuts?" Lund followed her, ignoring her indifference. "In *Jaws 2*, in a callback to the first movie, it opens with our first look at Chief Brody riding inside his car as he takes the ferry to the island, right? But back in *Jaws*, that was something they described him doing *before* the events of that film. Therefore, *Jaws 2* should have mixed things up and opened with him under the car. Or on top of it . . ."

"What do you mean, 'It's not real'?" Angie spun around to face him, checking the backs of her legs for cuts, happy to have something to do to keep her off the rail (and on the rails) for now, and to avoid thinking about the implications of Godzooky's murderous bilingual admission, and especially to distract her from dwelling on what they'd done to Janky, an incident that seemed like years ago.

If a thumbless kid falls off a fire truck in the forest and nobody's around . . . does it make a sound?

Angie was starting to doubt it.

"It's a special effect!"

"What?"

"All of this," Lund said. "It's a special effect."

"I don't have time for this." Angie said, giving her legs a last swipe for scabs, feeling something unusual on the backs of her thighs. But she wasn't ready to look at it yet, so she stared at Lund, arms crossed. "Okay, maybe I do," she admitted.

Questioning reality right now was balm for their situation.

"I know I am a ridiculous snob when it comes to CGI blood in movies," he said. "Like insufferable. Like if I had a glass of wine, and I sipped it, and then I sniffed the cork, and then I swished it around in my mouth, and then I realized it was just some CGI blood in there, I'd totally call the waiter back over and make him take it away."

"Does he ever shut up!" a voice came from behind him, then Lund bleated in surprise as he was suddenly de-pantsed, blue jeans yanked down and off before anyone could identify the culprit. His jeans twirled in the gray-and-black churn like they were riding an invisible bike.

"Did you shit yourself!" Ruck pointed at the jeans, his nose wrinkled.

"Leave me alone!" Lund said, moving away from everybody again.

"I think you need an oil change then, bro," Ruck said, kicking the jeans away from where they'd splashed down to reveal a strange rainbow of colors trailing from the back pockets.

"Good lord."

"What the hell . . ."

"Is that where the red was coming from?" Reeves laughed.

"What is happening to him?!" Beth screamed.

Angie backed up reflexively with the rest of them, Janky's murder forgotten as she thought about the solubility of drugs, and the wrong color of blood, and for a glorious moment, before a passing street light briefly illuminated what her fingers had found on her thighs, she was convinced nothing was real, not even the teeth marks of her friends on the backs of her legs.

"You drugged us," Amy said to Dan.

"No, not really," he said, shoulders up. "Okay, maybe. But how was I to know he wasn't going to take off his pants."

"Why would anyone's master plan involve guessing what Lund, of all people, was going to do with his pants?" Gaddy asked him.

"You should talk," Dan said.

"No wonder we're so fucked up!" Amy cried.

"Listen, I just didn't want to get caught with two hundred tabs of acid. I thought that was the cops rolling up on us at the restaurant. I figured I could retrieve it when the ride was over. To be honest, I forgot with all the—"

"With all the murder and all," Amy said, finishing his sentence instead of Angie's for a change. Everyone sat low in the water, trying to stay warm, and no one said anything for a mile or so.

"You know what they ought to use CGI for?" Ruck asked Lund to break a silence that was more noticeable than usual. "Puke. In movies, no one vomits in a believable way."

"He's right," Lund agreed, keeping a wide distance from everyone, as well as his pants, which he made no move to retrieve. His jeans seemed happier liberated from him, crazily animated in the waves like a car dealer's tube dancer.

"They always have their cheeks all puffed out as they run to the toilet with the fake barf chunks in their mouth, or they do this tiny little squirt of fake puke then spit, spit, spit. Nope. Not how that works. Just use some CGI geysers of gork and be done with it, am I right? Just go *blooooooooorp!* Or maybe just have them actually vomit like regular human people."

"Is there a point to all this?" Angie asked, hoping the question was limited to Ruck.

"What the fuck?!" Dan yelled, jumping up. Ruck was puking for real, an almost solid torrent of golden foam, and everybody screamed and sprang like they were spring-loaded. Angie stood on her tiptoes, eyes and mouth shut, holding her breath, expecting the drug-poisoned fluids to finally cover her head. But it never did.

This was the science of displacement, of course, and Angie knew nothing would ever change. Their water level was indifferent to everything they'd brought with them; beer, whisky, urine, blood, sweat, tears, drugs, even vomit. Forever unclean and unchanged.

To try and keep her gorge settled, Angie closed her eyes and instead of thinking about the LSD in her bloodstream, she thought about that new kid on her hayride, and how Lund was probably the newest hire at their school, definitive proof that her childhood infatuations had died. She laughed to herself at the idea of faking a fight on this ride with Lund. The days of kids turning on the first display of violence were over. Tonight, like everything else, human behavior was as flipped as their stomachs.

Everyone else turned from Ruck's display a split second too late, and the daisy chain of vomiting took hold. Both the boys and the girls ran to the rail, fighting unsuccessfully to stop the torrents of puke from racing like rapids over their teeth, displacing that mysterious rainbow from the back of Lund's jeans and onto the deserted streets. Godzooky fought the hardest to keep everything down, only snarfing double jets of milk from his nostrils. Angie nodded at him in appreciation.

When they finished passing along the technicolor yawn, they recoiled to respective corners and cliques, mostly looking deep inside themselves for comfort, knowing their bodies wouldn't be warm enough to offer themselves, or anyone else, much consolation for long. But they bounced back, like they always did. They understood that, no matter the outcome, this LSD-laced pool was their home now, and everyone's insides was family.

CHAPTER X

QUEEN EXCLUDER

New Kid Stories

When the second new kid came to town, it was dumb luck, really. It was such a relief to imagine that anyone I could lose would be replaced so quickly. And when I asked him about his relationship with his unusual phone, he swore he never got calls from the prisoners.

Impossible.

"Let me guess," I sighed. "You have the only magic number in the world."

"It's the telephone that's magic, actually, not the digits," he explained as I walked into his house for the first time. He placed it in the center of their mahogany coffee table, between two encyclopedia volumes marked *Q* and *R*. A gigantic, camouflage-streaked military telephone, just like the ones in war movies when they called in an air strike "on their current location," complete with the requisite two-foot-long, floppy antenna. It was the biggest phone I'd ever seen, and that's including the gigantic replica my sister made from tenderloins, rib eyes, and duct tape at last year's Meet the Meat Harvesters Festival (two tri-tips gave it something resembling that clamshell snap), but the crowd around her artwork was still pretty anti-phone from the prison's harassing calls, and they burned her sculpture at the "steaks." Sorry, I couldn't resist. I guess they couldn't, either.

But the New New Kid (or "NuNu," as I tried calling him, which didn't stick, either, though my sister helped all she could with snarky chants of "NahNah and NuNu sitting in a tree, f-u-c-k-i-n-g . . ."), he was new enough to retain a sense of humor about telephones. It still didn't stop him from quickly stepping between me and the enormous phone when I reached out to touch it, up on his tippy toes to keep it out of my reach, waving that green-marbled beast over his head like a trophy and telling me that you could wander five miles in any direction and still get "immaculate" reception. Then his father came into the room and wrestled it out of his hands. He introduced himself and apologized for his son at the same time, then he looked me over a moment, like he knew me, and used the giant phone to order us a pizza and some Dr. Peppers.

I stood close when he did this, and the voices on the other end of that giant phone were huge and scratchy, too, filling the room like those old speakers at the drive-in. I was afraid someone at the pizza place might overhear my new name, and I reminded myself to change it again as soon as possible, to keep up with our rotating home phone numbers. In our town, we were used to changing things around, and that included ourselves.

My name had been Nahla for a while, even though "Angela" was the name our mother wrote on my birth certificate. Ever since I was old enough to realize people were talking about me, I hated the name "Angie," even more than "Angela," and I worked on getting people to call me "Nah" as sort of a compromise. "Nah" as in "I'd rather not." But none of the new names ever seemed to linger on anybody's lips, and they constantly asked me, "Who are you today, honey?" so I just stuck to "Nahla" as a compromise. Our mother approved, explaining that this name was Arabic, even though our family was "German or Cherokee or something?" I never bothered to look this up because *everybody* always said they were Cherokee, and also our mother seemed way too proud of all this name changing. And since I was already one of those kids who changed their name more often than they changed their shirts, my identity rebellion was mostly dead on arrival.

While we waited for the pizza, the New New Kid told me that his family wasn't Cherokee or anything, but still pretty important, especially his father, a former government psychologist-turned-architect, famous in the '70s for some kind of experiment where he made college kids pretend they were prisoners. The New New Kid said we were "the only ones to truly appreciate this town's dilemma, the problem of the phone calls, and the synthesis of both prisoner and resident—"

"But it's got more to do with the design of the building," his famous dad interrupted. "A shape that will one day make the guardians of the prisons obsolete. Tell me, Nahla, what do you see when you look around this space?"

I wasn't sure what he was getting at, and I took a moment to walk the perimeter, checking out areas inside and around the house, letting him passively take the lead.

"Now that you mention it, there's sure a lot of dogs!" I said.

"Guard dogs, to be exact," he corrected. "Good eye."

I smiled at the compliment, but it didn't take a good eye to see that there were dog sculptures everywhere; an alabaster beagle guarding the mailbox, a crystal bull terrier guarding the terrace, a concrete Labrador at the base of a naked flagpole, and when they walked back to the front door, a wicker hound and a grass poodle guarding the porch that I'd somehow missed when I came in.

I guess calling them "straw dogs" before the sacrifice would be too on the nose.

"Do you collect toy dogs?" I asked, unable to resist minimizing the sculptures.

"It's not so much the dogs we collect," he said. "But the idea of them. The 'guard dog' has an interesting history. They are our guardians, yes. But more importantly, we are theirs."

The New New Kid finally rescued me from the dog tour, and out of earshot he told me that his grandmother actually collected all the canine art, right down to a Dogs Playing Poker black-light painting that, unsurprisingly, his father didn't bother claiming at the estate sale. They were actually from "here," he said. "Originally." At least his mom was. Not much of a new kid after all, as it turned out.

"Why was she into guard dogs?" I asked him, but he was already looking a little different to me.

"They go with our last name," he said, and I assumed their last name was "guard" or "dog," but I didn't care enough to ask. But I did very much appreciate how often both he and his father were saying "guard," however. I'd heard that repeating a word can make it lose its meaning, and I hoped this could help me forget about my brother and the job that killed him.

As I watched his father pay the delivery boy for the pizza and reassure him it wasn't a problem that he'd forgotten our Dr. Peppers, I noticed the New New Kid and his dad talked real similar, which made me want to stop listening to them completely. It was less what they would say, but how they said it. He had one of those fathers who just *sounded* very understanding of everything, especially anything that usually made other people angry, which was disconcerting to be around. No sighing like balloon knots. No punching phones off the walls. I guess I kinda hated it. His mother, if he had one, was nowhere to be found. But after sitting in on a quiet "normal" dinner with them, normally a ritual where the sudden urge to complain about everything and everyone who'd ever wronged me always boiled over (like that new kid who stepped on my glasses in second grade), all of my grievances got bulldozed by his father's gentle inquiries very fast. And by the time The New New Kid's calm and reasonable father finished asking about our day between evenhanded lectures, I was considering hugs and "high roads" as possible solutions to our town's devastating prank calls for the first time.

Then his dad blew my mind when he said I should relax and enjoy the pizza because no one would be calling their giant phone and interrupting *their* dinners. I could hardly believe it. I almost didn't remember a normal meal without threats from the prisoners. So when I dove in to help devour that sizzling carpet of extra cheese and pepperoni with them that night, I soaked up all the noble, high-minded topics swirling around the table as long as I was able. The atmosphere felt so receptive, so different from what I'd been growing up around lately, that I ultimately came back around to having an irrepressible urge to disrupt it.

First, I told them about my brother's tragic fate as a prison guard, relishing in their shock. They knew about the death of the bees, so, for no reason at all, I made up some story about being allergic to their stings, punctuating this by bending my fork sideways against my plate and producing an electric, teeth-grinding screech that was painful enough to freeze all conversation. But it didn't faze them.

Instead, his father wrote down a home remedy for bee venom, which I waved off, defiant.

"The bees are long gone," I reminded them. "I just felt like sharing."

"We know," his father said gently. "But everything comes back around." He smiled, and I couldn't stop my boot from reflexively kicking his shin under the table.

If he felt it, he gave no indication, but I felt myself flinch for both of us, right before my tears.

* * *

Wardens were originally convinced the new infestation of cellphone smuggling was going to be the catalyst for plotting escapes or organizing gangs behind bars nationwide. This had already happened in Brazil with a massively coordinated attack in 50 prisons that had left at least 700 people dead. But even if there was initially some hint of illegal networking, it was eventually revealed that our prisoners simply wanted to make a phone call for the same reason any red-blooded American kid did. To harass somebody.

After the first calls were reported in our town, prison staff seized a total of three phones from inmates, boasting about this in the news, claiming it proved just how efficient their contraband searches had become. But a shellshocked guard from one of the Brazilian prisons where the riots occurred scoffed in an interview, "If they only found three phones, they ain't looking very hard!" This sound bite was very popular on the national news, replayed every news cycle to shake up state corruption (there was even an auto-tuned remix), or trying to combat the complacency throughout prisons and local law enforcement. "Ain't Looking Very Hard!" laughed the headlines.

The next month, 200 cellphones were found. Then 500. Then over 3,000. Soon after that, the number of phones plateaued. But it was too late. It was estimated that in our town's new prison, there was at least one phone for every inmate.

And prisoners got much better at hiding them. No more phones were found by guards, but the calls were increasing exponentially. Now it was the national epidemic they'd predicted. Prisons everywhere—federal, private, even county jails—all reported inmates casually dialing up lawyers, local newspapers, sometimes their grandmothers, with complaints ranging from repressed civil rights to a lack of extra-crunchy peanut butter. At least one prisoner arranged the murder of a state witness in an upcoming trial. Some of them traded shares on the stock market. One Supreme Court justice had his dinners repeatedly interrupted with grievances about the poor cellular reception on Death Row and reportedly removed the battery from his phone.

"They're better than cash," my brother whispered once. "Prisoners are willing to pay nine hundred dollars for a phone. They sneak 'em in, sometimes in their . . ." he trailed off. "Never mind."

"In their what?" I needed to know.

"Do you know what 'rectal' means?"

"Of course. Wait a minute. You can't talk on a phone with your butt!"

"Shut up, stupid. But listen to me here," he said. "Nine hundred bucks? That's a lot of money, you know? Especially with the bees gone and all. So we tried jamming the signals," my brother went on. He whispered so much now that I forgot what his normal voice sounded like. And he told me that this new phone-suppressing technology was something they first experimented with in Brazil, where there were fewer legal hurdles. "The FCC claimed it was some sort of violation, but people were ready to try *anything* at this point."

Few knew this, but our town was the OG of the 5G conspiracies. I vaguely remembered the controversy surrounding the three ominous towers at the edge of the town limits, which, besides scrambling airport's radar in neighboring towns, had seriously injured more than 300 holiday travelers, even causing one kid to lose a thumb when the exit door slammed on his hand during a runway traffic jam evacuation. The towers also interfered with the guards' own communication and effectively destroyed almost all cellular reception outside the prison walls.

"Oops!" was that day's headline, next to a picture of our own shrugging warden.

That was about the time anyone obstinate enough to do so, like our mother, decided to dig their old rotary phones out of dusty attics or chalky junk drawers and mount them back where screw holes had been puttied and plastered over decades prior. Cellphones for civilians became a waste of money as most phones died within an hour of activation from the tower radiation anyway. Some residents tried to look at the bright side, citing studies where cellphones were causing brain tumors, or even linked to those lucky anencephalic babies being born brainless and therefore without anything in their skull where such a tumor could hang its hat. But the choices for the rest of the town were now clear. It was only soup-can telephones, *Doctor Who*–looking phone booths, or a big black phone like your grandma had, with its endlessly tangled cord wrapped around your neck.

Or a pea-green, person-sized Army phone that you could snuggle up to like your mother, something I was convinced was happening at the New New Kid's house.

"All we can do now is monitor illegal phone usage in the prison on this big-ass, blinking map. We just stare at it, impotent," my brother sighed, exasperated. Like father, like son with the sighs, I realized. But my brother never had time to master them, making this one a meager "Sigh Number Six," aka "Bubbling Emergency Tracheotomy."

"Most of us guards don't even bother watching actual prisoners anymore. We just take turns watching this huge TV screen where active phone calls pop up on the screen like bug bites. The little red dots quadruple at night, by the way."

"Why?"

"That's when rates are down."

"Wow. Right about when everyone sits down for dinner," I marveled, loving all these secrets and whispers in the dark. If I had to be honest, I hoped it would never end.

"Well, maybe that part was a coincidence. No one knows anymore."

"One of my teachers said this all started because the payphones broke at the prison and no one could call crying to their mothers that they wanted to go home."

"Bullshit. I already told you why! It was me," my brother said. "And I'd only loaned that inmate my phone because he seemed like a nice guy who needed to talk to someone. If I'd have known he was gonna *yell* at her, then yell at everyone else in the entire world, I never would have done it, I swear."

"Do you wish you never took the job?"

"What? Are you nuts, sister?" he laughed. "Keep working with invisible honey, making invisible money?"

Like us, most of the surrounding counties considered honey their lifeblood. At least one person in every family worked hard bottling it, harvesting it, spreading it on crackers, or drizzling it in their tea. But our bees vanished about a year ago, right before the prison sprang up from the ashes of our hives. No one could prove these things were related (not for lack of trying), as people were talking about the worldwide decline of honeybees long before colony collapse hit our little burg. I was more immature back then, and still stuck with the name "Angie" some days, but I was old enough to remember very clearly the last brick of honeycomb my brother and I savored together while he was still alive.

It was right when the temperature was getting cool, and the bees would be slowing down with the molecules. I remembered this moment like it was the first time, the honey dripping down our chins, the sticky webs tangling in the strings of our hooded sweatshirts, that yellow nectar colored more like mustard than gold from the heavy concentration of pollen, *never* the dead amber of refined grocery-store varieties that eventually ended up glazing our gloomy, post-colony-collapse carrots. Because of the glut of pollen in the area, my dad claimed our honey was packed with more power than a hundred B12 shots, more strength than fifty cans of Popeye's spinach, but we still would have indulged, even without such endorsements.

My brother and I cracked the geometrically perfect chambers in our fists, and we let the thick yolk run down our throats. Instantly intoxicated, a cassonade headache threatening in the backs of our eyes from all that sweetness, we would count to five until the last remaining taste buds were smothered. Then we would finally swallow a flavor so intense it was notorious for inducing tourists to retch just from the sugar overload. Amateurs.

"Tonguing the cell."

That's what my brother called it. And when he first said this, as he crushed the golden, brittle waffle in his fist, I felt like I was doing something bad, something dirty. I watched him closely that day, understanding how he really was just an extended version of my dad, and how I was a bigger version of them both, and I drank in our shared lifeblood until I dropped.

Soon after we shared those cells, before the bees disappeared for good, the honey began to turn red.

My father said it was nothing to be freaked out about, maybe just a new patch of invasive flowers in the area. But all our mother ever picked was the occasional wild white narcissus to decorate our dinner table (once or twice the raggedy pink variation), so he didn't sound very sure, and we went ahead and sounded the alarm anyway. No one could pinpoint where this red-tinged pollen was being harvested, or by whose worker bees, even after a search party of volunteers held hands and crisscrossed the fields looking for any hint of stray crimson. And the new honey tasted a bit like blood, but sweeter, just as I hoped it would. I had tasted my own blood when I hit puberty two years earlier, my body naked and folded up, arms clutching my knees, hidden next to a meticulously clean bathtub, tucked between an even cleaner commode. I saved some of that blood, too, but my brother refused to taste either.

This was the final autumn harvest, when my father noticed the red honey in our backyard hive. "It's the brood comb," he explained solemnly. "But it isn't dark enough."

"Is that bad?" I asked him.

"Yes, it's bad. It's supposed to turn black."

"Why?"

"It's from the bees' feet. 'Travel Stain,' is what the old-timers used to call it. But it isn't black enough this year."

"What does that mean?"

"It means there aren't enough bees wiping their little shoes at the door!" he yelled, trying to fake a laugh to cover his fear, but I was already obsessed with this new information. I thought about it often, especially when I was on long walks, trying to notice if the roads under my feet were being stained darker and darker and darker . . .

One time, I dreamed of a parade of winter coats coming down the street in the middle of summer, fuzzy black-and-yellow hoods like horse "blinkers" that forced everyone to focus on our toes. A whole town looking down in shame, trying to forget their phones. The opposite of a hopelessly cellular-obsessed populace just one short season before.

However, our friends and neighbors still refused to blame an invasive signal of those phones for our troubles, not even after the famous press conference (according to my dad, "the third most ridiculous ever broadcast"), where one scientist started crying like a baby. This scientist shared a name with another, more famous scientist, and I wondered why he never changed it, when changing names was the easiest thing in the world to do. My father refused to say his name out loud, instead becoming the first person I'd ever heard my father label a "chickenshit."

"We only have three years left," declared Larry Irwin Einstein, PhD. "The once mysterious Colony Collapse Disorder can now be safely attributed to cellular signals and the resulting navigational confusion of the hive." Dr. Einstein, the default spokesman for our local Royal Beekeepers Guild, spoke in front of a veritable army of scientists, who extended as far as the eye could see. But he seemed to be the only one who was so choked up, but with our shaky reception, I couldn't be sure. "In some states, up to ninety percent of the population has been affected," he sniffled. At the time, I had no idea which population they were referring to, ours or the bees, but it made no real difference.

Most veteran harvesters, with the exception of my father, simply refused to believe any of this dire news. Instead, they attributed the mysterious decline to the controversial use of "queen excluders," a precisely measured grate used to isolate the queens, allowing only worker bees to move freely in and out of the tiny bars. Originally designed as protection from invading insects, the vets initially suspected this filter made the queens irrational, unreliable, even self-destructive. Rumors of hives appearing with stranger and stranger shapes began to sweep the community; bewildering, haphazard sandcastle-like structures dripping honey from their open towers instead of cells, oblong hamster habit trails that went nowhere, dying larvae piling up with their nurses in this dead-end maze, dazed Minotaurs with nothing to defend. The mathematically pleasing hexagons of the old hives were now a thing of the past.

I secretly loved this theory and searched in vain for these purported hives shaped like toddlers' first Lego sculptures. I'd heard there was one down the street that was shaped like a maimed starfish, but I never found it. I thought it was hilarious that the geezers could be so indignant about excluders messing with a queen's natural life cycle when they routinely yanked the heads off the queens every five years to stimulate colony production. Striving for an immortal hive, they would unceremoniously replace them with young queens, unmoved by the drawings of tiny heads on tiny pikes, wearing tiny crowns, that some children were immortalizing in crayon at preschool.

But the phone calls from the prisoners quickly made the town forget about the odd behavior of the bees, and their subsequent vanishing act.

I was only able to answer about a half dozen threatening phone calls in the first weeks of the harassment, before my parents became more cautious. But I was still able to develop some rituals. I would transcribe every ugly, stammering threat of the prisoners, hoping one day to get a call worse than the one that interrupted my little cousin's third birthday party. Everyone still talked about it. My uncle Jim had made the mistake of reflexively putting this call on the speaker phone with tons of us kids in earshot:

"I'll fuckin' cut your head off and fuck it, cuntfuck."

I was the only one not crying into the yellow-and-black-striped bumblebee cake after the prisoner's announcement. Jim broke his phone in half right there, and the children cried even harder. Trying to salvage my cousin's special day, I explained to everyone that I was already used to such threats by now, so the rest of them should be, too. I told everyone they should just pretend the voices were renegade "time and temperature" recordings, that mostly forgotten phone number the older beekeepers like my father would call for updates, since the climate was so important to our hives. I still dialed the number on occasion, pretending the soothing voice on the other end was my brother's.

"It's the *tone*, not the *words*," I said to the party, but no one believed me. "'Tonight, partly threatening with the promise of rape and murder!'" I laughed at them, and then I blew out birthday candles that weren't mine, which is when you make the worst wishes, the ones that always come true.

CHAPTER XI

PEDAL PUBS
AND PANOPTICONS

After the mass gastral evacuation, they must have slept without realizing it, leaning against friends and enemies alike on the rim of the pool, soothed into their poisoned slumber from several miles with no turns. But when the fire truck crushed some night-prowling road critter under the rear "dualies," they all rose in shock, grabbing for each other to maintain balance.

"I think that was a possum," Amy said after a moment.

"More like five possums in a raincoat," Ruck yawned.

"Did anyone hear a phone ringing?" Angie asked, catching Ruck's yawn as she peeled off Jill, reluctantly exposing their clammy, sticky skin to the wind again.

"No, did you?" Beth asked from behind her, hope in her voice.

"There are no phones here," Jill said. Then, "Wait, we're missing somebody."

"Somewhere out in the world, we're all missing 'somebodies,'" Beth said.

"Shut the fuck up, Beth," Dan said, weirdly passionless.

"Hey, what happened to the lights?" Angie looked around, panicked back into full awareness. At some point while they were out, all remaining strobes, sirens, and even the feeble Christmas lights had been extinguished. The illumination had been inconsistent, which she initially assumed was poor wiring, but with their total removal, it seemed like another bad sign.

"Somebody is definitely missing," Jill said again.

"I counted twice," Beth said, pointing to the circle of stretching bodies as they woke. "The mayfly is gone."

"You mean the 'Gadfly'?" Angie asked?

"Yes, Gaddy is gone. Holly, too. Maybe Sherry . . ."

"What?"

"Who's missing?"

"Hold on, everybody sit still . . ."

There was another head count, eyes working to adjust and scan the ink-black water, with no more party lights to guide them. By the time they began their approach toward a possible streetlight glow in the distance, they were able to discern for certain that Holly, Gaddy, and Sherry were now missing.

"How?" asked Beth. "Holly was just here, telling me more of her money story."

"What are you talking about?" Angie asked her.

"She was curled up with me all night." Beth looked sheepish. "For body heat."

"What do you mean 'all night'?" There was accusation layered on the fear in Angie's voice. "It's still night, isn't it?"

"I don't know what your problem is, Angie, but she was right here with me. She told me the rest of the story about their big heist. It was amazing, actually. Dollar bills on the walls, dollar bills floating in the water like soup crackers. She said maybe we could follow them home."

"Crackers is right," Jill said. "I think this bitch was dreaming."

But then they saw the money all around them. Angie waved her hand through the soggy dollars floating on the surface, and Jill held one bill up like a dead rat. Ruck snatched it away, and Reeves grabbed it from him. Godzooky held one dollar up, looking for light. Lund shrunk from them as if they were alive.

"What the fuck is going on now?"

"We're missing people," Angie said, voice shaking even more as the truck grinded more gears. "That's what's going on!"

"Okay, so what, though?" Beth said, crossing her arms.

There was something new in Beth's voice Angie didn't like. Or maybe it was just that Angie was ashamed that her first thoughts weren't about survival, but instead a twinge of disappointment about hooking

Jill up with Beth, and despite not knowing Gaddy very well, she didn't miss her at all.

"Relax, I'm here, peeps!" Gaddy said, bursting up out of the water dead center in the group. Beth screamed her Sea World entrance, and Angie was surprised there wasn't a fish wriggling in her teeth.

"Do you live underwater now?" Reeves asked her. Apparently serious, he reached out to touch her face in awe.

"Do *not* believe a word Holly says about the robbery, by the way," Gaddy said, ducking Reeves's hands and ignoring his question.

"So who's dead, then?" Lund asked, splashing his face to wake up.

"Maybe nobody," Dan shrugged. "We were all sleeping, right? Maybe they just jumped off at a stop."

"There *are* no stops," Jill said matter-of-factly. "There *were* no stops."

"Janky didn't jump," Angie said, glancing around for any hint of shame.

"Fuck him," Dan finally said after a moment. "Didn't you hear that weird shit about his spider fingers or whatever?"

"Oh, is that why he had to die?" Angie asked him.

"I think Holly was a cop," Beth said, breaking Angie's train of thought.

"What?" Angie asked, as everyone turned to Beth.

"That story? About the money? She talked like a cop."

"She talked a little like a movie cop," Lund agreed.

"But why would you say that?" Jill asked.

"I don't know. Something about her I never trusted."

"I think you got her confused with me," Gaddy said. "*I* was the cop, ya dummies. And I wasn't a cop, I was in the Secret Service. Sorta."

"Some secret."

"Where are your two friends?" Amy asked Gaddy, but Gaddy had no answer. She seemed more troubled than anyone about their disappearance.

"Weren't *you* a cop?" Dan asked Beth.

"What? No."

"You totally seem like a cop."

"Yeah, I think I saw her wearing a badge or a uniform once."

"Me too!"

"When was that? Maybe a year ago?"

"Halloween?"

"Everyone has dressed as a sexy cop once in their life."

"A cop wearing a cop costume on Halloween is an actual nightmare."

"They are not cops!" Angie shouted to stop the interrogation. "All three of them were shooting up at the restaurant earlier tonight."

"We don't shoot up," Gaddy said.

"Last night?" Jill was rubbing her head. "Feels like last year."

"See? That's what I was saying!" Gaddy said. "Why is it always so weird for women to go to the bathroom together? Men are the only ones who make it weird."

"Hold on, I want to know something," Angie said, turning to Gaddy. "Back at the restaurant, did you or did you not flush a bunch of drugs down the toilet?"

"Wellllll, okay, we tried to . . ." Gaddy started to say, playing coy.

"What do you mean 'we tried to'?"

"Dan stuffed them down Lund's pants instead."

"Good God."

"We know this."

"How many drugs went down Lund's pants?"

"All of them," Gaddy laughed.

"Dafuq."

"But five seconds ago it was unfair for me to assume you were fucking addicts?"

"Fucking addicts or *fucking* addicts?"

"She's got a point." Amy hooked a thumb at Gaddy.

"I give up." Angie threw up her hands and turned to hang over the rail and look back out into the endless night. The glow on the horizon was a little closer.

"I think we are missing the forest for the fleas here," Ruck said. "Let's back up and look at the facts. At some point during the night, Holly and Sherry got off this truck. Did we slow down? Did we stop? Jill says no. And we're sure they're really gone, right?"

Reeves popped up out of the water, gasping.

"Every inch of this pond is present and accounted for, sir!" he said, spitting a fountain of water at Jill and doing a mock salute at Angie. "No corpses on the bottom, Cap'n!"

"Are we sure about that?" Amy asked him as he dog-paddled around.

"Listen to me. So last night . . ." Beth was saying.

"It's the same night!" Angie yelled.

". . . earlier *tonight*, some of us were talking," Beth continued. "And we think you might be able to shed some more light on our situation."

"Who?" Angie said, looking around. "Who are you talking to? Me?"

The moon was behind the clouds, and the pool was at its darkest.

"What was the name of your college dissertation?" Beth asked her. "The one about the prisons?"

Angie looked at Beth, then back at Ruck, then over at Dan, then looked around for Godzooky for help. But he must have been lying lower than usual. Impossibly, even lower than Reeves, their submariner, who was missing again.

"What is going on here?" Angie asked them all.

"Ooh! I know this one," Dan said, holding up a finger. "She read her dissertation out loud to me once. It's called *The Man-Opticon*, because of course it is."

This sudden scrutiny felt dangerous, but Angie couldn't help but smile a little. She was in a precarious situation, but, like most grad students, she welcomed any chance to talk about her thesis.

"Well, since you brought it up," Angie said, clearing her throat. "The full title is actually *Walls, of (Dis)course and the Panopti-Con . . .*

"Bit of a mouthful, Angie!"

". . . *The Problems of Self-Discipline in the 19th-Century Extracurriculum.*"

"Excuse you?" Ruck laughed.

"Is she still going?" Dan asked.

"Ignore them," Jill said. "I want to hear all about it, Angie. Continue."

"No. I want to know. Is this your master plan, Angie?" Dan asked her.

"Well, I was always more of a planner than a partier," she laughed.

"Ain't that the truth!" Jill said, gesturing wildly at . . . everything.

"Good one!" Angie clapped. "Now let me ask all of you, has anybody here heard of the Stanford Prison Experiment?"

"Duh," Gaddy said. "Where do you think we're from?"

"Well, in my thesis, I argue that the urge for voluntary self-confinement by students is inevitable, but not without its benefits. You see, even outside normal institutional barriers, someone who is not incarcerated will re-create their own walls, of course, the walls of—"

"Discourse!" Dan shouted. Ruck high-fived him.

"Oh my God, shut up," Beth said.

Angie chewed her lip at her.

"I didn't mean you, Angie," Beth said. "So wait, are you saying that your research tried to prove that people *want* to be trapped or imprisoned?"

"That's oversimplifying things a bit, but sure?" Angie suddenly had an idea where this was going.

"Nah, fuck all that," Ruck said. "There are only three possibilities here. One, we're in Hell. All these stories about money growing on trees and making cars out of skulls or whatever? That's shit you'd only hear in Hell . . ."

"I didn't make a car out of skulls." Godzooky said, stepping up from a corner and elbowing in between Ruck and Dan. Angie closed her eyes. Ruck had baited Godzooky so easily, she was surprised he wasn't holding a fishing rod.

"Well, well, well, look who's back!" Dan said, eyes and nose pinched, like he smelled a rat.

". . . and two," Ruck was still saying. "Remember when I said we did something wrong, and how we're being punished?"

"Yes," Angie said. "Every time you talk, we are absolutely being punished."

"I think the punishment might be Angie's experiment."

"I think he's making sense," someone behind Angie said. They were all way too close.

"What do you mean, *my* experiment?" Angie made sure Jill and Amy were nearby, too.

"Well, who else would be doing the experimenting?" Ruck asked.

"Glad you asked," Lund said, one finger in the air. "I've been thinking about that, and I think it has something to do with doubling up."

"What?" Dan asked, staring down at the top of Angie's head.

"Think about how many pairs there are here. We got Dan and Reeves, Angie and Amy, Ruck and Janky—"

"And a pair of your nasty pants," Dan laughed.

"Experiments on twins have a long, less-than-distinguished history," Lund said.

"But there were three of those chicks . . ." Dan was counting heads again.

"Yeah, and look what happened to them!" Lund said.

"You know, Angie *has* been real keen about pairing me up with Jill," Beth said, smiling for the first time that night. It was a bad look. Too many teeth. Angie wondered if it matched the bites on her legs.

"Did you just say 'keen'?" Dan snorted.

"Well, he said 'chicks,'" Angie shrugged.

"Ruck might have a point," Jill said, and the pool was deathly quiet for a minute.

"Well, slow down," Ruck said, laughing. "Because I haven't gotten to my final, competing theory."

"Competing with yourself?" Angie said.

"Exactly," he said. "And my third theory is this. I think this pool is affecting us."

"No shit, Spurlock."

"I mean, it's affecting us in other ways. Like our memories."

"What do you mean?"

"What I mean is, either everybody's lying with these wild stories, or we just happen to be the craziest motherfuckers to ever sign up for a party bus together, *or* this broth we've been marinating in has infiltrated not just our bloodstream, but our stream of consciousness as well."

"That probably made more sense before you said it out loud," Dan said, but Angie wasn't so sure. How insane was it to think that this hot tub, which was visibly tainted with a toxic combo of illicit substances and bodily fluids, could be literally messing with their minds? The triplets' story, Godzooky's confession, her own childhood memories of the prison? Could prolonged exposure to the pool manifest money on the water, lead to murder? Or, more likely, lead to the memory of murder? Suddenly, Angie wasn't so sure. But she was convinced of this:

Trapped on the back of a fire truck, unable to present any evidence of truth or fiction outside of a missing thumb or floating money, all that remained was the story itself. Words. Apocrypha further corrupted by an impossible situation and the oddest amalgam of unnatural toxins and environmental tortures, finally cut off from any grounding stimulus of the real world by an endlessly rolling sensory deviation chamber . . .

As the only remaining representation of their lives, even a fictional narrative would, by default, become their reality.

More silence click-clacked by as the truck rolled over some highway reflectors, punctuated by the grind of the transmission locating another gear for the steeper gradient. Then it took a turn hard, and for a moment seemed on the verge of tipping. But they were used to the jostling now. They were used to a lot of things, like a party that never slowed below 55 miles per hour, cold, filthy water up to rimming their bellies, and the increasingly distant memory of their lives before they climbed aboard. Beth broke the silence, pointing at Angie.

"It was her," she said.

"It was me, what?" Angie asked, but there was no answer.

Here it comes, she thought. *And nowhere to run.*

"What did you do?" Beth wanted to know, but they both knew it was a meaningless question, and not even a question for her, but red meat to satiate any future suspicions of the group. Beth lunged at Angie, who fell backward as more slippery bodies surged forward. Arms had her under the water long enough to hear her heartbeat in her ears, but when she came up, coughing, the lights of a new town were blazing on the skyline as they suddenly barreled into a populated area.

"Civilization!" someone cried, and the hands around her relaxed to help her back up.

They were rolling through a main street—townsfolk lined up around the corners to get into the bustling bars, joyously, gloriously partying in the streets, and upbeat music blasting from parked cars along the curbs. It was like they'd never left, and most everybody in the pool seemed to flip a switch, grinning at such a beautiful sight after hours (days?) of blackness.

They'd backed off Angie, and some of the bodies who'd swarmed her had drifted away and up to the rail. Consumed by a strange, new compulsion—or maybe it was the admiring gaze of the roadside spectators—they began to act as if they were having fun. Brains foggy with confusion, their hips took over, unconsciously swinging with the music from the bars. Even Angie felt her foot uncontrollably tapping the bottom of the pool. This urge to dance warmed her body back up as she questioned her sanity. But there was some rationale for this inexplicable response to their captivity. If revelries were still in full swing, then maybe they hadn't been trapped on the fire truck as long as they'd feared. Blame it on booze, or the oil stain of acid clinging to their skin. But even their missing friends, even their missing enemies, even what happened to Janky, it was all temporarily forgotten. And for a brief moment, it was if they no longer needed to be rescued.

It was just a party.

But just as quickly as the truck passed through that town square, spotlighting their desperate faces with a glimpse of normalcy, the engine under them sped up to a gallop again, and they roared past the bars at dangerous speeds, the blast of the fire truck swallowing any potential pleas for help before they could even consider escaping their mouths.

The truck bounced over a pothole, spilling some of them to backsplash into the pool, but Beth and Lund hung tight onto the rail. With them, the spell of the distant revelers had never really taken hold, and they both found the strength to scream.

"Hey!"

"Help!"

"Yeah, you!"

"Look up here!"

A couple drunks on the street turned. One yelled back, "Show us your tits!"

Instinctively, Lund reached down to stretch out his double-X, one-of-a-kind collector's item Outpost 31 T-shirt so that it covered his soggy, white Fruit of the Loom briefs like a dress. But Angie and Jill got on their tiptoes, both leaning over the rail together. They waved at pedestrians dashing by the fire truck, narrowly missing the front fender, and for a split second, Angie thought she saw her dead brother standing at a crosswalk on a cellphone, swinging a caged canary in his other hand. Then she blinked and the canary was replaced by a stray cat, mewling so loud, it pierced the din. Then it was a tiny skeleton. She shook it all away.

"What is it?" Jill asked her, turning her by her shoulders.

"I think I saw my future husband," Angie lied, and Jill smirked and shook her head.

A crowd of stumble-drunk young men pointed up at Angie and Jill from under a streetlamp rattling with the force of their passage. "Kiss each other!" they hollered.

"Did they say 'Kill each other'?" Lund asked, almost in tears.

Even after a decade in a college town, Angie was still amazed by the toxic intoxicated and their ceaseless demands for barroom pseudolesbianism. But, to be fair, they *were* in their underwear.

Beth pushed between them and leaned out over the rail, reaching for anything or anybody, and someone on the street shouted.

"Smile, bitch!"

Beth glared a moment, then turned away and slid down the inside of the pool until the stained water was licking her chin. She closed her eyes and seemed to locate a distant memory to satiate her anger, and Angie had no doubt that story would be perfectly nuts and just what she needed. But over her shoulder and out in the streets, arms and beers were still held high, though the voices were fading fast. Mobs stomped their feet like show ponies, snorting and chanting until their cries meshed with the chorus of grinding gears:

"Kiss her! Kiss her! Kiss her!"

As the lights of the town's crossroads winked out one by one, Dan and Ruck resumed colluding in their corner, hatching new plans of escape or dominance, while a drunken, bleary-eyed Reeves resurfaced silently in another. Reeves and Godzooky were invisible again, while most of the girls nestled in the remaining two corners, and Gaddy crawled ear-to-ear, whispering in every receptive hole she could find.

There was some sobbing, as many of them regretted not trying to jump or shout at that lively intersection, which possibly represented their last chance of escape, but Angie didn't blame them for being unable to resist their performance on the rails. She knew it was next to impossible not to act as a party was expected to, particularly when it knew it was being watched. That was the Panopticon. That was *science*.

The shit is smack-dab in my . . . wheelhouse, she thought, and she could have sworn she heard a foghorn blat from the driver's cab.

Someone spun a bottle, and Gaddy cleared her throat to finally tell her side of their story. But she parsed it out, one person at a time, and anyone who was actually listening to her betrayed no interest. Angie tried very hard to listen to Gaddy when she came around to her ear, but she was having trouble focusing on the shifting dimensions of the pool, suddenly convinced she could feel it swelling or shrinking at will, whether to expand and accommodate anyone who needed to hide or scheme in its shadows, or to closing in like an iris, steel rails eating their tails, forcing them all toward the center of the party when it was their turn to tell a story.

Or their turn to be punished.

In the last twinkle of distant streetlights, the fire truck careened past a Pedal Pub, one of those clanging, Rube Goldberg–looking abominations that did double duty as a mobile bar and tipsy transportation. It was more like a railroad handcart, really, and all of this, at first glance, made it sort of a miniature kindred spirit to their pool party. Two rows of sorority girls lined both sides of the contraption, pedaling and laughing for all they were worth. But to Angie, they looked oddly exhausted, distressed. Maybe she was projecting, but she was convinced they were being held captive, too, all of them lost in forgotten parties cruising the barren, blackening edges of town, spinning bottles like increasingly desperate tales, coerced by forces unseen to work smooth, tanned legs well past exhaustion and they drank for their lives, with no end in sight.

CHAPTER XII

GLASS HALF FUCKED

Gaddy's Sherry Story

They had a hard time believing what they'd just seen, but it was alright, because they found out later that they hadn't really seen anything at all. What's the old saying? Believe half of what you hear, half of what you see, and nothing that they pee? Okay, here's what really happened:

Remember a couple days earlier? When I whispered something mysterious in the ear of the Amish turned Yogi turned penis-guzzlin' master illusionist? See, whispering was normally Holly's job, but after some good-natured threats I confessed to her, and only her (she's not here to dispute this, of course), that what I'd given the Honorary Yogi was some very simple instructions to eat nothing but beets, berries, and rhubarb until the next time we saw him. Sure, it seems unlikely that I could relay all this information and convince someone to do my bidding in, what, three to six minutes? But the other explanation, that I exploited the Yogi's off-the-cuff story so effortlessly, isn't that equally insane? Sherry didn't believe it, but she never had the same vision as me. Or Holly. And neither of them had my level of ambition.

But he did it, drinking down my homegrown, farmer's market prescription, which, in turn, stained his urine that scary red, because maybe I promised him it was some freaky sex pregame thing? Like rhubarb makes semen taste sweet or something? Which is something one in three men will fall over themselves to obey if a woman asks them to. One in one if it's Holly. Coin flip if it's me.

Later, I tell Holly not to tell Sherry any of this (and they'd both totally back me up if they were still around), calling it a "need to know" basis, even though Sherry had been planning on just punching this guy repeatedly in the kidneys so he'd piss blood on cue, maybe dare him to take as many of her "Houdini slugs" to the gut as he can. This must have been Plan P, I'm guessing, so the Yogi, and the spectators, were pretty lucky we didn't go that route and sic Sherry on his bladder.

At least I don't think we did? I'd totally ask them if I could!

Here's the thing, though; when I think about the Honorary Yogi and the kids that staged the fight to smash the mirror, now I understand something I didn't quite grasp in that moment, something that makes me glad I always work so hard and maybe don't ask as many questions as Sherry, or keep as many secrets as Holly . . .

See, when someone tells you they'll make do with three people if they have to? They're actually making do with six. And someone who will make do with six, well, they'll probably make due with anyone.

"So last quarter I'm writing this story for my creative writing class about some kids stealing something, and it gets really complicated, and for three days I'm stuck on the last third and can't figure out how to get them to complete their robbery in a believable way. And on the day it was due, I finally just say 'fuck it' and had all the characters get arrested."

As I pull down another handful of dollar bills, I'm convinced Sherry is telling me all this to try and scare me. But I'm going too fast to worry about it now. I've settled into this fast, fluid motion, getting my lacquered nail under a business card and a stick pin, then *zoink!* up it comes, just like a magician swiping the tablecloth and leaving the dinner, just quick as fuck. Okay, so most of the dollars end up with a tiny rip down the middle, but I'm careful not to tear them any more than that. And who cares? There isn't an establishment in the world that wouldn't accept a one-dollar bill with a little mileage on it. So after I take one down, behind me, Sherry is putting one up, pinning new dollar bills under the business cards where I've torn them off. It's like shearing sheep, if sheep were money. And in some cultures, they totally are.

Anyway! We're swapping dollars for dollars, and I feel some skepticism in the air, but this will all make sense at the end. That's what I told them, too.

"Great story, Sherry," I say, still mowing down the dollars with my manicure. "So what you're saying is, we can't trust you and you're gonna get us arrested?"

"Calm down, ho, it was just a funny story."

"Well, from where I'm standing, the moral of your story is that this might also be the level of loyalty you expect from people in real life," I say, laughing, as I keep *rip! rip!* ripping 'em down.

I pause to look around, to make sure The Hut is empty, except for the four of us. Sherry and I up on our tiptoes, or each other's shoulders, working the walls and the ceiling. And Holly is back up at the bar, sipping on something pink and sickly sweet and making sure a hopelessly plastered Chuck never turns around.

It's weird that he's still in there, right? But keep in mind that Chuck is sitting on the brass rail like a bar rag, facing the silver teeth of his broken mirror again, resigned to keep trying the dick trick with the Long Island Iced Tea until the end of time. In case you're wondering, his iced tea wasn't all that "long," which wasn't doing his gag any favors. But the length of this insane bar bet becomes the time limit on our caper, like one of those little hourglasses full of sand. Except this hourglass is full of tequila, vodka, light rum, triple sec, gin, a splash of Choke-a-Cola, and, of course, someone's penis.

Oh! But remember, this is not an hourglass, it's a five-hour glass. And it's running in reverse. Or something. Forget that analogy. I didn't take Sherry's writing class, so I don't know much about metaphors or whatever, but it's kinda like what Holly's skeevy dad said to her once when she kept us out for three days straight:

"Are you girls 'intoxi-cans' or 'intoxi-can'ts'?"

The point is, we have some time. I pull down another fifty ones in rapid succession, way faster than I shoot baskets in bars—and I'm not slow at that, either—then we move to the wall under the jukebox where the money grows the thickest under all those nostalgia tears, and Sherry fills a new void I've left behind under the flashing NEW CASTLE sign, pinning those starched and ironed dollar bills back on up, stamping them like butterflies under all the business cards that those smug golden boys and gilded girls left behind. Too bad we couldn't fuck up their future while we were at it.

*　*　*

Fine. Here's how it works.

A couple nights back, while we were first fondling under-inflated basketballs and being all sneaky and bonding over our degenerate plans, after a couple of really *really* sugary drinks got us dizzy, I might have confessed to Sherry that I hadn't been kicked out of the Secret Service at all. I think Holly already suspected this (if you want to ask her in the afterlife), but yeah, I was only kicked out of SCU, just like everybody else, and kicked out for plagiarism, too, no less. Which is required by law at this point. Actually, I should clarify. My case was kinda something special. In fact, my plagiarism incident was so bad that the provost said I was "technically a counterfeiter." And that's where the Secret Service comes in. Fer real.

So, get this, my story about a Secret Service interview and all the crying? Technically, not a lie! I was actually on their hot seat for photocopying fake twenties in the basement of the library.

Whew! It's a relief to get this off my chest, I'll tell ya, and it probably should have been a relief back then, too, and maybe brought us all closer? But it's tough to get close to Sherry, especially after she's eaten fried food. And I was close enough to Holly for both of us. So when Holly starts missing every basket on the Atomic Dunk, and I'm thinking about all this with the timer winding down on the basketball hoop and each of us cradling our balls like the babies we don't want, and the buzzer going off and the red siren swirling . . . the counterfeit dollar signs in my eyeballs were just like these light bulbs flashing over everyone's heads.

Because that's when I suddenly knew exactly how to pull it off.

I came up with the most important part of the plan right there at the buzzer, right when it counted the most.

And even if they would never admit it, without me, they'd be nothing. Just ask them. Oh, right.

Check it out. If you're not trying to be too good at it, did you know that counterfeiting is super easy?

I only spent about fifty bucks on green toner to make all of our fake dollar bills, though that snazzy *résumé* paper wasn't cheap! But I'll get it all back. Like Sherry loves to say, it's a labor-heavy job, more than an all-nighter, but when we're all "sad and done," we will have earned whatever we take. Earned as in "deserved." No one can deny this.

So with my immaculate hands fluttering along with our hearts, I'm seizing dollar after dollar, and Sherry's slapping my homemade bills back up in their place, all while Holly cheers on Chuck still working on that drink between his legs. My fake bills aren't perfect, but they're good enough for wallpaper in a dive bar full of townies and college morons. And, just like Sherry will tell ya, I've been behind the scenes at the Secret Service, so she trusts my secret formula for making money that, hopefully, will withstand the harsh lights of closing time. To be honest, though, I don't care if they do or don't. We'll be long gone by then.

Back up at the bar, Chuck finally passes out from the strain, which is good timing because Holly can help us out pruning the walls and the roof. Even perfect hands get tired.

Once we've raked it all down, I walk across the bar, heading for the door, garbage bags of money rustling and bouncing off my thighs. I accidentally kick Chuck's Long Island Iced Tea with my open-toed sandal, and I flinch. Sherry gags. Holly squeals. I freeze and wait for the spill. However, unlike the Honorary Yogi, Chuck's glass is only half full, and I'm thinking, "Holy moly, did he do that trick for real?"

But Chuck's out cold and will never know or care what he achieved, which makes sense because, just from talking to him these past couple weeks, he was definitely more of a half-empty kinda guy.

I'm running for the exit again, but before I can even open the front door, it swings wide in our faces, letting in the first slivers of morning, and guess who walks in? Sherry called him the Honorary Amish, and Holly called him the Honorary Yogi, but he was looking like he'd need a new honorarium. He's straight-up intimidating in the morning, and maybe it has something to do with the spectacle of the sunrise, but he glances at Chuck's prone position, then scans us up and down, and I almost feel like apologizing. With his black jacket and white collar and the blazing sun framing his face, he suddenly seems more *ethnic*, more Jesus than Amish, anyway. And when he talks, a Spanish accent I hadn't noticed now peeks through with the daylight.

"What have you naughty children been up to?" he asks.

"Don't you worry about it," Holly practically spits. Dog tired in the light of day, Holly, "Our Girl Friday" (and Saturday), has shed much of her charm like snakeskin.

"I think you're taking down my offering," he says cheerfully, and I wrap the end of my black bag around my fist in case it's fight-or-flight time. He looks at the piles of new and old bills strewn about our feet.

"What do you mean 'your offering'?" Holly says, not sure what to do but buying seconds.

Honorary Jesus cracks his knuckles and strides to the center of the bar, polished boots clomping on the tiles like something heavy's coming down.

"Me and my flock spent years decorating this foul interior as part of an important lesson, but now you've decided to cut straight to the end of the sermon."

"Wow," Holly says, sarcastic. "You're gonna teach us a lesson, huh?"

"Fuck off," I say.

"I know I'm unable to learn new things," Sherry adds, not so sure.

"You girls sure like bar bets, but have you ever seen the one where you dip a twenty in alcohol and set it on fire?"

"Nope!" one of us says, probably me.

"Well, it is quite remarkable. When the fire goes out, and when the money stops cooking, it is left perfectly unscathed. The alcohol burns away, but the currency just stays the same."

"Fascinating," Holly says, motioning for us to pack up all the bags and get moving again.

"It has something to do with the fibers or thread count, you see, because they make *real* money to last. So if my church or my children wanted this place to burn easily one day, to, say, cash out on this town? We would have to line the walls with something else besides cash. We'd need something that looks like cash money, but burns up much more effectively . . ."

I'm not following completely, but I think I'm getting the idea. Holly, too. She picks up a fake dollar and sniffs it.

"What do you mean 'looks like cash money'?"

"I mean, all that time you spent, all that preparation, it was such a waste."

"You're sure different than you were last night," I remark.

"Are you in some kind of cult?" Sherry asks, almost cheerful.

"Oh my!" he laughs. "No, no, this is a fine Jesuit university. An upstanding, faith-based community. Santa Carla University has the highest post-graduate employment rate in this Christian nation, as well as retention! Those business cards on the wall prove it. Sure, the student population isn't as diverse as we'd like it, but it's getting there."

"Got a real plagiarism problem, though," I shrug.

"Sooo do you think you're Jesus, bro?" Holly asks him.

"Carry the cross long enough . . ." He just lets that hang there.

"Good talking to you!" Holly says, heading for the door. He steps in front of her.

"What I mean is," he says, arms wide to block her, "if you're stealing paper and replacing it with paper . . . well, this is admittedly sort of silly, but it doesn't really change things for us."

"What do you mean?" Holly asks, but now I think I get it.

"I mean, that wasn't money you were stealing."

At this, he unzips his fly, and a long, arcing stream of urine covers the counterfeits we've pinned to the nearby wall. Then, in a smooth, '80s action-hero motion, he produces an American flag Zippo, flicks it, and waves it over his head like a concert encore. I can just make out the upside-down cross on the other side.

By now we're moving in slo-mo, too, and the Honorary Jesus just keeps on pissing. He doesn't quite turn his water into wine that morning, but the alchemy is spectacular enough. We smell it right before it happens, and in the final moment before the fire, I'm still trying to wrap my head around the idea that he was drinking gasoline the night before, right along with those other colorful cocktails. Maybe it was Sterno. That's flammable, too, right? These bums will drink anything.

The stink of gasoline cascades from between his legs, covering the fake dollars surrounding us, as well as everything else. And when Honorary Jesus reaches in front of him to break the stream with his lighter, the flames boil up around him like dragon's breath, and the wall of the bar goes up like a righteous bomb.

An actual miracle, Chuck snaps out of his trance moments before immolation. He runs for a fire extinguisher, and he puts out the wall with an unceremonious gust of foam. Like it's his job. Which it is. Then he shakes his head to try and understand what the hell is happening. Honorary Jesus turns to walk out the door, but he calls back over his shoulder.

"Good work, Chuck. Today wasn't the day. But we'll try again at the next graduation."

"Okay, see you then! Have a nice flight!" Chuck yells, still confused but waving like the hapless dumb-ass he is. He sits on the floor, rocking the extinguisher and himself back to sleep.

We gather up our money and leave. We don't care that it's fake. We did the work, and it's ours. That's what these kids will never understand.

When we step out into the light, a Mexican maintenance man in a red jumpsuit zips by in his golf cart, the back end of his vehicle piled high with palm fronds. A storm seems to have rolled through while we were inside—typical unpredictable SoCal weather—and the streets are flooded. We barely notice. Drainage soaks my high-heeled tennis shoes and rushes over me toward the gutters, and for some reason, I'm convinced I could tread water.

Is this what church is like? I wonder. As a kid, I never wanted to go.

The maintenance man stops in front of us to idle, and he lets us cross the street to our waiting car, his head turning only slightly to follow the dollars peeking out from our bags and our belts.

We hold our breath.

Then he nods and drives on through the rain wreckage without a word. Maybe he thinks we're strippers? Or, more likely, maybe he just knows we're all in this together.

Walking down the sidewalk, workday done, Sherry asks me the question.

"Did you see that?"

I nod, though I'm not sure what exactly she means. She could be talking about a ton of crazy shit, but I do see the neighborhood, maybe for the first time. And even though it kicked us out, I'm finally looking at SCU with something like respect.

But I never shake her question. It seems like the most important question in the world, one that I'd never dare to answer, wired up to that lie detector or not

When I get home, I take off my shoes to wash off the whiff of tequila and rocket fuel, and I see a dead bumblebee trapped in the tread of my left sneaker, and I'm sad that someone got hurt after all. I mean, fuck those college kids, but we need the bees. I don't have the courage to check under my other shoe. What if we're all down there?

Slow down, this isn't a happy ending, don't worry! We rake in $5,379 dollars, yes, and we split that three ways. But a month after counting all that money on the floor of a hotel room between our wiggling toes, all three of us find ourselves in the proverbial hot seat, hooked directly to a certain government seismograph that caused all of my trouble back then.

So, just like us, it turns out that students regularly steal the dollars off the walls, too! A couple dollars here, a couple dollars there. But they're replaced so often by alumni, or by the hundreds of weekly celebrations about new jobs or snazzy internships that no one ever notices. And when some of my funny money ended up buying a freshman some condoms ("ribbed for her indifference") from the 7-Eleven across the street, it didn't take much legwork for the real Secret Service to backtrack those half-ass counterfeits to my already infamous photocopy skills.

As a bonus, the agents make sure to tell me that our heist was "by far" the least lucrative scam they have ever encountered, narrowly stealing the number-one slot from some halfwit who tore four corners off a twenty-dollar bill, just to glue them onto a single.

"Which means each counterfeit twenty he created cost him twenty-one dollars, get it?" they explain. Oh, we get it.

Epilogue. It's not much consolation, but we don't go down easy. If the interrogator remembers me from before, he gives no indication, and when the questions start flying, nobody cries this time, but the needle jerks and traces our jagged lies out on the paper like it's singing "Rocky Mountain High." I've been here before, so I fall back on what I know, meaning my Kegels. And, unlike the mythical urethra drink draining or gasoline pissing tricks that the false prophets of the world try to bamboozle us with, this is a real exercise that results in real *profit*, from a real, live muscle that any woman can strengthen to turn the tables. Or at least turn a table over? Or maybe it will just induce a barely detectable but no less significant seismic disturbance to that earthquake machine so you can get away with one last lie. But we mostly just squeeze our fists instead of our pelvis . . . aaaaand it doesn't move the needle.

We get sentenced to seventeen years. Divided by three.

I know, right? You know why that math doesn't work? Because this judge has a jar of candy next to his gavel, which betrays a sweet tooth, so he only gives Sherry five years when she tries some of those mesmerizing hair flips she learned from Holly, and a newfound confidence she learned from me—and no doubt he ends up buying her a big, goofy, girly drink or two after court. With sugar and alcohol mixed together, we always got away with murder. So sure, she might have been the MVP that night after her trick with the drinks and the dudes, but it's more about the last man standing, you know? Or the last woman swimming?

But it's still a man's world, and most of those men, honorary or not, are judges of some kind or another, so it turns out there was a lesson after all. Which is this:

Look around. We all end up in the same place. And we always will.

CHAPTER XIII

MACDADDY CUTS
THE RED WIRE

$\int$he's right. We all ended up right here."

A wad of dollars floated by, a trail of green ink whirlpooling in their wake.

"I call bullshit," Dan said. "Busted by the Secret Service, my ass."

"Just ask Holly and Sherry," Gaddy said.

"Was that a threat or a confession?"

"Did you throw your friends off the boat while we were sleeping, you crazy twat?" Dan kicked some water her way.

"Whoa, settle down, kids," Gaddy said, acting hurt.

"So what's the point of that story anyway?" Lund asked her. "Is the Honorary Jesus driving this fire truck?"

The group hadn't considered this, and Gaddy just smiled. "Why not? That theory is as good as any."

"So you got sentenced to how many years, Gaddy?" Angie asked her.

"Yeah, why aren't you in jail right now?" Amy was shaking her head, too.

"I am in jail," Gaddy said. "Right. Now."

Angie looked her over for signs of deception, but since there wasn't anything visibly wired to her groin to detect pelvic muscle spasms, Angie didn't know what to believe anymore. And she almost preferred it this way. With the sudden propensity for parables, she was developing a growing respect for any tall tale that passed the time, the more far-fetched the better. It was easy to imagine any one of them telling this story later, and nobody buying it.

There was more splashing than normal, and she saw a couple of the guys were cornering Lund against the rail, who was looking around for his floating clothes to shield himself.

"How come we haven't given this asshole more scrutiny?" Dan was asking.

"Even though he was just the drug mule, there's no denying he has fucked us up."

"For the record, I, for one, was not okay with that," Beth said.

"We didn't consent to it, either," said Angie, speaking for Amy as well.

"What's the harm?" Reeves said, joining them from out of the waves. He started to say something else, but gagged, stifling another volley of puke with a hand over his mouth. After a moment, he held up a hand to signal he was fine. "See? No effect."

"Hey, dosing the party was not anyone's intention," Ruck laughed. "How could we have known this fatbody was gonna swim in his goddamn jeans?"

"Don't worry, I didn't stash it all with this idiot," Dan said, a finger hovering over Lund's heart.

"Then where's the shit?" Ruck asked him, hopping like a kid who had to piss, which he did, right down his leg. "Holly! Where'd you put our shit?"

"She's gone, dummy."

"I hope it ain't in her butt!"

"Butts aren't strong enough to hold anything," Gaddy agreed from across the pool. "Compared to everywhere else, the muscles in the rump are nothing. You can hide an eight ball in your ass, but you need something else to chalk up that shot."

"Yikes," Dan said, and Lund actually nodded in agreement.

"Kegels, baby!"

"Oh my God."

"What are the implications here, really?" Lund asked, breathing a sigh of relief as the mob had stopped focusing on him for a moment.

"What do you mean?" Dan asked him, not ready to let him out of his corner.

"I feel like this is just an excuse. In movies, when the script inserts drugs into the narrative—figuratively, I mean . . ." he said, covering his ass with his hand, "it is always at the expense of the story, to rationalize the irrational. We don't have to do that. We don't need to suspend our disbelief. This is *real*."

"No, you shouldn't *not* have taken off your goddamn pants!" Dan yelled.

"That was a double negative. And it was incidental. There are other possibilities."

"Like?" Dan was pressing in on him again.

"Like the driver's business card?" Angie jumped into the debate, remembering Janky and trying to muddy the waters and keep the escalating tensions off the weakest of the group. "Remember how it had an old dollar bill pinned to it?"

"So?"

"So maybe the triplets stole the first dollar our driver ever made. This is payback."

"That was forty-five states ago," Beth said dreamily.

"Still more likely than our altered states of consciousness being the answer to everything," Lund said, thumb on the bridge of his glasses again. Angie thought he was making some sense, then he flashed her a crooked smile that she once heard described as "box office poison," and she turned away from him again.

And then, like the flame to a moth, Lund's nerdy eyeglass adjustment brought a fist from the crowd. There was a blur of water and no one was sure at first who threw it, as it wasn't a punch with a lot of power. But Lund's spring-loaded frames absorbed it easily, and there was another swing and a scuffle as everyone pulled Ruck and Reeves off him. But there wasn't a lot of passion in the intervention, either. Lund seemed used to his periodic abuse now, as was everyone else.

Angie surveyed the scene. For all the pent-up tension, it was way too calm. She thought of the newest variation of the contentious "Safe Spaces" on the SCU campus: soothing music, cool beverages, a place to lie down after any heated debate. Is that what this was? An extended safe space where they were chilling in bathwater and backwash instead of on a cozy carpet square? And just as those Safe Spaces were clearly behavioral experiments in sheep's clothing, she couldn't help but be convinced her own underlying fear that they were being controlled also had something to do with their hesitation to fully riot. Was Janky a one-off? Was their lack of control mistaken for safety?

What if the rest of the world had it worse right now?

She looked at Jill for signs of anything, but Jill never seemed rattled, either by the latest scuffle or everybody's string of confessions. However, Gaddy's eyebrow was up as far as Beth's eyebrows were down, obviously more invested in the truth of her own tale than the rest of the group, even though the closest thing they had to a lie detector was useless because, back in what seemed like a lifetime ago, they'd all proven once and for all that spinning bottles, or truths or dares, were inherently self-serving.

"No way," Amy said from behind Gaddy and Beth. Jill and Angie turned away from the boys to listen.

"No way what?"

"No way you were in the Secret Service."

"Did you even listen to her story?" Lund asked Amy.

"What else would I be listening to?" Amy asked him, annoyed.

"You only got part of her story," Lund said, almost nonchalant. "She threw them under the bus. Literally."

"That's one interpretation," Gaddy said.

Angie opened her mouth to ask Gaddy how she could have possibly pushed her two friends overboard as the rest of them slept without any help from anyone else. But when Gaddy turned away and Angie saw Beth's white flowers behind Gaddy's ear covering some fresh scratches, she figured she had her answer.

Some of them must have been missing the speakers and their suspenseful dance-music score, or maybe it was just the new lullaby of wheels clicking across the depressed lines in the highway, but a subtle beat was pulsing back through their bodies. Improbable as it seemed, some of them started to dance again, or at least writhe around a bit, not quite cutting a rug, but sort of rhythmically shivering along with the truck. Or maybe they'd just discovered another of the infinite and ever-evolving methods of warming up.

Ruck was humming, then beatboxing to the clicks and clacks, settling on a lurching rendition of Public Enemy's *Fear of a Black Planet*.

"Black man, White woman . . . Black baby . . . White man, Black woman . . . Black baby . . ."

Ruck reciting the famous Dick Gregory sample from that song was just about the most embarrassing thing Angie could imagine (and she'd heard Janky's airplane story nine times), and Dan and Reeves wandered away from Ruck to peer over the back end of the fire truck. She watched them closely as they engaged in a quick, animated conference about something. Then, shimmying their shoulders to his beats, they both slithered back over to Ruck like water moccasins. Angie watched all this with a growing anxiety, apparently the only one to remember what had happened to Janky.

Reeves and Dan were humming along with Ruck's rapping, Dan moving closer and closer until his lips were almost touching Ruck's ears. Ruck stopped.

"Hey! Keep going! I want to hear more about this Black baby, Ruck. Is that song about you?" Dan asked him. Angie didn't like the bizarre tone this was taking, this sudden concern for Ruck's ethnicity, and Angie remembered how her research had noted this was exactly the sort of destructive distraction that eventually dominated discussions between most long-term inmates.

"The song is about everyone," Ruck said, nervous but proud of his answer.

"Hey, Ruck, where are you from?" Dan asked him.

"Where am I *from*?" Ruck looked from Dan to Reeves and back again.

"I never noticed it before," Dan said to Reeves.

"Or maybe he's just sunburned," Reeves said to Dan.

"I might be a little windburned, now that you mention it," Ruck said, agreeable to the last. He tried spinning a nearby bottle as an excuse to tell another story, but Dan snatched it away. The flotsam around them that had become their makeshift conch shells for campfire tales was now eyed by most with suspicion or ignored. Angie looked toward Godzooky, who's antenna was up, watching from his side-eye. She imagined holding an empty beer can up to her ear and Godzooky putting one over his mouth, and the private conversation they could have.

"So tell us, Ruck, where are you from?" Dan asked again, adding. "Originally."

"His name is a rugby term!" Jill said from somewhere. "It means a pile-on, right?"

"You don't say . . ." Dan tried out his best villainous chortle.

"These are all great questions, but the answers might take some time," Ruck said.

"Got plenty of that!" Reeves snorted, letting himself fall back into the pool. Angie thought she briefly saw the bottom when he splashed.

Is the water even lower?

"Okay, great," Ruck said. "Here is a story about one small victory on the front lines of diversity in America . . ." As far gone as they all were, Ruck could still elicit a collective groan. Angie could tell that no one wanted an inspiring story right now, but this tactic made some sense. Maybe by playing an expected role (usurping Janky's previous job of class clown?) Ruck could remind them his designated place in their party. Previous poolside confessions had captivated the group, due to the inherent interest in someone making their skeletons-in-the-closet dance for the masses, but Ruck was going to have to step it up.

"Okay, so, all I wanted was a cookie. Three white-chip cookies, to be exact. You see, for lunch, I'd been getting the same turkey-and-swiss sub from Metro every day for a week, before I bit into one and the mayo burst from a bubble in the bun and filled my mouth like I'd taken a wrong turn into gay porn. But it was tough finding food close enough to my job and . . ."

"Where were you working?"

"He just said he was in gay porn."

"It was a summer job at the quarry."

"Yeah, motherfucker can't spell quarry but he got hired over me," Dan said, laughing.

"Yep, that's the one! So you know there's not a whole lot of lunch options around there. It's like those movies when someone's in a plane over the ocean watching the gas gauge so it will allow them just enough time to fly back. They always crash and, of course, turn on each other in exactly nine minutes, seven seconds, precisely how much time I have left on my lunch, you follow?"

"Nope!" Reeves said, but Lund nodded, always ready for a movie reference.

"Leave the airplane shit to Janky," Dan warned him. "Continue."

"So just when I'm about to give up, I see it, a tiny MacDaddy's I've never noticed before, and it's like finding Shangri-La connected to a rawboned drive-thru beer outlet. The left engine on my plane is already sputtering as I crash through the door chimes and, wouldn't you know it, there's a line . . ."

"Enough with the airplane metaphor," Dan said, lower.

"What the hell is MacDaddy's?" Reeves scoffed. "Is that next to Hard Ralph's Café?"

". . . even worse, the line is a bunch of kids, five of them ranging in age from nine, ten, maybe eleven-ish, kinda wandering around, chattering. Two getting food, the rest just screwing around. I start to get annoyed, but I'm fighting the urge, not because these kids are Black—later I'll justify the awkwardness of me adding this detail up front—but because I hate it when some hatchet-face crone 'tsk-tsks' kids for just jackassing around."

"Or maybe you've discovered that by only getting mad at people who get mad at people, you can cut down on the people that irritate you by half?" Beth offered.

"Good point," Ruck said, not really following her train of thought. "Anyhow, these kids are creeping forward, slow as starfish, so I occupy my brain by imagining the cash register boiling over with seahorses and hope this makes me late enough to get fired from that shitty job."

"Starfish? Seahorses?" Dan laughed again. "Where is this place, Atlantis?"

"No, *this* is Atlantis," Angie reminded him.

"Have you ever seen a seahorse give birth?" Jill asked them, shuddering.

"Anyway, I'm cracking my knuckles, preparing to go at this lunch like an octopus when I get back in my car: eating, driving, honking, and messing with the stereo all at the same time. So I declare, 'Three of those white-chip cookies, good sir! The ones with the nuts,' and he gets my change from the register, and it's not full of seahorses after all. So as I'm putting away my wallet, I do a quick assessment of the MacDaddy's workforce. One guy in a red shirt, two more in the green, and, of course, it's the middle-management punk in the red who has the distinct look of someone working up the courage to say something racist right now. So I pray to 'Oh Shit,' the Patron Saint of 'Oh No,' while I'm looking at this little girl who has just handed me a cup of ice for no reason except because she wants to be helpful. I've somehow managed to go all summer without hearing one of *those* jokes, even though I'm hauling rocks with some real roughnecks. But I know it's coming. It's like an airline's turbine whine building in the air all around us . . ."

"You just don't listen, do ya?" Dan asked him.

"... and I almost escape the gaze of the red-eyed bastard in the red shirt when he catches me squirming, and he says to me, 'The funny thing is, they all probably have kids of their own.'"

"Damn," Jill cringed.

"So I'm standing there thinking, *If I don't say something by the time they hand me my cookies, I'll be admitting I'm a complete pussy who is afraid of greasy fuckers in ballcaps with hamburger hands, just because I'm light enough to pass as white.*"

"You are white, bro" Dan said, emphasis on the "wha" sound. "Aren't you?"

"What's up with those baseball caps anyway?" Reeves asked him. "Makes fast-food workers look like the sorriest baseball team in history."

"The Bad News Beefs!" Dan said, laughing.

"So one of the toadies hands me my cookies, and even though my airplane has long since crashed into the ocean, I remain at the counter and ask to speak to the manager."

Dan was gritting his teeth at every airplane reference, and Angie now understood that Ruck was doing two things; using Janky's story as a defense mechanism to blanket Ruck in "uniqueness," maybe broadcast his value in a crisis situation, or to possibly sow some doubt about the casual murder they'd committed. She wasn't sure either was working anymore.

"'Can I help you?' Red shirt asks me, and I start sputtering like the Red Baron, 'You made a crack about those kids.' 'Nope. I didn't say nothin',' he says, but his face is as red as his shirt, and four more green shirts step out to flank him, enough to fill the infield. He asks them, 'Did any of you say anything to those kids?' And I say, 'No, *you* said it, something about "I bet those kids got kids" or some crap.' 'Nope, didn't say nothin'.' And I realize he's gutless, so I can get away with reaching over the counter to knock over their huge, anatomically correct hamburger sculpture and grab him by his red collar, and I almost do this! But this sweaty Burgermeister smells terrible, okay? An eye-watering combo meal of onions and ass . . ."

"You're making Dan hangry," Reeves said, tongue tracing his teeth.

"... and he says to me, 'I think you just heard us talking about a movie.' 'What fuckin' movie?' I ask . . ."

Lund was all ears.

". . . but there *was* no movie, so I slam-dunk my cookies into the trashcan for what might be the weakest civil rights protest in the history of this great nation, and I yell, 'Go count the seahorses in your cash register!' At this point, I'm half-expecting another manager to come up out of a trapdoor in a black-and-white-striped shirt and twirl a whistle because now they're calling the police. So I'm outta there."

"Cool story, bro." Jill said it this time.

"You are, without a doubt, the most important civil rights leader of our time," Gaddy said, giving him the sarcastic slow clap.

"Yeah, it was truly the *least* you could do," Beth added, almost smiling, and some of them laughed. Angie breathed deep. Ruck's story, as self-serving as it seemed, hadn't been entirely ineffective at dispelling some of the tension in the pool. When the laughs died down, Dan cleared his throat and spat. "But he never answered the question. You know, about where he's from?"

"Never mind all that," Gaddy said, sending Dan back and away from Ruck with a bump of her broad shoulder. "Tell the truth, Ruck," Gaddy said to him, arms embracing him from behind like serpents, long fingernails lightly brushing his temples. "*You* made that joke, didn't you? Up at the counter. About those little kids."

"Maybe." Then, "Yes."

Jill and Amy audibly gasped. Even Dan and Reeves looked impressed.

"Wow," Angie said, otherwise speechless. Ruck had contributed a confession after all.

"You know what?" Reeves said. "I'm sick of these stories." And the spell was broken with a rumble of angry agreement. Amy gripped Angie's arm in fear as they watched Gaddy circle Ruck again, her long, strawberry-blonde tresses swallowing his face like a Kraken. Her hair had miraculously tripled in size due to tonight's water-and-wind repeat cycle, apparently filling the vacuum left behind by the notable loss of Holly's fantastic Medusa mane.

Gaddy hauled Ruck back and down into the furious surf around her, angling for a kiss.

"One of us . . . one of us . . ." she was saying, laughing as he struggled harder.

One of the white flowers behind her ear fell into his mouth as he went under again.

* * *

"No more fucking around," Dan said, snapping his fingers for attention. "Here's the deal. We will climb down the side of this stupid truck, and then we will crawl under the chassis, and then we will cut the fuel line."

Dan waited for a reaction to the plan, taking a moment to squeeze his fists and wring the water out of his grip, admiring his own raised forearm veins in the process.

"That's crazy talk," Lund said, but he wasn't too convincing. Jill, Amy, Angie, and even Beth looked at each other in turn. Godzooky watched Dan closely. Honestly, in a night of bad ideas, it was the best idea they'd heard yet.

"Listen," Dan said. "Ruck has clearly led a cursed life, and he almost talked us into an early grave with his stupid cookie story, *but* remember what he said about his airplane running out of gas? He was onto something. Weren't you, little buddy . . ."

Dan pulled up Ruck by the hair, and he offered a cautious nod. He was still alive, but visibly shivering, less from cold and more from Gaddy's violent baptism. Ruck started to speak, but Reeves came around and clamped Ruck's nostrils shut to stop his mouth. He held up a finger in Ruck's face, then stood behind Dan, arms crossed, licking the water dripping off the end of his own nose. Ruck drew back away from them, but he was still nodding along, either on board with this new plan, or relieved to only be a peripheral focus for the moment. Gaddy was holding Ruck's hand tight, and after another forceful kiss, without the Atomic Dunk this time, he quickly stiffened his posture, along with his resolve, and soon he was standing tall. Even Lund relented, admitting that this sounded like exactly the right thing to do in that moment, like the big action scene toward the climax of the movie. Godzooky seemed game as well, daunting arms still crossed and stacking his chest like firewood, but he looked cautiously optimistic.

Reeves whispered something to Dan, who nodded slowly.

"Okay! Are we doing this?" Dan asked everyone.

Shrugs and nods all around.

They got to work.

Most of their clothes were gone, but they were able to fashion a relatively strong rope from their remaining waterlogged socks. Lund's acid-washed jeans were avoided due to the trickle of candy-colored poison

still emanating from the back pocket, but the sock rope seemed sturdy
enough without them. Reeves test-drove its reliability by whip-cracking
the tail end of it against Lund's red, freckled arm, laughing as the painful pink welts rose on his skin like bread dough.

"Ow!"

"I like it!" Reeves said, giddy. "You could climb down a building on
that sumbitch."

"It could work," Ruck agreed from slightly behind Gaddy. They
were holding hands.

"And we have our volunteer!" Reeves announced, and Gaddy thrust
Ruck's hand in the air to accept the nomination. Ruck looked ill.

"Don't worry," Gaddy whispered to Ruck. "You don't have to do
anything you don't want to do."

Ruck grimaced, chomping his top lip hard enough to draw blood.
Angie felt a twinge of pity, all these years later still associating any flinch
with a troubling mixture of cowardice and compassion. She'd never
been a fan of Ruck, and not just because of his prank call two years
ago, a gag she was convinced had been orchestrated by Dan after their
breakup.

Even though the modern prank phone call was a lost art due to
cellphones and their lack of anonymity, Angie understood that young
men constantly found themselves with that strange midnight urge to
reclaim it. Not just because Angie missed them, too. Sometimes she
found herself pining away for the early days of "star-sixty-nining," a
courting ritual officially recognized as "first base" east of the Missis-
sippi, according to her brother. Back before the siege of murderous,
disembodied voices in her hometown, prank calls were a welcome sort
of home invasion. It was hard for people to remember that a prank call
used to be considered the equivalent of teasing a girl on the playground
to show her that you liked her. But despite growing up outside of any
normalized phone rituals, she was not amused when Ruck's muffled
voice came through her cellphone speaker:

"I hear you like to fuck . . ."

Most days, any deranged phone call reminded Angie of her brother,
or that distant prison, or even the loss of the honeybees and the shut-
tering of their family's hives. And she told Ruck as much back then,
when he fessed up. She kept him on the line for a half hour, at least
long enough to drive thirty miles and chuck her cellphone through the

window of his downstairs apartment. She held eye contact through the hole as he picked her busted phone up from his floor and shook off the broken glass. He was pretty confused, and more than a little freaked out when her voice continued to whisper in his ear in a voice he'd never heard before or since:

"They're always listening . . ."

Terrified, he never even made her pony up for damage. Though he did wrap the broken phone in a pink bow and mail it back to her when her next birthday rolled around. As she watched Ruck's eyes search the group for help, it occurred to Angie that her own birthday was once a year, like a birthday should be. She also thought about how broken cellphones were perfect gifts. Especially when it came back to you as effectively as a boomerang, a toy that every child has owned but no child has ever successfully thrown . . .

I'm losing it.

She shook off the mental digressions to snap back to the present, where Ruck was trying to talk his way out of crawling under the fire truck.

"Hold on, man, just hold on," Ruck was saying to Dan as he pulled him toward the side of the pool. Gaddy released his hand. "Wait. Will you wait? I don't know where a fuel line is."

"It's the red wi-i-i-i-ire," Reeves sang.

"No, no, always cut the blue wire," Dan said, arm affectionately circling Ruck's head to keep him from slipping his grip. "Ruck, my friend, haven't you ever seen a movie before?" Dan asked him.

"He's right," Lund muttered, disappointed that Dan identified the trope before he did. "You always cut the blue wire."

"But I can't climb under this thing!" Ruck said. "There's no space between the wheels. The whole damn side of this fire truck goes all the way down to the road!"

Dan considered this, glancing at Reeves. Ruck's cheeks puffed out as he waited, as if he was holding back a scream. Reeves closed his eyes.

"He can go under from the back," Reeves grunted, opening his eyes again. That settled it.

"Let's go." Dan squeezed Ruck's shoulders, then hoisted him up and out of the pool, giving him a hearty slap on the back to gear him up for walking the plank.

"I have nothing to cut it with!"

"Then chew through it, Cookie Monster," Reeves said.

"No, Ruck, just yank on it," Dan said. "Just yank on whatever. A fire truck isn't a bomb, and this isn't rocket science."

"Yeah, it's 'fuck it!' science," Reeves laughed.

"And if I pull a brake line by mistake?"

"Even better," Dan said.

"How is that better?"

"You're doing this!" Reeves bellowed, loud enough for Angie to feel it vibrate the water.

"I'm doing this," Ruck repeated, unconvinced, looking to the crowd for sympathy. "I can do this. Let's do some rocket surgery . . ."

Reeves started tying the sock rope around Ruck's waist as Ruck took a long look up and down the empty road. It was too dark to make out any white lines or ditches, and, as always, they were going too fast for anyone to get a clear picture of the topography flashing by beneath the wheels. The bumps were infrequent now, which gave him hope, but any help from the streetlights felt years away. Angie tried counting reflectors on the road, estimating that they were traveling approximately . . .

"Five hundred miles an hour," Dan said, licking his thumb and holding it up to the wind. "Give or take a hundred. So don't worry. Before you know it, we'll be landing on Mars."

"Pennsylvania!" Gaddy said, laughing.

"No, seriously, Ruck, you're all good to go, bro. Let's do it."

They all avoided Ruck's gaze. He sniveled despite the brave face he'd put on for Gaddy, and he put one shaking leg up on the steel rail. Dan and Reeves each took an arm and started lowering him over the back end of the truck and into the ghastly red glow of the taillights and that hair-raising rush of an inviable path to nowhere.

Ruck climbed down to the bumper easily enough, then over the chrome trailer hitch, deftly spinning his body around and up, almost like a gymnast, until his stiff legs and torso were sliding under the truck. Dan and Reeves shared a glance, impressed by his surprising dexterity. They both held the sock rope white-knuckle tight, like they were a tug-of-war anchor. Water trickled from the knots under their squeaking fists.

Most of the party held onto the side rails, held onto someone else, or simply held their breath. Beth took the opportunity to bury her nose in Gaddy's mess of wind-tousled hair so that she could nip at the flowers perched there; two brilliant white narcissus bulbs remained, which she carefully extracted from behind Gaddy's ear, one by one. Incredulous, Angie watched all this in silence, amazed as Beth pecked, chewed, then swallowed each one, petal by petal. She seemed to work up the courage for the last bite, drawing in a deep breath, and Angie was convinced the flowers were recharging her somehow, bringing blood back to her face, darkening her pupils to a predatory glint.

Too late, Gaddy realized what was happening on the final petal, and she hauled back a fist and *popped!* Beth square in the mouth. Beth took this punch easily, but never stopped chewing. A thin stream of blood ran from the corner of her mouth and down her chin as she swam away, and something about her backward glance convinced Gaddy not to follow.

Angie turned back to the action behind the truck, gulping as they bounded over a strip of shredded tire tread on the road. Dan and Reeves staggered with their sock rope, and Amy and Jill moaned, but the pair held fast. Godzooky stood nearby, solid but ready to move, eyeing the last dangling sock behind the anchors' grasp, considering a helping hand if their grip slipped.

Angie strained to look over the side, and she could just make out Ruck, half under the rattling colossus, his upper torso still visible. His progress had stopped, and he was squinting up through the red fog around him, choking in the fumes as he searched the outlines of their faces staring down at him, as if he was looking for a way out.

"Do it!" Reeves yelled into the haze of exhaust, and Ruck backed under bit by bit, until his body finally vanished completely and only his desperate voice remained.

"I can't see anything!" he cried.

"Pull the blue wire!" Lund yelled back.

"Everything down here is red, you fuckin' assholes!"

"Red assholes," Reeves said, giggling.

"Yank on everything you see!" Dan shouted.

"Okay . . ." Ruck said. "Hold on, there's something . . . it's spinning . . ."

"No, wait, don't touch it!" Godzooky shouted as he sloshed up to the rail, and Angie saw some of the automotive knowledge he'd demonstrated earlier during his bilingual horror story now clouding his face with a frightening realization. He grabbed for the last sock.

Just then, the truck was weaving through an abandoned construction site, screeching to keep control as it ramped over a rotten dog carcass and the roadkill removal shovel still beneath it. The wet rope shot through all six hands like a bullet as the tail end of the fire engine bucked them a good two feet into the air and back down into a mad mound of gropes and shouts in the center of the pool.

Except for Angie, who, unfortunately, had held onto the rail. She watched as Ruck fell free from the truck and bounced to the side, where the back dual wheels eagerly found him to roll his body out like a screaming pizza.

"They're always listening," Angie whispered crazily before she could stop herself, and an unfortunately timed streetlight lit up the scene on the road in case she missed anything.

Angie had to decide between terrible sights or even worse sounds, so she ground her fists into her eyes so they wouldn't follow the unlucky adventure of his head, now free from his body, pinballing and pirouetting through potholes and pylons.

Instead, she very clearly heard the wet cracking and slapping of his lips over his chin and the heavy slop of the long bloody streamers that trailed from his whirling neck like a beached man o' war stretched out in the sun by hungry gulls. And just as those sounds finally faded, she could have sworn she heard his last words croaked from a spiraling voice box.

"It's spinning . . . it's spinning . . ."

"What's the name of that show?" Lund asked them, when the shock of Ruck's decapitation had died down. Judging by the way bodies shifted from her question, she guessed no one would answer. But Angie looked up.

"What show?

"That game show, where people get arrested and isolated, then offered the same opportunity to rat each other out. So if none of them confess, they're all rewarded with freedom. And if one rats but the others don't, only the rat is rewarded. And if they all rat, they serve a lesser term."

"That sounds like the worst game show of all time," Beth said.

"I see where you're going, Lund, but we're in no position to betray each other," Jill said, but she seemed to realize the ridiculousness of her statement as soon as she said it. She slumped forward again, head in her hands. Angie wondered if Amy had seen Jill kiss her at the rail. Angie had never kissed Amy, though they'd been known to get hammered and play drunken grab-ass at the occasional (land-locked) party.

"Jill's right," Amy said. "Everyone has already confessed. To something."

Angie considered this.

"All I'm saying is, we could have beat that game show," Lund said. "It would be easy. If we're not anticipating anyone making the same decision as ourselves, our own decisions cannot be influenced by the action of—"

"Shut up, Lund," Jill said, head still in her hands. "We're not talking about a game show here, we're talking about . . . what are we talking about?"

"Making a deal," Dan said.

"That's not the show," Lund said.

"Making a deal with who?" Angie asked him.

"I don't know his name," Dan admitted. "But I do know he's driving this chariot. And someone here signed his contract."

"Shit was rigged," Reeves grumbled, eyes blinking slow. "We never had a chance . . ."

Angie glared at Reeves, distressed at the sight of him so soon after Ruck's death. She'd assumed he'd lurk in the corners, or under the water, like he'd done after Janky. They stared at each other a moment, and then Reeves threw up his hands and laughed, moonwalking away until he tripped and fell backward. It was quickly becoming his trademark. Angie started to speak on the question of the driver's identity when Reeves resurfaced, teeth shiny, spilling an armload of unopened beer cans into their circle.

"Where did he get those?" Lund marveled, and reached for one out of curiosity. Reeves smacked it out of his hand and cracked it open, guzzling it down in seconds. Then another. Then another.

"Every generation needs their heroes," Angie scoffed, watching Reeves polish off six beers in succession, a bellow of triumph as he let the crushed cans rain down over his head.

"So are these beers coming from the bottom of the pool or—" Lund started to ask Reeves, but Angie reached to pull him back, convinced he'd be the next target. More and more, she had this inexplicable urge to protect him. Amy, too, who steered Lund further away from Reeves's drinking display as he continued to crack cans, burping and hacking and swatting at something unseen before eventually settling on a quick but vigorous bout of shadow boxing against the fiberglass shell of the hot tub. It was only when he was down on all fours, peering into the shimmer of the water, that Angie got up the courage to approach him. She hoped he would aim any sudden torrent of puke over the side, though she might welcome the splash of warm bile, even at the cost of what remained of her sanity.

"Hello, Reeves," she said. "So what's going on down there?"

"Do you see it?" he said, mouth close enough to the surface to send small waves rippling with each word. It seemed lighter outside, easier to see each other and the borders of the pool, though no moon or street-light was visible. Angie wondered if dawn was approaching.

"See what, Reeves? Your reflection?"

"No. The way out."

"What's the way out?"

"The door," he said, annoyed that Angie was missing it. He stabbed a wrinkled finger at the water. "Right . . . down . . . there. You don't see the door? On the bottom of the pool? It's marked with a flower, a red narcissus . . ."

Her pulse reverberated in her throat as she followed his finger into the murk, hoping he'd discovered some sort of hatch, which might explain the disappearance of Holly and Sherry, the alternating water levels, or even the occasional replenishment of alcohol. She squinted into the dark, then felt around with her own pruned fingers, but there was nothing. Just ribbed edges of a worn plastic pool liner and a whirling dervish of empty cans and mini-bottles, dancing and clicking and clanking against the rounded corners of their tomb.

Reeves blinked as he lost focus on whatever he had seen. He shook his head.

"I thought . . . I swear I saw a door in the floor."

"Shut the fuck up, Reeves," Beth said, and Angie turned to see her and Lund right behind her. Confused, Angie stared at their clasped hands, just out of sight beneath the waves, and watched them slip away together into the shadows, then Angie took Reeves by one arm to prop him up against the side. Dan observed this new pairing, but said nothing. And Reeves just kept sinking down. He'd been doing this for a while, but this time felt different. Despite her misgivings, Angie struggled to haul him back up. She wasn't sure why she cared if someone who was directly involved in the deaths of a growing number of friends (or friends of friends) drowned, but she tried to talk to him anyway. Starting with some small talk to keep him above water, anything unrelated to the popular topics of the night; mortality, crime, punishment . . . anything she was interested in. Increasingly dangerous and useless, Angie was somehow still convinced Reeves was important to their outcome.

"Hey, Reeves, do you remember back at U of L, when my computer ate all our old emails? Reeves?" He seemed to weigh a thousand pounds.

"I thought you lied about that," he said, laughing, his eyes half-lidded, and he slumped through her grasp. "So that your jealous, short-lived boyfriend Dave or whatever wouldn't be jealous."

"No, it was an accident. He was never my boyfriend, and that computer was evil. Remember? So you printed them out, and then you ate them for real?"

"You didn't even know how to surf the web," Reeves murmured, eyes opening a bit.

"And you should know, you're the surf master, right?" It was Dan, sliding over to splash them both with a forearm of water. He took one of Reeves's arms off Angie's shoulder to help keep him upright. "Right?"

"Shhh," Reeves said, slipping from Dan's grip, too. Annoyed, Dan stood up straight and let Reeves go, his limp body dropping forward into an ear-popping belly slap.

"Well, that'll wake you up!" Dan said. But Reeves was staying down again. One minute. Two minutes. Angie kicked around the murk to find him, and he sprung up, metal teeth gleaming, like a shark that nailed the seal.

"Shotgun!" Reeves shouted around the shredded beer can in his mouth. He bit off another chunk of aluminum, staring at Angie as he chewed. Her hands covered the teeth marks on her legs as she took a deep breath to calm down. For a second there, she'd thought Reeves had a gun in his mouth, or a knife, some sort of weapon from a secret cache under his "door in the floor." What troubled her the most was that, for a brief moment, she wished it was true, that in a drunken rage he'd facilitate a quick and brutal end to their night. Any ending would do.

As he stood there, eating cans, the roar of the night air drying his body, Reeves began studying his forearms again, then scratching, he moved up to his shoulders, straining to scratch the impossible spot between his shoulder blades. Angie saw Beth and Lund watching this manic display, Beth with a half-smile as the other side of her mouth angled toward Lund, was finally telling her story. He was her only audience, and, if his trembling shoulders were any indication, he wished he wasn't. Angie turned back to Reeves and his fingernails gouged fresh trenches into his ribs.

"What are you doing?!"

"Goddamn fleas," Reeves said, digging harder. "Are there fleas in here?"

"It's too cold for fleas. Stop. Stop!" Angie was saying, but Reeves was down on all fours again, looking for his mysterious door at the bottom of the pool. Then he was gone, and it was silent again. She looked around for help, but everyone was against the walls of the tub, eyes closed or vacant, with only the distant whisper of Beth's story filling Lund's ear.

Alone, she counted out time. Nine minutes passed. And when Reeves came back up this time, his eyes were changed, inky and recessed, but blazing with purpose. Angie joined the party against the walls, and with the pool to himself, he floated on his back and stared up at the stars, pushing off the sides, then their legs when he bumped them, from one body to the next, harder and faster, scooping the occasional floating mini-bottle for the distant taste of liquor lingering on its snout. He flipped over on his stomach, black eyes now submerged, mouth no longer bubbling, soaking in the salty brine of their dead party to sustain his momentum.

After a few laps, he kicked off the wall between Godzooky and Jill, halting his swim dead center in the circle. There he began collecting wads of the counterfeit money that rode the crests of his waves, ignoring the verdant hemorrhage that leaked from the bills to mix with the acid-washed spectrum of Lund's floating jeans, all of this staining the churn of their communal soup a living, venomous green. Arms full of fake cash, he kneeled, dipped his chin, and began to drink. He made note of who watched, who looked away, and who opened their throats to join in his communion.

Just as he'd tallied up the imaginary fortune, he counted everyone on his fingers, as if they were real.

CHAPTER XIV

THE SMILE POLICE

Beth's Story

It makes sense that I'd end up a tourist attraction, drifting along in the water somewhere, just like it makes perfect sense how I ended up at my last job. Do I think this is funny? You bet. Don't worry, I'm smiling on the inside. Do you know what a smile really looks like on the inside, though? You should peel one off some time and check it out, turn that rind inside out. Maybe this story will help.

All my life, men have been telling me to smile. "You're so pretty when you smile," they'd say. It made me feel like there was a second face waiting just under the surface, where my "real" smile was stashed, something I was unable to access. It took only thirty years, but men have finally stopped asking me to smile. I guess I'm too old to carry around two separate faces anymore. But I was in the perfect position for a new line of work, where, ironically, it was essential that you never crack a smile. Kinda like a cop, I'd be stern, so people would think they were in trouble, if only for a few seconds. It's all I'd have to do on this new job. So I took it.

"Excuse me! Sir? Come here, please, sir . . ."

Most days go like this. I linger near the street corners along San Francisco's Fisherman's Wharf, so anyone I stop will wonder if they got caught jaywalking. So many tourists stream across these intersections, desperate to watch drug-addled street musicians dance for their dinner, hilariously eager for some "fresh-caught" seafood that has long since turned to rubber riding a refrigerated truck all the way from Maine.

"Sir? Hello. We have a problem," I say. "I'll need you to step over here, please."

One day, I snag a guy who seems like the usual mark: skin soft as an uncooked fillet, draped with the immaculate track suit that indicates a white-collar fifty-something on a well-earned vacation. Like most people crossing The Embarcadero, his eyes are wide, searching the horizon for a glimpse of Alcatraz out in the bay, when he should have been more aware of where he was walking. And before he understands what's happening, he's letting me guide him by the elbow away from the crowd. These are crucial moments before the punch line, and it's so important to get the pen in their hand before the jig is up.

"What did I do?" he asks. There's irritation behind his eyes. He's a large man, but he allows my grip to steer him. They usually do. This is due to several factors: my mirrored sunglasses, my blue shirt with the sharp, pressed corners, my chrome name tag, the fact that I'm a woman . . . and, most important, my frown.

"Here, hold this, sir," I say, and I bring the clipboard up to his chest. I lean in as if I'm writing a citation, but I hand the pen to him instead. He takes it. This is the cue for my real face to "split." By split I don't mean "take off," I mean "crack open" (you say "tomato" . . .).

Have I mentioned that I show all my teeth when I smile? Men used to love this when I was younger. I have good teeth. At least I always assumed so, judging by how often men demanded to see them.

"You weren't smiling, sir!" I say through my completely unnatural grin. "And that's the problem. You see, you're in San Francisco now. It's a beautiful day, the beaches are open, and everyone is having a wonderful time. So we're going to have to ask you to start smiling!"

I hand him a cheap sticker that says I HEART SAN FRANCISCO, and somehow my awkward smile becomes infectious no matter how hard he fights it. They're like yawns in that way. I might not smile often, but that doesn't mean I've forgotten how (yet). He's annoyed, but visibly relieved he's not getting a real ticket. He starts to leave, and I point to my pen still in his hand.

"Before you go, sir, can I get your name and address to send you some information? It's for charity. To help the homeless."

Sometimes it's the "homeless." Sometimes it's the "unhoused." Sometimes it's the "unhomed." Sometimes it's the Unhoused, Unhomed Girl Scouts. Sometimes it's even the vets. Pick your war. Whatever dudes are into. And sometimes, when I'm real tired, I just say "to help the planet," which covers everything. And that last one isn't a lie. Once, I tried getting men to sign a petition to help save the sea lions basking on Pier 39, but I didn't get a single signature. I never should have tried this on Pier 38. One glance across the bay at that lazy, sun-soaked dog pile of elephantine creatures and people start thinking that sea lions didn't need saving. That they're actually doing better than most of us.

So this guy pauses for a good beat to comprehend the plight of the homeless in our coastal city, then he snatches the clipboard from my hand. He's already accepted the sticker, so he feels like completing the rest of our transaction is reasonable enough. I used to flash a cardboard badge with SAN FRANCISCO SMILE POLICE scrawled in the center of the star, but it was slapped out of my hand four years ago by a man in a Stuart Hughes suit. Now I just have my clipboard and some loose pages. Sometimes I draw lines on them. You don't need a lot of swag to do this job.

The man finds an empty space near the middle of my paper. I've already written some fake names and addresses at the top of each page so people hesitate a little less (no one wants to be first). But it's up to them what they write in their box, and the "personal" information that men give me varies greatly. But that's fine. All I need is a handwriting sample. If I could ask them to write "the quick brown fox jumped over the lazy dog," I certainly would, but what they don't know is that any combination of words will do.

He writes down an email address, then adds his signature next to it, dropping the pen onto my clipboard and thumping it against my clavicle, growing angrier with each step away. This level of frustration tells me our interaction was successful. Official. Necessary. Men *should* carry the burden of unease after our exchange, a little irritation mixed with relief, just like when we have to deal with them.

Once I've collected fifty names, I head under the pier. I can usually gather anywhere between ten and twenty signatures every hour. Or all fifty in half that time if it's a Saturday.

Despite the top deck being the center of all the waterfront action, the algae-streaked pillars holding up Pier 39 also enclose a subterranean ghost town. Tourist dollars swirl in all directions on the streets above, but this shadowy underbelly of Fisherman's Wharf is sort of like the

deceptively dead eye of a hurricane. There are beachcombers and homeless milling around most piers along The Embarcadero, all the way to
the boardwalk. But not under Pier 39. Part of the reason is the rotten
fish, but it's also due to a decrepit, long-forgotten tourist attraction
bobbing in the water nearby. Along a street of failed gift shops and gim-
micks, tourists seem to feel guilty around such a conspicuous failure.
And because he is there every day, as well, everyone avoids "the captain"
like his foundering is infectious. Except for me.

Listening to him explain it, his "Laser Boat" seemed like a good
idea at the time. And at first glance, it looks like a typical tourist barge,
with thirty or so seats positioned along its deck, ready for some good,
old-fashioned sightseeing. But the Laser Boat is actually a converted
Mirage luxury yacht, ratty and barnacle-ridden, the windscreen on the
flybridge cracked like a motel mirror. But even in this state, it was still
capable of an incredible 80 knots on the water, or so I'm told.

But most striking are the sides, where bright orange flames lick the
length of the hull, curling near the stern like the tail of the dog that
ate your graduation cake. The vessel is capped off with a huge yellow
spoiler, big as goalposts, where a pair of steel-blue doves have always
huddled. Before the Laser Boat went out of business, there had been
a line of tourists down the block buying tickets, mostly because of the
captain's unflappable enthusiasm. He pulled triple duty as a corny car-
nival barker, whipping up interest from the gawkers by pacing the deck,
or flagging down the families in the nicest track suits. But these days,
when there wasn't a solitary soul remaining who wanted a ride, the
captain still sat on his boat every day, his feet swinging over the gun-
wale, smoking a joint and chewing on toothpicks, twigs, and memories
of jam-packed tours. When he was still an active skipper, I remember
seeing the captain, aka "Laser Bob," just about every afternoon. And I
knew his outrageous pitch very well, which he still recites every chance
he gets. It goes like this:

"Are you tired of those *long* sightseeing tours? Well, step right up!
The Laser Boat will show you 495 San Francisco Bay–side attractions in
nine minutes or less! We promise to spend five seconds on Alcatraz . . .
three seconds on those stinky sea lions . . . and we'll cross under the
Golden Gate Bridge at Mach 3. None of that *lingering* nonsense. So forget those slow-motion tours and get with the *Laser Boat*. All to the tune
of your favorite '80s hair-metal hits. Back at the dock in three songs

or less or *your money back*. Ride the snake! Rocket Tours Unlimited is not responsible for, and expressly disclaims all liability for, damages or death resulting from use, reference to, or reliance on our amazing tourist experience . . ."

Something like that, anyway. And maybe the trip wasn't exactly that fast, but the boat was undeniably ridiculous. And this was the allure that kept the business afloat.

But just like the viability of the female of any species, the more modest charms of even the fastest boat have an expiration date. And even on the busiest weekends, it's now dead quiet around those sun-blasted orange flames. And with that silence (Laser Bob's reminiscing notwithstanding), I have plenty of time to study the names I collect in peace.

There are initials carved into the palm of my hand. They're often mistaken for a tattoo when I'm not making a fist, which is almost never, but this has cost me a legitimate job or two, even kept me out of the Air Force when the recruiter shook her head right after shaking my hand and told me, "Sorry, you can't have them where they show." Men liked to say I'll likely end up in academia, the last resort of the proudly illustrated. They turned out to be right.

But it's not a tattoo, and it's not a brand, though this is what it most closely resembles. It's a signature. Some experts think it's impossible to authenticate handwriting when the sample is a carving. They say it's because too much pressure exerted on any writing instrument, particularly a blade, will disrupt the natural hand routines and muscle memory. This would normally make etchings indistinguishable. But only if the writing surface is not stationary. And only if the knife isn't impossibly sharp.

Luckily, I was holding my breath when I did it, so I was able to remain perfectly still.

I hold the clipboard of signatures up to my palm for comparison. I study the peaks of the script, the valleys, quaver, and tremble of the authors' hands. A year ago, I took a handwriting analysis class online. It only took three months and twelve trips to a little library two blocks over, just off Columbus Avenue, the tourists' umbilical between the wharf and Chinatown. I got a certificate and everything.

I hear myself reading some names aloud, and I flip over my tongue to stifle them, but the voice is just in my head, searching for characters, not real people:

"Reeves," "Ruck," "Janky," "Dan," "Nahla"? What kind of name is that?

Today, there's still no match, and I'm back walking my beat before the sun goes down, nodding at real cops when they ride by on their bicycles. Eventually, I end up around Forbes Island, the ramshackle floating restaurant that the most ill-informed sightseers mistake for The Rock itself, and I manage to grab more elbows and hasty signatures. I hand out my dog-eared heart stickers and tell them to smile, sharing more awkward moments with suspicious men.

They always let me steer them by the arm. They let me play my game. I think it's because I'm short enough to get away with it. Ever since junior high, I've been mistaken for someone younger. But with the new lines on my face, and the new lines on my hands, those days are over. Thank God.

Once, when I was very young and living too close to the beach in Santa Carla, a surfer tried to impress me by saying, "Do you like this car?" as he angled a thumb at something with flames painted on the hood. But I heard him say, "Do you like this *scar*" instead, and I wasted six weeks in that relationship before I realized he was not nearly interesting enough to have any marks on his body at all.

Walking away from Forbes Island, a woman tries to ask me for directions, but I turn away. I never approach the women, and not just because it's not a woman's name that's carved into my hand. It's because I know they're onto me. If it's one thing a woman won't tolerate, it's someone trying to trick her into smiling.

I see a man watching from the splintered wooden rail, thick arms crossed, head tilted like an amiable dog. Another big guy, with mirrored sunglasses like my own and a red, jarhead haircut, so I worry he's actual local law enforcement getting ready to tell me to move on, something that happens twice a week. But something about this guy is different, too. But there's something wrong with all of them, to be honest.

I move on anyway, and the man frowns and walks toward me to cut me off, like an orange cat crossing my path (are they bad luck, too?), then he turns and walks past me again, seemingly waiting for me to give him my song and dance. So I do.

"Sir? Hello. We have a problem. Can I speak with you for a second . . ."

I go through my whole rigamarole, and he even takes the pen from my hand at the end, but he hesitates when he sees me make a fist to hide the initials. He continues to stare at the clipboard, but refuses to write anything. Even worse, he's already smiling, which robs me of the punch line. There's a bit of the tourist look to him, but maybe more of a professional vacationer. Like the owner of a beachfront home who also rents to others.

Exactly like the sort of landlord in charge of the bungalows along the beach where I woke up five years ago, my fists and shoes filled with blood and sand.

He fits the profile. But, of course, they all fit a profile.

I search every beach house along the strip after that morning, every seasonal beachfront villa in a ten-mile radius, backtracking through leases and rental agreements and floor plans, but I find nothing. Except for my hand, there's no proof that anything happened to me behind any of those emotionless, sand-pitted windows. But the houses are so similar, I can still gaze up from the surf and lock eyes with any of a hundred sunburned and saltwater-burned front doors and feel the distinct chill of recognition. It could be any of them. It could be all of them.

He hands me back my pen. He wrote nothing, but now I know it is him. I don't need a handwriting analyst. Why would I? I've got the certificate and everything.

I keep my hand on his arm, and he follows me under the pier. The benefit of being a small woman is that men will follow you anywhere. You only have to offer a smile in return.

And sometimes, I can.

There's good shade under Pier 39, and the smell of the bloated, snoring sea lions can mask anything, so it's perfect for my purposes. But sometimes a tough sell to others.

I've heard that the wildlife reeks twice as bad under Fisherman's Wharf, and I have no doubt this is from the sea life scrounging on leftover rubbernecker cuisine. Especially the skate. Skate's the garbage fish, a ray the tourist traps will sneakily substitute for whatever they run out of on the menu. Did you know that most times when you think you're getting salmon, you're really getting skate? Scallops and linguine? More like skate and spaghetti. Fish and chips? Try skate and fries. I've seen piles of dying skate under the pier, flapping desperately for the promise of an ocean an impossible ten feet away, cookie-cutter circles punched in their wings.

So this particular tourist's nostrils are flaring, and he's just beginning to wonder why we've come down there. His smile slips when he sees the size of my knife, which is even larger than my smile. Suddenly, I'm not as small as I was up there in the sunshine, especially carrying a hooked rigging knife with the dimensions and impact of a thresher's tail. I learned some time back that, down here, around the decay of the Pacific jetsam, a sailor's knife with a marlin spike makes a stronger impression than any gun.

Footsteps clomp across the slats above us, and I see Laser Bob peering down through the wide cracks. He blinks slow, pretending our eyes don't lock. He's chewing on a sprig of something, and now he's chewing faster. There's always something doing laps around his lips these days, one of the tell-tale signs of a captain who misses his boat.

I back the man against a pillar, my knife at his neck before he fully comprehends the situation. He's real tall, so I climb him like a tree, and I flick the blade against the corners of his lips. People think you struggle when you're afraid, but I've learned that it's just the opposite. Orange cat energy now gone, he's frozen like cold concrete as I tenderly brush the sand from his face. He barely blinks at the sudden "Arf! Arf! Arf!" of the sea lions above us. I always time things so Laser Bob is just starting to feed them, something that is against the law but impossible to discourage. The tourists feed the sea lions everything. The fish, too. And if they're drunk enough, it's that same skate that becomes their accidental offering. Pier 39: a cornucopia of thrice-digested leftovers and skate-on-skate violence.

The barking is deafening now, plenty loud enough to muffle a scream, but I don't cut deep. Not at first. I cut just enough to change the expression for good. And I always explain that I totally understand what they're going through.

It's not easy to force a smile when everything inside you says otherwise.

But with a little work, it's not impossible.

I sit on the edge of a boat that resembles a child's daydream doodle come to life, my feet dangling next to Laser Bob's as we share the last hits of his roach. The sharp edges of my mouth can finally soften as he tells me again how panhandlers ruined his business.

"But it was a mutual deception," he says. "People go through the motions and give us money, no matter the lie. Everyone plays the game. But up to a point."

I reflexively nod in agreement. Bob seems the wisest at the end of my workdays.

"Nowadays it's even worse," he goes on. "Now the panhandlers' signs have to say 'Not Gonna Lie, I Need Weed!' just to get food. Or they'll give you a business card that says 'Turn Over' on both sides and hope for a laugh to loosen up the wallet. But isn't that one lie too many?"

I take a draw and shrug, watching my fingers down the end of my nose for any sign of the shakes. And as we smoke, he explains that his teenage fantasy of a boat was always shaped like a shark, with the same disposition, but being docked so long isn't what killed it. He says it died the day the Wake Zone declared no one could go over 10 knots ever again. He adjusted his pants just thinking about the speeds he was capable of, and I'm reminded of the bulge in my jeans where my rigging knife is curled up, asleep.

"Seventy feet long, twin twenty-five hundred horsepower jets, speeds of up to eighty *smiles* an hour," he laughs. "It exists only to part Neptune's hair. Or stitch the Red Sea back together."

I'm never sure what he means, but for a man who used to get paid top dollar to pilot a craft that's 70 feet long and 2,500 horsepower, Bob has as many holes in his story as in his watchpockets. Once, he tried to convince me to move to Kentucky with him, his place of birth, to hone the skills we'd acquired out West.

"No disgrace going home," he'd said to me. "Everyone should move away from the water for a while. Or toward it."

"You could always take the water with you," I would remind him, and he would give me a smile that he never wasted on the tourists. A real one.

Back at the dock, I flick the roach into the sand and slap my legs to stand back up.

"It's true, we have to make progress," he says to me, hoping I'll stay a little longer. "We do have to keep moving, even if it's in a circle."

I laugh, and I throw him a smile for free. I try to keep exactly as many smiles as stickers, so there's always a couple extra at the end of the day.

He puts his head down, pouting a little, and I look him over, thinking back to when he first introduced himself as "Winnebago Walt," sputtering past me on the pier in his newly renovated food truck, adorned with FULL-TILT TACOS . . . on every side. His angle was to sell tacos from a truck that "Will Never Stop!"—tossing them out the window at people running to keep pace as they fumble for change. Unsurprisingly, it lasted half as long as the Laser Boat. Born and raised in Bullitt County, Kentucky (which explained the overalls), Bob always seemed a little out of step with California. "Did some time," he admitted once, snapping his denim straps with his thumbs. "Was a volunteer fireman for a bit, too, the only beast I ever rode where I made money!"

I wonder what he'll call himself when he switches vehicles again, and I decide that whatever his new identity, it will be closely aligned with the top speed of something. But I understand him more than I understand myself, and I'm envious of his life most days. To have such a clear reminder of failure bobbing in the water next to him.

Imagine the comfort in that.

He lights another roach from the gutter stash of his front overalls pocket, and he studies the embers.

"All that talk of a 'gateway drug,'" he says, laughing. "A real gateway isn't a drug at all. It's just a door in the floor, something that makes you take chances. You know what's a real gateway drug?"

"What's that?" I ask, cracking my back, itching to get back to work. I've heard all this before, but you're in it together when you're treading water on the coast, earning nothing tangible for your labor, but doing a job that's no less important. As if it's any answer, Bob plucks a horsemint blossom from a crack in the bow and thoughtfully chews a petal. He swears the weeds will pry his boat apart one day, and he explains to me that he's doing his part to chew back the inevitable. Sometimes I imagine teaming up with Bob and all of his amazing rides and slapping a siren on the windscreen as we zip through towns and chase down frowns and ruin everyone's day who makes the mistake of buying a ticket.

"Edible flowers," he says, taking another nip. "Now, that is a gateway drug. Much more dangerous than weed. Just popping a flower in your mouth and eating it? What's next? Kids eating each other?"

"Except the flower you ate was not edible, Bob," I say, but for some reason, he can't hear me. My legs tense for the jump back onto the dock when we drift close enough. Soon I'll head for another street corner, where men will cross against the light without thinking, eyes glued to a gorgeous but unreachable horizon, never noticing me until it's too late.

I'm running out of time to find them all.

Maybe tonight I'll grab a paintbrush and help Bob touch up his flames. And we'll finish just in time to begin painting the sun-faded scribbles on the opposite side of the boat all over again. And although this fire may never be finished, he'll never allow the colors to wane completely. I'll stay up all night, just like the night before. It'll look like a party, but it's more like work. And then tomorrow, I'll start my job early, toiling to remind the world that, just like a shark, we die when we're dreaming, and we smile without meaning.

CHAPTER XV

WRECKLESS EYEBALLING

Move away from her," Angie said. "She's just trying to freak us out."

Lund was huddled against the side of the pool, eyes on Beth, scared to let her close. He had that look Angie had seen in their pool before, an expression on his face that marked him as "next," and Angie was trying to keep him talking so others wouldn't focus too much on his outburst.

"Look at me. What's your name again?"

"Show us your hand!" Lund yelled at Beth again. Not quite smiling, she put her hands behind her back, watching him closely.

"There's nothing on her hand, Lund. I've seen her hands."

"Keep her away from me," he said. "She's a fucking serial killer. And she's friends with—"

"Look at her eyes," Angie said. "That crazy bint is somewhere else entirely, eating flowers, running with the rabbits . . . eyes and ears on me, Lund! What's your real name?"

"My name? 'Lund,' like the city in Sweden, means 'grove' . . ."

"So your name is 'Grove,' huh?" Angie asked. "That is very interesting. Did I ever tell you my other names?"

"No, no, not 'Grove.' The name 'Lund' is short for 'Lundegaard,'" he said, and Angie's heart hiccupped, as the mercury vapor swirling in the fluorescent tubes buried in the deepest recesses of her brain struggled to flicker on in recognition. She sank back into the water to stew on the memories that were bubbling up.

Had Angie known someone named "Guard" when she was a child, back at a crucial point in her life, between the bees and the prison? The word *guard* had always stuck with her, mostly due to her brother's fateful final occupation. But she didn't pay much attention to names back then, as she was too busy changing her own. And only the boys seemed to develop that *X-Files* last-name fetish that might have helped the memory stick. The possibility that *guard* had been a piece of Lundegaard—that someone could drop the engine instead of the caboose when it came to their name—had never occurred to her. Until now.

But this couldn't be the same person. The New New Kid was a formative moment, but she found it impossible to pull up a face from those memory banks. She hadn't given Lund much thought at all when he'd started orbiting her circle of U of L friends tonight. This pool party was the most she'd ever seen of him, but, admittedly, it had been a lot. Enough for a lifetime.

She squinted to look Lund over as best she could, but it was a lost cause. Just as it had highlighted their failings, the water had also smoothed their features. Trapped on the back of a fire truck with these quantifiable but interchangeable assholes, Angie wouldn't be able to pick half of them out of a lineup after tonight. They'd all been blended into the same pale, wrinkled, gelatinous globule, jouncing around the endless back roads of Kentucky until they became the soft, rounded corners of the same worthless blob.

"I can't believe you don't remember me," Lund said, pressing in, his hand like soggy Wonder Bread on her shoulder. But as he said this, Angie thought her heart had stalled. She coughed to get it going again, looking around for help, but most everyone was paired off and melted together, just as every party game predicted. Intense conversations with people they wouldn't have deigned to make small talk with out in the world. And she understood the instinct completely.

She slid closer to him. *Why not?* They were all in the same boat now, so to speak.

"Maybe I do remember you?" Angie said, a memory still on the tip of her brain. "Help me out. Honestly, I thought your name was short for 'London.' City names *are* the new hotness these days. 'Sydney,' 'Orlando,' 'Brooke Lynne,' that one's my favorite . . ."

"'Truth or Consequences, New Mexico' . . ." He smiled, spinning a bottle in the water next to his knee. Dollar bills radiated away from the bottle as it twirled, most of them white, the last of Gaddy's ink bled out.

"Slow down there, Orlando. We vetoed that Truth or Dare."

"It always just turns into 'truth' anyway," he said, sadly. "No one picks 'dare,' therefore, no consequences." Angie took the bottle from the water and pointed the brown snout at his face.

"Okay, then. Truth."

"I'm not doing that," he said. He grabbed the bottle back and held it to his ear like a phone.

"Almighty, Almighty, I'm calling in an airstrike on our current location . . . Ow!" Angie smacked the bottle away.

"You have to play," she said, eyes begging Lund to understand what was at stake. "Look around you. Look what can happen. Remember Janky? He was bad at the game, but you can keep it short."

"What game?"

"Don't you get it? You have to give them a story."

"I don't have any. You tell one."

But Angie's life wasn't on the line. Even if it was, Angie didn't really have a story to tell. It was Nahla who'd had all the adventures.

"But you're over here trying to tell me one right now, Lund."

"That story is about us. It's only for you."

"Listen to what I'm saying, Lund. Tell a story right now or they will kill you."

He glanced around the pool and got a couple "Don't fuckin' look at me!" from the corners. He turned back to Angie.

"Seriously, dude, who are you, exactly?" she said. "I'm dying to hear."

"I thought you said I was the one who was dying."

"Yes."

"So are you really trying to tell me that, to save my life, I need to tell a story . . ." Lund paused to savor the joke. "That says something about my *character*?"

"Absolutely." Now he was getting it, even if she wasn't sure what that was.

"Okay," Lund said, snorting at the fun, *meta* nature of it all, and maybe understanding the implications of the inability to entertain a mob. He cleared his throat, and Angie got as comfortable as she could in the cold water, and Lund began to tell her a story about the road, which was their bloodline now, as unknowable as the families they'd left behind.

"Angie, have I ever told you about our mother?"

"Our mother was the one who ruined Christmas for everybody. There wasn't much work in our hometown, unless you had a job at the prison, or boiling down the dead hives for the beeswax. So our mother thought 'outside of the cell,' and she came up with this idea. What if you could dial a license plate number and talk to any car on the highway."

Lund's voice was strong; evidently he had a story to tell after all. But the delivery was . . . off. Like everyone knew his story didn't really count, and Lund did, too. The fire truck took a slow turn into an area so desolate, Angie felt like they'd been dipped in an inkwell. But this also helped his story, too. Too dark to see each other, his confidence was growing by the second. Already, his narrative was impossible as the rest of theirs, but this one was starting out with a little something extra; details from Angie's life. So far, it was nothing too personal, nothing that wasn't common knowledge among her friends and colleagues. But his story had miles to go.

"You see, as long as you could read a license plate, you could punch in that combination of letters and numbers on your phone and be instantly connected to another driver. Actually, it was more like calling the car itself rather than a living, breathing person, which made you even more likely to do it. Also, making this a match made in Heaven, was the fact that most phone numbers and license plates had seven characters. Our mother claimed to have gotten this idea from the orientation video at her new job for the Kentucky License Bureau, an exaggerated history of licenses that mostly talked about that antiquated time before there were so many cars on the road, when an identification tag was just a short series of letters, or a word that could be easily remembered. She worked at the DMV for a total of forty-eight hours, the longest she'd ever remained employed, and, coincidentally, the average length of time between violent, gun-related, road-rage encounters in North America. Other mothers couldn't hold a job, either, but at least she held my dad captive with her crazy schemes . . ."

"Real quick, why are you saying 'our mother' but 'my dad'?" Angie asked him. "I mean, if you're going to do it, do it. It's bad enough you pull this crap on me this late in the game, claiming to be my long-lost . . . whatever. Keep going, but watch yourself, Orlando."

"I'm sorry. It's just this habit. I say 'our mother' because my mother had kids with several men before she married my dad, I mean your dad. I mean our dad."

"Rollin' those dice, huh," Angie said, laughing in spite of herself.

"Anyhow, back to the plates," he said. "'I've got it!' she declared. 'License plates equal . . . phone numbers!' Ecstatic, our mother shouted out her new formula, first to the mostly forgotten but still smug *Beverly Hills 90210* actor on the dusty screen of the VCR/TV combo in the License Bureau break room, then to whoever came in to grab a free cheese sandwich from the fridge, then to my dad—who was as supportive as he could be, as always. Then to anyone else who would listen. She tried to get through the next two days of DMV training without dwelling on her idea, but found this to be impossible. Her brain was a monsoon. This was the way back, you see? As you'll recall, our hometown was full of crazy conspiring after all the scary stuff that went down with the prison and the phone calls. And then the fire. I'm sure you remember all of it. But phones had already been weaponized once, in a way, so that was still on everyone's mind. But consider the possibilities . . ."

Outside, Angie was smiling, but he couldn't see it. Inside, Angie was screaming, and he could feel it. Prison stories were probably fair game, considering their situation, a logical outlet of a confined imagination. And she'd been talking about incarceration for most of her academic life. And, of course, she'd encouraged all of this just moments before. But it still seemed out of bounds. She knew where he was going with this, and Angie hadn't had a *real* conversation about her dead brother in years. Maybe a couple times with Dan, maybe once with Jill. But with private prisons everywhere now, and with phones as thin as Communion wafers, her anomalous family history just didn't seem so off-limits anymore. So she let him keep going. For now.

". . . most cars already had names, our mother realized. Phones, too. She realized that this was why old vehicles in movies were in such pristine condition, since you were more likely to take care of something with a name instead of a number. Maybe even give it an affectionate pat on the hood, maybe tell them damn kids to stop throwing their football over it, or maybe even stop to wipe off a patch of bird poop with your own hand? Take this vehicle we're trapped on right now. I have no doubt it has a name. That's the reason it has lasted as long as it has. And that's why it will outlast us."

Angie felt the temperature change in the water around her as some of them squeezed in to hear Lund's surprisingly engaging turn at the microphone. It was still dark as a dungeon, but she could make out the shadows of heads nodding along with his narrative.

"Actually, this vehicle does have a name," Angie said. "It's . . . 'Friar Tuck,'" It made her queasy to say it out loud, but even queasier hearing it.

"Of course it is!" Lund laughed until he coughed. "Perfect. Well, we didn't have the heart to tell our mother the only reason cars and fire trucks are so shiny in the movies is because they aren't real. They're toys, lining streets no bigger than a sandbox. Or worse, computer-generated facsimiles of toys. Virtual or physical playthings, all piled under the Christmas tree. But that was a Frisbee we were tossing around those fancy cars, not a football, and every real car ends up rusted out anyway, in lonely garages or abandoned car washes, no matter what name it was given. But toys can look big enough from the right angle, right? Just like these streetlights. Just like the priests who laid the first delicious little Frisbees on their tongues. But our mother never understood a forced perspective when it wasn't her own. She told us once how she stole a whole bag of Communion wafers, and when she got busted, she piled them on a plate for Santa on Christmas Eve, next to a tall glass of milk for him to drink with his penis. Just kidding!"

Angie slapped Lund across the face, hard.

"Focus," she said.

"Sorry. Okay, yeah, so, that's right around when she started trying to call Santa on the phone, accusing anyone who answered of a vast conspiracy! And that was on a rotary phone, too, and, as you know, the bigger and the more awkward the technology, the more the commitment to the conversation."

Angie took a deep breath, hoping his story maintained coherence. She felt slightly more heat in the water and knew that others were listening now, maybe more intrigued by her slap. But Lund was so low on the social totem pole, the blow may not have registered at all.

"But despite the collective urge to spin such a complicated lie as the concept of a 'Santa Claus' during children's formative years, our mother decided to make connections other people would never consider. And she was convinced her new idea would catch on fast, just like that crazy text messaging the kids started doing. And some Silicon Valley start-ups agreed she was onto something. Hell, they'd helped NORAD modify their Santa Sleigh Tracker, which, before their upgrades, had caused Kris Kringle to be mistaken for a Russian first strike on at least five nail-biting occasions by almost a half dozen of our dim-bulb presidents."

"Hey, 'Rock the Vote,'" Angie snorted.

"More like 'Rock the Boat.'"

"Yikes. Don't hurt yourself, Lund," she said. "So you were saying . . ."

"So it turns out, our mother's license plate idea was a huge mistake. As we now know, not only did it cause every driver's terrible instincts to surface, but it gave a convenient voice to everyone's worst urges. People quickly realized that the only reason highways weren't piled to the sky with road-rage wreckage was because anger for every perceived insult— cutting people off, driving too slow, driving too fast, just driving too *wrong*, etc.—could sometimes be quenched with a harmless glare or even a reasonably obscene gesture from the relative safety of another rolling shark cage, a threat that increased exponentially depending on one driver's perception of weakness, or 'baby on board' signs, or truck nuts, or that maddening new-car smell still perceptible from three car lengths away—the exact distance recommended to avoid tailgating, by the way. So except for the off chance that two hearing-impaired drivers would have a clash on the turnpike and start throwing page after page of hand signs and shadow animals out their windows, drivers normally had no voice for their frustrations. Just a fast 'Fuck you!' followed by the only logical response, 'Fuck you, too!' Message sent. Message received. But dialing the license plate in front of you, and instantly getting that car on the phone, that changed all of this. And hindsight is twenty-twenty, but they never ever should have debuted it during the holidays, when traffic and people were at a mental rock bottom, everybody trapped in gridlock, late for parties . . ."

Or trapped at parties.

Angie's shoulder was close enough to be pressing against Lund's arm, whisking off his meager body heat. But he wasn't shivering. It was almost like he was refueling his core temperature from the attention. She could tell this was a new position for him, fortitude soaring after first securing Beth's attention, then her own, and now even the group's, and she took advantage of his steadying heart rate as a temporary but not-insignificant source of warmth.

"Regardless of these obvious dangers, our mother's brainchild was greenlit, fast-tracked, and went national on Christmas Eve. Okay, maybe not quite coast-to-coast, but there was a big push, mostly due to a couple of those nakedly ambitious tech bros who—inspired by Hubris, a hugely popular ride-sharing app that accidentally turned the average Joe from a taxi driver into an unsanctioned rapist— worked night and day with our mother to achieve their lofty goal of connecting every single stranger on the road. Beginning with our town. That proverbial canary in a coal mine. Or the bee in the birthday cake? In any case, road-rage incidents multiplied by the thousands. But she was unflappable, claiming all of these incidents were just growing pains on the way to taking back the highways, opening lines of communication, a disarmament pact for angry travelers everywhere, breaking a few omelets to make some eggs . . ."

"That's not a thing."

". . . what you have to consider—and what she already knew—was the popularity of her invention with women. On the surface, it seems like the highway is a playground for the stunted boys and their toys, but in reality it's the females who dominate the road. Just look around. As our mother explained, this was not wishful thinking, or a political statement. This is simple statistics. Hard numbers. Hidden figures. They're just so hard to see them because, even with their driver's seats high, they remain invisible. 'But this will change,' she told us, with that permanent wink. 'They'll all see.' Look around . . ."

"I can't see shit," someone said.

"She didn't make a whole lot of money, at least not at the end. But the beginning was a little more lucrative. At least it was enough freedom to divorce my dad, start seeing some other dads, maybe find a new brood, or ready-made family, one who was hardwired by tragedy, injury, or indifference to ignore the moral implications of the collateral damage she could cause."

"Oof. Metaphor much?"

"In the first twenty-four hours, the bodies started hitting the off-ramps. We thought she'd be more sensitive when it came to inciting road rage, especially after she'd been so horribly injured during a red-light engine-revving session so many years ago. But even though she hated motors almost as much as the sounds we kids made with our mouths to imitate them, she convinced us that what happened to her eye was a feature, not a bug. I mean, a bee. Needless to say, the rest of the population didn't have her special sort of tunnel vision, or, you could say, her *drive*."

"Nice," someone said.

"Keep going, I'm on the edge of my nuts," someone else urged.

"So after lots of hand-wringing, after the bullet-riddled and tire-iron dented pileups in the drainage ditches, after the fist fights in the virulent clouds of car exhaust that rolled and tumbled through the cat-tails along the sides of the roads, after the blood-in-oil Jackson Pollocks across the yellow lines and the twisted strips of chrome decorating every gas-reeking bush along the highway . . . a new law was passed. And fast. You could no longer talk on your phone while driving—let alone call another car. 'Madness!' we all said, already missing the danger, but this law was quickly hustled through other state legislatures, too, the assumption being that phones had always been a dangerous distrac-tion behind the wheel, like driving while air drumming, thumb wres-tling, slug buggin', slapjackin', you name it. Even now, very few people knew the real reason for this law, fewer than the number of fools who still believed Santa Claus could really navigate holiday traffic without the help of NORAD. Seriously, you know why you can't talk on your phone while driving? Because of our fatherfuckin' mother. Because a phone was more a weapon than a tool during one particular winter in our hometown. Remember, Angie?"

Angie tried, but shook her head; her hometown was as blurry as the start of this day.

Except for the fire. Tonight, memories of the fire were coming back. She wondered if that's how Lund's story would finally end.

"So watch out!" Lund said, fingers wiggling, trying to be spooky. "If a cop sees you flipping open your cell Captain Kirk–style, you might find yourself in a quick-draw situation with Officer O'Malley. Bring that phone up to your head a little too fast? You could be tackled to thwart a suicide attempt. But who are we kidding? Today, cop will probably shoot you, then write it up as 'Seasonal Defective Disorder' pending 'retraining.' Didn't you know? Christmas is hard on cops. And for good reason; people on the streets today are pushing for even fewer restric-tions. Talk of the bans on tinted windows being repealed, incentives for stereo installations with the largest subwoofers, contests to award the most suction-cup teddy bears clinging to their windshields . . . anything to distract drivers from locking eyes at dangerous speeds and reaching for their godforsaken phones, anything to encourage fuzzier, happier thoughts on the road."

Almost on cue, a quick succession of streetlights illuminated the crowd. Hopefully, in time for the encore.

"He's funny lookin', but he's right," Dan said, almost convincingly. "I heard they were bringing back *Pimp My Ride*! And The Players Ball was simulcast live during Louisville's last town hall meeting. Our local church even endorsed Pimp Nation's blanket policy of 'no reckless eye-balling' because it could 'save a life, starting with yours'!"

"I heard pimps call their tricks 'Elves on the Shelves'?" Reeves offered.

"Watch it," Dan said. "This is no joke. Sure, car-on-car violence might never be as serious as putting our mother under 'pimp arrest,' but any punishment fits any crime if you're reading them off the Twelve Commandments on our courthouse lawn."

"What do you mean 'our mother'? You're not from my hometown, Dan," Angie said.

"They're there! Carved right in front of the double doors. Or maybe they *are* the doors. 'The Lord did decree, "Thou shall leer at thine feet, thine hands, or thine road at all times. Thou shall not make eye contact with trick-ass marks unless thine chariot approacheth. And thou shan't make eye contact with any pimp, under any circumstances . . ."'"

"Funny."

"'. . . something something thou shall not pull thine door, thou shall push?'"

"Okay, okay," Angie said, not wanting Lund to lose control of his monologue. She was torn between curtailing the mocking or letting any participation go on as long as possible, but Lund tapped his invisible mic and jumped back in.

"It's all true!" Lund said, voice booming like a kid who wanted to be a preacher but became a used-car salesman when he grew up. "Despite her pariah status, our mother had all Twenty-Five Commandments stamped on her business card, long before, and after, local governments permanently adopted them! And, even just yesterday, they were still calling our DMV the 'DMZ'! And in our high school's driver's educa-tion classes, you'll still hear statistics proving you're just as likely to have your eyes enucleated by car keys clenched in someone's fist as you are to be struck by lightning! Something that happens constantly when you're in a car! Only we can't feel it. The lightning, I mean. One of the benefits of being electrically grounded by rubber tires, which, as it turns out, is *almost* as beneficial to our upbringing as being grounded by our mother. But the silver lining they don't mention when you receive your license is that a human eye hanging from the optic nerve actually makes the perfect, wonderfully expressive souvenir for any vehicle, as long as it retains ciliary muscles around the cornea, of course. It can hang from your key chain just like that tiny personalized license plate, or hang from your rearview mirror like your fuzzy dice. Some religions maintain that memories are stored in the iris rather than the brain. And some people believe that taking a Christmas cookie is tantamount to taking Communion, but who are we to play favorites? Believe in what you want, right? Satan, Satin, Santana before Rob Thomas . . . because here's the deal, kids, as horrific as our mother's injury might seem, it brought us all closer together. We aim better with one eye. Ask any sniper. Or . . ."

"Or you could end this story?" someone suggested.

"Oh, this is still going on?" Another sigh.

But even as Lund veered further into fantasy, Angie respected the mythmaking on display, as any effort to entertain now mattered more than truth.

"One more thing," Lund said. "Scientists originally thought the human head sent signals to the body for up to five minutes after detachment. But it turned out an eyeball from our mother's skull can and will report back to the brain for years. So getting one plucked out during a roadside assault is the ultimate handshake. More than a handshake, actually. More like the hazy final impression of a life lingering in the liminal classroom of the best *pupil*. And for anyone carrying a key chain like our mother's, it's a grim but life-affirming reminder that you've been through it before. Like the fake testicles a female squid flashes so the males leave them the fuck alone. Like those eyes on the backs of caterpillars that trick birds into thinking they're snakes. Like the reindeer's nose that glows as red as a taillight if a perfectly preserved Frankenstein bumper on a '69 Caprice punches that baby just right. Because too hard and his nose blinks out forever, right along with that eyeball. But too soft and no one learns anything . . ."

Another streetlight drifted across his own pleading eyes, and Angie felt a sudden wave of sadness. They both seemed to understand that this story was sounding more like an Oscar speech after the orchestra cut it off, like a rambling Dutch Shultz drowning in his imaginary bean soup as death loomed. Another light burned past them, and Angie thought Lund's face was finding more streetlights than usual, as if they were just for him, another indicator that he was *next*, for whatever fate awaited them all. But in that moment, he did feel like a long-lost brother, or maybe just lost. But he was someone she could finally mourn, and she decided she would finally let him go if necessary. Even if that meant letting him go over the rail.

"Did you know that our mother tried to pitch her original idea to another phone company! It was the next town over, I think—some backward burg where they shoot traffic lights to make them change . . ." Lund said, faster and faster. In his desperation, he'd morphed into an auctioneer racing that final mallet. ". . . and for a hot minute, she was pretty sure they were gonna go for it! But without enough license-plate combos to work with, it simply got too convoluted. Kinda like this story. But new forms of communication are traditionally revered! Everyone knows this. But if calling the right number could be dangerous, then calling the *wrong* number would be fatal for both drivers, no matter how much road was between us. She could not, in good conscience, play matchmaker to humanity forever! But she did continue to sell her key chains for some time after that, sending lost eyes on adventures. They were great stocking stuffers, she would explain, and she made a little more money than the honeycomb jewelry and beeswax candles she'd cobble together from dead hives. And there were always plenty of eyeballs to harvest on the sides of the roads during the holidays, when everyone looks at everyone all wrong, when everyone sees themselves reflected in each other's anger, and when she saw herself reflected in the shiny change in their pockets. But she'd wink with her one good eye and remind us that when you see the lights on the horizon, those aren't motorcycles coming down the road. It's just every car in the world with one headlight out, a small price to pay to forever aim toward the future. And we believed her. Believed *in* her, you could say. Like Santa!"

"Take a bow!" Amy said, clapping a little too vigorously—as she was the only one doing it.

Lund gave a little "m'lady" flourish to show his appreciation as the fire truck took an uncharacteristically slow turn, and the light from a lingering streetlamp besieged by insects flashed the shadows of their winged assault across his face and neck. If he knew he was in trouble, he was hiding it well.

It suits him, Angie thought, before it went black again.

"Cool story, bro," Dan said. Most of them seemed unable to process his story, or unsure whether to even bother.

"Thanks?"

"But maybe don't pretend you're my brother?" Angie said. "Resorting to a twist that relies on genealogy is a narrative breakdown. It's also a bit of a sore spot."

"Not as sore as 'our' mother's eye," Jill laughed. "I mean, your mother."

"She's right. Have you been on Pornhub lately? Why does everyone have to be related?"

"Longest 'your mom' joke ever," Dan said.

"Did he say he didn't believe in *Santa Carla*?" Gaddy wanted to know. "Because I was totally there, and it's real."

"Does your mom really have only one eye?" Amy asked Angie. "That's not true, is it?"

"An eye for a thumb and a thumb for an eye," Angie mumbled.

"Is that an answer?"

"Yes, it's true!" Lund said. "At this point, it is true that everything is true."

He wasn't wrong. It wasn't important what anyone had done, or what they would do next. Eyes readjusting to the rural dark, Angie could tell by the slumping heads that final plans were being discussed. Amy and Jill were pressing up against her, and reluctantly she pushed away from their warm doubts and suspicions and stood in the wind again.

"Attention! How many of us are left?" she asked them all.

"I don't know," Dan said. "Seven? Six. No, seven. Why?"

"Do you remember what the vanity plate on this truck said? When we climbed aboard?"

When we climbed aboard, she thought. *A previous life!*

"Oh God," Amy said. "It was something terrifying, wasn't it?"

"No," Angie said. "But maybe it's a way out."

"Don't you mean a way 'off'?"

"How is it a way out?"

"Shhh," Angie said. "Okay, I'm pretty sure the plate said, 'BCUZ-789.'"

"So?"

"You know, like the old joke? 'Why is six afraid of seven . . .'" Silence. "'. . . because seven *ate* nine,'" she explained.

"I don't get it."

"Bullshit, it didn't say that."

"And now we're down to seven people," Angie went on. "See? Maybe this is what they wanted."

"Uh, actually it's nine people," Lund said.

"No, there's eight of us," Dan announced, counting all the heads he could see.

"That's what they want you to think," Angie scoffed.

"Who the fuck is 'they'?!" Amy cried.

"Maybe we just use our mother's idea and call the number on the plate," Lund said. "It's exactly seven digits?"

"Don't say 'our mother,' and you're forgetting three things," Angie said.

"What?"

"One, our phones are gone. Two, our phones are gone. And three . . . you get the picture."

"Oh, right."

"I thought every fire truck in the world was required by law to have a plate that says, 'RMBR-911,'" Jill said.

"Never forget!" Reeves was back, grabbing a drifting bottle and taking a swig of pool water. They hadn't noticed a full beer or whiskey bottle in quite some time. Suddenly inspired, Lund grabbed two empty beer cans from the water, shook them out, then handed one to Angie.

"We can still make a phone call," he said. "Go on over there, as far as you can, and put this over your ear. I know you remember . . ."

Lund put the empty can up to his mouth, but he didn't drink. Angie glanced at Jill and Amy, slightly embarrassed, then placed the opening of her beer can up against her head.

"You look exactly the same, Nahla," Lund whispered into his hole, twenty feet away, and Angie heard her real name spoken out loud for the first time in decades, clear as a bell, clearer than Hell, even with the cold wind howling around the aluminum like the midnight surf in a seashell.

* * *

When the cold first threatened to overwhelm the party, they made an important discovery. No body *really* had to shiver. The main thing they learned about shivering was this: You could stop doing it at any time. All their lives, they'd been told that your body needed to shiver to warm you back up. But all it really did was remind them of their misery. Once they forced themselves to stop doing it, they adjusted to their plight that much quicker. And with the water level so unpredictable, being submerged became the most immediate remedy to their suffering. So they learned to adapt to this as well, flattening their bodies on the turns to find the deepest patches at any given time to press their chests and bellies under. Angie, who still shivered regularly when she lost concentration, watched them flounder from the shallow ends to the deep ends, picturing tadpoles desperate to stay below the safety of the surface tension as sunlight devoured their puddles after the storm.

Lund was slithering on his back toward the deepest corner when Angie accosted him, tenderizing his gut with a barrage of punches.

"Tell me right now," she demanded. "You tell me where you heard that name!"

"From you! Calm down," Lund said. "That's why I applied here. Because Mom said you moved to Kentucky. She's doing well, by the way. Sort of a mess, but at least that prison is gone. Remember the fire?"

"Knock that shit off," she said, hauling back her fist at the mention of the fire, then hesitating.

Lund was sloshing in circles around her, nervous but cogent, more aware than the others, who'd slipped into a sort of accepting catatonia as they slid around the pool. Angie had to resist a sudden urge to reach out and gingerly touch his face. So she knocked him upside the head instead. One side, then the other.

"Hey!"

"You're not him," she said. "Not just because I count two ears on you, dude."

"You told me all about that kid, remember? He was one new kid before me. And the soupcan telephones our neighbors tried to rig up?"

"I didn't tell anyone about that. Not tonight, anyway."

"How would you know?"

Angie had no answer to that. "So you're my brother, too? Thanks, I hate it."

"More like a half-brother."

"Do you want to die, Lund?"

"Angie, listen, I'm the New Kid! I mean, the *New* New Kid, at any rate."

Angie had a hard time believing any of this, and she wondered if there had been a third new kid, back in those prison days. Either way, judging by the impressive detail of his rambling fable, he'd clearly rehearsed this moment. And, for now, anyway, maybe it was all confusing enough to keep him alive. Another streetlight flash revealed nearby skirmishes, and she saw Dan and a snookered, noodle-limbed Reeves huddling together, roughhousing as Reeves tried to get Dan to acknowledge one of his elusive "doors" on the bottom of the pool. Beth, Jill, and Gaddy were grappling with something, too. Everyone was shoving, slapping, accusing. Amy, however, was alone. And Godzooky was standing in the hot tub, affectionately running his thick hand along the inside seams of the fire truck's trailer.

Then they were back in the dark again. Then the light. Then the dark. Angie felt safer without the streetlights. And as she sat in the water she'd adapted to, she wondered if a soup can could really contact her dead brother.

Will the real New New Kid, please stand up . . . please stand up . . . she sang in her head.

"To be honest, I used to prank-call you all the time," Lund said, sheepish, next to her again. "My dad had our mom's number, but it was her real number, from before."

"What number?"

"Do you remember when you made me do that? Call everyone with that big phone?"

"That wasn't me," she said, eyes pinched as if it mattered. "That wasn't us."

Suddenly, Angie was upended onto her back as Reeves muscled up between them.

"You ready?" Reeves asked them, but he was nose to nose with Lund.

The truck was slowing.

Alarmed, Angie moved back toward Lund when a new kind of light flashed over them all. It was low, vibrating, alive. A motorcycle, by the sound of it, pulling a U-turn in front of them. Or maybe it was just a beater with one busted headlight. Whatever it was, its wobbly gaze "tharned" them all, but it finally gave Angie the perfect snapshot of Lund that her mind's eye could map onto her slippery memories. Lund was a chubby kid, and would look young all his life, with that white-blond hair you see in the background of country-music videos. And with his sallow skin, and the wet T-shirt clinging to it, he was white on white on white. "Toe-headed," he'd say to every mirror. Not "tow-headed," which referred to the color of flax or wool or whatever you'd stuff into your teddy bears to keep them alive. "Toe-headed," he'd insist, because "I look like a toe!" Angie thought about her own moth-eaten childhood toys, hanging by a thread onto their turn in the rotation, stuffed and restuffed with whatever garbage was handy. She guessed Lund reminded her of that, too. There was something in those doomed eyes after all.

Maybe he *was* the boy she knew a long time ago. Or all of them.

Sometimes, Angie resented the lack of scrutiny little kids gave each other. *Everyone* didn't deserve friendship, right? But stuck on a fire truck, hellbent for nowhere, it was tough to maintain such hierarchies. She used to laugh at people who resigned themselves to "loving some-one like a brother" when "the friend zone" seemed too cruel. But after her brother was killed, this became an impossible dream. So why not him?

Angie took one of Reeves's arms in her hands and pulled him away. His skin felt weirdly dry, like sandpaper, and she recoiled.

"Just hold on right there," Reeves said, almost lucid, but still on a delay. "He made you call whoooooooo?" The last word got stuck on the bug strip of his alcohol-soaked tongue again, and he grabbed Lund and spun him around by the collarbone, his wet Outpost 31 shirt snapping like balloon skin. Reeves pointed to a space just beyond his head. "Are you behind this? Or are you?" Lund laughed nervously as he squatted down to try and wriggle free of Reeves's wavering grip, newfound con-fidence long gone.

"Th-th-th-th-th-this is nuts," he said, and Angie noticed with dis-may that Lund's stutter had returned. Or maybe he'd just forgotten to stop shivering. "I knew her when we were kids, that's all."

"Leave him alone," Angie said without conviction, persuasive abili-ties drained, but Reeves backed off anyway. Then he flopped onto his washboard abs with an impossibly loud *thwack!* They were passing under a string of empty but illuminated billboards, and it felt safe to try and help Reeves up. But when Angie looked down at his face, she froze.

There was something happening to his eyes.

As she watched, they changed from gray to black to blue. She rubbed her own, which only made his head flash blood-red, then spin and throw sparks like Catherine wheels. She shook off this vision. Then Reeves sat up, eyes blinking back to blue, then black, then gray again. He stared past her, fully engaged with something unseen. He swatted the air and scraped at nothing on his shoulders, then more nothings off his elbows. His scratching sped up as he worked his way down his body, past his skinned knees, past the torn athletic shorts that clung to his thighs like electrical tape.

"Knock! Knock!" he yelled from the center of the pool, then spasmed away to a corner, swimming as if chased.

"Reeves! Hey, hey . . ." Angie was reaching for him. Dan, Jill, and Amy gathered around.

"Rip grom on da switchfoot, ya gurfer!" Reeves screamed nonsensically between gulps.

"Anyone got that Martian dictionary?" Dan asked, backing up.

"Knock! Knock!" Reeves shouted again as he swam through Jill's legs. The lack of a response infuriated him, and he curled up like a lobster in the pot and began thrashing out frantic sit-ups until the water was a cyclone around him.

"Knock! Knock!"

"Nobody answer that maniac," Amy said.

"Knock knock knock knock knock knock knock . . ."

"Who's there!" Lund could never resist it. He was also excited about his apparent reprieve.

"My time!" Reeves said.

"'My time' who?" Angie shrugged.

Reeves tilted back his head, soaking in the last of the blank billboards' glow, then he flicked a thumb under his chin, tongue clucking to imitate the click of his imaginary flashlight, mouth wide and as uninviting as a lantern shark's underbite.

They all saw the flashlight's beam.

"My time to shine!"

CHAPTER XVI

A PRAYER FOR
THE SURFER BOYS

Reeves's Story

I thought it would be funny to walk the beach with a door under my arm. I was home from school and had a whole summer to kill, so I decided to hit the water and wait for a surfer to harass me, maybe record it all on my phone or something, and this would finally out these punks for what they really were: a buncha entitled trust-fund babies who were way too old for this shit. Way too old to claim a section of beach as their own and needle any and all comers to make outsiders never want to surf or swim there again. Way too old to be posting videos of themselves on TikTok, messing with the wildlife.

And absolutely *waaaaay* too old to be dressed like sharks while doing it.

"We'll burn you every single wave," the first shark muttered, shuffling past me and aiming his surfboard at my face like a weapon.

"Nice day, isn't it!" I shouted, stabbing the base of my door into the sand and leaning on it to catch my breath. It wasn't the heaviest door in the world, but it wasn't easy to trudge up and down the shore with it, either. The door was essential for my joke, though. My brother had given it to me, scrap lumber from his side gig building houses for Habitat for Humanity, where they were currently tearing down an old apartment building just so they could hammer it right back up again. This beautiful door didn't match the newer, cheapjack doors they were installing, so my brother figured it wouldn't be missed. It was old-school, too. Rich mahogany, speakeasy-style, capped off with a knocker and a big, gold doorknob like a brass Big Mac. The previous owner had disfigured it by drilling a peephole, but the rest was cherry.

"The day will be a lot nicer when you're gone!" another shark said without looking over. The shark trailing him paused to spit at my feet.

Now, when I say "shark," I mean the online rumors were true. These were grown-ass men in black wetsuits with big dorsal fins jutting out of the middle of their backs. I wasn't sure if the wetsuits came like that, or if it was some next-level San Jose Sharks hockey gear, or if their long-suffering mothers had sewn them on before cutting off their crusts and packing their lunch. But I hoped to get close enough to touch a fin before the day was out. And everything was going as planned so far—buncha sharks fucking with me right on schedule! But I was a little confused by the rivalry. They were scoffing at me like I was really going surfing with them. Like I wasn't carrying a goddamn door.

Another shark stomped past, flipping a foot full of sand my way, followed by another shark throwing me a half-hearted raspberry. The next shark ignored me completely. Worried they were losing interest, I tried another tactic.

"Hey! Got a joke for you," I said, and the nearest shark whirled around, almost catching me in the chest with the skeg of his board. "What's the difference between a pizza and a surfer?" I asked. He just blinked.

"A surfer can't feed a family of five." No reaction. "Unless they're a family of sharks!" I added. Still nada, but there were plenty more where they came from, these walking, talking Dr. Moreau hybrids. So, inspired, I stepped back behind my beautiful door and rested my ear against the wood.

"Okay, here's a good one," I said. "Knock! Knock!"

I rapped the gold ring on the door as I worked to keep it balanced in the sand. "Who's there?" I answered myself, knowing they probably wouldn't.

"'To!'" I just kept going. Then a voice came from the other side of my door as a shark finally took the bait.

"'To' who?"

"To *whom*," I corrected, and the shark yanked open my door and rightfully punched me in the face.

* * *

I'd first learned about "localism" after the internet-famous incident involving my brother. The term referred to the escalating turf wars where local surfers would vandalize your vehicle, whip starfish or sand dollars at your head, or simply threaten to beat your ass for even setting foot on their precious beach.

At the time, my brother was down in Palos Verdes working environmental cleanup for the city. He was a good guy but a sucker for seedy beachfront life, fascinated by the deceptively biblical nature of a homeless population near the ocean, all those sandals mixed with surf, right? This was a plight I accused him of never acknowledging in the city.

Even though the surfers fought so hard for the area, they didn't think twice about leaving bottles and half-smoked Swisher Sweets everywhere. My brother told me that in surfer slang, *pollution* referred to interlopers trying to drop in on their waves. Always ready to give people the benefit of the doubt, he wondered if they had simply lost all concept of pollution after they'd hijacked the word, and I'd say, "No, bro, they're just dirtbags."

The day of the big drama, he'd been following up a report of a beached shortfin mako struggling in the surf. He'd found the adolescent shark quickly (this is a *real* shark, by the way, not one of these weirdos), as well as the circle of a dozen or so long-in-the-tooth surfers holding the shark's chin up for selfies as its gills flexed in vain. By the time my brother got to them, they were chasing each other with it like a squirming football, and he could already see it was long past saving. He calmly explained that interfering with protected fish or wildlife like this poor mako was against the law in California, when one of them tried to snap the shark at him like a wet towel in a locker room, effectively turning the poor creature's stomach and intestinal track inside out. My brother reeled back in shock. Years of volunteer work had steeled his resolve at the sight of roadkill and oil spills along the coastline, but the glistening purple ropes of innards vaulting over those serrated teeth like spring-loaded snakes from a jar of nuts was just too much for him, and he collapsed, mercifully unconscious for the fish's remaining violations and indignities before it expired. A random beachcomber called my brother an ambulance, but he was lying there getting sunburned for a while, and, of course, his encounter with the surfers ended up on YouTube, where it quickly went viral. This is where I saw it, like everybody else did (I didn't talk to my brother that much). I'd actually had to backtrack to my computer after catching his name on the local news, where reporters identified the gang as the "Bay Boys," though news cameras revealed a nearby beer-strewn, concrete-and-stone fort tagged with WARLORDS, a more embarrassing name the Bay Boys apparently couldn't get to stick.

On the internet, I saw that everyone knew the antics of the Bay Boys very well, and I even read about an El Segundo cop involved in a lawsuit to oust them, but none of the cases went anywhere. Most of the local police actually sanctioned their shenanigans, and any tourists who complained were told, "Sorry, plenty of beach elsewhere." The cops in Palos Verdes Estates, where their intimidation was by far the worst, openly encouraged the Bay Boys, letting them out of speeding tickets and other traffic infractions. According to some of the more coherent YouTube comments, on my brother's video, anyway, which had turned into a support group of sorts, where more and more people shared stories of their own run-ins with the gang. The victims included dozens of members of the hapless Aloha Point Surf Club, who were finally forced to disband after twenty years of the abuse.

They were the ones who first described seeing the fins.

I guessed it was probably in the local fuzz's best interests to keep the beaches thinned out. The Bay Boys were idiots, sure, but law enforcement probably figured they were the lesser of two evils compared to a thousand vacationers and the rise in more tangible types of "pollution." So, with the cops secretly behind them, and their insults flying as fast as the bottlecaps of their bottom-of-the-barrel Saint Archer beer, the Bay Boys broke zoning law after zoning law as they stacked their clubhouse higher and higher with earthquake rubble and driftwood. Tired of adding layers to their fort, they decided to modify their bodies instead, slapping fins onto the backs of their wetsuits for quicker identification on the ocean.

More videos of the Bay Boys cropped up in the following weeks, including drone footage orbiting the massive clubhouse, right up until the tiny helicopter was shotgunned out of the sky. One clip showed vicious brawls in waist-deep water and tourist faces being held under for way too long. I couldn't believe what I was seeing, as a fistfight in the surf looked an awful lot like attempted murder.

I tried to egg my brother into joining the class action suit when this was all peaking in the local news, but he was having none of it. He was a good Christian, turning the other cheek and all that shit. So he was off to his next mission, helping some other stranger or stranded beast in some noble way. But I wasn't that into selfless acts all that much, so this incident was driving me nuts. So when I stopped by to pretend I was helping him rip down that apartment, it was easy to spot such a majestic door surfing his scrap pile. He said, "Go ahead, take it," even though he wasn't sure why I even wanted it. But the next day, I pulled up my big-boy jorts and tossed it into the back of my pickup to smuggle home. My dog was in the window, watching all this, head cocked, back leg scratching a chronic infestation around his ear. He always seemed confused, not just because I never named (or discerned his breed), but because here's this dumb door walking around his yard. Doors are like a dog's mortal enemy, right? They sure yell at them a lot.

And though this probably doesn't make as much sense out loud (to a dog or a human), taking a door surfing just felt like the perfect juxtaposition, like showing up to an ex's wedding by dribbling a basketball down the aisle. I just wanted it to be clear that I was there to cause problems, and hopefully this door maximized the chances of someone documenting an online sequel to my brother's infuriating viral moment.

I didn't tell my brother any of this. Remember, he was a good guy, and he hated confrontation. But those qualities don't run in the family.

"Landshark," a voice whispered, and I squinted at the rainbow halo of ocean droplets orbiting the shadow looming over me. I was laid out on top of my door, knocker ring resting on my head like a crown, still reeling from the punch. Another shark high-fived the perpetrator, then they both ran toward the water as I sat up on my elbows and rubbed my bloody nose on my sand-coated knuckle.

I stayed on my door and soaked up the rays for a bit, waiting for my next move. Truth was, I didn't really have a next move. I'd totally forgotten to record the pummeling on my phone, which I'd left in my truck. And that's when I realized that I hadn't thought very far past my original plan of walking a beach with a door under my arm like an asshole, just trying to coax surfers to harass me. But even with me sitting with my toes anchored comfortably in the soft pebbles and pulverized shells and showing no incentive to go out there and steal their coveted waves, the Bay Boys still couldn't help themselves. Dozens more shark-fin-sporting bros rose up from the surf in front of me and high-stepped it back up onto the beach to give me shit.

"You lost or something, Stu?"

"Nope."

"Wrong place for you, guy!"

"I thought this beach was for everybody," I shrugged, shading my eyes for a better look.

"Naw, man." One burly shark smiled through his white handlebar mustache, tucking his gray hair behind his ear as he stepped up closer. He was wrinkly but big, seemingly too big to ride anything except a toilet seat—further proof of the ultimate paradox of localism: the better the fighter, the worse the surfer? But somehow this was their leader.

"That's where they lied to you, bro," he said. "People around here hassle outsiders. They might even work your car over."

"Really."

"Oh yeah, and if you take it to court, that shit costs, what? Ten grand, at least. Pain in the butt!" he laughed. "I sure don't want to go through that again. I mean, I'll waste so much money after kicking someone's face in. But I'm stupid like that, you know?"

"Right. So you must be the Aloha Point Surf Club, then?" I asked, knowing full well they were rivals.

"Fuck no! We fucked them up!"

"Good," I said, and laid back on my door again, arms behind my head. This seemed to soften his demeanor. The prospect of a shared enemy changed everything, and the wizened surfer stared down at me another second, then extended a hand.

"The name's Noah," he said as I shook it, flinching at the sharp sand in the webbing between his fingers. "You wanna stand in the soup for a tick? Great. Now, you're a Jake, so I can't let you in the real water, even for an ankle-buster, but you might get a treat seeing one of the boys tombstone it on a cruncher."

I wasn't sure what any of that meant, but I was all about this "tombstoning," since it sounded lethal. I stood up and started to brush off my knocker and blow sand out of the peephole.

"Naw, naw, leave the door, Jake."

"Hey, how'd you know my name wasn't Jake," I grinned, and Noah laughed back, clapping me on the shoulder. He didn't get the joke, either. We were gonna get along just fine.

* * *

Standing in the surf boil and watching the Bay Boys bob around trying to line up a good wave, I cupped some water and sloshed a mouthful of salt, then spit it back out to get the sunbaked blood off my teeth from my earlier cuff to the chops. The brine burned much worse than expected, and I remembered my pregaming before I'd headed out, when I'd tried to get into a more *nautical* state of mind by eating my first bowl of Captain Crunch in decades. Judging from the soreness of my tongue, I was pretty sure that breakfast gave me thrush, and the geriatric shark's punch probably didn't help any, either. As if that all wasn't enough of an assault on my mouth, I'd slurped down some leftover coffee still on my counter from the day before—slamming it cold because I'm an animal— but apparently this tiny squirming nightmare creature had been treading water inside the cup all night, kinda like Magnum P.I. in that episode where he got stranded at sea without a life jacket. If Magnum P.I. had eye stalks and legs growing out of his head, I mean, which was possible (my brother says that sex symbols in the '80s had a much tougher look). But the kicker was how I discovered the thing, surfing saliva straight for my tonsils when I coughed it back up and swished it around, thinking it was a chunk of Captain Crunch. I even pushed it up against the roof of my mouth, where I'm guessing it did tiny bench presses with my tongue until I finally spit it into the glass. I'm no scientist, so I still don't know what it was, but I'm pretty sure I swallowed the rest of its family and any tiny life preservers they were wearing because my coffee never twitched again. Could a day start off any worse? Luckily, a breakfast like that guarantees everything else will be an improvement. And it was.

Because I was right on track. I'd made my first friend, outside of work or school, that is. That was growing up, right? And anyone named "Noah" had to be in charge of something big.

I'd assumed that showing up to the beach with this dumb door under my arm would be so ridiculous it would immediately neuter the Bay Boys' bluster, as I'd be neither competition nor a threat. But this was a new wrinkle, as I never expected I'd be lucky enough to befriend someone so high in their ranks. I decided to play out my hand, eager for things to escalate any way they could for maximum chaos. Because if there was one thing I was good at, it was betraying friendships, especially one only an hour old.

I stood in the ocean a long time. And when the sun started sinking and it got harder to see their fins zigzagging on the horizon, Noah invited me back to the clubhouse, where they were stoking a fire. Their famous headquarters was tucked around the side of a jetty, way shittier up close than it was on the news, barely a lean-to, really, but the merman shadows dancing around the flames made it feel much more sinister.

With the sun down, their original name, "Warlords," almost didn't seem so idiotic. Almost. I sat down on a milk crate next to Noah, and he nodded, clearly impressed with his prehistoric crib. I noticed scattered piles of what appeared to be spent shotgun shells, and I stiffened. I jokingly asked what Dead Presidents mask was trendy for surfer bank robberies that year, and two sharks stood up, spit in the sand near my foot, then left. Noah ignored this and my question.

"Hey, can I touch that?" I finally asked after a couple more beers. I was pointing at the dorsal fin protruding from Noah's back. One of the biggest sharks, with black still streaking his beard, stopped cracking driftwood for the fire and slowly looked up at Noah, skeptical.

"Why not," Noah said after a second. I gave his fin a good squeeze.

Maybe it was the cheap Saint Archers, but my heart was ready to take a vacation from my chest because this fin was not at all the texture I was expecting. I thought maybe it would feel like plastic, or cheap rubber, maybe like a chunk of surfboard. But this was leathery, spiny, like snakeskin boots if they had a pulse. Like petting it the wrong way might be dangerous. I tried to bend the tip of the fin, and Noah's shoulders suddenly hitched as if in pain, and he jerked away.

"Sorry, man," I said, wiping my hands on my trunks.

"Careful, brother. It's real."

It's real?

"What's real?" I asked, trying to sound calm.

Noah shared a glance with the biggest shark, who smiled and went back to cracking wood. Noah looked me up and down, then sighed.

"Yeah, man, they're totally real! Real, live shark fins. Illegal and expensive. So don't bust it. That would . . . hurt," he said, basking in my confusion. He leaned in closer to whisper, "Okay, see, this cop we know sniped a box of these off a truck during a drunk stop. Gave them to us as tribute. The fins were headed for some high-end stewpots in San Fran Chinatown. Cures boners, fuck if I know."

I looked at his fin, black but sparkling in the firelight, studying the seam where it seemed to push through the thick skin of his suit, and

I didn't know which possibility was more horrifying: that they wore poached fins like trophies after the still-living sharks were sheared and chucked overboard to starve, or the suddenly more reasonable prospect that they had fins growing actually from their backs. Who am I kidding, real fins would be way freakier.

Either way, I decided more drinking was the best option.

I got pretty drunk, but some crucial things I learned that night include . . .

The clubhouse wasn't littered with shotgun shells after all. They were spent poppers, aka "anal" nitrate, a recreational inhalant popular in the disco era for enhancing sexual experience and facilitating anal intercourse by relaxing the sphincter muscles. And at first glance, it seemed the Bay Boys must love poppers, but not for the reasons I would have guessed. They loved them because hemorrhoids were the secret scourge of surfboarders. Sitting so long on those boards, or hunkering down on sandbars to take a shit before they buried it like a filthy sand crab, these were real problems for some real men. And these guys weren't spring chickens, either. Clearly, the outlaw lifestyle was wreaking havoc on their butts.

Noah confessed his crew was once enlisted in a dubious scientific study, an upstart professor's blatant attempt to gain notoriety equal to the "Stamford" (Connecticut) Prison Experiment, though his study was the much-less-infamous Stanford "Prolapse" Experiment, which, if you watched the films, appeared to be nothing but twenty-five college students straddling surfboards in their biology department parking lot. Nothing compared to that experiment where they tried swapping license plates with phone numbers, though. I'll tell ya, if there was one thing I learned from living in California, it's that locals loved to talk about unethical behavioral experiments almost as much as they loved surfing.

I almost wished I hadn't heard it, but that night, Noah also confessed that the combination of swollen anal nerves in a desert climate like California's resulted in an even more extreme condition, revealed when his predecessor awoke one morning with an engorged sand flea nursing blood directly from his anus. Noah swore up and down that they had saluted this flea's tenacity and bore it no ill will, however, squatting over the bonfire to burn it off was the only real cure. Sadly,

222 DAVID JAMES KEATON

this resulted in the retirement of the original Warlord. And they made me drink a toast to the man, nodding respect toward Poseidon's spray-painted memorial, where I finally noticed the grammatically incorrect apostrophe in WARLORD'S. Hey, they might be dumb, but with a name like that, they *owned* it.

"Not to demystify our sport or anything . . ." Noah smiled as I was fighting valiantly against the urge to make jokes about insects crawling two by two up a ramp into Noah's ass. It was tough. Until they started *really* talking about fleas.

Sometime during the party, one of these *Lost Manboys* passed me three tabs of acid with tiny googly-eyed cartoon insects drawn on them. I'd never dropped acid before, so I pocketed the papers. But because my shorts were tight and wet against my leg, the drugs soaked through my skin and hit my bloodstream as effectively as someone licking some Woodstock commemorative frogs and mailing them directly into my brain.

But I retained enough of my faculties that night to learn all there was to know about water fleas.

Such as how they had a record 31,000 genes jam-packed into their DNA, making them the most adaptable organism on the planet. I also learned how a certifiable, self-proclaimed "broceanographer" such as Noah could always find the beaches with the most waves *and* the fewest fleas, and that the only way someone like Noah lost status as the reigning king of the Bay Boys was if "Neptune sent him packing." And Neptune could do this just by "stamping their passport," which translated as evidence of any bite marks on their boards or their bodies. A shark bite, that is, not a flea bite. Any visible proof of a shark attack and they started at the bottom of the crab bucket all over again, the dreaded "civilian status" reset.

Contrary to popular opinion, a shark bite on a surfboard was not a badge of honor. In this town, it was bad luck, Noah cautioned. No, even worse than that. It was a curse.

He said just one bite and no one would catch a wave on that break for a hundred years. Imagine how low their balls would be swinging by then.

As the infinite beach bash dragged on, I paced myself and tried to hang. I've been known to close down even the most relentless party, but these guys out-drank me easily. They'd been up for days already. Remember, these were mostly ancient, trust-fund "boys," and without real jobs their waking hours weren't just reversed, they were perpetual. They'd be riding new waves again at dawn. Then again at dusk. They called catching every rotation of the sun without a wink of sleep in between "staying home." And they sure loved to stay home.

To take a break from my undercover work, I went down to the water alone, walking through the cold salt and foam to clear my head. The surf was oddly fragrant at that hour, like I was walking through a spicy skillet the morning after grilling the Catch of the Day. I sloshed another palmful around my mouth and spit. But this time, I swallowed, unconcerned with the dangers of dehydration. Daydreams of fish popping in skillets were making me ravenous.

Then I saw the mako.

Upside down and tugged at by rival seagulls, long streamers of viscera flaring from its mouth like a cartoonist had tried to draw it singing a song. I shooed the gulls and shook off the crabs and gathered the shark up under my arm and took it back to the water. I was still more than a little drunk, but I had a new sense of purpose after such an endless night of bro'ing down. And I'd be lying if I said I wasn't wanting my own fin. I was convinced I could truly infiltrate the gang with a black fin on my back, and as I swam with that shark, I gingerly rolled up the guts and put the outsides back inside. I'd read on the internet that sharks sometimes ejected their stomachs out of their mouths when hooked, so except for a few puzzle pieces the seagulls had pulled loose, it looked good as new. That's the amazing thing about sharks. No one feels the urge to brush a hand over their eyeballs so they can "rest in peace."

Alive or dead, those peepers remained the same.

You wouldn't think swimming with a dead shark would be so *intuitive*, but it was the most natural thing in the world. So natural that I began to wonder if that's why we were created, to swim the seas together. My upper arms fit perfectly under its pectoral fins, like we shared the same skeleton. Do sharks have skeletons? Who cares, because the two of us glided through that water like a sleek, sputtering motorbike and its smooth little sidecar.

I looked back toward their fading bonfire through the fog of daybreak inebriation, and I remembered my mission. I was there to get payback for my brother, not play with the locals. So I started thinking about faking a shark attack to curse their waves, and how that might be the easiest thing ever. All you'd need is a shark. And I had that in my hands! Okay, if the shark was dead, you might need something like . . . a bear trap? Yeah, that's the ticket. A bear trap stuffed into the mako's jaws and voilà! It lives again. The ghastly prow of the ocean's top predator back in perfect working order. It almost felt wrong to supplement the muscle power of its mouth with a metal trap, mad scientist mash-up of water and woods, but then I decided that was probably just overthinking shit. It was two tastes that went great together! And it would teach Noah a lesson. It would teach them all a lesson. Just one toothy snap and the resulting deep stamp on a body or a board (their surrogate bodies, let's be honest) and that's all it would take. Under their own bylaws, page 69, subchapter *blorp*, they'd be banished from this spot for a century.

I rolled my body to swim on my back awhile, pulling the dead shark up onto my belly, its dorsal fin dividing the waves and waterboarding my mouth and nose. I hacked and coughed, but I kept on kicking. My fin was small for now, and it rode my chest instead of my back, but I wore it proudly. Because I knew it would grow.

Legally impaired, I stumbled up to my truck, threw the mako and my door into the trailer, and drove to my brother's house. I knew he'd be up. Though he worked for a living (when he wasn't volunteering), he didn't keep normal hours—just like the sharks—mostly due to his unbridled humanitarianism as well as his late-night film obsessions. My brother might have hated confrontations, but he sure loved *movies* about confrontations, especially in those wee hours. And Peckinpah's "video nasty" *Straw Dogs* was one of his favorites. In fact, he loved that one so much that, in order to honor its most important nonliving character, he'd gone out and gotten himself a bear trap to nail over his fireplace. I already knew he was all about this movie because it was at its heart a cautionary tale about a timid guy rising up (not to mention being full of more haphazard carpentry than *Unforgiven*). But he swore he was just into the love story. Yeah, right. It's crazy, but of all the religious people I've known, the vast majority of them regularly viewed the most fucked-up films.

Years back, I helped him set the spring and hang the bear trap (in real life, they're a lot smaller, just like bears), after my brother brushed off the chunks of fur and anointed it "Chekhov's Trap," vowing that if he died before it went off, he'd probably wasted his life.

When I got to his house, I went right for those metal jaws, telling him I was the answer to his prayers, without an ounce of sarcasm. But it still took a little convincing.

"Why would I let you take this trap, Reeves?"

"Because I'll put it to good use, I promise."

"Doing what?"

"Getting back at some assholes."

"Whose assholes?"

I sighed, looked up, looked down, and finally just unloaded it all:

"I want to use your trap to mechanically reanimate a dead shark and then use it to chomp on those surfer punks who thought it was funny to turn an animal inside out and piss on you while you were unconscious and immortalize your piss face forever on the World Wide Web."

Ten minutes later, I was walking to my car with a bear trap under my arm.

"You could come with me, Jake," I said, loading up my truck while he watched, knowing full well my brother would never do this. I respected his pacifism, but I'd always had more backbone. And this was no metaphor. My last MRI revealed I had an extra two-centimeter void between my vertebrae and spinal cord. The downside of this was that I was prone to ruptured discs and spinal fusions. Meaning manual labor was a problem (okay, maybe that's an upside), even though that was all you could find on the West Coast, even with my nine years of college and an undeclared major. Now, that was a fuckin' pickle, am I right? My back simply didn't have the right *mettle* for the only kind of work I was qualified to do. It sorta made sense in California, though, where a word like *sick* can mean at least three entirely different things. Just like the name *Jake*.

"Forget it, Jake. It's Surfer Town!" my brother said, laughing, as I started my truck and backed out. I assumed this was a movie reference and gave him a consolation honk. Weirdo.

Though not visibly drunk anymore, I still probably shouldn't have been driving. But I figured I could just drop Noah's name to the Palos Verdes police if I got pulled over. It didn't matter, though, because the streets were empty.

Tonight the streets are ours! I thought, dizzy at the idea of the ready-to-assemble shark in the back of my truck. *But the beach is theirs.*

I parked in the lot on the cliff and trekked down to the sand carrying a door, a dead shark, and a bear trap. Like people do.

Dawn broke right when I got back to the clubhouse. It was empty, and the Bay Boys were already back in the water lining up for their waves. In the morning sun, I saw the beach was littered with shotgun shells and the "poppers" were gone, and I smiled at all the disorientating bullshit Noah could sling. In the warmth of that sunrise, I looked to the skyline and thought I could almost believe in their god, whoever it may be. I was never a religious man like my brother, but he did teach me some prayers . . .

There were prayers of veneration, prayers of supplication, prayers of worship, prayers of consecration, prayers of intercession, and prayers of imprecation. Probably more prayers out there, but that last one was my favorite. It was when you prayed for God to fuck up your enemies. Well, more like judgment for the wicked, but it was the only one I ever used, and I whipped out that prayer so much, it was essentially the only voice in my head. But on a beautiful beach at sunrise, I was afraid everyone could hear that voice, and I pursed my lips and plugged my ears just in case. Then I climbed into the bed of my truck, and I forced the bear trap deep into the slack jaws to lock teeth upon teeth upon teeth upon . . .

Then I prayed for something in the water to fuck them up real good.

For the kingdom of Atlantis, and the power and the glory of shark-on-shark action, now and forever, amen.

I couldn't be the only one praying at that moment, and I wondered if maybe this was why surfers were always getting chomped. How many surfers sang psalms to the sea to smite their rivals? Must be thousands. Millions?

My brother would have been upset. He once scolded me saying that any ol' dude using a prayer of imprecation was out of context, unjustifiable, unforgivable. "Just plain wrong," he said.

But if he was here, I would have told him, "Don't worry, bro! These dudes are totally sharks."

I laid my new shark and its metal smile out on my door, then placed them carefully onto the beach break. Straddling the door, I walked us into the ocean until my feet no longer gripped the bottom. As I kicked straight toward the shoal of black fins in the distance, I realized that this was what walking on water felt like.

Even from fifty yards away, I could see something was very wrong. Or very right. The Bay Boys were arguing, fighting for the same waves, and at least three of them had just been axed, the lip of one wave catching them in the grill and chucking them backward, head over fins (it's amazing how quickly you internalize the lingo). Whatever it was that was causing this chaos had them paddling in all directions. I locked eyes with Noah, and he did a duck dive under a surge to lose the crowd, then buttonhooked back toward me.

"Are you kidding with that sponger, Jake?" he said when he got close.

"Oh, you like my longboard?"

"No, I just wanna know why the fuck you're clam draggin' again."

I could see in his face that he couldn't believe I'd busted out my door again, but he was more confused about the dead shark to even acknowledge it. He waved me away.

"Go. You'll get your ass chopped out here, Jake. Take your 747 and get the fuck out."

"My funboard is here to stay," I said, still willfully obtuse. The slang was coming fast and loose from all those fireside tutorials. For example, I now suspected "Noah" was slang for "shark," which was kinda obvious, except that it was also the closest surfer slang came to Cockney (see, "Noah" equals "Noah's Ark," which rhymes with "shark," get it?), so this all made sense. Cockney rhyming slang originated as a way of coding conversations to confuse law enforcement, and its use here was logical, since actually shouting "Shark!" on the water was an invitation for trouble, like yelling "Movie!" in a fire. The word *Sharky* could also describe a lot of chop, but here in California, it more than likely described a buncha goddamn sharks. This was the most direct bit of jargon ever conceived, as it circled right on back to its origin, sort of like someone handing you a "piece of cake" that was really easy to bake. Or someone pretending to have no food to share, then literally spilling a can of beans on the floor.

Or you get tricked into spending the rest of your life in a hot tub and call it "dirty pool."

Something like that.

Okay, maybe just one more example. How about riding shotgun with a shotgun? Because this was the weapon I was still expecting to see a Bay Boy wielding before the end of the longest day on record. Anyhow, I was still a little drunk, but bobbing on the water somehow helped me keep steady, so I paddled over to Noah again.

"You again, huh," Noah said, distracted and uncharacteristically solemn.

"You see this right here?" I told him, knocking wood between my legs and deciding to ignore the dead shark for now. "This is a goddamn door. Like, right off a house."

"Yes. Yes, it is."

No time for me, he shook his head and paddled away, starting to line up again for a run. He was wearing a pink-and-black "shortie," a sleeveless wetsuit for the hottest days, but his fin was visible. And in the small of his back, just under this fin, I noticed a second bulge. Possibly the weapon I had been anticipating.

"Drop in on me with that fuckin' door, and you're dead!" he yelled out the side of his mouth. "And that's not code, Jake. Out here, dead means *dead*. You'll never stand up on our watch. This is the surface. All you get is the dick-drag, gurfer."

Gurfer? I wondered. "Surfage," I'd heard, though. Short for "surf age," it sounded more like "suffrage," like if women fought for their right to vote for the sickest burns.

I nodded and stroked my mako, careful to keep my hand out of its spring-loaded maw. The bear trap gave it a gleaming, wicked grin, but it didn't look too unusual after its implant. I had a feeling a bear trap would look reasonable in any shark's mouth. Maybe even our own.

I stayed where it was glassy, did some push-ups on my door to keep the muscle spasms in my back at arm's length, and I watched the Bay Boys continue to have trouble. Missing wave after wave, they pleaded to the sky, and then to the water. But opportunities never came. Listening to them mutter crazy shit like, "That grom won't rip switchfoot in the slot unless you cutback, waxhead," I closed my eyes to soak up the alien chatter while I waited, imagining my door sliding along the surface of an icy moonscape. It was a nice vacation. Then a sizable wave separated Noah from the pack and brought him close to me again, so I put my plan into motion.

Noah was on his knees when he veered next to my door, and I carefully pulled my shark's new iron jaw wide and locked the pin. I got down on my belly and did the terrier trot to bring him even closer. I was off Noah's radar, and his back was turned so I could use his fin like a gun sight to line up for the perfect bite. Ocean bubbling in my mouth, I slid my dead shark out in front of me and into the water, aiming for a hard snap on his squaretail.

Then I saw his hand reach around his back and pull the gun from the long split in his shortie as he spun a leg over his board to face me. He took aim. Fired.

I had just enough time to think, *Thank Christ, it's a toy.*

But not quite. Not a real gun, but a flare gun, and still pretty dangerous. It nailed my dead shark right in the mush, and its metal teeth snapped shut, jets of sparks roaring up through its eyes and nostrils. Noah smiled like someone who'd shot hundreds of robot sharks looking to nip his board, and he tucked his yellow gun back into his wet suit and kicked away like I was never there.

I sat with my burning mako, watching the orange fire gush from its gills. The lining of its mouth began to smoke and cook, the water in its snout popping like a fish fry, and it kinda smelled delicious. I was contemplating a bite of my own when I felt the bump under my feet.

Whatever it was, it was big.

Big in the way a shadow that slides silently under you is big. Big in the way something that can kill you with indifference is big. I looked to the Bay Boys and saw them clustered tight. They were looking around, looking down, as if they were being herded. I'd seen something like this in videos, when the amateurs clashed with the locals, and the gangs formed a sort of prayer circle in the ocean to frustrate anyone paddling for a wave. But this was different, more like the ocean was working to keep the surfers stacked up, like the water itself was functioning in concert with an unseen beast of prey, rounding up the quarry into a squirming nucleus of life ripe for the picking.

I pointed my toes and felt the same huge something still gliding by under my feet, with no end any time soon. Somehow, I was excited to be corralled with the rest of them. My prayer had been for the ocean, and now I was part of it, too.

The prow of the creature ascended in front of me, breaching directly behind Noah, sheets of water raining down from its summit. At first, I thought it was a whale. But it was transparent. No, *translucent*. Under the surface, I had no doubt it was invisible, but in that moment, my look of awe was refracted in its massive head. My brain was still mapping the titan onto more familiar forms when a mountain of ocean rolled toward me, then smoothed out as it dove deep.

The air was silent. No sea breeze. No gull made a sound.

Noah was gone, and so was his gang. I searched the horizon, but not a single Bay Boy could be found. Then two huge, luminous fins suddenly broke on either side of me, rotated high in the sky, until one crashed down dangerously close, narrowly missing a devastating slap over my suddenly puny door. I pulled my feet on board and closed my eyes, clutching my dead shark and its burning orange smile for warmth.

Then I remembered the peephole. This seemed like a good compromise. Not a true violation of its domain. I cupped my hands around the hole to take a look.

There was an eyeball staring back at me.

One lone eye, emotionless but intent. The size of a tractor tire, insect-like and buried in a living, crystalline structure. Two pairs of segmented antennae branched from the eye, which reached out to tickle my door. They traced the length and shape of it, then pierced the waves near my legs to brush the metal hinges. I tried to make myself small, as the antennae crawled up and stroked my shark, tentatively tapping the heat of the flare still hissing in its mouth. Then they jerked, whiplashed, and retreated back into the water. Peering down through my tiny fish-eye lens, I saw the giant in full, sinking low enough to finally chart its pellucid, seemingly limitless borders, and I realized how mindsplittingly humongous the creature really was.

The huge, segmented carapace spasmed and curled to pick up momentum for a dive, as the otherworldly mandibles in its crown spun their fluttering hardware like the mechanical movement of a watch. This mouth wiggled and thrummed, terrifying tendrils and bristles drumming like fingers, fanning, then coming back together like the shuffle of an invisible deck of cards, and I realized it was working the outline of screaming men through the strange machinery of its expanse. Men with fins, but still men. Going down hard. I watched every Bay Boy being swallowed and rustled and hustled through the maze of its body, and this helped me to diagram the rest of it and finally recognize the species. Or at least its tiny, familiar descendants.

I've often pulled the monster's offspring from my dog. Specifically, from the corner of a canine eye, whenever they've abandoned the easy blood meals of his belly to crawl through the forest of his fur and finally rest to drink fresh tears from his corneas. And when I would catch and hold a minuscule intruder up to a light, I would have only a moment to study the downturned, crawdad-like face and marvel at how much the land-based nuisance resembled a denizen of the sea. I understood now that flea collars were actually a castle wall, the last line of defense, as all fleas must yearn for a colossal, prehistoric past, but settle for the holy saltwater baptism of a mongrel's eye.

I stared through my door, the reflections of the sunlight sketching the tail end of the great insectoid form line by line, hook by claw, a body as vast and decorated as the Nazca Lines. I imagined these huge creatures were always in our oceans, invisible away from the scrutiny of the sun. Or until they needed to feed. I decided the surfers would also become transparent as they were digested, only perceived as real until the moment they were devoured, like every ration.

Two crystal wings flanking a pulsing ramjet broke the surface, and the two great fins rose high again, touching their tips in prayer, then they slapped down, their waves knocking on my door, upending my perch, throwing me for a loop. I wiped the water from my eyes, and I saw the thing oscillating downward, the wake almost flipping me over again as my eardrums popped from the force of its breach. But I held fast, and when it was finally below me again, I gazed through my peephole to see the huge creature descend, and I saw Noah's final struggles in the labyrinth of his invisible prison. The fins beat just once more, and it was gone into the depths.

When I pulled my face from the door, I looked around the still water, and I saw a fleet of unmanned surfboards, purposeless but dancing. They had a word for it.

Tombstoning.

One board was trembling violently, then it flipped twice until it was still, and I knew that signaled the last of the Bay Boys and a foot finally free of its leash to surf an eternal glass throat forever.

Alone, we caught the final wave in on my door. We stood up high.

It was everything they said it was.

* * *

I was arrested in the parking lot that same afternoon. Cop cars everywhere. Even a fire truck, which always looked insane on a beach. At least until I saw a beach on a fire truck.

The news reported I was holding the smoking "gums" in my hand; the steel-toothed grin of a dead mako flickering like a jack-o'-lantern, which the cops had to wrestle away. I couldn't explain what happened to the Bay Boys even if I wanted to, especially why I had seven of their surfboards stacked in the back of my pick-up.

Someone placed a hand on my wet head to guide me into a police car, or maybe it was the fire truck, who can say? I blacked out for a second when my forehead bumped the roof. And while I was gone, I traveled back to the moment I was surfing my first tube, when I was in the "green room," as they call it, the Jade Highway, also known as the Pope's Bedroom, sometimes referred to as the Astronaut's Garden, that emerald oasis deep inside a wave where a "Jake" has no business being. Forever, I am standing up strong while the ocean rolls around me and my prayers keep me safe, until the tail of that great invisible behemoth descends into the endless dark beneath my door.

When I can find it, I still knock on that door. It drives everybody nuts.

I used to knock on the plastic window when my brother came to visit me, and he always played along. He mocked the new streaks of gray in my hair, which I thought at first were the result of locking eyes with a terrifyingly prodigious aquatic mystery, but it was just frosted tips from the citric acid in the power drink that one of the surfers had chucked in my face. My brother didn't believe my story, probably because of the acid in my pockets that had bled through my skin. And I didn't come down for days. But, of course, he forgave me. And he played my game.

"Knock! Knock!"

"Who's there?"

"Will you remember me in a year?"

"Yes."

"Will you remember me in a month?"

"Yes."

"Will you remember me in a week?"

"Yes."

"Knock! Knock!"

"Who's there?" he would croak, knowing what was coming.

"See, you forgot me already!" I would say. And it will be okay when he does. It really will.

One night, I dreamed of plucking an engorged flea from the dusty lunar crater of my navel and flicking it through the bars of my prison cell, where it bounced across the concrete floor like a marble. In the morning, when we filed out for breakfast, I stepped over the comet streak of blood it had suckled from the scar tissue of an umbilical cord we'd always assumed long dead. This is the life cycle of incarceration. This is the best life you can hope for.

Locked up in here with everyone now, watching the guard drop his key ring and then kick them down the hall and around the corner before he picks them up (so as not to show weakness), I realize everything outside of the water is an illusion.

How else could a world remain frozen outside my window as my prison rolls by? It should be the opposite.

Even now, I still do my push-ups, sometimes in the shower, sometimes in the rain, anywhere there's a pool or a puddle, to get ready for the ocean again someday, to hopefully take my turn drinking from that leviathan's eye. Sit-ups are more difficult now, as the knob of bone in the middle of my spine continues to grow. It's painful to roll it against the concrete floors, or the metal-ribbed wall of a fire truck. My back hurts worse every day, but somehow, where alcohol isn't allowed, I remain drunk on these experiences. And the pain can be wonderful, too.

The driver of our prison bus does get angry sometimes, when I slice holes in all my shirts for my future fins. But as my spine pulses and swells, I will tell them it's okay, even if I have to fall back on the slang I learned from those surfers to explain that, in every sense of the word, I am "sick."

Even now, my back aches as I dream on my stomach, longing for the deep end of the pool, for any surface that yields, a flexible world that allows flippers and fins and encourages our invisible bodies to grow unhindered in every direction. To finally be free.

CHAPTER XVII

GOT MILK?

Except for Reeves, who'd belched out a string of mostly indecipherable surfer lingo, blasted through a flailing but passionate exercise regime, and was now splayed out in a corner of the hot tub studying the waves as if they held the secret of the cosmos, the remaining males were all up in each other's faces. Every mouth shouting a worse idea than the last. The remaining females, however, avoided this latest impending outbreak of violence, leaning against the rails to think about jumping again. Ironically, the more connections that their wild stories teased regarding the group, the more they realized they were strangers after all. Desperation was at a tipping point.

Hair whipping around her ears, Angie felt guilty ducking Amy's attempts to clutch her for comfort as she, Beth, and Jill continued to circle the edge of the pool, looking for signs of life outside the truck. They were deep into the countryside, with just the occasional tree, so they were back to considering the mystery of the driver again, and the business card Angie was holding up in a welcome sliver of moonlight.

"I think they're about five seconds from drawing straws," Gaddy said, pointing to the boys. "If they had any straws."

"No way this is a real name," Angie was saying, flipping the card over, then back. "Winston Payne? Come on."

"'*Winced in Pain*'? No way. Seriously?" Jill said, snatching the card from Angie. "Our captor's name is . . . yeah, don't make me say it again."

"So embarrassing."

"No, *I'm* Spurtacus!" Reeves shouted from somewhere.

"Should we really be scared of a guy named 'Pain' if it's spelled wrong?" Jill asked.

"Yes," Amy said, with a "are you kidding me?" thrust of her neck. "Look around!"

"What do we know about this driver?" Jill asked, the tone of her voice betraying a lack of interest in any answer. Beth just watched them all, as usual.

"I don't know," Amy said. "He liked dad jokes?"

"He had a vanity plate," Lund said as he joined them, ducking past the nearly catatonic Reeves, who was shadow-boxing a stain on the trailer, between punches yelling, "Please!" and "Fleas!"

"What were all those fools arguing about over there?" Jill asked Lund.

"About who gets to climb over the cab to knock on the windshield." Lund said, and they shared a look.

"Who won?"

"Well, that's the problem," Lund said. "You ever notice how every time there's a 'drawing straws' scene in a movie, the big moment is ruined every time because of a lack of an establishing shot regarding the length of the straw?"

"No, but I definitely noticed you noticing stupid shit like that," Jill said.

"Well, for clarity, people in films should always draw five straws and, for the sixth, say, one animal. Like a magnificent dove that flies from their fist. Just so the audience will know what happened."

"Then how about you head on back over and draw that short dove, Lund," Jill sighed, and they turned to see if that argument has resolved. Dan was squeezing three mini-bottles of Jack and one White Claw in his knuckles, labels down, though the "short straw" here was pretty visible due to the White Claw's rounded bottle, so things were going about as well as expected.

There was more shoving and shouting, and then they tried one more time by shaking out six empties until the "loser" found the can with the wriggling silverfish. But Reeves opted to chug the pool water in the cans instead, and when he coughed up the insect, no one understood the results, so they were back to square one.

"You said this thing had a vanity plate?" Angie asked Lund, taking his chin to turn him away from that scuffle to face their conversation. "What did it say?"

"I don't remember. Something 'nine-eleven' related?"

"Good for him," Beth said, arm around Amy.

"No, it was more conspiracy-minded. Like 'MLT-STL?'" Lund shrugged.

"The fuck is that?" Gaddy asked.

"You know, like 'melts steel' or something? Like jet fuel can't melt steel beams? Get it?"

"Bit of a stretch."

"No, that's a World Trade Center reference, I'm telling you."

"Oh, great, look who's joining us," Amy said as Reeves plowed into them.

"We're on our way to prison!" Reeves announced after doing a spin and a spit-take, blowing a fountain of warm pool water into all their faces. "This is a prison bus, you know."

As they wiped away the spittle, Angie thought he was making as much sense as anybody.

"That's how they do it, ya know?" he continued. "A sorta last hurrah. Big bash on the outside before lockdown, to curb violent tendencies on the inside. It's real! A prison party bus makes for happy incarcerations!"

"Maybe it's a tour?" Amy said.

"We're not prisoners. Or tourists," Beth said. "We're victims."

"Because prisons don't give tours, do they, Angie?" Lund asked her, and she frowned. If he *was* from her town, then he'd remember the tours the prison handed out while it was being built, and how these hugely popular and informative visits were still going on, even as the buses brought in the first prisoner transfers. Angie and her class took a field trip, which included a stop in the middle of this slowly awakening prison, the command center and hub of the panopticon, where they looked down at the newly bolted tables in the recreation room, where the tour guide and head guard pointed out a certain tradition among prisons, to gather in tight-knit groups and entertain themselves with far-fetched, self-mythologizing, campfire-style stories.

She'd been thinking a lot about those structures lately, how they were likely driving in circles, to creating their own mobile panopticon, subconsciously adopting the roles of inmate and guard, depending on which lap they were on.

What goes around, comes around . . . and around . . . and around . . .

"How do you know we're not prisoners, Beth?" Lund asked, holding her disorienting gaze. "Did your Smile Police police tell you that?"

"Her what?" Reeves asked, sputtering more water. Before she could respond, Dan was grabbing Reeves under his arms and spinning him around like a dancer. Nose-to-nose, Reeves gave Dan a quick kiss on the lips, then slipped a hand down the back of Reeves's shorts, coming back up with a snap, his wet underwear clinging to his backside like shrink wrap.

"Gross," Amy gagged.

"He's got more drugs down there," Dan said, letting Reeves slip his hold and backstroke away. "No way he's just drunk."

"I thought you put the drugs in Lund's diaper last night," Gaddy said.

"It's still the same night, dummy," Dan said.

"Is it?" she asked him.

"Good question," Dan said. "We're probably half-hallucinating all this shit, including you."

"So? That shit's in the water, fucking us up," Dan said. "We're half-hallucinating this."

"Okay, okay," Angie said. Her panic always cranked back up when too many of them were too close. She grabbed the business card back from Jill. "How much money did Holly give this guy Payne?"

"I don't know," Gaddy said. "Way more than three hundred bucks. I figured it was a tip."

"Maybe he mistook that extra money for extra time," Angie said, trudging over to a corner where a white-and-green-streaked roll of former one-dollar bills was doing a pirouette with a bottlecap.

"Or . . . he might just be mad because she paid him with Gaddy's Monopoly money," Amy added, and Beth nodded. Angie noticed that Beth and Amy had hooked the crooks of their arms together in either a show of camaraderie or combined silent hysteria.

"Well, unless it's raining in that cab, he wouldn't know my money's fake," Gaddy said.

Tired of standing and fighting to steady herself, Angie sat down to watch them throw around more theories, noting that the conversations that were the quietest—like Beth and Amy's—seemed the most dangerous.

But communicating in a hot tub on a highway often required a mouth against an ear, and in no time, everyone was pairing off or crowding into tight, sneaky units again, with Jill's name riding the sideways glances of at least two groups. Angie distinctly heard Dan bring up the leap-year-birthday thing again as an opportunity to discuss Jill's possible culpability in their abduction. Some of the drunker ones weren't quite convinced she was responsible for everything, but the drunkest of them all—meaning Reeves—was somehow convinced that their very existence depended on her safety, and that her death should be prevented at all costs. Godzooky also endorsed this position, which was fortunate for Jill. This earned him a glare from Dan, but he didn't make a move. Possibly because, despite pickling in the water with the rest of them, by all appearances, Godzooky remained stone sober. Perhaps he'd inoculated himself earlier by slamming all that milk.

But Jill, easily overhearing all of this, laughed it off, or occasionally agreed with their worst suspicions just to "keep the party going." But as she dipped in and out of conversations, Jill began to focus on Amy, watching her cling to Beth's leg, noticing the red wings of irritation in the corners of her eyes where she'd rubbed them raw. Angie wondered if Jill had it in her to pick a new target of misdirection and take the heat off herself from their resident dumb-asses, or if this was just the inevitable green-eyed monster, always rearing its head at the worst possible times.

Then Jill found the extra gas tank.

"What? Where?" Godzooky asked her.

"Right here," Jill said, sliding on her knees to the front of the pool, then standing up to lean down behind the cab to rap on the huge steel coffin between the trailer gap.

"Knock! Knock!" Reeves laughed from somewhere.

"No way. That's just a toolbox," Dan said, shaking his head.

"Then why does it have a hole that says 'FILL UP HERE'?" Jill asked him over the wind, hands on her hips.

Beth and Amy snickered at this, and Angie looked up, hopeful. Dan rushed over and shoved Jill out of the way to check it out for himself. Sure enough, there in the middle of the diamond pattern of metal Xs was a hunter-orange arrow and the unmistakable wide hole for a fuel spout.

"Oh my God," he muttered. All the peripheral plotting had ceased.

"What does it m-m-mean?" Amy asked, teeth chattering and dry mouth clicking.

"Carlos, how long do you estimate he could drive on an extra tank like that?" Angie asked Godzooky.

"How should I know?"

"I thought you were the gearhead."

"I am?" he asked her, as Jill came over to Angie's side.

"You're a bus driver," Jill said. "In my book, that makes you the 'large-animal vet' of the road world. So what do you think? When will this thing run out of gas?"

"I couldn't say." Godzooky breathed deep, scratching the back of his crewcut, uncomfortable to be the center of attention. "How long have we been driving?"

"That's the zillion-dollar question, ain't it?" Dan said.

"Well, maybe if you hadn't busted Janky's watch . . ." Amy started to say to Dan, then stopped, remembering how they busted Janky, too.

"I just don't know." Godzooky rubbed his big hands together to warm up his brain. "We got what . . . a truck that's averaging fifty-five miles an hour . . . and probably gets about five miles per gallon . . . with two fifty-gallon tanks . . . taking us five hundred miles . . . or ten hours, tops?"

"Oh man," Dan said. "Ten hours?"

"We've been in here longer than that," Amy said.

"Either we run out of gas or the sun comes up," Godzooky said. "But one of those two things will be happening very soon."

"You can't hold your breath for ten hours?!" Reeves taunted Dan. "Sissy!"

"Why would I want to do that?" Dan asked him.

"You tell me, fucker!" Reeves said, making even less sense. Reeves punctuated his accusation by smacking Dan hard on the back, leaving his hand there to rub between his shoulder blades as if he was looking for a hidden weapon beneath his skin.

"Get off me, ya lush," Dan said, ducking away from another slap. But Reeves just stared, occasionally scratching a red streak on the inside of his elbow. Then he dove past him, cracking his knees on the bottom, and did an approximation of body-surfing to the nearest wall.

"You know something, Reeves?" Dan called after him. "You suck in a crisis!"

"Wheeeeeeee!" Reeves swam corner to corner, like a pro wrestler stalling for time before the next gag. But as one of his laps brought him near Dan again, he jumped up and lunged for his throat. Dan sidestepped him easily as a matador. Both seemed to be moving in slow motion.

"I believe in Santa . . . Satan . . . Santa Carla . . . all his anagrams," Reeves was saying, hunching over to find a deeper spot to hide in.

"Focus, you idiots!" Angie said. "Don't you understand? We're all in this together!" She was embarrassed by saying this, even before Dan and Reeves blew snot water out their noses in response. "Can we drain the gas tank or not," she asked after a moment, not expecting a serious answer.

"Yes," Lund said, stepping up tall, eager to participate and more coherent than most.

"How?"

"We just siphon it out, then let the gas dump over the side."

"With what?" Angie asked.

"Yeah, with what?" Dan asked.

"Are you kidding?" Lund said, smiling, already relishing the attention he would get at this reveal. "Just where do you think we are?"

He walked to the rail and strained over the side to grab the ladder anchored to the side of the truck. Then, steadying his body with the closest rung, he reached even farther down to flip a chrome handle and open a long hatch with his free hand. Grinning and wheezing, he came back up, splashing across the pool with the tail end of a thick fire hose bundled against his chest.

When the congratulatory back-patting died down a bit, Lund christened the flank of the truck with a mini-bottle of Grey Goose, which didn't come close to shattering. Another attempt with a mini-Smirnoff had the desired effect, and he wrapped a glass shard in a swatch of fabric from the side of his stretched-out shirt. Realizing that the woven flax fibers of the fire hose were much harder to cut than he thought, he enlisted Godzooky to saw away on it instead. Dan watched the muscles dancing in Godzooky's powerful forearms, and he motioned toward him with his chin.

"Bus driver, huh? I still feel like we should be blaming you for something."

"Funny you should say that," Godzooky said as he sawed faster. "I feel like we should be blaming *you* for something. But you do what you think is best."

Dan's face softened, and he offered his version of an olive branch.

"So you're into Johnny Cash?" he asked. "Have you accepted the Man in White as your Lord and Savior?"

"JC in the house." Godzooky smiled, looking up from his task. He offered his free hand. "A 'Man in Wack' reference is my kryptonite, brother. Represent."

"You're not that much bigger than me." Dan surprised him by slapping away Godzooky's "glad hand" and slinking away. Lund quickly popped in to replace him.

"You know, we could have used that hose earlier with Ruck," Godzooky said to Lund, but Dan disagreed, from a safe distance.

"That wouldn't have made any difference!" he said.

"Did you know that before 1890, these things used to be leather?" Lund was saying to Godzooky, who was no longer looking up as he got closer to cutting through the hose. Beth and Amy were openly clutching each other, and Angie breathed a bit easier. A unified goal lightened the dread in the pool again, maybe incited a minor power shift. And the moon had come out from the clouds. They could see each other more clearly than they had in miles.

"I believe we're being tested," Lund said to Godzooky, but he directed it to all of them. "I realize that a person who is no longer with us had a similar theory, but I really think it's true."

"No longer with us," huh? Angie thought.

Reeves was back in their shallow end, busying himself with gathering up bottles and cans to locate any remaining alcohol. He enlisted Dan's help with this, and that seemed to relax them both a bit as well, until Dan overheard Lund's observation and seemed to notice him all over again.

"What the fuck did you just say?"

"I just said we were being tested," Lund said, still riding high on the victory of his fire hose discovery. "Like, this is a test, or whatever." He turned back to the hose. Godzooky had stopped cutting and ripped his section of hose the rest of the way, and Lund gathered up the coil from around Godzooky's feet. He strode toward the gas tank, but Dan headed him off, standing in his way long enough for it to get awkward.

"Excuse me, please," Lund said, and after another couple seconds, Dan moved to the side. Lund unscrewed the cap on the tank and crimped the end of the hose to feed it into the hole, inch by inch. Angie thought he was dragging out his big moment in an almost sexual manner, but decided he'd earned it. If it worked.

How many more chances in the spotlight would he get? she thought.

None, as it would turn out.

For his last trick, and for his first drink of the night, Lund sucked the venom from his canvas snake until the diesel filled his mouth, burbling and coughing amid the cheers. Fumes filled their nostrils, almost re-inebriating the group, as the hose pumped fuel over the rail onto the road. The truck sped up in response to losing its lifeblood, and this felt even more like a win.

"Well, we bought ourselves some time!" Dan announced to the crowd, trying to take credit, and Angie ground her eyes with her fists, surprised that she was missing the memory of intoxication that came with the dissipating gas fumes.

"Actually, just the opposite!" Lund laughed. "Now we wait."

"Wait for what?" Dan asked.

"See that?" Lund pointed to the sky. "The stars are visible now. Draw a line from the Big Dipper to Polaris, then a celestial sphere around them. The vernal equinox, our new reference point on this sphere, will trace our passage, a total of twenty-three hours, fifty-six minutes, and four point ten seconds of solar time, which we break down into—"

"I can't wait to kill you," Dan pretended to joke, but Beth, almost smitten with Lund all over again due to the effectiveness of his plans, almost let her smile slip for free. She wrenched her arm away from Amy and handed Lund a triumphant full beer she'd squirreled away somewhere. He took it, cracked it open over his head, then moved next to Angie to celebrate as he took a swig, then offered her one, too. As he leaned in, she saw the moonstruck and brainsick look on his face that she'd recognized from suitors before, the sort of queasy attention a girl never courted. And under that watchful moonlit sky, she noticed an irrational anger refueling Dan's eyes as he glared at them from a distance.

Angie took a drink, and it went down easier than she expected. She decided that, when it came to be Lund's turn under the wheels, she would mourn him. But it would be easier this time, like it never was for her brother.

Sleep came for them again, and when they awoke, they used the stars to estimate that eleven more hours had passed. But there was still no light in the sky. A hint of sun was always threatening to crack the horizon, but they were cracking instead.

"Impossible," someone said. No one argued or double-checked the math, not even Lund.

"Loose lips sink ships!" Reeves spurted and splashed and sank as if deflating.

"Just remember, everybody, we're all in this together!" Dan laughed, mocking Angie's line from earlier.

"Wait, where's Gaddy?" Angie looked around the pool. Sometime between when they awoke and counted the stars, the water level had climbed to chest level again. "When's the last time anyone saw Gaddy?" Angie was frantic.

"Don't throw bones in glass houses!" Reeves burbled, then sank again.

"Gaddy?" Angie cupped her hands over her mouth. "Gaddy!"

"Shhh," Reeves said, seeming to reinflate on top of her. "She lives underwater now."

"Get off me!" Angie shoved him to the side, and then, heart hammering, she dunked down to paw and kick around the bottom of the pool, looking for a body. Everyone kicked her away from their legs, until she came back up, panting.

Illuminated by the moonlight, the water, mixed with the waste products of interminable revelry and unthinkable stories, was now a color no longer found in nature.

It's like a nuclear brown, Angie decided, spitting into her hands and trying not to retch.

If there *was* a door in the floor, she guessed it would never be found again.

"'In this corner . . . weighing in at eight hundred and fifty pounds . . .'" Reeves was herding bobbing mini-bottles to a side of the hot tub as he hiked down his shorts to piss freely into the pool. ". . . Chums and Hoses!" The wind of the highway kept the bottles clinking closely in shared turmoil and a wide turn helped keep them floating together as a unit. A big bounce of the fire truck's shocks, and the mini-bottles switched places, enclosed in Reeves's outstretched arms, but they scattered again.

Just like us, Angie thought.

And there were bigger bounces, more severe strain on the shocks. Ever since they'd drained the gas tank, it had felt like the fire truck was doing at least 100 miles per hour, on a straightaway to nowhere.

Angie looked at Amy, water up to her neck, hand up and holding the side of the pool. She'd said nothing since Beth abandoned her. Angie kept to herself, picked glass shards from her skin that she'd picked up with her palms when she'd dredged the bottom for Gaddy.

"Hey!" It was Jill, yelling at Reeves, who had popped open a fresh mini-bottle of Jack to pour into the neck of a half-empty Blue Moon. Holding eye contact with Jill, he slurped it down. "Where are you getting those?!" Jill screamed.

"Sick," he said, smacking his lips and swimming to Jill. "You made your cake . . ." he told her, then slapped her hard across the face. "Now lie in it."

At the slap, Amy reactivated and thrust her way between Jill and Reeves. All night he'd been mixing his drinks and his metaphors, and she'd had enough.

"Move, twat," he said, but she stood firm, hands on her hips. "I said 'move.'"

Jill and Amy both hopped up to sit on the edge of the pool above him, his face now at their feet as they glared down at Reeves in disdain. He climbed up to the rim to join them.

So Amy climbed to her feet, with her back against the rail. Reeves stood up with her.

Too late, Angie felt the energy of the party shifting again, and started to swim their way.

When Reeves palmed Amy's head for the shove, he was probably intending to send her violently into the pool, maybe into a corner to think about what she'd done. But he pushed her face much harder than anyone expected, and Amy tumbled backward over the rail, legs flying up above her center of gravity. Before Jill, Angie, or anyone else could even react, her feet were over her head, and she was lost. They never even heard her hit the road.

"My God!" Angie screamed.

"Motherfucker!" Jill said, diving at him from the rim. He moved out of her way, then swirled to see more of them approaching.

"You killed her!" Lund was splashing over, Godzooky close behind.

"Oh, *now* they realize we're dying?" Beth asked a visibly shocked Dan, and Angie had a split second of guilt with her rage and disgust, wondering if the previous casualties had seemed unsubstantial compared to the brutally swift erasure of Amy, her "work wife," so-called twin, and supposed best friend, a loss that was finally too close to her own death.

Then Godzooky was holding Reeves's head in his hands like a basketball he'd seized at the jump, and a battle that had been a long time coming was finally joined. And it was a pretty good fight. For a party.

Reeves was beyond drunk or worse, but he was also a former athlete, meaning he was someone who had consolidated years of motor tasks into memory through repetition. So instinct was probably the reason he was able to get so many quick shots in on Godzooky's face, hard, fast punches that would have ended most brawls. But Godzooky's body was cloaked in years of working-class resentment and brute force, and he never would have gone down if Dan hadn't joined in, slashing the side of Godzooky's face with the jagged throwing star of a broken longneck. The surprise gash was enough to loosen Godzooky's vise-like double grip, which had moved down to Reeves's more vulnerable throat, and both Dan and Reeves were able to get under him and piston their legs—just like they'd been taught on surfboards and linebacker sleds half their lives—until they could force Godzooky's body up and over the gas tank until his hard, slippery limbs were sliding up the back of the cab, frantically scrambling for purchase. He was able to grab the air horn mounted on the roof, which honked for the very first time in appreciation of the fight. Godzooky had been dangerously close to plummeting over the front of the fire truck, but his chest swelled with the clarion call, and he spit a wad of blood that had filled his mouth from his slashed face, and he fought his way back down the cab and into the pool. Reeves and Dan piled on his back, but he struggled back to his knees to get his head above water. Then he was up onto his feet, standing tall, as one of his glistening, power-lifting haunches revealed a tattoo no one at the party had noticed before.

It was a giant rainbow koi, riding a thigh roped with trembling muscles, a golden hook piercing the pulsing oval of the fish's mouth.

Godzooky took one powerful step forward, with Dan and Reeves in the crooks of his arms, manhandling all three of them toward the side of the pool. Impossibly, he scaled the wall, carrying the two of them like trash. Dan and Reeves stopped pulling at his arms and both grabbed the rail instead, all their fingers slipping as Godzooky bore down to launch them free.

Then somewhere in that cab, Winston Payne, their unseen escort, tapped the brakes.

The lurch of the fire truck dunked them all, and when they came up, gasping, looking toward the rail, Dan and Reeves were there, staring at their empty hands.

Godzooky was gone.

Angie closed her eyes, hoping he'd somehow survived, maybe crawling down the grill Indiana Jones–style, where maybe he could make his way all the way under the truck, busted sock ropes and red wires and gas lines and spinning axel rods be damned, and soon she'd open her eyes to watch him climbing back up through the red fog of the taillights or the white glow of the headlights to save them all.

The fantasy was shattered when, beneath their feet, their toes felt the seismic thumps of their friend's horrible journey. Like a captive pinball, Godzooky rebounded off the mudflap flippers, then through the 100-point bumpers of those unstoppable dual wheels. Full tilt.

Angie watched the vibrations of his death ripple the water around her, tickling the gooseflesh on her legs, feeling every second of his hopeless battle all the way up in her throat.

Jill wept silently as the truck plowed on, taking a series of turns during their mostly silent, shared moment of mourning, until Godzooky returned, in one final, passive act of resistance, to verify what they'd feared, that they'd essentially been driving in circles the entire time . . .

Across the red glow of the road, Angie saw what remained of their party; the long trail of wallets and smashed cellphones, Lund's jeans, Gaddy's designer camo backpack, Reeves's Aquaman Converse hightops. All their belongs that Godzooky had swiped from the pile on the chrome stairs. He'd told them he'd stolen from every job he'd had, so they couldn't say he didn't warn them, and some of the items he must have pilfered when they first climbed aboard, then somehow hid during the commotion. Or maybe he'd just thrown it all over the rail when no one was the wiser. Angie noticed a small smear of white dust near the traffic lines, and she was convinced this was a sand dollar she used to carry in her purse for good luck, something she'd been relieved to find fit perfectly in the unfortunate ring that an unused condom had permanently stamped into the leather pocket. This sand dollar had been a gift from Dan, but the condom was from Reeves, and the symmetry of the revelation made her stomach heave. She started to laugh as she realized that the only "valuables" Godzooky hadn't liberated from their party were the hundreds of counterfeit one-dollar bills.

Past the long trail of their belongings was Godzooky himself, a body once as robust as a cartoon bulldog now horribly extended like Silly Putty that was pulled too fast, the silent screams of the faces of Sunday comics heroes fractured and fragmented across their newspaper stain. And past this was another PowerWash of gore that must have once been Ruck, and past that, barely visible, the tiny mechanical splashdown of Janky's giant wristwatch, and past this, another outline of carnage revealing a strange, inscrutable embrace, possibly Holly and Sherry, or Gaddy and Holly, or any and every combination, both clinging to each other as they'd been ground under and over, under and over. But no sign of Amy, who Angie figured was small enough to ragdoll into a pothole or ditch. Or maybe she hadn't landed yet.

Farther past this roadside gallery of horrors was the evidence of something else entirely, a bright, shining stripe of substance that generated real hope.

At first, Angie thought it was just the double-white line of the road, a reminder that there was still a world of rules and responsibility. But then she realized she was seeing a triple streak of milk, blood, and honey. Three long, vibrant strokes that were clear evidence of life, still glimmering in the moonlight, dividing their highway far into the distance, but eventually to merge into a rich, shimmering golden stream under their waves, mapping their way to that freshly painted pathway where they'd be begging for their turn under the wheels when the infinite party circled again to come back around.

CHAPTER XVIII

TONGUING THE CELL

Angie's Story

After the catastrophic loss of the American honeybee, my "new kids" were next on the chopping block of endangered species that society had neglected to protect. When I was little, I wasn't sure how I felt about the attention a new kid would get when they disrupted the hivemind of our town, but I understood that sometimes new boys were just as interested in me as we were in them. Our mother said it was my constant name changes that kept them on their toes.

"No one has ever had as many names as us!" our mother would say, usually followed up with, "Now look up the meaning of your new name, or I'll stop writing it on your lunch."

But I didn't need to look them up. They didn't have to mean anything. My new names were just one more thing that seemed to interest the new boys in direct proportion to how much the other girls would exclude me. So, by default, that sort of made them mine. Or, at that point in time, made them "Nahla's."

The last time I changed my name, it took me years to admit I'd done this as a way to dream of a life away from my family, as well as my hometown. It was so much easier to do this than it was to consider *why* I was doing it. Eventually, it got to a point where I couldn't predict which of my deadnames would show up in my dreams. Or who would wake up.

* * *

"You wanna hear a secret?" my brother asked. "I took a phone book to where the murderers were lifting weights, and none of them could tear it in half. I can't prove it, but I think this was ground zero."

I didn't understand the implications of this story, mostly because I wanted to say that these prisoners were sure pumping *irony* by letting a phone book, of all things, conquer them.

But he went on to explain that, once the prisoners got ahold of that phone book, they had us. Every resident was hit hard and fast with the calls. And changing your phone number worked for a while. "But they have so many ways to find us," my brother whispered.

I can't explain it, but this was all very exciting to me. When you're somewhere between a child and an adult, the world doesn't seem so big as so . . . attainable. Everything is possible yet off-limits, especially a prison, whether they're state sanctioned or of your own making. But another secret even more closely guarded than those cells is this:

Kids thrive in confinement.

"You know the guy in prison movies who says he's the guy behind the guy who can get you things?" my brother asked me one night when we were supposed to be sleeping. "Well, there's a guy behind a guy behind a guy who can get *any* unlisted phone number. And it's those numbers they want most. They're more popular than cigarettes. Way more than pornography."

"Why can't they just wave that magic wand to find out who's hiding the phones?" I asked him. "You know, that long gadget they smack your butt with at rock concerts?"

"Phones aren't metal anymore—guns, either," my brother, Greg Junior, said. "For God's sake, some of them are half candy! That doesn't mean there's no security, of course. They still search all the visitors. So you know what they did? They decided it had to be a guard sneaking in the phones, since it's too hard to get past visiting-room security, so—"

"What about flying one over the wall, like with a remote control plane!" I interrupted.

"Ridiculous."

"Or . . . tie one to those seeds that flutter down from the trees like helicopters?"

"Shhh!" My brother was always shushing me, and somehow I missed that, too.

"Or . . . send the phone in like a puzzle. Little pieces in everything."

"You know what? That just might work! The cons have gotten so good at hiding them that they can disassemble even the most complicated phone into ten to twenty-five bite-sized pieces in zero point two seconds. And a puzzle could be scattered and stored *everywhere*."

"Like their butts!"

"Butts are so passé," he laughed. "I'm talking stashing phone parts in their books, potatoes, boomboxes, you name it . . ."

"Wow. What's a boombox?"

". . . then, when everyone is sawing logs after 'lights out,' they slip out those pieces and assemble a working phone as fast and mindless as our mom making our favorite sandwich."

"Our mom doesn't disassemble and reassemble my sandwiches."

"She could, though," he said, trying to sound scary.

"Stored anywhere, huh?" I giggled.

"Knock it off with the butts. What do you know about that anyway?" he said, laughing, too. "But, no joke, those handheld security scanners you were talking about? Post 'nine-eleven,' they've modified those wands so they're much smaller now. So while you're at the door shaking out your boots or your purse, they can slip one into your mouth, nose, anywhere, and you won't even know it. It's up one nostril, down the other, then up the crack of your ass before you can say 'boo.'"

"'Boo!'" I said, thinking the order of this sort of scan would be crucial.

Then we were both snickering into fits, trying in vain to be quiet, watching the hallway for a light under our parents' bedroom door as we tried to get serious again.

"It's crazy, but you know what the best way is to find phones on prisoners? Cats. They used to have dogs sniff out the phones, but there's something about cats and their urge to zigzag around the legs of someone when they're trying to have a long-distance conversation, or trying to drive a car, that is *clutch* for law enforcement."

"Okay, now you're just making stuff up!" I said, slapping his arm.

"Nope! Truth is stranger than *friction*!" he laughed. "And phone calls are like catnip to cats! Just try talking on a phone with a cat nearby and watch it run over to trip you up. They say it's because they think you're talking to them. Or maybe they just love phones so much, they're trying to kill you to get it, which makes sense, too."

"Just like the prisoners," I said, and he pondered this until we were stifling our laughter again. The distant sound of muffled ringing was the only thing that stopped our sniggering from finally erupting uncontrollably, and Greg Junior grabbed the phone to hang it up as fast as possible.

But he couldn't resist listening. Just for a second. This was the problem.

He cupped the receiver to protect me, but I always heard the voice anyway.

"I can't wait to fuck all your cocksucking fucking asses with this fucking phone, you . . ."

I swear I tried not to enjoy the contractions of his body as he cringed. I tried every time.

Later, I was walking around with the newest of the New Kids, trying to show him how certain sidewalks were getting darker by the day, the ones that drew the lines between our tallest buildings and our dying trees. But he was too busy telling me about his insufferably reasonable father, how he was convinced that phones gave the prisoners an illusion of escape from their incarceration that was "nearly as addictive as drugs." Maybe it was his dad who got me into my research field later in life. Tough to say when everyone you meet is an expert at what ails them.

But he also said the phones had just made it all too *infectious*, and that was the real problem. Then this kid started going on and on about something called a *pan-op-tuh-something*, a word I didn't recognize at the time, and how his dad said this was a "horrible idea for a prison, never mind the waste of riverfront property" (which sounded a lot like my dad). But his dad said this was why everyone was acting so crazy around here, because they had a guard tower with tinted windows smack-dab in the middle of a circle of cells, both the prison and the town, and no one knew when they were being watched, "or by whom." He said our town brought it on themselves by "inviting architecture that highlighted false authority," whatever that meant.

"Invisible omniscience," he said that he said that they said.

Then he asked about our mother. He said that his dad remembered our mother from school, way back when they were still "just a couple of larvae."

That's exactly how he put it, like they were snug as bugs in a rug.

I had no answer.

* * *

I made the kid call me "Nahla," and he would be the last one to do it.

This one reminded me of the first New Kid quite a bit, with no moms and extra dads and fierce opinions. He was paler than the previous, sandy-skinned boy I'd considered new, so distinctly white and hollow-eyed, he seemed like he'd wandered in from a silent movie. But he talked way too much for that. Between him and his dad, they talked so much that their names seemed pointless. If I ever asked them their names, my brain quickly purged them in place of more pressing information, like all the crazy things they were saying.

Other people's names were for when you wanted to get someone's attention, and this was something I already had.

That night, as I walked with the New New Kid down Main Street, crunching on a strawberry sucker with the promise of a chewy center, I almost held his hand, but the distant echo of a thousand phones interrupting a thousand dinners snapped me out of it.

"And your dad feels sorry for them?" I asked him.

"We both do. They're just making prank calls. Everyone does that."

"I never did that."

"You never ordered a pizza for a neighbor, then watched out the window?"

"Nope."

"You never called up some teacher and made airplane noises?"

"Nope. Also, I've never heard an airplane go, 'Fuck you fuck you fuck you with my foot,' have you?"

He flinched beautifully and changed the subject.

"Someone told me you used to hold hands with some other kid. Do you still talk to him?"

"Heck no." I wiped my nose with my arm. "You can't talk to someone who stutters, not for too long, anyway, even if he hadn't left town. And he couldn't hear me if I did. Did anybody tell you how his ear got all messed up?"

"I heard his dad tried installing a payphone in their house to stop the harassment."

"Yeah. That didn't work. It just ate all their Canadian quarters. Stupid duck money. And it started ringing off the hook about a day later anyway."

"They find every number," he said.

They sure do, I thought.

"Someone must have given it out, though," he said.

"Maybe," I said, then turned away to keep from smiling.

My brother wasn't just the first person to be murdered in our prison. He was also the first person to be murdered in our town. Our mother first told us that he was "killed by a phone call," refusing to elaborate, and understandably I thought this was some sort of metaphor, like when my dad would say, "Always check your feet in case you stain the honeycomb!"

Luckily, I was able to get the facts from the library archives.

The headlines screamed PHONE BITES MAN! as I fluttered through the microfiche to read up on how, on the day he was killed, my brother had been checking toilets for weapons, or weapons for secret pyramids of margarine cubes (which I later learned were for masturbation purposes), when an inmate went berserk and stabbed him in the throat with something called a microphone filter, the tiny piece of cellular innards that screened out background noise to allow your voice to pass through unmolested.

The King Excluder, I thought, awestruck, as it sounded so much like a recently mothballed tool of our trade.

And I'd be forever convinced my brother had been betrayed by that first phone he'd gifted a prisoner. It just *had* to have been a piece of his own phone that killed him, and I wanted to tell our mother what I knew, or my father, but I was unable to lure anyone into any more conversations regarding my brother. Soon after, my father turned to the internet and immersed himself in conspiracy theories, something that seemed harmless enough.

Comedy cut to a mushroom cloud shaped like a clown.

I remembered my brother telling me in detail about how pieces of cellphones were being used for everything behind bars, from utensils to sunglasses to abstract art. The Birdman of Alcatraz had nothing on their dedication to cellular technology. Some prisoners even *married* their phones, in lively but clandestine ceremonies disguised by the endless hiss of the laundry room. But when those honeymoons were over, the arguing would start, sometimes coming to blows with these phones, when the person on the other end of the line wasn't around to present themselves for physical abuse. Remember, cellphones were bigger back then.

At home, the honeymoon was over, too, and my father stopped talking to our mother, and everyone else around me was either crying or sleepwalking or both. I buried those impulses by replaying our midnight conversations, over and over.

But the most obvious lingering effect of my brother's death was how it brought our town enough attention that outsiders who weren't shellshocked by the loss of the honeybees could now work on solving our problems with the prison. This was a moment of solidarity, press conferences, promises made if not promises kept, and even talk of all telephone harassment being permanently ended within one year. But the year came and went, and, as always, any collective effort against the prison just made things worse.

We were back by the river when I had my worst idea ever.

Me and my NuNu Kid were staring at the shadows in the distant windows when I turned to him and said, "Hey, we should call my dead brother's phone."

"Why?"

"To see if he's still being passed around inside the prison."

He was afraid to do it, so I held his hand a while. Then I told him to go home and bring me his dad's monstrous, green-eyed phone. He still resisted, so I told him my brother's biggest secret, about how it all started. And I said that maybe we could be heroes and end it all tonight, that maybe my brother's phone really *was* the only phone in that prison, that maybe there was only one sad, wrongly imprisoned man making all those calls. And maybe we could call this prisoner and reason with him, "Talk him down like cops do with those guys on the ledge?"

Eventually, the NuNu Kid was convinced, and we sat back on our elbows, holding hands and kicking up insects in the overgrown quack grass, where we uncovered a lone honeybee, dead as long-distance discourse. I was amazed to realize I'd almost forgotten what they looked like.

"What came first?" he asked me with his dad's serious voice. "The phones, the bees, or the prison?"

"That's like asking 'the chicken or the egg or the chicken?'" I shrugged. "It doesn't matter. Not anymore. Probably never really did."

I flicked the dead honeybee at him, then scowled when he scrunched it under the heel of his sneaker. So he told me an even bigger secret, about a telemarketer who accidentally called the prison during peak hours and, legend has it, was put out of business by the flood of return calls and, eventually, employee suicides. Then another story about how the unluckiest people in our town were saddled with the easiest-to-remember numbers, a town now plagued with so many calls that no one could walk down the sidewalk without setting off every phone booth or glowing pocket that they passed by. We were now inhuman, he swore, sad magnets for these devices, and soon even the telephones in the backgrounds of our television shows would be ringing to interrupt the action . . .

Before I could scoff at all this, he told me something else, about how Native Americans hated, *hated* bees. He said they were the worst European import ever. Besides us.

"'The White Man's Fly,' they called them."

"Mm-hmm."

"Because they recognized honey for what it was. Spit and bug shit, maybe a little blood."

I was starting to hate this kid. Not just because that combination sounded incredible.

"Did you know that Citizen Kane's sled was actually called 'Nosebleed'?" he asked me, on a roll now. "You have to look real close. I mean, he was delusional, and the paint was peeling off, so it was sort of a *Star Trek* 'V'ger' situation, and . . ."

And just like that, I'd had enough of him.

"So are you gonna go get your dad's Army phone or what?"

"I don't know," he pouted. "How about I sneak his gun out instead?"

"Don't be a pussy," I said, trying out one of the words I'd heard from the prisoners.

"Whatever," he sighed, sounding less like his father and more like mine with a perfect rendition of Greg Senior's Seventh Sigh, one I called: "Snake Who Realized He Lost His Body."

The NuNu Kid stood up and brushed nothing off his knees all official-like, and I sneakily tried to trip him as he trotted his bike up to speed to get through the tall grass. I stayed staring at the prison, not really expecting him to come back, certainly never expecting him to be cradling that giant green phone like a baby when he did. I still hated him, but I also loved him a little, too.

He dialed my dead brother's phone number while I leaned on his soft shoulder.

A small, soothing voice answered, just like I'd promised it would.

The voice sounded calm, harmless, maybe a little older, like right at that age between Greg Junior and Greg Senior, and we took turns talking to the voice for hours, chatting about our hopes, our dreams, his dad's theories, then some more of my hopes, until I asked the tiny voice in the giant phone what it would do if I rubbed the sides of the receiver hard enough to set it free.

I was never sure exactly whose that voice was, but there was no reason it couldn't have been my brother. If anyone deserved to live in that phone it was him. Or me.

We talked so long that we fell asleep by the river, a giant phone nestled silently between my knees like a pillow, a position that my dad once said could help align my spine (even though I never flinched, I certainly slouched). Clutching the phone, I'd roll away from him, then back, as the gray dandelions, already dented and sagging from the head wounds we'd inflicted on our way into the clearing, were now crushed completely.

I may have dreamed of doing the right thing for once in my short life.

The phone rang, and I answered it, expecting to hear the same voice again. But it was a woman, whispering the digits of the new phone number our household had just received.

And when I finally understood this was our mother's voice coming from somewhere deep inside my house, hiding from my father so she could talk to his father instead, probably curled up in a dark corner with the curl of our phone cord pulled to its absolute limit, I hung up.

The next morning, I stood on the bank of the river, writing on imaginary paper with my secret pen, then I sealed the imaginary message in an imaginary bottle, and I threw it in the water. It was a story for my town, and by my town, and I didn't care who found it. Satisfied with the splash, I turned to head back, but when I glanced behind me, I saw a beer bottle pinned between a branch and a jagged piece of concrete, spinning and spinning, never to catch the current and deliver my story to anyone.

Then I heard the thumping of music, a robotic, heavy beat. I looked across the river and saw a fire truck. The sound was coming from a pump and the hose that was dangling into the fast-moving water, downstream of the prison. I remembered what my brother said about all the piss, shit, and blood that polluted that water, and I wondered if this is how a fire truck filled its tanks. And what would happen if it sprayed this malignant run-off into a fire? Would the flames just change colors? But it didn't look like it was filling a tank, more like it was pumping the river water directly into the back of the fire truck, like when my dad used a hose to fill our kiddie pool.

I walked back to where the giant phone was sleeping. The NuNu Kid was, too. By the time he was stirring, his dad had driven out to find us. My father did not. His dad didn't seem very angry, however. He just gathered up his giant phone and asked if I'd join them for breakfast. It was just as pleasant and interesting as any family dinner before the prison. Sure, there was an empty chair where his wife would have been, but I imagined my brother in it instead. Mostly so I wouldn't picture our mother sitting there.

And when the giant phone began to ring, his father bounded happily over to it, hefting that secure line up to his head with both hands, saying "hello" through his confident, cavernous smile. At the time, I assumed he wasn't expecting anything except further orders from other big, important men like himself. But later, I understood that he was expecting a call from our mother.

So I sat back to take in the full effect of this man realizing that the prison had his number now, just like the rest of us. The color drained from his face, like a pen my brother once confiscated from a prisoner to slip secretly to me during dinner. One of those naughty pens with the water inside and the girl whose dress melted away when you flipped her over. I looked at his dad's face and thought of that girl, both of them now naked in perpetuity.

There was a small incident, long before all of these things happened with the prison, when my little sister was running away from me, fumbling to open the cellular phone we both shared and pressing it tight to her face as she prepared to inform our mother of one of my misdemeanors. I had snapped the clamshell shut at the exact moment my sister stuck out her tongue in triumph, catching it across the numbers while it still quivered from her raspberry, hearing a clap more satisfying than any wet hand that our mother would send flying to routinely turn our cheeks red. When my brother asked us later why our lips were bleeding,

I explained we'd been playing a game called Tonguing the Cell, and it had gotten out of hand.

"It's like slamming a piano on someone's fingers," my little sister agreed, still sniffling but backing up my story.

My brother's eyebrows went up in recognition of the name of our game, but smiled at her instinct to hide truth from authority. Then Greg Junior got serious again, warning us to never swim in the river downstream of the prison. He said it was polluting the town with runoff from not just the prison showers and toilets, but from dumping every fluid and excretion that those hundreds of inmates could spawn. And while I was still repeating the phrase "Tonguing the Cell," in the hope that it would stop sounding so unusual, he grabbed both our faces at once and whispered intimate details of a prison ritual with this very same name, something he'd recently observed among the worst cellmates, on the lowest levels. He said it was a medieval punishment, where one of them was forced to clean every squalid inch of the concrete floor they shared when the glaze of their filth grew too thick and began to stain their feet. And they had to do this with their tongue.

My sister accused him of lying, but I ate it all up, in both senses of the word.

Maybe it was my brother who told me that movie theater floors were covered with the same ingredients you found in honey: spit and shit, and maybe a little blood. But it was the thought of never tasting it that made my first real movie one of the saddest experiences of my life.

It was years after he was gone. After we left town for good.

After the fire.

Everyone thought I was crying because of something I saw on the screen, never noticing that I couldn't take my eyes off that gloriously sticky floor.

One last thing. And this feels important. During that final breakfast with the new kid and the new dad and the new phone, I didn't take a single bite, as my breath had been locked down behind my tongue in anticipation of that call. The upended bottle bubbled in my fist, gilded veins of maple syrup crawling unnoticed through the perfect grid of my waffle, molten gold pooling around, down, and finally over the edges of my dish and onto their floor. I remember the moment well, but mostly because it was such a poor substitute for those wonderful fresh honeycomb-cracking mornings with my dead brother.

I could hear the threats coming through the giant green phone, now forever compromised, but there were specific instructions from the voice this time.

To use the syrup like spit, and the phone like a fist. It seemed that now that prison could see us, as well as hear us.

And while his dad tried to be strong and protect us by keeping the phone down hard over his ear, I waited for the receiver to loosen from his head from the sheer violence of the voice behind it.

Or maybe this voice would fade over time, spreading out over our skulls like the crack of a golden egg, to become another slow, soothing reminder of my brother's final resting place between my ears, free to whisper all of his old secrets like he had the night before.

The inmate raged on, and the phone finally dropped. Regardless of my young age, I'd still had a rich fantasy life, but I couldn't comprehend the savage promises of this prisoner, just as I couldn't imagine any voice suffering imprisonment, no matter what horrible things it might say. And despite the strange fathers or shared mothers who surrounded me, old or new, widowed or abandoned, or however many new kids or new families or new names I could give myself, I was certain I'd always be the only one at the table who never flinched.

CHAPTER XIX

HAPPY POOL PARTY
BUS FOREVER DAY

For the final game, they used the first bottle of whiskey they'd all drained together, back when the fire truck first rolled away with thirteen of them dancing in the pool. Happier times.

The empty bottle of Jim Beam Devil's Cut bourbon had come back to their circle a couple times since then; passed around, then discarded, it was also used for their first party game, until they realized it wouldn't stop spinning.

This clear violation of the laws of physics was different than the paradox of their journey, as this was something they could affect. It was also getting to Beth, who couldn't bear the scrutiny if it stopped to point at her. So she seized it from the waves, quickly screwed some sort of tiny message into its neck, and then tossed it out into the night. Reeves, all eyes and bubbles, made a half-hearted slap to intercept it, but he was rarely more than alligator-level above the surface anymore, and too far gone to make the leap.

They all heard the bottle shatter on the river of asphalt, her message presumably gone.

According to some sketchy astronomical calculations from Jill (which were really more astrological, and therefore not *logical* at all), her birthday party had been going for approximately twenty-seven hours, and she tried to hide her terror mixed with something like pride. It was Godzooky, ironically, who continued to provide the most definitive information regarding their situation, as every so often the speed bumps of his ever-flattening muscles under the wheels were morbid proof that the fire truck was continuing to travel in circles. Just like how their shivering had ceased, they also rarely looked up anymore, either due to the false promise of an impending dawn or because they'd finally become physiologically accustomed to a permanent situation.

They lived here now.

"What did the note say, Beth?" Jill asked her.

"It was a map."

"To what?"

"To the graves under a pier in San Francisco."

"Good God," Angie said. "We need you acting crazy like we need a hole in our head."

"We need a hole in this *boat*!" someone burbled, probably Reeves.

Beth turned to Angie's tear-streaked face. She'd taken Amy's death harder than even she'd expected.

"When we first climbed aboard, you called the driver a 'Rocketeer.' Why?"

"It was on his business card," Angie said, turning away.

"And what else was on that card, exactly?" Beth's hands groped Angie's body, presumably searching for it, but the wind had flipped it out of Angie's hands thirty miles back.

"Get off me. I lost it." Then she remembered something. "It had a tiny hole."

"Where he pinned his first dollar to the wall!" Jill cackled. She was under them somehow, even lower than Reeves, belly against the bottom.

"What else do you remember?"

"It didn't say 'Rocketeer.' It said 'Raconteur.'"

"As in 'Rocket Tours' . . ." Beth whispered, and then she moved off. The water was lower again. So they could lie down and still breathe. So Angie did this, watching Jill crawl to Beth's side.

"What are you saying, Beth?" Jill asked.

"Nothing. I just knew a guy who drove a boat is all. His business was called 'Rocket Tours.' He also did time—"

"We know this. You told us all about it."

"No, actually I didn't," Beth said, sitting up.

"Do you think it's the same man?"

"I think they're all the same man."

"Who's all the same man?"

"Did you see the driver?"

"No."

"Then what are you even saying?!"

"I'm saying I knew a man who drove a boat. No, a fire truck, but it had fire on it, and some of these names sound the same. His business failed." She looked around, not sure what to add.

"Okay?"

"He did boat tours around Alcatraz, but his boat was much too fast, and the distance was much too short, and the tour was over before anybody knew it. So, as you might expect, everybody wanted their money back."

"Yeah, sounds like exactly the opposite of what we're dealing with!" Jill said, rolling over to Angie, then starting to rub her shoulders. Every time she remembered Amy's death, she tried to keep Angie's spirits up after the loss of her "better half" by touching Angie in some way. It mostly just irritated her.

"Listen, everybody," Jill said. "A lot of us are in shock, I know. But I just wanted to remind you all of something. It's still my birthday."

"Are you joking?" Angie shook off her hands and flipped over to look at her.

"I just want people to make the most of this," Jill said, and Angie and Beth, and any others who had been listening, crawled or slid away.

"Relax, everybody!" Jill yelled after them. "They'll know we're missing soon enough, right? I mean . . . I mean, the sun can't just refuse to rise!"

"Exactly. How has the sun not come up?" Angie said, but she wouldn't look up. Beth, however, stood to scream at the sky.

"Where are you?!"

"Calm down. Shhh, it's coming," Lund said, and his empty reassurance made Beth sob.

"There's no dawn," Beth said, head in her hands.

On her back, Angie snuck a peek at the sky spinning above them as the truck took another turn, and she tried to remember anyone else in the world. She'd have given anything to hear her brother's voice, or even a hateful call from the prison, if it hadn't burned down.

Reeves surged up between them, and if all their pupils hadn't dilated, too, she might have sworn his eyes rolled over black and his lips parted around a double triangular grin before he slid backward under the water that shouldn't have been deep enough to hide any body, let alone his.

Their circle constricted for a bit, to protect themselves as he prowled; sometimes they'd try to grab him and pull him up, but he'd contort his body and slip their grips like a salamander. All of this increased the heat somewhat, but they were all shivering again when the Devil's Cut bottle returned.

"Fuck it," Angie said, giving it a spin. "Let's play."

". . . and they drank like their *lies* depended on it!"

Jill was making a toast. Even though the alcohol was gone, they found themselves drinking whatever filled any bottles and cans that bobbed past their faces. They used their new hands, with tire treads for fingertips, snagging these treasures as if born to it.

They used the Devil's Cut as their Ouija planchette, and it was surprisingly effective. There was even less resistance in the water than on a table surrounded by skeptics, which usually hindered a traditional wooden heart's speed across the board. And adopting Lund's method of assigning letters to the remaining bodies in the pool, they were deciphering messages in no time.

"There Is No Fire," was the first thing they translated, which was kind of a head-scratcher, and Beth halted the game a moment to stuff another message into a bottle and whip it out into the hissing, crimson waves of exhaust.

"Where are you getting . . . *stationery?*" Lund wanted to know, but she had been peeling labels all night. She handed another mini-bottle of Jack Daniels to Reeves, a tight tube of the black label now on the inside, and he seemed honored to have been given the throwing duties. All bleary eyes upon him, he dramatically held the tiny bottle in a practiced baseball grip, flexed everything he had left, and hurled it overhand into the night.

They didn't hear this one shatter, but Angie caught a glimpse of it splashing safely into the cold comfort of a drainage ditch. Lund was skeptical, as always. He explained to her that what she likely saw was just the rows of reflecting retinas watching them pass. Still, there was a momentary celebration as they all imagined themselves tucked away in the soft, brown earth of those ditches, all that terrible momentum gone. But more importantly, even if the truck drove on forever, there would always be some solace, even in such a one-sided correspondence.

When Beth composed her next note (with the help of a perfectly timed lightning strike), Angie was close enough to read it, and she saw Beth didn't need a writing implement after all.

"There Is No Fire," is what Beth was scratching into the backside of the beer labels with her thumbnail. Angie guessed it had something to do with alerting people that there was a fire truck that refused to stop, though it seemed like an unnecessarily cryptic way to scream for help. But Angie was more fascinated about how this message revealed Beth as the dominant hand of their final party game.

"Okay, hands on the Ouija bottle," Beth said, just as Reeves resurfaced, blowing a thin stream of water into their circle.

"Ask me anything," he said.

"Oh God, it's back," Jill said.

"I want to talk to the spirits," Reeves laughed, tonguing an empty beer can. "You know, like, the . . . *spirits.*"

Instead of acknowledging his joke, Beth weaved it into the game.

"We ask the spirits . . . are we in Hell?"

Three shriveled hands rode the bobbing bottle around their circle, pointing at them in turn, until another answer took shape.

Lund deciphered it again. "It said 'Yes'."

"We ask the spirits . . . where is Hell?"

This took a little longer to translate, but the answer came. Lund shook his head as he interpreted it.

"This spirit said, 'It is ice . . . Smirnoff Ice.'"

Beth scratched this important message into a label and threw another bottle off into the night. Enigmatic answers to overly dramatic questions became the thing to do for a stretch, until Reeves straight-up asked the pool if "everyone was going to die." He struggled to point the bottle at himself, even though he'd been designated the "Yes," so he went back under.

Peeling labels was infectious, too, trying to tear them off in one solid piece, but Angie ripped every label she attempted—a sure sign of bad luck—as she worked to guard her legs from Reeves's teeth. Beth proposed a game of Marco Polo, only because she knew no one would risk closing their eyes around her. Jill suggested climbing on each other's shoulders for a game of Chicken, but it would be too easy to get chucked overboard. But Beth said she was onto something, that a tower of bodies on bodies on bodies could get a look farther down the road. She was climbing on Jill's back when Reeves rammed her legs. Jill flung Beth off and squealed.

"What on earth was that?" Jill was looking at her hand like she'd been bit.

"What was what?"

"On his back!" Jill was pointing to a mass between Reeves's shoulders. It was too dark, and he was moving too fast for Angie to get a good look, but there was something there. Jill splashed after him, but he flipped over and bared his teeth and his belly instead.

"No, seriously, there is something growing on this crazy mother-fucker's back!"

"Like what?"

"Like a fin!"

"We've been poisoned," Beth decided once and for all, and she threw away the label she'd been working on. "If not by the beers, then the drugs. If not by the drugs, then by the water. And if not by the water, then each other."

"Obvi," Jill said.

"It's all punishment, remember?" Dan said, eyelids heavy. "We've been through this."

"Correction, we are *going* through this."

"He's right," Beth said. "Everybody's right. This was never a party. We're on our way to prison, and this is just a normal bus, filled with urine, sweat. booze, and unsolicited and unearned mythmaking. Which is a bus's natural ecosystem. If the lights ever came back on, you'd all see we're handcuffed to each other in this gruel and telling bullshit stories and puking and pissing all over a floor that sloshes with every turn and—"

"Stop!" Angie said, fingers in her ears.

"But are the crimes really so bad?" Jill asked them all. "Gaddy stealing dollars from rich-ass alumni? That's a righteous cause if I ever heard one. And my Spanish is rusty, but Godzooky rescuing that guy on the assembly line? He's totally a hero. So what if he stole my phone. These are not sins, is what I'm saying."

"No, those were sins," Angie laughed. Her Spanish, if not her barometer of right and wrong, was clearly better calibrated than Jill's.

"I haven't sinned shit," Jill said.

"If all sins aren't created equal . . ." Lund said, "they will be by the end of this ride."

That seemed to settle it. Angie closed her eyes and popped her fingers out of her ears, feeling the highway wind in her hair as she swayed with the rumbling imperfections of the road. Just as they all did, she now understood that she knew the wheels beneath her more intimately than her future.

Angie started counting overpasses, and got to nineteen without turning. Jill claimed that the position of the Morning Star meant they were now heading west. Though their final game had spelled it out for them, few people remembered that the final circle in Dante's *Inferno* was frozen, but Angie did. And if they were no longer circling, she didn't miss it. It had been vaguely comforting for a while, but now she preferred the illusion of progress.

She guessed they'd left Kentucky and had entered Indiana. Or worse. With Dante on her mind, she was worried they were headed for the Tenth Circle of "Heckfire," that baby-talk hybrid state of "Kentuckiana," where the worst people she'd ever known lived, breathed, but rarely worked, a magical place where she'd been drunkenly assaulted by authority figures at least twice in her life. There would be no help there, she decided, and she vowed to end the journey by any means necessary before she crossed that line.

With less than nothing to do now, some went back to the Ouija waterboarding, others flinging bottles with liquor-label messages nestled inside.

The last word their last game spelled out together was *Yield*. Or maybe it was *Wield*.

Either way, it was enough of an incentive for some of them to begin secretly stockpiling their corners with the best bottle shards they could use as weapons.

"Do you want to know what really happened?"

Angie and Lund had found a quieter corner of the pool so he could tell her about the prison, for what she hoped was the last time.

"Yes and no. And no."

"Can you remember what happened to it?" he asked her.

"Of course I can. It burned down." There was no emotion in her voice.

"A modern prison can't just 'burn down,' Angie."

"All I know is, one day, the prison was gone. There was a smoking hole where it used to be, and just like that, the calls stopped."

"Prisons are concrete. They don't just burn."

"I saw the fire truck parked next to the rim of the crater," she said, neck stiffening even as she said the words.

"What kind of a fire truck?"

Angie considered her answer carefully.

"Yes, it had a pug nose like this one . . ."

"You realize you're probably describing a 1955 American LaFrance Series 700 pumper, the only fire truck our town ever used."

"If you say so."

"But even if a fire truck was there, it wasn't there to help."

"I know. I saw it from across the river. It left too soon, while everything was still burning. And that includes concrete. And if a fire truck was there, that means there *was* a fire."

"It didn't put out a fire, I'll grant you that. That truck was there to give the illusion of rescue, that's all. But the death of those prisoners had more to do with a . . ."

". . . with a bomb. Okay, I remember it now. My mother didn't let me watch too much of the news after the explosion, and we moved away after that, but there was a man with a bomb. He was taking one of those popular tours of the prison, and he got all the way to the center of that Tootsie Pop. Boom."

"That's not what happened, Angie," He took her hands, and his were as soft and insignificant as she remembered. "What really happened was this. Yes, a man walked into that prison with something, but it wasn't a bomb. It was a giant phone. And it wasn't just any man. It was my father."

Angie remembered the night on the river, when she gave an inmate the number of that big green military phone. And she remembered the next morning when they called it back. But Lund wasn't there for any of it. Somehow, he'd heard the story in the pool. Even if she didn't tell it. But the story was in the pool. And any story in the pool was everybody's story now.

"Let me guess. Your dad was so upset that he called in an airstrike on his own location?"

"Exactly. That was always the contingency plan. That's why they gave him that special phone in the first place. In case the calls went nationwide. In case the prisoners started prank-calling the White House, or worse. Which they did. One call from that big green phone and a surgical drone strike secured the perimeter forever. With fire. The sort of fire that can burn concrete 'to the ground' and beyond."

"All that because I did the equivalent of writing your dad's phone number on a restroom wall?"

"It might have had more to do with our mother."

"You know, Lund, you're better at this than some of us, but I'm surprised you didn't go the 'Our Father' route instead. Has a different *ring* to it, doesn't it?"

"I don't know. It seemed like stepping on the punchline? Like taking a second bite off the same apple."

Angie decided to keep playing along because, why not?

"So did all of the prisoners die? Because of me?"

"Only one prisoner lived, a man who had been outside in the yard playing basketball, and he thought what he saw was a toy helicopter flying over those walls. He walked right out through the hole it left behind. Then he started up that fire truck—this fire truck—and he drove away."

"That's not what happened. I saw it on the news. There was a fire, yes, but it engulfed the town. We lost our house because the one working fire truck we had failed us at a crucial moment. I rode my bike down to the river, and I saw the fire truck again. Except this time, it was parked up at the burning prison, black smoke pouring out of the cells. And it did nothing."

"How many times did you see this thing at the river?"

"Never." She shook her head hard. "Every time."

"Maybe that happened, too. Maybe it all happened."

"I can believe that in here, in this pool," she admitted. "Everything happened, fine. But I don't believe any of it happened with you."

"Why?"

"You can't even keep your 'new kids' straight, Lund. Remember when you were the other one, with the soupcan telephones."

"I'm that one, too. In this pool, I'm all the new kids, and all of the stories, and all these possible endings, these *reasons*, they're all true."

"No. It's like Ruck said. We conjured something up in this pool, all right. But we just conjured up more conjuring. More rituals. More dumb party games. More nothing."

"I know it was you, Nahla."

"You know nothing," she said. "You only know what you heard."

"But that's all anyone knows," he said.

There was no arguing with that.

* * *

Angie was well on her way to the sweet embrace of hypothermic sleep when she opened one eye and saw Lund standing over her with a triangular claw of broken glass.

She jumped up, startled, but he put a gnarled finger to his lips to shush her, and then he began working on slicing through another stretch of long canvas hose. Angie watched Lund labor away. When he'd cut a new piece free, he pointed to the water and pointed over the rail. After a moment, she understood his plan.

He was going to drain the pool.

He'd managed to empty the reserve gas tank, so this seemed a reasonable play, though every idea seemed reasonable when people around her were snatching empty mini-bottles that floated by and sniffing them for booze like desperate grizzlies during a trout run. But as she watched Lund suck on one end of his hose, siphoning the toxic soup of the pool around them to pour it out onto the street, she realized some of the partiers who remained weren't on board with this new program. And once the pool water dropped even more, putting their bodies even more at the mercy of a wind already whisking any remaining moisture from their grey gooseflesh, the shivering they had vanquished had returned. And now no one was looking at Lund like a hero anymore. And just that quickly, Spencer S. Lundegaard's luck ran out.

He wasn't targeted by the ringleaders, Reeves and Dan. It was Beth who punched him in the mouth first, and Lund spit a blob of blood red and heavy as organ meat. Angie gasped, amazed that the human body could continue living after ceding so much. She watched Beth hit him again, this time with knuckles full of mini-bottles, and they shattered along with his face. Another fortuitous flash of lightning allowed Angie to follow the journey of Lund's eyeball over the rail, a comet trail of optic nerve and white lidless surprise riding the force of her blow. Beth stepped back, visibly shocked at her own power, hands out in mock surrender, and Angie saw the initials carved into the palm of her hand.

No, wait, those aren't initials . . .

At first, Angie thought her hand read *bed*, remembering one of her students saying this was the only word in the English language that looked exactly like what it was. Then she thought it was Beth's own name marking her skin. But no, it was something that rhymed with *Beth* and, etched in blood, it also looked exactly like what it was.

More bodies wormed in next to Lund to join this frenzied but solemn liturgy, and, so far away from repercussions, so deep into the depressing, blackened, blasted-out *nothing* that was Kentuckiana, Angie stopped trying to identify the assailants. She heard at least four wet bodies slap and tackle Lund to the steadily draining pool floor, then, against his pitiful protests, drag him toward his turn in the taillights.

She tried to cover her eyes with her hand before the ritual was fully illuminated in red, but she couldn't help but peek through her puckered fingertips at the absolute worst moment.

She saw Lund's glasses divided as neatly as his head, between a weeping ocular crater and his remaining dejected eyeball. Teeth bared, he was hurled off the truck grill-first, his last headlight snuffed out, his cranium sailing unswerving into a towering steel street sign that read YIELD. And, agreeable to the end, this was exactly what his skull did to comply with its unflinching yellow blade.

It was unthinkable, but the fire truck was going faster, even though they were now hurtling down dirt roads instead of asphalt. They huddled together even closer, their bodies on the verge of shaking apart. Angie felt her ears pop from a change in air pressure. In the black of the dwindling pool, she was blind again, though sometimes she could make out the starlight winking in the deep black of Reeves's eyes, or a faraway headlight that never got closer, reflecting off the glint of Jill's perfect teeth. When she asked Jill why she was smiling, she started saying something about time travel finally being proven and how that meant her leap-day birthday was "historic," and Angie tuned her out. It was just darkness and engine squeals for the rest of them, their quiet panic having evolved into catatonia. After straining to talk over the rumbles of the road for so long, they'd developed a new form of communication, one that lacked language but was no less comprehensible. It would have seemed inscrutable to outsiders, but their final congregation spoke volumes. Hugging themselves and each other, periodically holding their breath to stop chattering molars, they would silently mouth the words as someone pointed their hooked finger at everyone in turn. They read their bodies as they read the wheels. All of it was roughly translated as, "You're all in this together," or sometimes "You're fucked," which meant the same thing, really.

She'd heard a dueling message like this before, when she first learned to answer a phone.

After what felt like 500 miles of country road at Mach 10, Angie attempted a final head count, anticipating more women than men in the end. She thought of their fables, and she attributed their survival to many things, such as the ability to stay under the waves, or the strength to tread water, to work those same muscles they developed in secret when they were cutting Zen gardens into their palms with their own fingernails, or facing the lie detectors and party games of the opposite sex, all the while smiling, smiling, smiling through sharpened eyeteeth.

Jill grabbed the sides of Angie's face and kept trying to talk for real. Angie tried so hard to listen to that old language, but she was captivated by a sleek, slack-jawed visage floating by that somewhat resembled Dan's stolid face, now sinking beneath the suds, dragged down to be passively consumed by an unseen force, never to resurface again. Angie hardly even recognized Jill now, who was wearing Lund's acid-washed pant legs on her arms when she wasn't standing on her head to spin around and around as she recited some other incomprehensible incantation. Angie wondered about the combinations of drugs that had spiked their clothing and how mixing them together in this stew of experiences and life stories and obvious lies had affected them all.

"In a swimming pool, it's almost impossible to make forward progress when your body divides the surface of the water between the tips of your toes and your nostrils," Jill was explaining in this foreign tongue, sounding more than a little like Lund, or at least Lund's venomous blue jeans, which she was now puppeteering. She said all this like it was the answer to everything, and it sort of was.

"Forward momentum is an illusion!" she shouted. "And from the point of view of the road, we've always lived our lives in reverse." And with that, she was done. Her objective had been fulfilled. Jill had listened closely to their stories, gratefully accepting all of these gifts she'd been given tonight. And she had made use of them in the most obvious way possible. By making her own memories.

Spent, she tumbled down on top of Angie.

Angie did understand those words, though, and she believed them, even before their embrace, even before their kiss, even before they stopped each other's mouths and their alien tongues and together discovered the last two warm places in the world.

* * *

They sailed past something huge. A gargantuan, glowing conflagration fluttering across the horizon. Visible even from where their knotted bodies lay on the pool floor, this mammoth monolith flickered and taunted them through the trees, until they understood the massive flames were just projections on a movie screen doing its final drive-by. They could just make out their own names in the end credits scrolling up toward the sky.

Angie considered the average length of time for a drive-in double feature, and realized that three hours was exactly the amount of time they'd paid for. But she told no one, and her calculations dissolved in her brain just as quickly as they'd crystalized, any remaining coherent thoughts draining out of her ears and into the pool and through the hose and finally out onto the indifferent highway.

One of the strobes was working again, and quick flashes of light illuminated the following desperate actions; someone springing up like a porpoise with a purpose, only to slip and crack their head like a joke; someone trying their luck ripping off their own head; someone saluting the group and diving off into the night. If Angie had to hazard a guess, she would have said that last launch was Reeves, judging by the perfect form of the dive. And even after all the violence at his hands, she was sorry to see him go. The pool would certainly miss him, at least.

At some point, Beth finally snapped and never came back, a break that was barely figurative, as it began slowly with a deep gash of a frightful grin that virtually severed the globe of her skull, carving off her personal southern solstice from her Tropic of Capricorn on down. Like everyone on the truck, this last smile was really a surrender, a clear supplication that she'd accepted a torment designed for her and her alone. And, like everyone on the truck, a case could be made she was right. Self-inflicted punishments would always be more effective than whatever the party had in store. Didn't someone say a surprise party was never an act of compassion?

Angie could *hear* this final smile of hers, at least the jackhammer chattering of her unsheltered teeth. A grimace peeled back to her gumline like a Hollywood chimp, exposing Angie to a distinctive sound every one of them had buried under their own pursed lips, hanging onto whatever kinetic energy and warmth their own combinations of psychological rock bottom could generate. It made sense, though.

Smiling should be hard. And it was.

Beth smiled, and then she screamed until she was hoarse. And when she hit top volume, bottles shattered, then their shards fragmented to pebbles and rode the waves over their shins and into their mouths, and they were suddenly driving past another vehicle, a real, live school bus, crammed full of kids' asses instead of faces, on their way home from a much more reasonable game, their pink-and-yellow flash of skin and metal heading in the opposite direction, like a snapshot from the yearbook of their former lives.

The kids screamed back at Beth, thinking it was a party. Which, of course, it was.

It was the last party, where every party in the world ended up if you tried hard enough.

They wanted it to be over. So they ended it. They walked to the back of the fire truck, where the red glow was blinding now. And anyone who remained held hands in the supernova of a thousand taillights, that colossal crimson haze that had signaled dead ends and eternity for most of their ride, but now marked the doorway to their escape. Their eyes watered in the wind, so they closed them. Their fate was unknown, but no one flinched. They knew how important it was to stick the landing.

They jumped. Together.

But they didn't hit the road.

They touched down somewhere else. Intact. Alive. Eyes still shut, they could smell the green instead of the black. They opened their mouths first, and they could taste the grass, breathe in the soft, wet soil. Then, one by one, they opened their eyes.

The fire truck had stopped.

"That's it?"

How long they had been parked, no one knew, but numb from the wind and the drink and the drugs . . . time had proven meaningless.

But they were deep in the woods. On someone's carefully manicured lawn.

It was a party.

Colorful streamers and balloons were tangled high in the trees, a huge HAPPY LEAP YEAR BIRTHDAY! banner scrawled in childlike letters and glimmering in the flickering light of a crackling bonfire. Anyone who was left picked themselves up off the lawn and milled around the flames, silently circling to warm their bodies back up. Through the smoke, Angie saw power lines, and a bundle of transformers, possibly a security fence surrounded by coils of barbed wire. But it was tough enough to focus around the flames, and her bloodshot eyes worked overtime to adjust to a new world no longer constructed of wet skin, highway slaps, and only the occasional cagey wink of the moon. Lightning flashed again, but the storm was so far away, always moving in the wrong directions.

The cab door of the fire truck opened with a weary creak. The driver stepped out.

He was wearing headphones, the wire unplugged and dangling. A black eyepatch hovered indecisively between his brows and a pair of eyeballs that looked equally ruined. The wad of dollar bills they'd given him at the beginning of the night fluttered from the chest pocket of his dirty overalls, corners flapping in the breeze like a rattlesnake. He pulled out the money roll, fanned the bills in annoyance, and the dollars took flight, one after the other. As he walked, he left a rustling wave of cash whirling in his wake. On the dashboard behind him, Angie could barely make out a crackling TV monitor, with the now-empty pool flickering on the tiny screen.

The driver frowned and looked over the scant remnants of their group, mouth working silently as he scanned bodies naked and stained with streaks of their toxic soup. Angie swayed with everyone in the firelight, wild-eyed but indistinguishable from the rest: ageless, sexless, mindless.

"Goddamn, you kids sure know how to throw a birthday bash!" the driver said, sliding the eyepatch over his left eye a moment, but settling on his right. He unbuckled the only remaining rivet of his filthy overalls to let them both drop and hang below his waist. He spit something black and laughed. "Though, of course, most people would argue a surprise party is always an act of aggression . . ."

Around the fire, hands started to rise, first to find each other and the numb ridges of their fingertips, to gently, almost imperceptibly, caress the rough, heart-shaped edges of their worst ideas, an invisible planchette now hovering among them. And though no one could hear anything but the sounds of timber splintering and rupturing with the bonfire's heat, a silent message was sent. And received.

Arms wider than any honorary Jesus, the driver beckoned them close, and they left behind the warmth of the flames and fell upon him, hands and mouths ripping and rending and biting, tearing him down to the ground, down to their wrinkled and webbed feet, down to their level of understanding, rendering him unrecognizable but, ironically, now the perfect decoration for any party:

Ribbons.

Once the driver had been worked into a warm pile of streaming party favors, they placed what had been his body on top of a long metal coffin behind the fire truck's cab; the gas tank they had sucked dry to no effect. Angie searched the abyss of the revelers' gaping faces for her brother, wishing he could take part in the communion. Then someone took a flaming branch from the bonfire, living leaves still spitting and popping, and the fire truck went up like a bomb, redder than ever, burning like it was its birthright.

But there were other trucks at the party, too.

New vehicles with gleaming chrome and no rust, not burdened by an extraneous sound system, hot tub, or other recent conversions to mark it as an embarrassing dance wagon. These were the first and last responders; well-muscled men and women crammed into the trailers, thick coils of hose between their legs, tool belts riding powerful hips, all of them throwing back beer and popcorn and making no effort at all to stop the blaze.

A phone rang in the distance, and no one moved to answer it.

But Angie focused on her own pumper. Even though its fire was climbing to impenetrable heights, she wasn't ready to leave it behind. She remembered this very same truck visiting her school when she was a child, how she rode in the back with one of the new kids, and how that ride seemed like forever, until they staged a fight to freak everybody out, and how, under that pile of bodies, she'd watched the black road sliding under the tires and found acceptance. And when the fake fight was over, she asked if their chugging red vessel had a name. But the new kid said it wasn't a ship, and more like a lifeboat, and lifeboats never had names. She'd looked at his face and thought of her brother, remembering days of honey and distant prisons, the acrid smell of the afternoon when her father burned their hives.

He said they were sick, that they would infect the rest, and it took her some time to realize he was talking about the bees.

He burned them with a homemade flamethrower made of WD-40 and an American flag Zippo, and as she watched the cells engulfed while the squirming honeybees smoked, all of their striped abdomens fighting the reflexive death curl, she curled right along with them.

But that day, she realized her father was right. There *was* something wrong with them. Because they didn't fly away. They didn't fall to the grass. They merely burned, locking compound eyes with her own as long as they could, not moving, not flinching, and once the fire was extinguished, they went about their business all over again, crawling over and around each other as if they'd accepted a life in the rubble. She decided right then that if this was dying, maybe it wasn't so bad after all.

More faceless jumpsuits and fogged-up visors arrived, finally beginning to douse the flames, the torrents from their hoses filling the pool in the back of the 1955 American LaFrance Series 700 pumper back up to the brim as it was washed clean. Naked, Angie ran through the blinding glare of their flashers and the roar of the billowing black smoke and climbed the first chrome steps she could find. Safely aboard a vehicle painted black instead of red, she sat in a seat facing the wrong way, next to astronauts with mirrors for faces, and she offered her hands for them to lock behind her back. Hidden away, she smoothed the remaining valleys from her wrinkled fingerprints. She spoke with her breath and the tip of her nose by drawing a heart on the window, dreaming of celebrations teeming with secrets, hidden highway ceremonies tucked away at every unreachable vanishing point, the wind blowing out the birthday candles along with the blood from her hair before it could dry, and she inhaled a world that no longer existed.

Behind her, near the husk of the smoldering fire truck, she saw Reeves reemerge from the trees, slick and gray as a baby before its first breath, striding through the billows of the bonfire, now a wildfire, climbing back onto the engine that had forged them. Indifferent to the pyre, he stepped up the hot, hissing stairs, back up into the boiling cauldron, now seething with red flames instead of waves. She watched the fin on his back cut through the breakers like he was claiming the deep end of the pool, and Angie leaned out into the wind with her handcuffs rattling, as far as she could go without falling, still able to sense him despite the growing distance, fighting to penetrate the distortion and shimmer of daybreak on the road.

Somehow, she could still feel his cold skin pressed against her own, warming him but cooling her, until they were perfectly acclimated to every temperature. Formless, impalpable, and, ultimately, truly invisible.

And any world that tried to confine such a celebration would recede from them like their reflections on the water.

ACKNOWLEDGMENTS

Big thanks to the Podium team, especially Stephanie Beard, Brian Skulnik, and developmental editor Wes Miller for helping me twist this balloon animal of a manuscript into shape.

Thanks to Amanda Shaffer for the cover and Tony McMillen for the title. And thanks to all the editors who published early chapters of this, like Richard Thomas (who liked the bee story), Cameron Pierce (who liked the shark story), Tim Hennessy and Rusty Barnes (who really liked the dollar bill story), and Ross Lockhart, who published a little chunk of this while asking the question: "Can a Ouija board work on water?"

Thanks to Amy Lueck and our families for support during the all-nighters, JDO for brainstorming during conception, and Gabino Iglesias (aka Godzooky) for proofreading his own dialogue. Thanks to the novel and film *They Shoot Horses, Don't They?* for inspiration (even though I hadn't read or seen it before I wrote this).

And shout-outs to the original ride-or-die party crew who risked it all that night on Louisville's real-life Pool Party Express; including Birthday Girl Megan B., Ashley, Meghan, Adam, Stephen, Kathryn, Caroline, and Ben. Even though that fire truck didn't have water in the pool, we were never really sure if the driver was going to take us home.

ABOUT THE AUTHOR

David James Keaton's award-winning fiction has been widely published. His first novel, *The Last Projector*, was featured on KirkusReviews.com, and his collection of horror stories, *Stealing Propeller Hats from the Dead*, received a starred review from *Publishers Weekly*. More recently, his novel *Head Cleaner* was recommended by both *Booklist* and *Library Journal*. Keaton teaches in California.

 **Podium**

DISCOVER
STORIES UNBOUND

PodiumAudio.com

.

Printed in the USA
CPSIA information can be obtained
at www.ICGtesting.com
JSHW020709220724
66718JS00010B/1

9 781039 467477